PRAISE FOR

BLACK AS DIAMOND

"*Black as Diamond* is haunting and ethereal, balanced with the warmth of found family. This is a cast of characters you are bound to fall in love with as they fumble their way toward one another, seeking connection in a world that is falling apart."

—Andrea Stewart, *Sunday Times* bestselling author of *The Bone Shard Daughter*

"U. M. Agoawike combines truly epic world building and breathtaking action to create a wholly original, harrowing dark fantasy. *Black as Diamond* is a gut punch of a debut novel."

—Chelsea Abdullah, author of *The Stardust Thief*

"With vivid prose, bone-rattling action, and a queer romance as tender as it is thunderous, *Black as Diamond* is a dark fantasy gem from the glittering heart of the genre."

—Sophia Slade, author of *Nightstrider*

"This is the sort of fantasy I love. Layered, detailed world building, lush prose, lovable but flawed found family, and a central magical mystery tying it all together. *Black as Diamond* is a triumph!"

—M. H. Ayinde, author of *A Song of Legends Lost*

"A wickedly original epic fantasy bound by the familiar threads of friendship, family, and fate. Agoawike's masterful world-building is in rare balance with characters who shine bright within a world where nobody quite fits, and nothing is as it seems. Dark but boldly hopeful, *Black as Diamond* is fantasy at its most brilliant!"

—Fiona Fenn, author of *The Crack at the Heart of Everything*

BLACK AS DIAMOND

U. M. AGOAWIKE

Published by Ezeekat Press, an imprint of Bindery Books, Inc., San Francisco
www.binderybooks.com

Acquired by Jaysen Headley
Edited and designed by Girl Friday Productions
www.girlfridayproductions.com

Cover illustration and hand lettering by Christian Chang

ISBN (paperback): 978-1-967967-00-1
ISBN (ebook): 978-1-967967-01-8

Library of Congress Cataloging-in-Publication data has been applied for.

First edition
10 9 8 7 6 5 4 3 2 1

Printed in China

For anyone terrified of living up to
legacy, heritage, or expectation

I

IN THE ROUGH

ASARU

The bodies were fresh. They hadn't been dead more than a day.

They were strewn about the room, the corpses. Six corpses frozen in the throes of death like grotesque statues of onyx.

Darkening the doorway of the embassy, Asaru loomed—and saw only death. Sunlight streamed around him, his silhouette painting the ground with long shadows. He glanced back at the valley in the distance. Sterrock was filled with tiny dots, as humans, Estyrians, bustled by unaware. His ears twitched at the faint din of their laughter, chatter—*life*.

His hands were clenched so tight a thin line of blood welled where his claws pierced the skin. As he stepped inside, the furred tip of his tail whisked at his heels. Rigid brown wings dappled in gray and white were tucked close to his back.

The floors were wet with a tacky black substance, which stained his feet as he examined the embassy. Both the interior and exterior had been built to resemble an Aedyton temple, a slice of the island incongruous with the Estyrian landscape. Four round columns stood at the middle of the room, painted with symbols in an eggshell white that matched the color of the walls. On either side of the room lay overturned tables and seats, and sunken into the far wall was a false door with several trunks beside it.

In a certain light, the embassy actually resembled a charnel house more than a temple, decorated with bodies rather than jars of ash ornamented in gemstones.

Though his heart ached at the resemblances to home in every corner, Asaru refocused.

None of the bodies, at first glance, looked to be his brother, yet they were his kind, eresh keyel. Necks ringed in jewels that formed halos, limp tails, cracked horns, and wings—what was left of them—a broken menagerie.

This was the familiar part.

Unfamiliar were the creeping black marks speckling their arms and their cheeks. A faint scent clung to their flesh, sour like maggot-infested meat rotting in the heat. Terror was etched into their faces, eyes wide open. Some had their hands near their necks, reaching desperately for something in their final moments.

Asaru crouched by each body to confirm that none were Alvarys.

The four wearing broad collars of faience beads appeared to be ambassadors of Aedyton, recently sent over to do what they could to make life a little more bearable for those back home on the island. The other two, though . . . Asaru's jaw worked as he rubbed the wejat tattooed on their inner wrists. The empty eye stared back at him, barely distinguishable from the hard material coating the dead skin as if it had been brushed in ink and frozen.

Their faces—he knew their faces. They made up half of the four members of the elite Tetrarchia. Both were missing the gems that should have formed their halos. Asaru tilted the head of one to peer at the bloody gaps left behind by the fallen stones. The threads of khetry that usually surrounded a body—the web of life that wove itself over the world, visible only to those who could manipulate it—had rotted away. Limp string curled like dry, gray worms away from the dead, while still-living threads clung that much harder to Asaru himself.

At the back of the man's neck was a triangle of black diamond, still warm. Touching the gemstone didn't burn Asaru like it would other eresh keyel—a trait that had always set him apart, since it was dangerous for his kind to encounter black diamonds. *Death is a commonplace of life,* he reminded himself. These were once his kin, his comrades. To see them in such a state, in such a strange land, tightened Asaru's throat with remorse.

But these deaths were unnatural. Worse than unnatural.

He followed the dark liquid to the center of the room, where it was thickest, seeking out the source. A cracked vial was buried under a congealed mass of the substance, and when Asaru reached in to pluck it out, it felt distinctly like old blood. The vial, crafted from a single faultless piece of glass only slightly longer than a finger, had cracked in two, leaving little of the substance to examine. Raising the glass to the light, Asaru watched the way the spots of black clung to each other. The fluid reacted strangely, as if it were magnetic, unlike any substance he'd seen before.

Beneath the smell of rot lingered something else. Something he never thought he'd encounter, even as a warrior.

A curse.

Asaru dropped the vial. If that was truly what it was, there was the possibility it could spread. It might have already. Some curses could be disseminated through touching a cursed object. They were rare—a nuisance at best, fatal at worst. This was the first he'd ever seen in person.

He quickly strode to the false door, threw open the largest trunk, and hissed. It was empty, the Chronicler's beacon nowhere in sight.

When the warden had tasked him with finding his brother, he'd been told the Tetrarchia's last known plan had been to make their way to the Chronicler. If Alvarys and the other warrior weren't among the dead, they must have escaped with the beacon. That was good, but not great.

He glanced back at the bodies and knew he couldn't leave them in this state. Not without respect, not without some semblance of the proper rites, which they wouldn't receive so far from home.

Khetry hummed as if sensing his intentions. Asaru grabbed the red strands in the air, manipulating them between his fingers as if they were silk on a loom. Like a spider's web, the woven strands reverberated with the motion. Faint red lines shone, connecting him to the living world, and the living world to him. In rote motion, he brought his hands, palms flat and fingers threaded with khetry, to the sides of his jaw. Heat pulsated in the back of his throat as he cast the spell. It grew, from a bulb into a tongue of flame that enveloped his own. Fire spilled from his mouth and shot toward the bodies, drawn like a devouring beast.

Colors swirled to create a golden flame that consumed and cleansed. He spit out the last of the spell and watched the fire do what it did best.

"Your mind by Hukhetyel, your body by Chert Ouadjet, your aether by Khertote. Return home to dwell in the Red Web of Life once more."

Asaru's voice was thick with emotion and warped from the smoke that clung to the insides of his throat as if it were a refinery. Jaw clenched, he watched the fire spread hungrily. Flames danced in his eyes, turning the hazel suns bright. Soon Asaru stood amid a garden of heat and hurt, able to think only of his brother as he forced down this loss, squeezed it as small inside himself as he could. Emotions had to be contained, controlled, and commanded lest they derail his duty and compromise him.

His pointed ears flickered, picking up the footsteps of the White Sand soldiers who had escorted him from the Sea Gate. Only after he glared them into submission and, more disappointingly, fear did they stay behind to wait on either side of the embassy's pylons.

"Everything all right, sinj—*sinjorno*!"

Asaru stepped outside and extended his wings, ignoring the frantic shouting of the soldiers as they tried to stop him. Their senseless racket slipped from his mind, like water streaming through cupped hands. Nobody could stop him—there was work to be done. With a powerful pump of robust wings, he soared into the clear Romian sky.

Both he and the embassy burned.

Wind across his cheeks, lightness singing in his bones, Asaru scanned the lands below. Even so far above, he noted the threads of khetry connecting him to every living thing on the earth and in the sky. Never again would his kin fly. And he was determined to find out why.

At the border where Sterrock Valley met the hinterlands, Rhodiola Palace came into view, perched on the outskirts as a symbol of humanity's tentative control over nature. There, he would find the human king; there, he would find the start of his path, and answers.

Rhodiola Palace sprawled in a wide arc of manses columned with marble that cast an impressive shadow over the fountain at the center of its courtyard. Each manse was crowned with a dome of unmarked glass, and every inch of the structure spilled with the lush blooms of its namesake. Crimson rhodiolas clung together in massive bouquets that, even at Asaru's height, smelled of wealth.

As the sun trailed beneath the horizon, preparing for dusk, Asaru descended in a scatter of dust. With hooded eyes, he traced the path that led around the courtyard fountain to the central manse, before landing among four sentinels of the Black Order.

Once their shock wore off, three of them drew their swords, their gazes as sharp as their steel. Leather straps across their armored chests held more blades. The fourth sentinel stepped forward, hand over her chest in salute. "Lieutenant Maruroze Silje, sinjorno. Where are the White Sand that were escorting you?"

Asaru ignored her, contemplating how much force it would take to bring down the doors behind them. The lieutenant repeated herself, and a bubble of irritation fizzed across his skin. They were not going to make this easy, not that humans historically had a habit of making anything easy.

The Sea Gate was a testament to that.

When she tried to speak again, he stopped her. "I do not care."

In an instant, Asaru shifted his stance. Khetry wrapped around his wrists, invisible to the humans, as one of the sentinels charged. Asaru was quicker. He threw his arms forward, palms flat, to cast a simple but powerful air spell at the sentinels. Unable to react fast enough, the four were blown back by a barrage of sound, pinned against the ironwood doors. The doors groaned under the pressure, cracks forming along the edges.

Arms outstretched, wind gusting around his form, Asaru crept closer. He closed one hand around a thread and, with a motion like pulling rope, wrenched it over his shoulder. The humans went flying as if grabbed by the indelicate hands of a child. The doors bent, then burst, ripped from their hinges with frightening ease.

Groans of pain arose behind him.

Above, the sky was a bruised purple. Cold hands of dread warred with the anger within. An itch crawled up his nape as *something* prodded the edges of his mind for an entrance. He shook his head to focus.

Inside the manse, rows of wide-eyed humans watched as Asaru strode past. Ambassadors, dignitaries, nobles of all types and dress in the middle of discussions he couldn't care any less about. Though his eyes flickered across their faces, he didn't really see them. He had only one target.

Portraits of the seven past rulers of Estyria, each as regal and severe as the last, loomed high on either side of the throne room as he entered. In each space between the paintings was a sentinel standing like a column, weapon drawn. At the end of a narrow carpet spanning the length of the room, the king of Estyria sat upon his simple throne on a tiered dais. The king stared from behind the crossed swords of two sentinels at his sides. An arbalester behind the throne nocked a bolt and pulled back the winch on her crossbow.

To Asaru's surprise, the king raised a hand to placate the sentinels. "Rest easy."

After a long moment, and as if it pained them, the sentinels sheathed their weapons. While the swordsmen beside the king complied, the arbalester only lowered hers. The bolt sat loaded in the channel.

Silence, long and winding, filled the room. Then King Zaosha du Velanescu addressed Asaru directly.

"If we recall, sinjorno, the White Sand were meant to escort you from the Sea Gate to the embassy—not the palace." Zaosha leaned forward and stroked his sparse beard. His gray-touched hair was braided into thick twists with a few strands draped loosely over his shoulders. A golden circlet rested above his brow with an opal so bright it could only have come from Aedyton. "What *are* you doing so far from the embassy?"

"Your Majesty!"

From the faceless crowd a man shot up. A human, Asaru noted, with salty black hair tied into a short tail and an ametrine brooch pinning his cloak over his shoulder. "Surely we—you—can't be suggesting to let—"

"Sit down, Governor Devall." The king almost sounded bored, his baritone tinged with what Asaru registered as a long-standing threat. The king turned back, looking amused, as if the uselessness of nobles was something they could commiserate over.

Instead the embassy burned in Asaru's mind. From the blazing flame, red, red hot, a presence grew. Its unseen hand caressed his mind, testing, claws like needles that sent static along his senses. He clenched his fists but couldn't feel his fingers.

Focus.

"Why have you disrupted high court with such fury?"

A barrage of thoughts—the bodies, the black, the beacon, *his brother.* Pain traveled down his spine and into his seizing hand as Asaru regarded the king.

"I found everyone in the embassy dead. All with the indicators of a *curse.*"

Someone gasped, several others murmured in shock. He held himself from rolling his eyes. They didn't truly care about the eresh keyel. This was a spectacle, a play at empathy for them, and nothing more.

The numb static of his hands slowly spread to his legs, feet—everything that he was. He gripped his wrist, pressed his heels into the ground. His mind was a battlefield as the presence pushed and pushed and—*Possession,* he realized. Someone was trying to possess him. And he didn't know how to fight the presence as it pawed at his vulnerabilities, prying into his thoughts with malevolent ease.

Zaosha tapped his chin. "A curse, you say. In our own realm? Curses are complex spells, are they not?" In the twilight, the king's eyes seemed to glow gold. A thin stream of green smoke escaped the king's mouth, visible only to eresh keyel. Only to Asaru.

The man was lying.

Asaru stared over the opal crown. Unbalanced, he staggered as he took a step forward, trembled against the unbearable pressure squeezing the margins of his skull. The room blurred, a fuzzy canvas of light. He shook his head to try to clear it, but the presence of the possessor increased. They exploited the vulnerabilities that left him raw from thoughts of his brother. Tamped down on his sense and self until he was at the mercy of their sole command.

"They are." His words were faint and strained.

Static and pain. All he knew was static and pain. Then his body was no longer his. It was as though there was an impenetrable barrier between his mind and his actions. A nightmare he was horrifically all too aware of but could do nothing to wake from, his limbs bound like a living doll.

On light feet, Asaru dashed forward, too quick for the

sentinels. He struck the one on the right with a quick jab to the throat that had them stumbling back, gagging. Then he pivoted and swiped the other sentinel's leg, sending them tumbling. The movements felt distant, almost foreign in his own skin. *No*—he tried to drop his arms, tried to shake the static away. The possessor's will, their mastery over him, was stronger, its control absolute. He was a useful tool and nothing more. He could hardly string together a thought, much less resist.

Against his will, he grabbed at khetry and punched a spell toward the arbalester. A wave of pure khetrical energy struck the weapon from her hands. Before him, a third sentinel planted herself in front of the king, brandishing her sword with one hand and shielding her charge with the other. Asaru narrowed his eyes—no, he was *made* to narrow his eyes, knees bent into combative readiness.

The high court erupted as humans rushed to escape. Heels tore at silken trains as they ran like headless fowls, and petals fell to the floor alongside cracked gems and other frivolous adornments, hairline fractures shattering them to slivers. Lieutenant Silje staggered through the doorway against the tide of people. Her temple bled profusely, and she clutched her right arm, which was bent at a wrong angle. She yelled something incomprehensible beneath the din of the mob, then every sentinel pulled out their sword as they leaped in front of the fleeing crowd to face Asaru.

He observed them with distant eyes, a scream muffled in the back of his throat by a will that wasn't his own. This wasn't what he wanted, wasn't what he was there for. Possession pulled him deeper. The box in his mind that still belonged to him grew smaller every moment, replaced by an expanse of want and hunger only spoken of in history tomes—

The whistle of a blade caught his attention.

Asaru stomped down on the fallen sentinel's leg, ducked beneath the oncoming sword. Steel met silver cloth as he blocked the sword with crossed arms. The sentinel struggled to push her sword down as he tightened his arms. Even as the sword cut through his arm wraps. Even as the edge kissed his skin. Even as he started to bleed. The possessor pushed power into him, and he shoved his arms up, knocking her off balance. He seized her sword by its blade when she fell.

The sentinel's face flashed with surprise for a brief second, then broke when he trapped the sword between his fingers and pulled. Their eyes met; she gritted her teeth. He planted a solid foot against her sternum, and her skull slammed against the stairs. Blood pooled around her head as her body rolled to a stop at the foot of the dais.

Golden blood dripped from Asaru's hands where he gripped the blade. It streamed hot down the inside of his elbow to his fingertips, then to the carpet. Turning to the king, he flipped the sword to grip the hilt. It was solid and well made—the presence in his head deemed that satisfactory.

Zaosha tried to stand, hand extended, his palm tattooed with an intricate circle. Asaru kicked his chest, sending him back into the throne and searching for breath. The king stared, fear burning in mismatched eyes. Up close, Asaru saw they were not quite the same shade of brown.

Fear turned to terror as Asaru plunged the sword into Zaosha's chest. It happened in an instant, like a snap, and everything fell apart. Rending human skin was almost as easy as striking down a remnant. Red and gold blood mingled, a deathly bronze painting the blade. Asaru stared unflinchingly into the king's eyes as he watched the light in them fade.

There was a scream, a long crescendo of a wail.

As he pulled the sword from the dying man's chest, he whispered, "Your mind by Hukhetyel, your body by Chert Ouadjet, your aether by Khertote. Return home to dwell in the Red Web of Life once more."

Asaru tossed the sword aside, and it clattered to the ground.

The hazy pressure faded, the static dulling to a faint itch. He blinked, took a breath. The dregs of possession chilled him as the cold horror of reality began to settle in. He stepped back and looked upon all that he had done.

The king's body slumped on the throne, broken by Asaru's hands. Those empty eyes stared up through the glass dome at a flock of birds flying in formation.

"I . . . What? What did . . ." Asaru stared at his hands, the bloodstains. He couldn't kill a human. As little as he thought of them, he would *never* kill a human. He was made—*born*—to kill remnants. That was good, like his brother; he was good, like his brother—he had to be.

Moving his limbs freely, Asaru took in the chaos below the dais. Lieutenant Silje stood at the head of the sentinels, face ablaze. Despite her broken arm, her gaze seared him with such vehemence that he flinched.

"Lieutenant, I—"

"Detain this eresh keyel by whatever means necessary."

Trying to placate them was a lost cause. With no time to think, Asaru unfurled his wings to take flight. He had to leave, find Alvarys. Fix this. Khetry swelled, thrummed as if strummed, a tight energy alive with anticipation. It flared in his vision, burning red through his body.

The sound of cracking bone filled the air. With a gasp, he lurched forward as a crossbow bolt lodged in the meat of his wing, bending brown and gray feathers. Stunned, he stared at the wound before pain splintered every nerve in his left wing.

He heard the telltale click of the crossbow being loaded with another bolt. He turned, watched her level the weapon at him, place her eye on the sight.

"Wait!" Asaru reached out in panic, pleading.

She pulled the trigger. An observer outside his own body, Asaru watched the bolt fly from the channel at a snail's pace before tearing through his abdomen. Skin parted, and the metal wedged itself into flesh.

He watched himself grasp the bolt, watched himself scream and double over in agony. Fear and guilt blended in his voice. He was lost in the pain, unsure where he began and the anguish ended, if at all.

He watched as the arbalester nocked another bolt and wound the winch with lethal intent.

Then he watched himself disappear in a shower of sparks, feeling nothing more as he faded into resolute darkness.

WREN

Through the windowpane, sunlight dappled the curly black forest of Wren's hair as he scrambled between the projects on the apothecary's main mixing bench. One side of the bench held a basket of flowers, flasks, and strips of linen; the other, a small burner, atop which sat a weathered metal pot with a blackened bottom.

In the middle of this mess, Wren yawned and adjusted the lens of a microscope. Through it, he peered down at a slide holding the flayed seed of a water dropwort flower. It resembled a brain, or perhaps an insect skeleton. White tendrils of growth were mushed against the inside seed coat and looked nowhere near as dangerous as they truly were, but the sight sent a twinge through the poison burn scarring the side of his face.

The wrinkled brown flesh, faintly purple, of the scar crawled up the left side of his neck and petered out over his cheek as though he'd been splashed by a poisonous wave, which in a way, he had. He shook his thoughts free from the incident playing out in his head, returning to the microscope.

Wren was determined to distill a philter, some sort of temporary antidote for dropwort poisoning, so that what happened to him would never happen to anyone else. A deeper part of him knew *he* had happened to himself and that this was all he could do to salve the painful memory. Grasping at any possible chance of returning to the Guild of the Living Body—that esteemed place of learning where journeyers became apprentices, and apprentices became healers.

He wished to be more like the mythical and gentle Mator, the greatest healer who ever lived; or perhaps like Eírtat Warda, founder of what would later become the guild itself. Instead—he was the only person he knew to fail at becoming a healer.

He very, *very* carefully set the slide aside and breathed a sigh of relief.

As another yawn forced its way out of him, Wren caught a glimpse of himself in the mirrored window. He looked as dead on his feet as he felt. His hair was unkempt and its tail half out of its blue ribbon. He seemed to carry the weight of regret across the broadness of his back, as well as in the deep, dark bags beneath his mismatched eyes. The right was brown, the left—the khetry eye—a startling, vibrant gold. Drowsiness fluttered at his lids, threatening to drag them down, and him right alongside.

The air smelled of lotus, chamomile, and moonglory—and burning herbs.

Shit.

Wren darted to the other side of the bench and turned off the burner, coughing as he waved away the thick smoke of his failure. The substance inside had congealed to a sick-looking green, and from the bronzing crust at the edges, he was sure the bottom had burned too.

With a frustrated sigh, he pressed his palms against the

bench. His hands were black, as were the rest of his forearms up to the elbow. They were permanently stained by antimony kohl such that his tattoos seemed to melt out of the darkness into the rest of his skin. Not an accident, just an unfortunate consequence of his first year at the guild.

Wren plucked a pen from his apron, then flipped his primer to a blank page to quickly jot down a note of the day's failure. Where primers were spellbooks for the modern lulaik, usually passed down within a clan or family, his was more of a haphazard commonplace book, cobbled together from a plant identification guide and scrap paper he'd bound together with twine. The looping curves of his handwriting covered the pages front and back. Ink smudges and doodles of concentric spirals from the times he lost focus while contemplating a salve or a spell filled in the remaining space.

His nose twitched at the lingering smell of burning, so he pushed open the window to air out the last of the acrid odor.

Soft larimac branches twined in an embrace with the climbing ivy from the various woven baskets strung across the beams of the low ceiling. Nastradona truly was a beautiful place, even if apothecaries were nowhere near as highly respected as healers. Luckily for his job security, he hadn't burned it down—yet. Every day he strayed closer to that line, saved only by the fact that he was the only—and therefore best—apprentice of its owner, Zanna.

Pollen floated through the air along a gentle breeze from Zanna's upstairs apartment. Yellow flecks settled in Wren's hair as he dragged a hand through it, grumbling. He was burning through their supplies instead of doing his *actual* job, which waited in a basket at the other end of the bench—filling the medical swatches with a poultice meant to clot blood . . . or stop inflammation. He wasn't entirely sure, due to how much space the guild took up in his head.

As he pressed his pen to the page, Wren worked over what he was doing wrong—which was a lot. *Regarding* this *particular situation,* he reminded himself, *not life in general, dumbass.* He could study on his own all he liked, but he needed access to a proper, *ancient* primer. One that collated the knowledge of several generations of lulaik, ideas expanded by the invisible hand of collaboration.

A tap on glass drew his attention. Just outside the window, a brown starwren perched on the sill. Beady eyes met his unflinchingly, and for a moment, Wren had the fleeting desire to hide away. It cocked its head, something clasped within its jagged beak. Even with its mouth full, it tried to warble that scratchy tune that had, on more than one occasion, startled him from a few minutes of dreamless rest on the mixing bench.

Hopping forward, it dropped its prize onto the bench and hopped back. Its talons clicked like rain on wood. The feathers on its fist-sized chest puffed almost in pride when Wren picked up the offering. Slowly, so as not to startle the intelligent little creature.

"I have no idea where you found this, but, um . . ." He looked at the trinket—a piece of bone resembling a needle, eye and all. "Thank you?"

It chirped like a pair of shears in response and took flight. Dappled brown-and-white wings disappeared into the cloudless distance. He stared listlessly after it, his namesake. What a peculiar bird.

The creak of the apothecary's back door preceded a high, clear voice.

"Every day I wonder if this job is a joke to you," Zanna said as she jostled through the door with a crate of jars rattling against her chest. "We're the only apothecary in Sika, and apprenticeships aren't easy to come by in Valyn. Yet here you are—*my best employee.*"

Your only employee, Wren thought, running a hand through his hair. He smiled sheepishly as she placed the crate on the bench. The jars were filled with yellow bedstraw and drellow; he immediately recalled their uses for spirits and serpent venom. He also immediately recognized they were for Governor Khaas's house healer, a frequent customer.

"Sorry, Miss du Allopei." He shoved the primer and loose petals into his apron. "I *was* trying to do both at once."

"You were failing to do both at once. These swatches aren't done. Poultice hasn't even been mixed. Drier than my damn eyes from all this smoke."

Wren ducked his head, duly chastised despite her unaffected tone. She stared him down—*up,* really, as most people were a fair bit shorter than him—with a cutting look. Her eyes displayed her lulaik heritage, amber on the right and molten silver on the left. It was a comfort to be in the presence of another lulaik. Usually it was just him and his mother. And when he wasn't at Nastradona or at home, he often felt out of place, disaffected from the loneliness. He didn't find his melancholic thoughts to be great company.

"You need to take this more seriously." Zanna continued. "It's my job to keep you out of more trouble, and you just keep wanting to get yourself back into the same problems that got you discharged from the guild."

Wren kept the wince from his face. His next apology was a whisper, more to himself than her. *Sorry for always being the way that I am; I wish I could be someone else.* Instead, he gulped and said, "Then I'll try to do more of that. Working, I mean. Starting now—" He gestured to the crate, not wanting to seem too eager. "I can take that to the governor's manse if, um, you'd like."

Zanna paused untying her apron to look at him. He squirmed under the assessment and looked away, tangling his hands together as he thought about the package that was hopefully waiting for him at the governor's manse. Staring at the dissected dropwort, he was blindsided by the smack of her balled-up apron against his chest. He sent her a confused look as he tripped over himself to catch it before it fell. "All right," she said carefully, "I need to prepare a delivery for Governor Devall's daughter, anyways. I'm counting on you, Wren."

He clutched her apron to his chest and nodded. "You can trust me."

Waving him off, Zanna tied her braids into a topknot, already halfway up the stairs that led to her apartment.

When her footsteps had faded, Wren untied his own apron and hung both up by the back door. He scrutinized the bench, weighing whether it was worth it to clean since he'd be in early the next day, before deciding only to clear away the dropwort for the sake of his neuroses. As he cleaned, his finger brushed the bone needle, and he held it up with an appraising hum, a crooked smile gracing his lips at the thought of his little friend. Its visits were sporadic, but its gifts were plentiful. They filled many pages in his primer—likely the reason why his own book was less than useful in the pursuit of his medical endeavors. Wren liked pretty things, shiny things. His mother likened him more often to a magpie than a starwren.

Tucking the needle into his shirt pocket, he grabbed his satchel and stuffed his primer and coat into it. He hefted the crate against his side, taking a moment to adjust to its weight before stepping outside into the late afternoon sun. He kicked Nastradona's door shut behind him, mentally apologizing for the mark his boot left behind. Nothing unusual there, though; he *was* known for making a mess of things.

Looking up, Wren shaded his eyes from the sun's glare and found the governor's manse. Half an hour's walk, plenty of time to ruminate upon his inadequacies and catalog the day's many mistakes. *Exciting and entirely deserved.*

He made his way down the much smaller hill where the apothecary was tucked away, passing businesses of a similar nature—herbalists, healers, and needle specialists. The dirt path soon bled into cobblestone as he entered the busy market of Sika Major. Wren squeezed through the thicket of merchants crowing in the Akiki tongue, which flowed like water, while children jostled the crowd with chalk in their hands. Across the rooftops, some of the more adventurous youths dropped rocks into the baskets on fruit sellers' heads in competition, only to run off laughing when one would accidentally knock the nose of a passerby.

At a corner was a hexe being tended to by an elderly human. The shrine was dedicated to Bahdab and Jalorun, two of the six gods that composed the Six Facets of Being. He didn't observe the Estyrian religion—those foreign deities were not his—so he walked right on by, too distracted by his own anxious thoughts to even spare a glance at the empty offering bowl.

Cobblestones gave way to a grassy switchback path at the base of Sika's largest hill, surrounded by the primeval Kingswood. Such large mounds were common across Valyn. In Sika, it was where those of status resided—lords, ladies, wealthies, and most importantly, Governor Aliandrix Khaas. The governor was rarely seen interacting with the common folk. His Lady wife, Rozenline, was much more personable.

Occasionally, a carriage rumbled by, drawn by horse or choramelo, and he was pushed to the side of the makeshift road, where he gazed out over the Valynian landscape. The distant mountains, hazy and indistinct, set a nice backdrop for the verdant rolling mounds the city was built into. If he squinted, he almost imagined he could spy the highest ring of Aedyton between the adjacent mountain faces, though he had no idea what it truly looked like beyond his own conjurations.

As Wren readjusted his hold on the crate, his mind wandered away from Estyria and into Aedyton. He was the last person to care about politics, but he wondered about the snippets of gossip he'd caught in the market. Apparently the Sea Gate was lowered that morning for some ambassador—or was it a warrior? He knew many Estyrians were wary of the eresh keyel, preferring them to be bound behind the gate "for the safety of the realm." The reasons were as trite, in his opinion, as they were foolish.

Thousands of years ago, the eresh keyel had come into contact with the humans of Sterrock Valley. And as people are wont to do—as he'd been told by others with such physical drives—they mated. From that mingling sprang the lulaik. It was the eresh keyel he had to thank for the ability to cast spells, manipulate khetry, and see the red web that pulsated between blinks like breath.

Then, as the tales went, one eresh keyel grew angry or bitter or mad—sometimes all three. There were ten different ways to begin the story. They all ended the same.

This eresh keyel, Oprekhet, betrayed her kind and her sibling, created the remnants, and started the war that Rhenitha ended. She put up the Sea Gate in a treaty with the drakes and was lauded as Good Queen Rhen forever and ever and ever—so history spake.

Whatever.

The gate had been a horrible decision; it deprived lulaik of their kin due to misguided fear. But hindsight was worthless when looking back on the past.

Sighing, Wren fingered the smooth blue crescent of his necklace and hurried along. There were heavy footprints crushed into the grass from those who had gone before him. He stepped gingerly into each of them.

A manse emerged between the trees, built right into the grassy mound as if born of the earth itself. Call him simple, but it was by far the largest home he'd ever seen. It was like a new sight every time he made the climb.

Thick brush bracketed even the highest window, and violet-dotted ivy clung to the stone walls in patches like the spots of an illness. Nature intruding upon the man-made. A path of stone led to a distinctive iron gate between two guard towers from which the Black Order casually surveyed the path. Into the top of the gate was wrought the Eye of Estyria in splendor, with six rays behind it and the diamondglass sword Velanu atop.

As he approached the sentinels, they acknowledged him with a nod before returning to their conversation. The imposing gate swung outward slowly, and Wren made his way inside. He moved through the courtyard, weaving around the denizens of the manse as they went about their work. Sentinels milled around, conversing as they avoided their duties; servants rushed to and fro; and yapping children and animals ran by underfoot, splashing through the fountain.

The governor's healer lived in a tower separate from the

main manse. It stood out in terms of both location and architecture. Shining with chrome ornamentation and metal statues whose eyes were inlaid with jewels, the style marked it plainly as Eihron, sister Norvatti tribe to Wren's own Rosatay. It wouldn't be as obvious to others, but the tribes did what small things they could to keep their motifs and traditions alive.

The noises of the compound faded to a murmur as Wren scaled the winding steps. At the top, he rapped on the door until a petite woman dressed in a healer's changeant green flung it open. Blue threaded her cuffs, and an eglantine in the same shade was embroidered at the neckline.

"You're impatient," Floret hissed, tugging him inside by the collar. She snatched the crate with an unsurprising amount of strength and set it atop her mixing bench. Compared to the flaxen-headed members of House Vas'lile, Floret stood out with her amber hair and comparatively quiet demeanor. Few words, for action did all the speaking instead.

Wren watched her, fingers dancing together at his back like impatient spiders. He wanted to be polite, but he also *really* wanted what he'd come for.

"Do you have it?"

"Yes, I have it, you utter child," she snapped. Floret frowned at him with stormy gray eyes. Her hands spasmed before dropping to fiddle with the feathers of her robe like an antsy bird.

"Well, um," he ventured, trying to sound measured despite his glee, "can *I* have it?"

Massaging her temples, lips flattened into two pale lines, Floret moved to a chaise by the window. From beneath a blanket embellished with rhodiolas—a sight at which Wren frowned, though his annoyance died before it could bear fruit—she drew out a wrapped package.

"Found by a Solsuqa antiquarian excursion in Sterrock," she said, her brow furrowing as she stared at it. "No one claimed it before it was put up for auction, so here—"

Wren held himself back from snatching it like an eager child and instead, being the polite young man he was, graciously accepted it when she pushed it against his chest. A chest that felt like it was going to burst as he finally, *finally* held a proper primer. But a find like this was not without cost—so he asked hesitantly.

Surprisingly, Floret waved him off. "Think of it as your very own new family heirloom."

"Whose family?"

Her answer was a thin smile as she gestured to the door and turned back to her bench. A clear dismissal if he'd ever seen one.

Wren clutched the package as he rushed home, fingers hot as if he'd committed a crime. It almost felt like one, for him to hold a primer that hadn't come from his clan. Like stealing the legacy of another, one so ancient it had taken antiquarians to uncover it. He could barely restrain a grin as his heart thumped erratically. Warnings, reminders, sense practically sieved from his mind.

Finally, *finally*—he could begin to claw his way out of the shadows of failure and into the light of atonement.

Wren traced a line on the page, feeling the ridge of the weathered ink beneath his finger. Incredibly old, with a frayed spine, moth-eaten pages, and centuries of knowledge, the hefty tome of a primer sat in his lap. He flipped through the pages and found himself back at the bookplate. Spidery writing inscribed a name. Rhenei Velanescu ci Sterrock. Another lulaik named after Queen Rhenitha, as most believed he, too, was. He grimaced and scratched at it until all that remained was Rhen ci Sterrock. *Much better.*

Under the light of a black candle, he thumbed through the rest of the primer. There were pages of dry theory, drawings of spell circles annotated in red ink, and—most pertinent to his interests—notes on obscure plants, their properties, and the places they could be found. Already, his mind spun with iterative ways to accomplish the next version of his project.

He had just finished copying a line of text into his sorry excuse for a spellbook when a scrap of colorful paper poking out from near the back of the antique primer caught his attention. Turning to it, he paused to read what appeared to have been pasted in from another, much newer, tome. The page was simple: a neatly printed paragraph and beneath it, just as carefully drawn, an elaborate spell circle. But it was dotted with fingerprints as though someone had tried to rub it out. They'd succeeded only in smearing the red ink.

Wren tilted his head, reading the spell circle. The shapes were disjointed, but he could make out something about luck.

A luck spell?

He'd never heard of such a spell before, was not even aware something like that existed. Lips quirking wryly, he thought he could do with some luck. And he was never one to shy away from appeasing his own interest. Undiscovered new spells were always interesting, like the jewels his mother kept in a cabinet he wasn't allowed to touch as a child. Besides, curiosity ran in the family, from his mother and his . . . father.

In casting the spell, perhaps he might, through its mechanics, learn how it was made. And in turn make something of his own. Something that might bring him back into the fold of the guild. His scar throbbed, and he brushed his cheek absently.

He paused to listen for the telltale sounds of his mother walking around their home. Though he'd left Nastradona early, he hoped her deliveries would keep her out later than usual that night. He loved her—he just didn't want her as a witness if this all blew up in his face. Certain there was no one else home, Wren cleared a space on the floor to draw the spellwork.

As the diagram instructed, he lit six black candles around himself. With a white stub of chalk, he connected them. For each candle connected, the flame blazed brighter. Khetry seemed to thicken as he went, the energy enveloping the room in a tight cradle as the last candle was joined.

Khetry shone in Wren's vision. He blinked, his golden eye constricting as the Red Web of Life pulsated. It was connected to him—from him to the candles—from him to the bone needle in his hand. He'd forgotten he had it until he saw the use of it in the spell's description. Things had a strange way of working out like that.

Wren glanced at the primer, reading the last part of the paragraph. It was the hardest to understand, but from what he could glean, blood was required for stability. A deep prick to the finger would do. Blood was more often used to draw spellwork, rather than as an additive to augment a spell.

It's a new spell, he thought, convincing himself, bringing the needle to a finger.

Six drops of crimson. One for each candle. *One, two, three, four, five, six.*

The flames rose higher still. The low light cast him as an otherworldly figure within a circle of fire, chalk, and blood. The heat within him spiked to the point of discomfort. Blood dripped from his nose like a font. When he licked his lips, he tasted iron.

Using his clean hand, Wren took the chalk and completed the

spell circle. The spellwork was a complex tangle of sacred geometry, lines forming symbols with separate and connected meanings—triangles and stars, squares and curves. The symbols in the circle spoke to the functions of a spell.

Satisfied his work matched the drawing, he pressed his black palms against the smooth cherrywood of the floor. A silent voice chanted in his head as he began charging the spell. All around him, khetry thrummed, red-hot threads drawn to the circle. The larger the spell, the more charge it needed. He was no eresh keyel who could grab the threads directly and cast as they pleased.

Cracks raced across the floor as the circle began to glow. A gust of wind roared. A crease notched his brow. He shuddered with the sluggish euphoria of a spell almost charged.

Someone once told him to make good choices. He couldn't remember when—or who. Maybe he was, maybe he wasn't. But he *needed* this luck spell to work. It *had* to work.

Wren raised his hands and flicked his wrists, casting the spell. The lines of the circle glowed ever brighter until the white expanded outward, covering the entire floor. When he squinted at the web of khetry, he saw the threads that banded around him. There was one particularly bright one, corded almost like a rope, that connected him not just to the world, but to something else. That wasn't quite right—not a rope, a chain?

A chain.

What have I done?

This wasn't a luck spell. This was something else. He was performing a *summoning.*

The vibrant string looped itself around Wren's wrist, squeezing tighter as he pulled against what lay at the other end. Tendrils of electricity lashed his skin with tiny painful shocks that all together formed a chimera of hurt. He was weak, always had been.

The spellwork dimmed before it flared again, even brighter. A miniature storm ravaged the room, with him at its eye, knocking down candles and breaking the circle. Breaking the circle would break the spell.

The circle was broken.

The circle was *broken.*

And so too would Wren break—torn apart by the red substance spilling from the overheated cracks in his aether.

White chalk across his fingers and flames in his veins. Khetry tightened around his wrist, paralyzing him from the khetrical backlash. A heat as cold as ice crawled down his spine. He pulled himself free, clutched his stomach, and *screamed.* It hurt like a dagger drawn deep through his flesh. Something had gone terribly wrong. He'd broken one of the three cornerstones, those nigh-inviolate rules of khetry, and now he was paying the price.

Through blurry eyes, Wren bore witness to a shower of sparks. Tiny white stars popped like catching fire as a figure took form.

The sparks surged—a body fell—lightning grew.

Khetry bit at his chest, branding him with a malicious fury. The searing pain lasted for a lifetime and a second. Inside and out, gales ricocheted, in his mind, his own personal chaos. A tiny, lucid part of him hoped his mother never had to see this. The commotion died, wind ceasing and candles hissing out. A weight bore down on him.

He pressed a hand to his throbbing temple. Touching it only made it hurt worse.

The weight moved. His eyes shot open.

Wren came face-to-face with a mouth full of fangs—long, sharp canines and even longer, sharper incisors. Above that mouth were eyes clenched shut, dark lashes trembling. A tear leaked from the corner of one eye, splashing onto his cheek, followed by a cool gasp of air.

Something wet and warm soaked the clothing between them.

Lying overheated amid dust and blood, Wren must have been going mad, for the last thing that flickered through his mind was a delirious *Huh. Pretty.* before he lost consciousness.

PALENISA

Palenisa woke in fits and starts as the world came together through a blur of color, blinking her blue eyes blearily at the sky. Overhead, the sun shone directly into her face with the personal vendetta of hired knives. Based on its position, it was about midday. She felt a thin crust streaking her face, and when she reached up to her cheeks, she found salt there.

Oh, she'd been crying. For a moment she blanked on the reason why, until it all came rushing back.

The night before, her career—and life—ended.

Water gathered in her eyes. Furiously, she scrubbed at them, irritation warring with her mounting despair. The merciless sun glared through the canopy of trees above, and a headache beat inside her skull—as if she wasn't already falling to pieces.

Curling into a ball, Palenisa pinched the bridge of her nose, which was pierced by a silver barbell. Everything hurt, in a disaffected way, as though she were still drunk. Her jaw creaked, teeth and fangs grinding in her cottony mouth. As she moved, something wet squished, and the hot air was made worse by the smell of rotting waste. She was in the gutters.

Of course.

She supposed it was fitting for her to have spent the night among the refuse. To be discarded, to be unworthy. They were alike in that way—for how could she claim to be anything *but* unworthy after what she'd done?

Cursing herself, Palenisa struggled to make sense of how suddenly everything had fallen apart. One moment, she and the rest of the Crocodile Coterie had stumbled across the seaside camp of a Vana clan; the next, she found herself crossing blades with Yinka to stop the Sister of Might from striking down a crouched Vana, even while their fellow sisters cut down the rest as they fled.

The coterie had more free rein than most guardsmen, as theirs was an exclusive order under the sole command of Kharess Dust. They'd been left to their own devices more often than not, to pursue targets of their own choice when not dealing with the kharess's enemies. But never in a million years had Palenisa thought they'd *choose* to eradicate—to *attack*, she corrected, shying from the loaded word—the Norvatti, as rogue Aspects had during the Crusades. The Crusades were over. Had *been* over for about eight hundred years. And the coterie was far from a gang of unruly rogue Aspects who had nothing better to do with their spirits-blessed power.

The memory played on repeat as she ran over every aspect of her disobedience, examining it from all angles to pick out her innumerable faults. She was supposed to be—had been—the Sister of Faith. Dedicating her time within the coterie to the Zodiac, those twelve spirits of her faith who blessed Aspects, like her, with their powers. Then she'd gone and disobeyed a direct order while on duty. And for what—just because it felt wrong? It had, but it hadn't been her place to disagree.

So she was, once again, nothing of status. She'd been stripped of her emblem—a symbol of one's rank in the coterie—and unceremoniously dumped into the street by her former sisters. Effective excommunication.

Her chest squeezed, and she humored the grim thought that it meant she was dying.

Better she hadn't been discharged by way of woman-to-woman combat. Yinka was strong, but Palenisa didn't want to see how much worse the consequences would have been for killing her opponent.

Through a headache-induced haze, she recalled drinking herself into a stupor and not much else. Crying too, but that was a given, considering her sorry state.

The stench of effluent wafted to her nose as soft sewage oozed beneath her. She could barely find it in her to care, more content to wallow—wallowing was good.

Vines from behemoth trees crept their way into the gutter by her feet. Above her foul bed, the denizens of Okiro went about their day. From a structure built high in the trees above, someone tossed gray water out a window. She rolled to the side, barely missed by a stream of liquid shit, though the splash still caught her.

Though wallowing was good, she couldn't wallow forever.

With a resigned sigh, Palenisa ran a hand through her usually white braids, stained with refuse. Unwilling and unable to stand just yet, she pulled herself to her knees. She paused, examining the suvaugrams on the backs of her hands, marked there since birth, identifying her as an Aspect. The left bore a crossed circle;

the right, a sunburst formed from lines of varying lengths. They were the symbols for the earth and sunlight spirits, respectively, two of the Zodiac that could also be found on the suvaunoors of her faith.

She tried to find comfort in the fact that even without *being* the Sister of Faith, she still had hers. Could still pray to each spirit of the Zodiac at their suvaunoors.

A few wraiths cast strange looks her way as they walked past the gutter. She sent every one of them as withering a glare as she could muster. When they looked away, she was dimly satisfied. After taking a moment to breathe and gag—and force down the bile that followed—Palenisa pressed her feet into the ground and anchored herself like an adamant rod.

Drawing on her earth Aspect and the earth spirit, she pointed to the gnarled vines. Like snakes, they wriggled into the ground. The roots raced around her as she shifted her feet sideways. Cracks broke a circle in the wet dirt, and she bent her wrist back, finger pointing straight up. The ground gave way along the cracks, a small patch pushed up by the giant vines beneath them. Once high enough, she grasped the lip of the gutter and pulled herself out. She waved a hand that sent the vines wilting back into place.

She collapsed face up in the middle of the road. Fellow wraiths—with snow-white hair, dark skin, and ears pointed like dainty leaves—stepped over her, but she could not bring herself to move.

To think a thing is fine; to speak it aloud made it thus. So her mind predictably returned to her loss, encircling it with the coils of an obsessed viper. She couldn't help but think about how it had immediately rent her in two. One's title within the coterie was a legacy passed down from sister to novice, but *she* needed it more than the rest of them because she'd done worse. Her misdeeds followed her like an omen she believed only service to the coterie could heal.

The sun baked Palenisa a deeper brown as she collected herself and banished the thought of omens with a quick, furtive prayer to the chaos spirit. *I still have the Zodiac always watching over me.*

As usual, the capital city was a crush of noise and movement: dusty streets packed thick with all manner of vehicle, hawkers carrying wares on their heads, and open-air establishments, eateries, and tavernas. Structures built into the base of Ilon's abundant trees climbed all the way into the canopy, where a tangled net of rope bridges swayed as people moved from branch to branch. Stalls unfurled like flowers to display goods of gold and thunderstone, synthetic hair and an eclectic rainbow of wax cloth, dyed Mauriidan rugs, and fish marinating in baskets of salt.

As she sat up, the heat made itself known in the form of an insistent drop of sweat rolling down her spine. The cloak that pooled around her like a circle of night didn't help, yet Palenisa donned her hood, then tugged her sleeves down to her palms until none of her was visible, save for her fingertips and mouth. She felt at her back for her staff, tucked in its holster to charge, and along her thighs for her daggers. Then, with a grunt, she stood and wiped off as much of the gutter as she could.

As she picked her way down the street, the points of her ears twitched at the occasional whisper from an onlooker who recognized her. They knew her as Sister Gleissa. Before long, the news would spread and she'd forever be the *former* Sister of Faith. She clenched her fists hard to stop herself from lashing out, her nails biting into her palms. This didn't stop the worst of her hangover from settling in like the initial icy-hot searing of a fresh wound. It was becoming harder to think, and she needed to forget again—at least for a while.

Palenisa stole her way around the side of a familiar taverna. Well, it seemed familiar enough—maybe it was one of the many she'd been at the previous night, but they all blended into a kind of inebriated slurry. Waiting for the barkeep to disappear back inside, Palenisa hung in the shadows behind the taverna. Before the door swung shut behind him, she darted forward to grab it and slipped inside the dark storeroom. She grabbed as many bottles as she could carry, leaving a stack of aur as payment in the place of each one. Her dignity was already torn to shreds—to *shreds*—so there was no need to add guilt and shame to the mix by stealing.

Bottles hidden within her cloak, Palenisa made her way down to the shore. Head held high, she ignored the stares, even as the overwhelming miasma of being watched suffocated her. She let out a breath she knew she'd been holding and melted into the crowd as a tall, formless black shadow.

The beach was more of a small spit of sand just large enough for four, maybe five wraiths to splay out comfortably. It had the Lizardwood for shade, beached flotsam, and an obscured view of the kharess's manse. The beach wasn't empty when she arrived. Where sand bled into dirt, a couple sat hunched together beneath ashen cloaks in hushed conversation. Ignoring them, Palenisa pressed her cheek to the moderately sized driftwood at her side. The scents of brine and piss wafted from it. Even though she wasn't alone, the secluded view made it all worth it. It was why the previous Sister of Faith had shared this spot with Palenisa. It had been their little secret reprieve when she was still a novitiate.

She missed Ada with the force of a million suns, almost as much as she missed her mother. The latter grief had healed in time and blood. The former simmered in her stomach, some days drowning her in a bright grief where she saw the older woman in everything.

Against her will, Palenisa found herself thinking of the way her sisters had hissed at her when they'd taken her emblem. They'd turned into a den of snakes in a split second, black hoods and moon-pale hair surrounding her as eleven pairs of electric-blue eyes glared her into submission. Shaking her head, she uncorked a bottle and drank the memory away in a sweet wave. The tears she'd tried to hold back earlier spilled in earnest.

She cried, she imbibed. She cried some more and imbibed the day away, watching midday shade to afternoon, and afternoon into evening. Spirits, she was a fucking mess. As twilight approached, her streaked cheeks were wet again. The sun had almost lowered beneath the horizon. Fading light streamed across her face, momentarily dazzling her vision.

Her head lolled away, and she was too spent to do much more than take another deep pull that dribbled from the side of her mouth. Palm wine was too weak to dull her enhanced sense of smell, though she tried. Seven bottles lay empty at her feet. She had *really* tried. As sleep threatened to lower her lids, Palenisa ran a claw around and around a large whorl in the driftwood trunk she was leaning against. Faint voices arose where her bare skin touched it, the wood reaching out to speak to those who could listen. An ability all earth Aspects were blessed with.

Humming, she listened as the wood recounted the aural ring of its history in a hushed croon. From growing unfathomably large among its kind to the people it had met in its time: a couple seeking solace under the forgiving shade of its leaves, a foreign orphaned child clambering through its branches, the woodcutter whose axe had downed it with a single reverent swing. Listening to what was once living earth speak, the haze in her mind grew, a creeping line of comforting mist.

Until it came to her. *That smell.*

Startled, Palenisa sobered up almost immediately. The world practically slowed to a crawl as the pungent smell of khetry came in like a bolt from the blue. Like spiced water, like iron and water-beaten stone after a thunderstorm. An unappealing combination. Beneath the khetry was the undertone of blood, rich and heady.

For such intensity, there had to be lulaik in the vicinity.

Palenisa vaguely noticed the wraiths at the other end of the beach sit up when the smell grew stronger, surging in strength before dropping to baseline. Vertigo overcame her, like waves crashing against a cliff. It took all her waning strength to dig her claws into the driftwood, unbalanced by the sudden change.

Raising her chin, she sniffed the air, and her nose cleared, as did her languid mind.

The smell lingered in the near distance, like gazing at far-off mountains. It resembled the sensation of the sun's warmth on one's skin—always there but never noticed unless searched for. It wasn't *close* so much as it was pervasive, shot from elsewhere and leaving her to track its aftershocks.

So if the lulaik was not close by, then where was the smell coming from?

She pivoted, trying to pinpoint a direction. Not south to the badlands, nor to the Lethean Sea ahead.

There, north. The realm of Estyria.

For the scent to carry so far, someone—*multiple* someones—must have been casting an incredibly strong spell. To what end, she did not know. Perhaps they wanted to die or were simply unaware that their actions would catch the noses of Aspects so far south. Did group spells even exist? She knew very little of lulaik save what khetry smelled like. But as she examined her thoughts, a plan began to coalesce.

After becoming a sister, she'd sunk into her faith and vowed to protect—in Ada's memory. The previous night was a failure, yes, but one she could rectify. Anything made through spoken word could be reversed by an act of devoted commitment. This was her opportunity. She'd wallowed, and now it was time to take back what she had foolishly lost.

Palenisa rose and closed her eyes. Bathed in dusk, she was formed of pure senses—smell, touch, sound. Her braids fluttered in the sea breeze. The dregs of the sun's glow called to her connection with the sunlight spirit.

Her eyes snapped open. A thrill rushed through her.

Somewhere out there, the most powerful spell any Aspect living had ever sensed had just been cast. She needed to find its source, find the lulaik before another Aspect could.

It was time to repent.

For the Vana. For her disobedience. For the spirits. She would—she *must*—do it for the spirits. With their approval, Palenisa could show the coterie—and the kharess—just how deserving she was of her stripped title.

Redemption was a bramble path. And she had just taken her first step into the dark. All it took was just one.

RISHÉ

The Silk Screen temporarily closed for two hours every single day; brothels were open continuously, but even those who sold sex needed sleep. Not that they turned away any patrons who came in during the "after hours."

Rishé was sitting behind the front desk fifteen minutes before one such closing. The Screen had a front desk because Erazill, its often-absent owner, was a real *visionary*; he wanted customers to see a kind face before slipping into the arms—and between the legs—of his Butterflies. Rishé, on the other hand, didn't care too much for all that.

Instead, she was hunched over, focused on her lap rather than the small coffer of aur she needed to sum for morning pickup. The golden coins were piled neatly for her counting pleasure, in magnetized stacks of five and ten.

Technically, she *was* doing the brothel's books. In reality the thick accounting ledger sat propped up on the desk to shield where her focus truly lay: the pamphlet on her lap. Across the pages that hid her were neat rows tabulating finances from the many years she'd been working at the Screen after amicably parting ways with the guild.

Her eyes were drawn back to the pamphlet, which was a study published by the Dugantu Archives in Ilon. She'd been waiting to read this particular issue for a while, but responsibilities had piled up, and unfortunately it had tumbled all the way down her list of priorities. So she had to carve out any time she could to get her reading done. She leafed through thin pages in fascination as her teeth worried at a fingernail.

Absently, Rishé reached up to brush aside the hair from her forehead, remembering at the last minute that it had been messily cut into a short crop at both sides and front. Her fingers looped around one of the three braids behind her ear as she read.

Past the dry abstract, she avidly soaked in any and all knowledge the pamphlet had to offer, eager to reach the details of the study.

> *Considering such unusual characteristics, it is not too implausible, then, to speculate on some power arising prior to the spirits-blessed Aspects of Peskelos and the Ilonese protectorate, or even khetry—that most ancient of substances, which eludes the sight of all sapient beings but eresh keyel and lulaik.*

It had been moons since she'd sent a missive to the Dugantu Archives inquiring further about this theoretical third power. And this article only served to further her theory that her necklace was more than *just* a unique stone. Rishé lifted it to scrutinize the pendant—a bright red stone covered in silver whorls that resembled writing. It didn't look particularly ancient, but that was half the thrill. Uncovering the depths of what appeared, at first, to be mundane.

As she squeezed it, a phantom heat warmed her palm, feeling almost like another hand in hers. As the necklace was the one thing, aside from her face, that she carried in memory of her mother, she wanted—*needed*—to know if there was something deeper to this, Jarha's last gift to her daughter. It was all she could do to keep her mother alive beyond the impassable borders of death.

Rishé thought back to her last conversation with the madam. The accounting of sex was a dependable business, but not her final vocation; as such, Parianne had offered to fund her higher education in Fa Djain. Though a gracious offer, Rishé had dithered, politely asking for time to consider. She wouldn't have been the first person employed at the Silk Screen to be extended a change of scenery. One of the former Butterflies, Rayet, had become a pirate, last she heard. Perhaps accepting wouldn't be such a bad idea. The University of the Commonwealth *was* known to have a robust library, and red stones—often called thunderstones—*were* slightly more common in the south. Yes, it almost sounded appealing.

But Estyria was her home. Even with a father she hardly ever spoke to, this was her home. Where her mother lived on in memory.

At the sound of footsteps, she glanced with amber eyes over the top of the accounting ledger. The last patron of the night, rosy cheeked from imbibing Anticarta-imported topalinca, shuffled out as he tucked himself back into his trousers, ignoring her completely. Once the door shut behind him, Rishé's stolen reprieve was over. Butterflies melted from their rooms to fill the space like water in a bucket. Topless, bottomless, draped in glitter, feathers, and missing a heel or two. Verdant hemplock smoke wafted to the ceiling from long pipes, to cover the scent of sweat and spent bodies.

Rishé brought her knees up. She quickly skimmed over a few more words before she could no longer ignore her duties. Hard to do when Butterflies kept flitting over to the desk. They draped themselves over her back and ruffled her hair as she half-heartedly listened to them gossip about their clientele. When it became nearly impossible to focus on the words on the page, Rishé slipped from the chair. She slithered through the swarm and ducked past a curtain of shells into the dimly lit hallway. A few Butterflies lingered there too, chatting quietly in the low light as they passed a pipe between themselves.

Grabbing a broom, Rishé quickly swept through each of the empty rooms. They'd been themed after different species of butterflies because Erazill was nothing if not consistent. The monotonous drip of a water clock accompanied her routine. She shuffled the pamphlet between her hands while juggling sheets, silk garments, and the occasional shoe shucked off to the side and forgotten. Folding what she could, she set the rest to be laundered or discarded as appropriate.

As she worked, Rishé found herself thoroughly entranced by an intriguing line of theory in the text. Carrying a precarious armful, she shoved the back door open with a foot and collided with an equally surprised figure. It was the madam, hands on her hips, only half as amused as the smile on her lips would otherwise suggest.

"Rishé." Parianne sighed, tossing her scarf over one shoulder. Tiny bells sewn along the ends rang with the movement. "Distracted, are we?"

Pausing, Rishé shuffled her haul—pamphlet under her chin,

arms overflowing with cloth that trailed on the ground behind her.

"No, Madam," she signed, shaking her free hand with three fingers clasped. Signing was automatic: a language she was fluent in since her mother had been hard of hearing. When her hands talked, part of her mother still lived. *"Some light reading."*

Parianne regarded her with cool coral eyes. She appeared ageless in the way that any guess of an exact number was always off by a few decades. Parianne paused a moment before she signed back. Not many were proficient in Eslang. Some, though, like Parianne, knew enough words to speak with her. Slow but understandable, and very much appreciated.

"Join me for tea?"

Rishé would rather lock herself in her room and read the entire pamphlet cover to cover while furiously jotting notes in her journal. But she prided herself on her affability, her ability to adapt to people after watching them, and it wasn't like she could *say* that to Parianne's face. *"Busy."*

Clearly not believing her, Parianne hummed in fond exasperation and turned crisply on a heel to enter the Screen. Rishé lolled her head at the door, huffing softly. She gathered up her bundle and picked her way to the laundress a few streets over.

A chill rolled in across Carbon Bay. The cliffside cities of Ausre often grew icy at night, but this night was more humid than most. Wisps of hair clung to the side of her neck, and Rishé tasted salt on the back of her tongue. She walked a dangerously thin road between cramped buildings and the stone barrier at the edge of the cliff. The path was lit by lanterns strung between windows, candles flickering on doorsteps, and early-morning revelers smelling of mead, with fusion globes in hand. A glance below revealed Porto Goniver, its ruins reclaimed as the dwellings and establishments of common folk. The rest of Ausre was much the same, cities dotting the sheer cliff faces of the mountains that bordered Estyria's western coast.

Stars winked in the Sky Court, a wide net of darkness. Along the horizon was a faint band of blush light.

Dropping off the bundle was a quick affair, the laundress already expecting her, though she was none too pleased by the tackiness that bound the cloth together. Rishé smiled apologetically and rushed out, her nose already buried in the pamphlet once more.

She paused beside a hexe, utterly engrossed in a passage theorizing about the "hidden mental powers of gemstones," when the watery mumbling of voices caught her attention. Not the voices, but the language they were speaking: Inachie, the Ilonese tongue. They grew louder, closer. The conversation came in snatches of what she could understand.

Lowering the pamphlet, Rishé watched the wraiths. One held a blue ball of starlight above their palm—a starlight Aspect, then. And both were clad in green capes pinned with the golden crocodile of the Ilonese standard at their shoulders. They, on the other hand, barely seemed to notice her in the shadow of the hexe. One of the many advantages of not being so vertically gifted.

"I could care less what some lulaik is up to or what rogue Aspects do with them—that crusade shit's too old-fashioned for me."

"It's 'I couldn't care less,' dipshit."

A clipped laugh followed what sounded like a playful shove. "Screw you! I'm just trying to say that Sister—*former* Sister Gleissa—"

They turned a corner and went out of Rishé's range of hearing.

A thought popped into her mind, and Rishé snorted at its absurdity. For a moment, she had the strange notion they were speaking of Wren, the one lulaik that she knew was foolish enough to tempt danger and cause such an utter commotion. An old . . . *friend.*

She frowned as a weight settled across her shoulders like two uneven buckets of water. He hadn't crossed her mind in years. Not since their falling out—and the dropwort incident, of course. It hadn't been anything spectacular, quite the opposite actually. One day the man had been there at the guild; the next—he was gone, and with him, their friendship, as well as anything that might have developed from it.

Bitterly, she shook away the memory. It wasn't *her* fault *he* left.

As she made to leave, gold glinted in her periphery. Pausing, she turned to scrutinize the hexe that shaded her. Religion was not something she bothered to partake in. She was not a follower of Nature and Light like her father and most Norvatti, nor did she care for the Estyrian gods. But their shrines were a feast for the eyes.

The hexe was a small thing, unlike those dedicated to Armasin, Mab, or even Disan. On a pedestal, a statuette of Gadgifah, the goddess of fertility, stood with its hands outstretched. Across them lay a sword not unlike Rhenitha's legendary Velanu. On its gray stone forehead was painted a pale hexagon of the Six Facets of Being. It was said that as long as Armasin's moon beheld the world, the rivers ran, the oceans flowed, the Six watched over everyone—Melarhone and Norvatti, human and lulaik alike.

Rishé knew all this from reading; it wasn't as though she'd ever participated in a ceremony to the Six, beyond watching from afar in mild curiosity. She fingered the coarse veilari awning over the shrine. It was painted with flowers as numerous as those that fell from Gadgifah's mouth—jasmine and marigold and common rhododendron.

Looking up at Gadgifah's face, she tilted her head with a wry smile.

Gods required prayer, offerings. And she *was* already there.

While the rest of the Six demanded flowers, favors, or food, oblations to Gadgifah took the form of parts of one's own self—a breath of air or a piece of hair would do. A holdover, Rishé assumed, from an ancient time when the goddess had been known as Chlorisha, smiter of the One Before All.

Rishé twisted a brown lock around her finger. She didn't have much hair, but she had life in her chest. So she lowered her head to the deity's hands, ignoring the carefully laid out offering bowl at the statuette's feet, and exhaled.

One for the lulaik those wraiths were gossiping about. One for Sister Gleissa because why not. And—she glanced down at her necklace, the pendant an almost virulent red—one for the pursuit of knowledge. *Why not?* Divine intervention couldn't hurt. After all, it was mock prayer in complement to her joke of an offering.

Mortals tended to the cruel. Laughing, she unfolded the pamphlet and continued on her way, wondering if—should they exist—gods were the same.

ASARU

It was darker than darkness when Asaru opened his eyes—at least, he thought he did. The color of sleep—not one shade, but that indescribable hue that lay behind closed eyes.

Am I sleeping?

He did not know, but he was not dead.

He did not see the outstretched hand of Khertote, masked in death, there to guide him to the Triumvirate and whatever lay beyond the veil. Instead, ahead of him, someone walked. Someone walked away. Someone familiar was walking away.

That hair, those wings feathered like a moth's, the unsteady gait born of a leg badly healed. He knew that gait.

Alvarys.

In sleep-darkness, Asaru imagined a face. Almond eyes lined with black markings, edges crinkled up in a cheeky grin. His brother. He opened his mouth to speak, but nothing came out. Voiceless, he tried to run but did not move. He did not move because he could not move. He was stuck in place by the spiderweb threads of a ruby maelstrom around him. Ruby and every other color that did not exist behind one's closed eyes.

But his eyes were open.

Something caressed his face. Revulsion shuddered up Asaru's spine, raising the hairs at his nape. He felt them around him, over him, clawing their way out of him. More caresses covered him, like hands. Three, four, five fingers on intangible hands crawling across his sides. From his sides to his neck. From his neck to grasp his face, two of them, in tender embrace. So familiar was their touch.

They dragged him down—and down. There he heard his mother's voice.

Come home. Come back.

His mother's voice was chanting. Tenat was chanting.

Asaru, warrior, brother, son.

From the void rose whispers and shouts, her distorted voice melding into a toneless ooze. The same, yet all so different. The chanting rose, climbing atop itself in frenetic crescendo. Insistent hands pressed at him. Pressed and pulled at him, apart, together, unbecoming while being remade. Reforged there in the ideal image of the darkness according to the plans of a presence far beyond his knowing.

His mother's chant wrapped around him. Wrapped around him until he couldn't breathe. Her voice was against his face, trickled into his ear until it came from within. Asaru's mouth unstuck, and he struggled to form a sentence through the slow warmth. He joined his mother, continued her chant.

Son, Son, Son, come home, come back, wake up.

But that wasn't him.

He turned his head. Or he *thought* he turned his head and met the decaying face of the king. Black flesh clung to a broken skull. Golden light—a shocking brightness—shone from hollow sockets.

Come home, come back, wake—

"—up!"

Asaru jolted awake and nearly collided with the person above him, who drew back with a start. A sharp gasp caught in his throat, his back bowing as he seized. A horrendous piercing pain radiated from his abdomen. It coursed through him, liquid fire in every nerve.

His mind reeled. *I am not here—wherever here is—but still in the palace.* It felt as though he were not with his body, merely a passenger for the pain. The shadow of an ominous presence loomed over his brain, and unable to feel himself, he thought, for a moment, that he was still under its possession. Panic swelled as someone pressed him tight against the hard, uncompromising floor. Supine, he was vulnerable. And when vulnerable—of both mind and body—he was a danger.

Asaru wrestled for self-control and lifted his head. Through a bleary film, his eyes landed on the crossbow bolt impaling the side of his stomach. Sluggish blood seeped from the wound, staining his ayashif and his leg wrappings in a garish gold. It took an age for him to blink. When he peeled his eyes open again, a man straddled his knees and kept Asaru from bucking as he twitched in pain.

The man cringed when their gazes met, quickly averting his eyes as his features melted to worried determination. "Put this in his mouth so he doesn't bite his tongue."

A pair of arms encircled his waist, and a gentle hand drew his head to rest in someone's lap. The image of a wary woman sharpened above him. She dabbed a cloth along his brow. The touch grated at him, but he could barely raise his own head, much less object to the unusual conduct. How very different they were from the healers back in Aedyton, whose hands hovered above the injured as they cast the spells of their trade from a distance. Much more formal than this blood-soaked mess, skin on skin and sweat and spit.

With the woman's grip to ground him, Asaru feverishly took in the entirety of his wound. The bolt had pierced his abdomen cleaner than expected, only a raised ring of flesh around the shaft to indicate the violence with which it had ripped through him. Jagged lines of bronze and violet crept from the point as if the skin was already halfway to necrosis.

"Oleander poisoning."

Asaru dragged his gaze to the man. A veritable jungle of black hair obscured mismatched eyes, and there seemed to be no part of him left untouched by freckles. Along the left side of his face and wrapping gently beneath the curve of his jaw to his lower neck splashed a scar, as if he'd been burned by a lavender wave.

Asaru blinked when he realized the man was speaking to him. "We removed the bolt from your wing while you were, um . . . *asleep*."

Shivers inadvertently traveled up Asaru's spine to the golden tattoo where his wings were tucked away beneath the skin. The fracture would heal in time, but already he ached for the sky.

"As for your stomach"—the man continued—"we had to wake you. To check for poisoning." Pause. "And, um, make sure you wouldn't go into shock. But I swear I can get it out safely! It's just that you were looking, um, pale and—"

"Wren," the woman said in affectionate frustration.

"Right! Sorry, let me just . . ."

The man—Wren—pressed around the wound, following the snaking path of poison, then felt around the bolt. Asaru's eyes drooped as he tried to pull away. A gasping pain struck him still, so with a tight throat, he looked away.

Supplies littered the floor. A bowl of spiced water with bandages hanging off the sides, a strip of cloth covered in herbs, and a wicked-looking pair of shears. Wren dipped the shears in the water. With an exhale, he snapped the bolt shaft as short as possible. Then he cut a cross in the skin around the base and began slowly working it out. The wound widened, more gnarled with each inch revealed. The wriggling discomfited Asaru, an incessant untraceable itch.

Tension seeped from his body when the last of the bolt was freed. He felt flayed, too spent to do anything more than watch the healers work. Above him, the woman drew a spell circle in blue chalk on her palm. She was lulaik, and Wren had to be too. Bands of khetry clung to her wrists as she charged the spell. Interest tugged at his weary mind at the differences between lulaik and eresh keyel spell casting, but he was no scholar.

In Asaru's distraction, he missed her casting of the spell. Bright red khetry flared, strumming before a pair of burning hands pressed over the bloody gap on his stomach.

Praise be to the Triumvirate and all other gods that exist.

A scream erupted from his throat, tearing free so suddenly he thought it came from outside himself. Lighting arced through him as his body contorted in remorseless, concentrated pain. Cold flames licked up his core, a bonfire raging across his skin like a thousand frozen suns.

A twin scream mingled with his.

Through tears, Asaru looked up and found Wren curled over his knees, racked in tremors and heaving as he scratched at his chest. The woman reached for him, burying her face in his hair until they looked more like one being. Wren shook under her touch, and Asaru felt himself shudder in kind.

Gulping down his pain, Asaru rose to his elbows. Moving was like pulling teeth. An ache rocked through him from gullet to gut with the force of spears stabbed in purposeful precision. Shaky hands pressed to his wound, claws running across the raised skin.

Wren keened as he frantically tugged at his shirt, wrestling with the material before seeming to remember the buttons. He wrenched it from his skin and tossed it aside to glance down. There were flowers tattooed across his skin: across his collarbone, entwined with a wheel on his hip, two on one biceps, and one tumbling down his other upper arm. None of those caused Asaru's distress. Instead, it was what lay starkly on the left side of Wren's chest. There, in tender-looking welts, was branded a wreath of acorns.

Asaru's eyes widened, denial and disbelief racing to the forefront. He felt at his own back, growing horrified when he discovered a twin brand etched across his shoulder blade. It felt as though a swarm of shadowflies had filled his head; an army of the tiny creatures buzzed into static between his ears. As he touched his own mark, a shock ran through him. Fingers stilling, he gaped as Wren twitched in response.

They seemed to come to the realization at the same time, their harrowed eyes locked on each other. *A backlash.*

Which meant one of the three cornerstones of khetry had been broken.

Manipulating khetry was all about maintaining order with the world while entangled in its animate strings. One cannot alter the body of another living being, their mind—Asaru thought of his possession and cursed the vulnerability that had allowed the possessor a foothold—nor the natural laws of consensus reality.

Something had been done that was horrible enough to warrant that binding brand. In all he knew of backlash, it *always* began with a brand. A permanent mark on the perpetrator for all to see.

There were only a few instances that came to mind—because people tended to be smarter, more careful than that. Asaru wasn't even sure if they were simply legends or held some grain of truth. In the tale of the eresh keyel bound to a human—long before the Founding War and the Sea Gate—they had drawn vital energy from each other before the strain took its fatal toll. There was the story of the lulaik piper who sought total ownership, mind and body, of their lover, as well as the one about the eresh keyel who vied, then died, for immortality. All branded with some ill fate. And Asaru had found himself bound in backlash to its next senseless victim.

Resentment flooded inside his racing brain. He hadn't been saved by these healers. Instead, through no fault of his own, he'd been bonded. With only one person to blame.

"You . . . fool," he spat hoarsely.

Wren shied away in reply. Shame coated him in generous strokes as he pulled his shirt back on with trembling hands. Clutching his stomach, he curled over his knees, forcing himself smaller as Asaru continued to glare. Pain flowed through their bond in a feedback loop—his physical, Wren's of the mind.

"By Ignante's blessed name, Wren. *Backlash?* What have you *done*?" The woman's whisper was laced with tangy surprise and sour anger. Looking more disappointed than angered, she kissed her teeth and grabbed a small bowl. She resembled Wren, with slightly more sun-browned skin and much longer hair. But they both shared those doughy, down-turned eyes.

"You're dehydrated." She handed the bowl to Asaru.

The coolness was much appreciated by his dry throat. It took a moment to come back to himself. He shivered as sensation returned, along with a dull, constant ache. His pain was managed for the time being.

As he drank, the woman rubbed a cool, sticky substance across his stomach. She dipped strips of cloth into the spiced water and bandaged his cauterized wound in swift but harried motions.

"D'ya." Wren sighed. "I'm sorry."

"Don't," the woman snapped. "Not right now." She kissed her teeth again, but her face softened. "Just—just go bring our guest some paprikash."

Wren nodded and left. The kitchen was through an arch attached to the main room, allowing Asaru to watch him stir a pot while looking like a thoroughly scolded puppy. Glancing between the two, there was a weight of assumed family history. Even with the quarrel, it hurt how familiar it all seemed. His claws bit crescents into his palm as he willed childhood memories from blooming. Those times were gone—and wouldn't return for as long as Alvarys remained missing.

"I am not a guest," Asaru said, sitting up with a grunt. It hurt to speak so brusquely, so he kept his tone low and flat to spare his throat.

As though she hadn't heard him, the woman dusted chalky hands on her thighs and spoke. "Please call me Sabine."

"*Sabine.* I am not a guest. I will not be staying here much longer, as I am searching for someone."

As Sabine assessed him for a moment, her braid fell over her shoulder. His mother wore similar braided locs that tumbled loose from the crown of her head like rain. At the reminder, Asaru's heart ached.

"Well, first of all, perish the thought. You've been out and unresponsive all night," Sabine said. "And second, we haven't seen or heard of any eresh keyel in the area. Can't imagine we would, considering the embassy is in Romia and we're in Valyn."

Asaru's tail whipped at his side. "What."

"We're in Valyn."

He gaped, unable to formulate a quick response. "That is impossible."

The curious sound of an animal stalled his confusion. Asaru stared dumbfounded at the strange furry creature that climbed into his lap, settling across his legs without a care in the world. It opened an eye to stare at him, seemingly unamused. After a pause, it blinked before stretching with a liquid ripple and turning over. Thin membranous wings sagged at its back. Strangely enough, he felt seen and judged.

He was petting the creature, mind racing, when Wren returned with a bowl and folded himself onto the ground a little ways away. There was an air of discomfort about him, forlornness. Gaze downcast, he radiated self-loathing. And Asaru was not sure why, but for all his anger at the man, he couldn't quite look away.

"It *is* possible," Wren said, still avoiding his eyes. "Because I . . . I summoned you."

"You"—Asaru blinked—"summoned me."

His eye twitched as he struggled to understand. But like flint that failed to ignite, he couldn't grasp logic where there was none. To summon someone—to even think of such a preposterous idea—broke the laws of reality, and the first of the cornerstones. No one was that foolish. Or at least, he'd *thought* no one was that foolish.

"If it helps, it was an accident."

"No, it does not help," Asaru snapped.

"You have no idea how sorry I am." Wren sounded miserable.

His shoulders rose to his pointed ears, and then he hunched, as if trying to make himself smaller. He looked a wreck, with dark bruises beneath his glassy eyes, his hair limp as seaweed, and a tiny, cruel part of Asaru deemed it good. A larger, kinder part of him—that sounded suspiciously like Alvarys—thought better of it.

A flurry of noise erupted outside, slashing through his thoughts.

In the sliver of sky visible through a nearby window, Asaru made out fireworks exploding against the setting sun. A ribbon, the wavy shape of a snake, a bouquet of flowers—all burst like colored jelly across the sky, disappearing in sparks.

"Words will not fix this." He ran a hand through his loose hair and down his nape, ignoring the triangular protrusion among his halo stones there. "Very little can fix this."

Asaru dully picked at his leg wraps. They would have to be redone like the ones on his arms. There were flecks of dried blood in the cloth. Red blood. *Red.* The color mingled with visions of gold and the feeling of static. The lingering possession gripped him by the throat. Warm eyes glinted luminescent with terror as a silver blade rent flesh. A scar in the ground wound serpentine over an ever-watchful eye.

He shook the images from his head. "I have to go," he said, looking at Sabine. He'd forgotten she was still there, too caught up in himself and Wren—and their unfortunate bond. "I need to find my brother."

Sabine frowned. "Look. I apologize for the backlash my child has caused. I can't begin to understand the enormity of your task—losing a sibling must be a terrible thing—but as lulaik, I feel as responsible for you as the sun is for the earth. And as a mother, I'm *telling* you, you aren't running off anywhere half dying of oleander poisoning like that."

"You do not have to," Asaru said, frustrated. "You do not have to help anyone but yourselves."

"I want to." Sabine made to touch him but thought better of it. "We can if you let us."

He pressed the heel of a palm to his tender forehead. "I cannot. I did something regrettable. I killed your king—"

"He was not *our* king," Sabine snapped, her voice a venomous barb.

"But he was *a* king," Wren said weakly. He focused on Asaru. "Regardless, you should rest. Let us heal you as best we can. I don't have the materials to make an antidote for the poison, but . . ." He touched his scarred neck almost absently. "There's a place where I can get them. If that's, um, what you want. And then I . . . can help you find your brother?"

Wren looked at his mother. A conversation composed of raised brows and squints took place across their faces. Sabine held her child's cheek, pressing their foreheads together before standing. She moved to the corner of the room, by a tapestry of a figure lying on a bed of clouds, and pulled down the ladder to a trapdoor. A square of the sky opened in the ceiling, and she disappeared through it, leaving the two of them alone in tense silence.

"Fine."

Wren blinked. "What?"

"Fine," Asaru repeated. Though reluctant, he wasn't foolish. Legends of khetrical backlash may have been just that, but the brand felt every bit as real as the wound that twinged at his side. "You bound us together, much as I am loath to admit, but even I am not willing to further test my luck with khetry."

The other man seemed to perk up at that.

"Oh!"

Then he slumped.

"Oh."

He dithered, charcoal-black hands flexing around the bowl on his knees. Then as if remembering himself, he thrust the bowl at Asaru, startling the creature in his lap. It yowled and swiped a paw at them.

"*Scavite,* Dakazna," Wren apologized as it stalked off, tail swishing. He shyly passed the bowl over. "This is for you. Um, to eat, I mean. Obviously." He cringed, mouth shutting with a click of teeth.

Asaru reached for the bowl, and their fingers brushed, a simple light touch that was like a cold shock to his system. He froze, then recovering just as quickly, he took the bowl and turned away. He felt as though he'd been mercilessly thrown into a frigid lake, forced to swim his way to safety. There was familiarity in this unfamiliar space, and the dissonance rankled him.

The bowl had cooled to a pleasant warmth that seeped into his hands as he ate. Savory, the paprikash was flavored with peppers and garlic. Chunks of meat swam in the sauce, and there was an almost rose-lemony aftertaste. Asaru ate ravenously and soon found himself drowsy. Setting the bowl down, he stared at the lulaik long and hard. He was reminded in Alvarys's voice that even for all his anger, he'd still been healed. They hadn't needed to grant him such kindness.

"Thank you."

Wren's head shot up. "You . . . you're welcome?" He looked at him strangely. "I'm sorry, I still don't know your name."

"Asaru."

"I'm Wren!"

Asaru raised a brow. "I know."

"R-Right." Flushing, Wren ducked his head. He took a

well-loved quilt from the stack that surrounded them and raised it. "Um, may I?"

Asaru shrugged and let the man adjust the blanket over his back. Before the lulaik could leave, he grabbed Wren's sleeve, careful not to let their skin touch, and pulled him down until their eyes were level.

A frisson ran through him as their gazes locked. The brand prickled, and Wren winced as though he sensed the same. Asaru looked between Wren's mismatched eyes, searching. One strand of khetry stood out from the rest. An unbroken line of red, it was knotted into a loose braid, a clear sign of the brand connecting them. Life to life, Wren to him.

It wasn't something that could easily be undone, easily untangled.

"I pray you do not forget the consequences of your actions," he said, freeing the man. He did not wait for a response, deciding to curl into himself despite his injury. If Wren left, he did not notice.

Asaru let the open window draw his attention again, to the violet sky interspersed with dim rays of sun that filtered into the room. An orange band of light shone across his thigh. As the medication turned his bones to lead, fatigue lowered his lids to half-mast. His heart slowed until it beat in time with the dripping of a nearby clock. The brand still throbbed, but the less he focused on it, the more its itch faded.

He watched motes of dust flit through the air and tried not to think of his dream. Tried not to think of Alvarys, too far to catch. Walking to a place he could not follow. Walking past the veil.

Soon the colors of sleep welcomed Asaru back into their many intangible hands.

PALENISA

Palenisa trudged through the Ausran city, already-thin streets constricting as she went. Grunting, she struggled to keep her unsteady feet in line with her cottony mind. Both staggered sideways, so she pressed against the rocky walls for balance and took a breath. She swallowed down the taste of the absinthe she'd been—very much counterintuitively—drinking to keep her going. Or perhaps she'd been using it to try to make herself forget about anything that wasn't solely forward movement.

Her body was wired and her head spun. She'd been traveling almost nonstop for a number of days—*three, four?* She couldn't quite remember. The only thing that kept her on her feet was the Zodiac, and the smell. That *smell.* It still hung in her nose with an all-conquering air, guiding her north, and then farther north.

Regardless, she had made good time and passed quickly through two provinces. At this pace, a few more days might find her in Valyn. For a moment, she let herself wonder what she'd do if the scent took her to Sterrock, heart of Norvatti country, where the eresh keyel were said to have first made contact with humans centuries before the Founding War.

Can't be. It wasn't a thought she let linger long. Running on the instinct of her senses more than any accurate form of way-finding, it didn't quite seem plausible. She doubted lulaik in the valley—if they settled rather than traveled in clans—would be foolish enough to cast such a powerful mass spell. Well, she hoped they weren't.

That night, she found herself in a small seaside town called Porto Veli. It was set low enough into the Ausran mountainside that the Lethean Sea lapped at the walls, spraying over the cliff-side barrier to slick the cobblestones. Half of it jutted out into the water atop an uneven tumbling of rocks and the remains of the long-destroyed city of Porto Goniver.

Pinks, blues, and oranges turned the sky into a painter's palette. Under the setting sun, blurry figures filtered up and down pathways carved into the cliffs, moving among flat buildings set into caves. From a distance, the cry of violins and an incessant bell reached her ears.

Estyrians all across the kingdom were celebrating the first night of Kestrel, dressed in their finest clothing and bearing red strings on their hands to commemorate the coronation of their king. Or maybe it was to celebrate their gods. She knew little about the other faiths on the continent save for their names—the Zodiac were all that mattered to her, all she needed to know.

The salty air was sobering her up faster than she liked. Her vision cleared as the taste of aniseed fled her mouth with the evening winds. Clutching her head, Palenisa groaned against the sudden awareness of her body and all its aches. Her blistered feet, her screaming calf muscles, the twinge in her lower spine, and the horrid scratch in her eyes. Even her own musk threatened to envelop her.

She grimaced, half wishing she still had aur to find lodgings in a taverna. If only so she could scrub herself clean, rinse, and do it all again. But the last of her coin was back in Okiro, perhaps still glittering in a dark storeroom. *No matter—better to remain inconspicuous.* With wraiths uncommon in Estyria, better she kept on her way.

The sun dipped below the horizon, and the last reserves of her energy faded with it. Sunlight Aspects needed sunlight, so without its rays, she felt like a boneless sack. A thing made from dusk and twilight. With the sun gone, she was steadfast and unwavering, yes, but also dead on her feet, falling asleep between blinks. She hoped the spirits wouldn't begrudge her a short rest for the night. Even a cave would do; so a cave was exactly what she found.

It wasn't a particularly comfortable cave, not that she imagined they tended to be. It was one of many dotting the beaten cliff face overlooking Carbon Bay. Palenisa crawled inside, careful to avoid the foul water, which was dark from the carbon leaching out of underwater caves. It's why Ausre was known even in Ilon as the hottest place on the continent, despite the badlands that lay within its own borders.

Wincing at the sight of the choppy waters, she slid away from the lip of the cave. Sometimes accidents happened—most times the consequences were a fate of one's own making. *But better safe than sorry.*

She tilted her head against the wall, closed her eyes, and just let herself . . . breathe. Her heartbeat slowed, but her mind spun in a slow stew of mild intoxication and bitter images.

Screaming Vana, hissing sisters.

A nest of vipers writhed in her gut. Forlorn, Palenisa touched her braids where her emblem would—should—have been. She'd always used it to tie her hair up, and without it, the braids swayed loosely around her waist.

Palenisa unslung her staff and twisted it open at the middle. It split in half. From one end she pulled out a small tube no longer than a finger and no thicker than two and brought it between her eyes. When empty, the solar battery more resembled glass than the hard light it was made of. She curled her claws around a single point to generate a faint ball of sallow light. It flickered with her weak connection to the sunlight spirit, tenuous whenever the moon rose. Barely there shadows rose on the wall opposite her.

She pressed a finger to the tube, and it filled with solar energy. Once the battery was fully charged, she pushed it back into the staff and twisted it shut.

As she set it aside, her vision swam. Cradling her face in her cool palms did little to quell her headache, which throbbed like dancing bones. The pulsing heartbeat in her head from that mild use of power reminded her—very much against her will—of how deeply tired she was. It was as if she were already asleep, just waiting for her body to receive the message and catch up.

She removed her cloak, folded it, and set it down to rest her head. Still on the fringes of being tipsy, Palenisa swayed forward, backward, forward—and suddenly her senses sharpened.

She dodged the silver-blue ray of starlight that shot by, inches from her nose. It whipped past with the tail of a comet, so cold and so close her cheek burned. Out of the corner of her eye, Palenisa caught the glittering ray as it faded into the rock and formed a crack. Then another. And another. Until the wall was a net of lines, and the cave filled with a dangerous rumble.

She heard the earth cry out beneath her palms before she saw it.

Palenisa snatched up her cloak and rolled aside, avoiding the wall's collapse as part of it imploded in a growling spray of rock. Carbon dust rose from the rubble that composed the back of the cave. Throwing on her cloak for cover, she whipped around to glare down the figure climbing into the cave after her.

A freelancer. She seethed. There was no one piece of distinction that identified one as a freelancing Aspect, but from her encounters with them, they always had a *tell* up close. On this one, there was a line of raised scars along the freelancer's forearm, from the starlight suvaugram on the back of his hand to the inside of his elbow. She didn't doubt each one counted his completed kill contracts. Surprising how few there were for someone who came at her with the force of a brash, young lion.

His stern eyes met hers over the unwavering point of his lunar spear.

"Well met, Sister—*former* Sister Gleissa," he said with a tilt of his head. A faded cloth tied his matted locs into a waterfall over his shoulders. Palenisa's lip curled back at the practiced slowness of his voice, and she knew he was most definitely green, and she began to doubt the veracity of the cicatrix tally on his arm.

"Can't say the same. What's the damage?"

"Got a contract to fulfill, Gleissa."

"I'm no longer of the Crocodile Coterie, nameless freelancer." There was a pause as she steeled herself against the hurt of admitting it out loud—not just to herself in the quietness of her tears. *To speak something makes it so.* She laughed, a bitter half sob of a thing. "I have it on good authority they want nothing to do with me."

The freelancer didn't waver. "Special contract. The client wanted you informed of the details before completion. Strange, but nobles're eccentric like that. Does the house of Da'Sanjam ring any bells? *Chiroyn?*"

Palenisa's eyes widened to shocked rings of blue.

That was a name she hadn't heard in well over twenty-five years. Once she ended Chiroyn and the other pathetic men who had murdered her mother, their names had faded. They hadn't crossed her mind, because they were *nothing* to her. Just targets of revenge. But Ada had washed her clean of holding on to that memory by giving her solace in the coterie. So it was a uniquely cruel game the mind played that she was able to recall *his* face, burned in lines of sunlight, more easily than her own mother's.

Clenching her fist, Palenisa prayed that the spirits were on her side in this. Sought comfort in the knowledge of the presence of the Zodiac.

She reached for her staff, but the freelancer was faster.

He vaulted over the cave debris, sliding and knocking the staff to the side. The steel rod rolled to a stop near the edge of the water, hanging precariously close to the waves, and a sheer, sudden drop. Starlight shot past her ear again as she dropped to the ground to dodge the crescent ray. As the energy impacted with the rock, her mind snapped into focus. A razor-thin line of blood oozed from her hairline. Violet, it dripped onto her lips and trailed down her chin, a pale imitation of her tears.

The freelancer's spear glowed a dull blue, the edges of his form fading as he drew on the power of the night, making himself invisible. "Have to say," he said mildly, "I look forward to seeing how fast a sister of the coterie can die." The freelancer twirled his spear and drew into a defensive stance, open hand splayed out with a ball of starlight floating above his palm.

Palenisa's eyes narrowed. From her throat came a hiss like crackling embers. The sun had set and yet still she burned. Blood had been drawn. There was no time for dawdling bullshit. Fine, she had no staff—*Don't need it.* She would make do. She would kill this man with her bare hands if she had to. A vicious smile threatened to overtake her face as she pulled a dagger from her thigh. She planted a hand against the floor, and the calls of the earth surged up to meet her. From the clarity of their voices, she could tell most of the alcohol had left her system.

Good.

Aspects worked better clearheaded. Plants and stones and metals were her domain. Even if her dagger failed, the earth spirit would not. Palenisa dashed forward, blade aloft, a furious bolt of sun in the night.

Dawn always brought with it a sense of rejuvenation. Morning light brushed Palenisa's face tenderly. One would think sunlight Aspects would be early risers; but as in many things, she was, most days, an odd exception. She yawned and cracked her back in a feline stretch, rubbing sleep from her eyes. A particularly forceful flick of her tongue prodded where her canines had split her lip, opening the wound afresh.

The taste of blood unsettled her gut, violently and with horrific speed. She rolled over, scrambled to the ledge of the cave, and vomited the sparse contents of her stomach into the bay. She spat bitter acid and held still a moment, waiting for the nausea to pass. As she glanced over the ledge, she grimaced at the freelancer's corpse floating face down beside the rocky shore. Soon it would sink beneath silent waves, and all trace of him would be gone.

"Fuck me sideways," she cursed.

She sat back, scrubbing blood that wasn't hers from her forehead. Salt and blood and brine mingled in her nose. The scent may have stretched thin but was still within reach beneath it all, like a beacon on which her entire being was locked. Standing, Palenisa kicked up her staff, then grabbed and holstered it. She swung on her cloak and donned her hood, taking comfort in being covered nearly completely. She felt almost like herself and knew soon enough she'd need to get drunk again to forget that feeling.

As she drew closer to whatever awaited her at the source of the scent, she prayed—*hoped*—they were worth it. *Spirits,* she thought, this time more reverently. Between apologies for the previous night's delay, Palenisa dutifully asked the Zodiac for guidance. *I pray I'm close—I do this all for you.*

WREN

Wren tried—with very little effort—and failed to still his bouncing leg as he pored over the primer before the hearth. He went from page to page, skim reading the text for something, *any* answer that would solve the problems he'd caused for himself.

The brand throbbed over his heart at the thought.

He lowered his head miserably and rubbed his hot eyes, trying not to cry. It was only fate that his mistakes would eventually culminate in something he could never take back. A violent response as the world lashed out at his foolishness, his unthinking audacity.

Always failing. Always making a mess of things. But this was more than a mess, wasn't it?

This was backlash, a violation of the three cornerstones of khetry. And he didn't even have enough heart to argue that he'd been tricked by the primer, for the fault was his alone. Curiosity was a vicious monster endlessly eating at him, feeding his inability to know when to stop, when to think, when to *feel* the danger simmering in the air.

The worst part was that the consequences were *not* his to bear alone.

A lump of regret formed in Wren's throat as he glanced at Asaru pacing by the window with a contemplative frown. A stranger whom he'd saved and condemned in the same spell. He'd summoned the eresh keyel and, in doing so, bound them together in the worst transgression known to khetry.

A punishment shared by two.

What use am I to anyone? Dark tendrils of a familiar melancholy began to invade Wren's mind. His heart turned to lead, and he wondered if he could sink into the floor, disappear completely, and ease the lives of those he cared for.

Compared to his current lot in life, the dropwort incident had been an innocent accident. Though he wondered what the guild would have to say to him when he brought another poison conundrum to their gates. His misdeeds tended to mark him permanently. His hand rose from his chest as he grimly clasped the side of his neck. The wrinkled scar gave under his touch, though it was slightly firmer in some places. It had grown taut over the years, but there would always be a tenderness to the skin.

As if sensing his stare, Asaru turned to him, still frowning, and Wren looked back at the primer. Words swam in his vision. Nothing-letters with nothing-meanings. He pressed a hand to the page, willing it to steady him. Meditation would have been the best thing to do, but he could hardly clear his mind even for a second.

The trapdoor to the rooftop garden swung open, and his mother climbed down, carrying a basket of flowers. Kestrel strings were wrapped around her wrists, with knots that represented the Estyrians' Six. Despite her distaste for the death god Disan, she still wore the costume of Kestrel yearly at the end of the sun season. "Too much worship of death," she always complained, "not enough of nature, not enough of life."

Shame darkening his cheeks, Wren immediately shut the primer and shoved it inside his satchel. Sabine's curious gaze turned to him, and he could only look away as the horrible son he knew he was. The best mother in the world deserved much better than him. Even though she'd pop him lightly on the head if she ever heard him *say* that around her.

As Sabine carried the basket into the kitchen, Wren tentatively approached Asaru, slowly, like one would Dakazna when she was half asleep.

"Can, um, can I . . ." he stuttered, already tripping over himself. By all that was sacred, he was a true mess. Asaru seemed to think the same, tail whipping in what had to be agitation as he stared at him. He was a decent bit smaller, though he had the aura of someone twice as tall and ten times more aggressive—no doubt that was true too. "Need to reapply the salve on it. Your injury. If that's, um . . . OK?"

"As you wish," Asaru huffed. Settling down by the open window, he tugged off the tunic Sabine had given him and set to watching the fireworks. Exasperation radiated from his tense form, which Wren knew was directed at him. Any other time, he might've complained he didn't deserve it—but he most certainly did.

Crouching, Wren examined the garish patch. Sallow purple lines flared from the raised entry wound. It felt warm as he rubbed in a tacky kingsbane salve. It indicated the man's body was pushing itself to heal as best and as fast as it could, despite the poison. As Wren worked, he was reminded again of the guild, of his aborted study to become a healer. He loved healing, loved helping people. Wished to have it all back, a time and a place when he knew what he was worth.

"Are you done?"

"Ah. Yes." Blinking from his stupor, Wren pulled away to eye his handiwork. The clean bandages were tight on Asaru's lower stomach, separated by a small strip of skin from what appeared to be a binder. The bandaging would be serviceable for a short while but would need to be reapplied as the poison spread. Unless they reached the guild before things got considerably worse.

"It is getting late," Asaru said testily. He pulled the tunic back on, chain belt at his waist clinking with the movement. "You said a few more days, I gave you a few more days. You said the evening, I gave you till the evening. Let us be going before my patience fully runs dry."

Asaru's intricate braid rested over his shoulder, auburn tip brushing the pale scars on the rest of his honey-brown skin. The marks of a warrior. Wren wondered what kinds of remnants he'd fought to receive them.

"Soon?" Wren looked over at the water clock, willing time to move faster than this sluggish crawl. "Yes, soon. I promise."

Dakazna trotted over to them. The wolvencat patted insistently at Asaru's calf until he picked her up. Her body lolled long and liquid across Asaru's lap as she flicked a pink tongue out at Wren. He returned the gesture. She was such a spoiled little thing.

"Anemone?" Sabine called, strolling from the kitchen, hands fisted on her hips. "Remind me again where I put my needles—"

"On the table, D'ya. Where you left them yesterday."

"Ah, maiks vuti, I'd lose track of my mind without you!"

As Sabine passed by Wren to her workstation, she cupped his chin in gratitude. She pulled out her ironbone needles and rolled a slate cloth over the sewing table. As a seamstress, she performed similar tasks daily, but every so often she needed him to remind her of the little things. Sabine pinched a thimble onto her thumb and rolled up her sleeves. Black dahlias common to their tribe, the Rosatay, were stitched into the meat of her forearm by an expert hand—hers. They twined with her tattoos, depicting a cornucopia of thorns piercing rhodiola flowers. Tugging a thread from her wrist, she drew it through the needle and, with nimble fingers, began to sew a spell circle into the fabric spread over the table.

Ever since Wren was a child, his mother had preferred to sew her spellwork into objects rather than simply drawing them. She claimed that blood, water, and charcoal were far too messy. A quick glance down at his hands proved her somewhat right.

"Anemone?" Asaru asked.

"It's my, um, blessed name. All Norvatti get one at their naming celebration."

Asaru hummed. It made an intriguing picture to watch him scratch Dakazna's curled horns a moment—*almost domestic,* a silly little part of his brain supplied before he summarily quashed it.

A soft glow arose from the circles Sabine had stitched as she charged the spell. Spiderwebs of khetry clung to her wrists, glistening like dew. Light rose and she flicked her wrists, casting the spell. What once were simple swaths of cloth now resembled snakeskin capes. Gray with faint dappled bands across their length, fading in and out of visibility as his mother held them up to the light.

The sight made everything much more real. Not that the brand wasn't real enough, but Wren found himself snapped back to himself with a cold discomfort, as if his mind were a stranger and he an unwelcome intruder.

"Refraction spell," Sabine explained to Asaru as he slid his on. It fell to his knees and had slits cut into the back to allow his wings to stretch. "Stick to the shadows and you should be relatively imperceptible. Be careful, it isn't perfect. Light has a way of uncovering most unexpected things."

Wren clutched his cloak and blinked, surprised to find his eyes damp. "Are you sure?" he asked quietly.

"Scavite," she sighed dramatically. "I've gotten tired of seeing your face—you're sixty, it's time to permanently leave the nest, vye?"

"D'ya," Wren said gently.

Sabine's impish smile faded, and she wrung her hands, toying with her fede ring as she often did when her mind wandered. Her crow's-feet deepened around her eyes, and in that moment, she looked decades older. "Just watch each other's backs. And please hurry to the guild, all right? No need to worry your dear d'ya any further."

Elsewhere in Sika, a water clock spilled over with the sound of rain pattering against metal, and a bell rang. Asaru's ears perked, hazel eyes alert. "It is evening. Let us *go*."

He moved to the door and looked back expectantly, but Wren was rooted in place, seeing the glassiness in his mother's eyes, the invisible yoke across her shoulders. She inhaled, exhaled sharply, and enveloped him in her arms. He wanted to stay there forever, where it was warm and where he was loved despite all the many careless things he had done wrong. He buried his face against her shoulder, breathing in the peppermint of her hair.

Pulling away, Sabine pressed her forehead to his in a Red Desert kiss, cradling his face as though she held the world. Like the rings of a tree, the marks on her hands spoke to her years. The scar from when she first taught him to use a needle, the healed-over traces of many sewn spells, the calluses from her work.

Since being cast out from their clan, they'd been alone, but they'd been alone together. The first, and only, time they had separated was during his stint with the guild, and they had not been apart for long since then. All they had was each other.

"Dorai, randu tios vua'foms'is," Sabine whispered. *I shall see you, my son.* Then she let him go, slowly, as if it pained her, and touched her cheek. "Come back to me."

Words were hard to come by, so Wren nodded. No tears would be shed. That felt too final. This wasn't to be their last goodbye. For as much as he yearned for the guild, he knew he'd come back. He always did.

"I always will."

Sika was in the throes of revelry.

Fluttering streamers in various shades of red hung across the road between boxy mansard roofs. Ropes were knotted for the Six, and scarves of fox feathers were looped around hexes. Music blew in like wind, and fireworks, flashes of sudden color, burst in time with the beat of distant drums. During Kestrel, Disan took on a lighter mask, smiling with the knowledge that fate would inevitably lead all life into the wide net of his arms.

Wren and Asaru passed hawkers at street corners trying to sell last-minute costumes. They passed vendors pulling sticky sheets of taffy and handing spun raspberry cream to children in cones of crosshatched waffles. Wren led them through Sika Major to Nastradona. They clung to the shadows, hurrying along a familiar path he could probably chart with his eyes closed. But even under the cloak, he remained wary, his gaze eagle sharp, scanning for signs of the Black Order. Some sentinels were wraiths, but thankfully, most were not Aspects. *They* truly were the stuff of lulaik nightmares.

As they trekked up the hill to the apothecary, Asaru seemed to grow agitated. Wren glanced back and found the other man glaring, his eyes almost aglow under his hood. "What is this, why are we wasting time here?" he hissed as Wren unlocked Nastradona's back door with the key atop the lintel.

"Need to grab some supplies our garden didn't have," Wren replied, biting his lip and pushing the door open. He winced at the creaky scream of the hinges that always accompanied it. Zanna had told him more than once to oil it out, and he was regretting putting off that particular task. "What I have now won't last all the way to the guild. It's not a particularly . . . brief trip."

Inside, the room was dimly lit by the city below and the wide-eyed moon above. Familiar shapes in the near darkness turned to obstacles, which he felt along to avoid. The door to Zanna's apartment was shut tight, but he moved slowly anyway, pausing between each step to lessen the risk of drawing any attention, from her or the other establishments nearby.

Though "quiet" did not necessarily mean "safe."

As politely as he could, Wren searched the cabinets above and below the mixing bench. Though he was not a healer, he knew the tools of the trade, being that he *almost* was one. More kingsbane, along with marigold and geranium, a roll of silk as thick as a fist for wraps, vials of oils. The entire time, Asaru loomed at his back, tapping a clawed foot as he muttered in impatience.

Wren wanted to apologize again but found himself distracted by the sound of shuffling outside. Wood bowed as the back door creaked in a sudden wail. A warning blared in his brain. Instinctively, he grabbed for Asaru's hand. It seemed they both did, palms pressed tight by some base instinct.

A jolt traveled through their bond, and Wren gawked at the falcon wings protruding from the slits in Asaru's cloak. They fluttered, injured wing drooped slightly lower with broken feathers. A breath later, Asaru not so gently snatched his hand away. His brow dipped into something more frazzled than a frown. The points of his ears flickered the same way Dakazna's did when she was caught off guard.

"Do *not* do that," Asaru said curtly.

But you reached out for me too . . . "Sorry."

"Wren?"

Zanna stood in her doorway, holding a candle. Her eyes bounced in disbelief from Asaru to Wren and back again, caught on the massive twitching wings. Asaru folded them away and met Wren's gaze with a look of mild inconvenience.

Why had he ever hoped for this night to go well?

"Miss du Allopei, I can—"

"Don't." She bit her lip and raised a hand. Frowning, she hummed for a moment. "Don't tell me. Despite your inadequacies as an apprentice, lulaik stick together. Take what you need and leave before anyone else sees *him*."

But it was too late.

One of Nastradona's nosier neighbors must've peered in at the initial commotion and spotted Asaru, or perhaps Wren's luck was worse than he had already assumed. The sound of sentinels stomping their way up the mound filled his ears. Panicked, Wren clutched his satchel, unsure. Afraid. His ears rang, each tone building like concentric circles in water. Louder, larger, until he barely felt himself in his own body.

Asaru shoved him out of his spiral. *"Focus."*

"Go. Down the other side of the hill, to the woods." Zanna gestured hurriedly, pushing them out the back door.

Wren's heart pounded loudly in his ears as they raced into the Kingswood, where cobblestone merged into underbrush. Behind them, the sentinels rounded the corner of the mound road, torches and swords in hand. Silver steel glistened in the moon's light, hungry to whet its edges. A shout sounded, an unintelligible cry as the unit noticed them fleeing. The faster of the two, Asaru sprinted ahead, cloak streaming behind him as he ducked beneath low branches and leaped over logs. If he'd had his wings spread, he'd almost look like a beast.

Chancing a look back, Wren shuddered at the sight of an archer behind the rest of the Black Order unit. With strong, skilled arms, the sentinel pulled back on her longbow . . . aimed . . .

Wren called out a warning, and they both ducked in time to avoid the steel-tipped arrow, which embedded itself in a nearby tree. Thick trunks obscured every possible juncture of the wood, and she still managed to almost hit them. She must have been trained by the Chain Archers, the most accurate and deadly in the world.

The archer nocked another arrow, advancing after the rest of her unit. They were trained, armed, deadly, and at this rate they would overtake him.

Liquid panic coursed through Wren's veins.

Asaru slowed his pace and spun on a heel, growling at Wren to keep running. He brought both hands to his jaw and khetry brightened, thickening, warping—almost *singing*. Sudden exhilaration overtook Wren like a free fall as Asaru breathed out a wide arc of fire. Golden flames cut a line through the earth before the archer could release the second arrow. The tongues roared, a lion rising to lick the canopy and the sky between him and their pursuers. The wall of fire forced the sentinels back. The sentinels skidded to the side to avoid being burned where they stood. But it didn't stop them completely. The thought of them closing in had Wren swallowing down stomach acid with the fear.

Their distraction, if only momentary, gave him and Asaru time to disappear into the tall grass. They ran farther and ducked beneath the drooping veil of a willow. In the tiny clearing obscured by its low-hanging branches was an inconspicuous entrance to Birinuyi, set against the trunk of the false tree. Accessible only to those who knew where to look, the underground tunnels of Birinuyi were a many-armed creature. In this one thing, at least Wren's father was—had been—useful, for the trunk was marked with a distinct crossed-out circle, originally set aside for him and his mother should they ever have need of it.

"Do what you must, but hurry." Asaru tilted his ear up and stepped closer to the tree. He barely seemed to have broken a sweat, while Wren came to a staggering stop by the trunk. "They recovered faster than expected."

Quickly catching his breath, Wren pulled off one of his earrings and worked it into blue chalk between his fingers. He spared a nervy glance through the net of the willow's pendulant branches. The steps for the spell floated into his mind's eye—chalk for the spellwork and a small splash of blood as an additive. The mixture gleamed on the mossy trunk as he finished painting the circle. It was a light one, and the lighter the spell, the faster the charge. He just needed to *open* something that already existed. He pressed his bloody palm into the circle, and it glowed white. As though being drawn, the sketch of a door impressed itself into the wood. Above the sound of his own panting, Wren heard the groan of some deeper mechanism working beneath the false tree.

Creaking on dry hinges, the impression sank in with a click, click, click. A curtain of moss rustled over the entrance that appeared. Wren swung his hand through the greenery and discovered it was an illusion. Asaru followed suit before stepping through the illusory moss without hesitation and disappeared into the tunnels beneath them.

Wren made to follow but paused. Hesitated, just for a moment. His heart was a moth threatening to beat free of his chest; the sentinels sounded even closer. He found himself looking back. Past the branches and through the trees, his home, Sika, was a green smudge in the distance. He thought of Floret, Zanna, his mother. Each left behind by a string of his own misgivings, each innocent to the chaos his curiosity wrought.

I'm sorry. Wren slipped through the hidden door. The last thing he saw before the door shut was a firework bursting across the sky, sparks like the horror of a summoning.

I am so sorry.

II

UNDER PRESSURE

ASARU

Time was hard for Asaru to quantify in the dank tunnels. It felt like they had been traveling for over a day, ceaselessly walking, sometimes half running in his case, as they moved farther and farther from Sika. Closer and closer to Alvarys.

There was little time for talking or sleeping or eating. As such, silence reigned, though his ears were filled with the sound of the rushing inside himself. Every part of him was alight with residual adrenaline, alert and wired as his fingers and toes still buzzed from the lingering effects of that fire spell. Perhaps he would crash soon, until then he had to keep moving.

It was only when his shoulder blade prickled in irritation that he slowed to a stop and looked back. In the dimness, lit faintly by a trail of bell-shaped blue flowers that cast the tunnel in moonlight, Wren lagged behind farther than Asaru would have liked. One would assume, for having such long legs, he would be able to walk at least a bit faster.

"We should . . ." Wren said, hand over heart. "Rest, just for a little while. Please?"

Asaru frowned. Most of his time as a warrior he'd fought remnants on his own, dealing with only himself. With just himself for company, it was easy to forget that other people weren't the anomaly, he was—both on Aedyton and elsewhere, it seemed.

"Fine," he said begrudgingly as the other man planted his hands on his knees and gulped stale air. He had to wonder, with the walls of these tunnels seeming too tightly packed, where the air came from. Those entrances like the one they had come through? If he closed his eyes and stood in place, he could almost feel a thin stream of warm breeze trickling from somewhere farther down.

Leaning against the wall, Asaru crossed his arms and allowed himself a single moment of stillness, like dew that hung on the end of a leaf. He shut his eyes, held his mind closed from vulnerabilities. The drop fell. Hazel eyes fluttered open, slit pupils dilated in the low light.

Wren tilted his head back. The column of his neck formed a smooth curve, covered half by the scar and half by freckles he was unable to see clearly in the semidarkness. Frowning, Asaru glanced down where they had come from. Both sides of the tunnel were nearly alike, earthen floors and dirt walls embedded with a lusterless gray rock that seemed to disappear among the vines that hung from the ceiling. It looked like a place between places, its only purpose a temporary passage.

"Where are we?"

"Birinuyi," Wren said, rummaging through his satchel. He pulled out the rolls of bread Sabine had given them and handed one to Asaru. "These tunnels were used as a safe haven during the Crusades, for lulaik fleeing rogue Aspects. The walls, um, the flintrock, it's said to dampen the smell of khetry." He bit into his roll thoughtfully. "And Weavers too. But I doubt *that* part."

Weavers. Those rare, pitiful lulaik who sought power beyond

what they knew, even at the cost of great, unknown sacrifice. Tenat had told him Weavers were legends, mere tales to laud the achievements of those daring few lulaik who had fought in the Founding War, if they ever truly existed. The doubt rang true—after all, *the power over life and death*? That went against every single one of the cornerstones.

Though he tried not to entertain conversation, he found himself inquiring further, compelled by a simple curiosity. Gathering information, as it were—he *was* a stranger to this continent. "And after these *Crusades*, what happened to the lulaik? I did not see many of you during my . . . time in the capital. And you"—he raised a brow, taking in all of Wren's unassuming nature, finding little that hinted at his eresh keyel ancestry, save for the leaf-shaped ears—"seem to try very hard not to stand out."

"We're still around. As you can—I mean, well, um, you know." Avoiding his gaze, Wren picked at the half-eaten roll. Wren ran his tongue across his small sharp canines. "History isn't my strong suit. I have—used to have—a friend who would know."

Asaru's throat was thick with bread—and some emotion that he wanted to force himself not to feel, but it still came over him, nonetheless. An emotion far too close to sympathy for his liking. He didn't know why he'd asked. *Because it's something Alvarys would do.* Prying the answers he needed from others in all his charismatic congeniality.

"So, um, your brother." He blinked back his surprise as Wren continued. "You said you were looking for your brother?"

Uncrossing his arms, Asaru cast a pensive look at the ground. The bisected end of his tail dusted the earth as confusion swelled within him and determination calcified in his gut, weighed down by an anxious dread at what the missing members of the Tetrarchia could mean. They'd taken the beacon—but the vial, that *curse,* had devastated every other person in the room. His hope was that the wretched violence hadn't touched Alvarys. It was a hope to which he held fast because he *had* to, for his own sake and his brother's.

"I was sent to the embassy on an assignment and found every single person there dead from a curse," he said flatly. *Relay the facts, force down your feelings.* Like he had taught himself to. "My brother and one of his squad members was missing. Along with a beacon they were sent there to find."

"Ah," Wren replied.

"Do you comprehend *why* I cannot afford any delay?"

"Well"—Wren pressed his pointer fingers together, chewing his lip—"getting you to the Guild of the Living Body isn't a delay. You're, um, poisoned. And you're being . . . pursued by the Black Order. We—you—can lie low in their neutral territory until the search dies down."

"No." A growl rose sharply in the back of Asaru's throat. The brand tingled, an almost familiar static that sent a shiver up to the base of his skull. The presence wasn't there, but its tackiness would forever linger. "I will let you take me to this guild. I will let you treat the poison. And then, I *will* find Alvarys."

Wren reached out haltingly, surprise coloring his expression before he timidly stepped closer. "Oleander poisoning can be fatal. And curses are rare. How do you know it's really a curse?"

"Because I have *seen* it. And eresh keyel cannot lie." Before Wren could respond, Asaru bared his teeth and snatched Wren's necklace, wrenching him down with a cry. "Listen close: I was sent here to complete a task. You have bound us, and that is something I cannot fix. Finding my brother is the most important thing there is. If you derail me further, I will not hesitate to leave you behind—backlash or not."

For a moment Asaru glanced at the moon-shaped pendant between his fingers. The stone was cool and luminescent against his scar-riddled hand. He brought his gaze back up to Wren's wide, startled eyes. He was close enough to notice that the left was not completely gold—a few carmine flecks swam in the iris like a banded gem.

"Nod if you understand."

Wren nodded.

Asaru shoved him away and kissed his teeth.

Cowed, Wren stared at him with a strange look. Trepidation and a not too small amount of fear were plain on his face, and something like regret tightened Asaru's throat. He forced himself to swallow it.

"Is"—Wren coughed, rubbing his neck—"is violence always the answer?"

Staring at his trembling hand, Asaru clenched it. "If needs must. They often do."

Phantom touches brushed his jaw, and a chill ran through Asaru from head to toe. He flexed his hands to ward it off. *Strange.*

They rested far apart that night. The next few days—maybe two, maybe three, maybe more—were spent in a similar suffocating silence. The walls were too close, the ceiling too low. With each step, the pain in Asaru's side intensified, and he slowed his breathing to compensate as the wrappings grew wet. Dutifully, he overlooked the pain. Pressing a hand to his stomach, he forced himself onward as the subtle ache soon sharpened. It was the worst he'd had, he could not lie, but he'd overcome it regardless.

After a few more hours of walking, Wren finally led them aboveground.

Like flowers peeking through the dirt, they climbed through

an overgrown trapdoor. The span of the sky was a welcome sight, and Asaru's wings longed to greet the clouds. They had emerged in a glade dotted with trees beside a babbling creek. The pale trees were ringed with brown spots that resembled eyes, hundreds of them, watching, and Asaru could almost taste the grass scent in the air. They walked a little ways, light morning mist clinging to their ankles in the underbrush.

Asaru doffed his hood and let out a sigh. He closed his eyes, and when he opened them, Wren was kneeling by the creek, collecting water in a flask. Wren had replaced the snakeskin cloak with an embroidered woolen coat conjured from his satchel. Under the sun, he looked unassuming for someone who'd broken one of the cornerstones.

Tempted to touch his brand, Asaru frowned.

"I need to clean your wound and replace the bandages," Wren said.

"I am fine."

Incredulous, Wren stared at where Asaru kept his hand pressed to his wound beneath his cape. It bled, fresh gore seeping through the soaked bandages. Both men winced. "You're not even *trying* to hide it. Sit down and just let me help."

It seems someone has a hint of a spine. As he perched on a moss-covered boulder, Asaru was mildly impressed by the firmness of Wren's tone.

Wren bound his hair into a low tail and unfurled a roll of supplies. He selected a few violet petals striated with gold and mixed them with soap and oil in a mortar to create a salve pink as the dawn. He worked efficiently, tactile in his healing practice. Grimacing, Asaru wanted to shed his skin, wanted to shy from his touch as the bandages were removed. Hands made of dream-darkness and a chant by a familiar voice congregated in the corners of his brain. With each layer removed, the strips of cloth were more blood soaked.

Asaru held still as the gold was wiped away, salve slathered in its place over the faded bronze starburst of his injury. As he was wound back up in clean bandages, he couldn't help but watch Wren's focused expression. There was an intimacy to this kind of healing. Hands on skin, fingers across flesh, red strings taut between healer and patient.

A pinching sparked down his back between his wings and he doubled over, shoulders quaking from the sudden rush. Eyes wide, his hands flew to his nape, clutching at the lifeline of his halo. Startled, Wren hissed, rubbing at his own neck as that spark of hurt flared through the bond.

"What's . . . happening?" he croaked with pained eyes.

"The curse," Asaru muttered through clenched teeth. *I must have been infected, perhaps even the moment I stepped inside the embassy.* With trembling hands, he pulled aside his braid and hesitantly brushed the shard of black diamond that had sat among his halo stones for as long as he could remember.

Other warriors had found it impossible—*unnerving*—that he could wear in his halo the same mineral that burned the rest of them with a single touch. "Unnatural," he'd been called each time he plucked black diamonds from the corpses of remnants and tossed them into the sea. All but shunning him, save for Alvarys at his side.

Does it feel bigger? He couldn't tell without seeing, but he could feel tendrils of raised skin, keloids snaking from the stone like some parasitic growth. He prodded around the shard, but each scratch of his nails only hurt him more.

A glance down at his hands confirmed what he knew to be true. Matching those on the corpses at the embassy were black marks like hard stone crawling up his wrists and speckling his scarred skin. Death already clawing at him from beyond the veil.

Bumps rose over his skin. A deadline he hadn't even known loomed.

Resignation was easy to bear. Asaru looked up at Wren, who had been staring at Asaru's newly blackened fingers. "Do you believe the curse exists now?"

Tense and quiet, Wren nodded.

A wet sensation streamed over his lips. Confused, Asaru brushed his nose, but it came away dry. He looked up when Wren cursed. Twin crimson rivers flowed down Wren's chin, staining his teeth. He tilted his head down and wiped a bloody smear across his face.

This bond was getting thoroughly irritating.

"Are *you* well?"

"Just overheating." Wren pinched his nose. He ducked into the brook and splashed water over his mouth. Blood drifted on the slow current, then disappeared. "When lulaik go too long without casting a spell, we overheat. Side effects include headaches, cramps, and bleeding, unfortunately."

Not the curse, then. *Good.*

Drawing his knees to his chin, Asaru looked aside. "Where are we? How soon can we continue?"

Wren hummed a moment. "We should be near Anseme. It's the closest town to Sika and the Ausran border." He donned his hood and slung his satchel over his shoulder. "There's a morning market there, and I really need, um, I really should refill our supplies. I'll be quick. I promise."

"Do not make promises you cannot keep."

"Don't you want to eat something other than days-old bread?"

"I eat what I am given." He shrugged. He wasn't picky.

"All right . . ." Wren furrowed his brow. "Well, I'll just be . . . down there . . ." He gestured vaguely over his shoulder. "You probably shouldn't go past the tree line."

"I am quite aware I am a wanted man."

"Um, right! Yes, OK—I'll just . . . I'm going now." Spinning, Wren trekked down the slight hill on which the glade rested. Even as he grew smaller in the distance, his hunched shoulders seemed to radiate embarrassment.

For a few minutes, Asaru made a round of the glade, redoing the wraps on his arms and legs, before he grew too curious to be quelled. He stayed well away from the tree line, but from atop a rock, he could make out the town on the slope below.

The creek flowed to a river beside the town, dotted with figures milling about in the market. At the center of its major was a fountain, a plinth with a statue sitting atop sprouting from it. He squinted, and its features sharpened.

It appeared, from this distance, to be a veiled woman clutching something in both hands. But its most striking feature was the familiar disk of gems that framed her head like a sun. He recognized the motifs from a story Tenat once regaled him and Alvarys with. About the human who wanted to become eresh keyel but turned to worshipping them instead. *Abbess Ariadine.*

Many humans had taken great interest in Aedyton's first warden, Madib. If he recalled correctly, Ariadine had been particularly devoted, proclaiming Madib a goddess rather than the mortal—however great—she was. Her faith spread virulently, but the story ended when the Sea Gate rose, and Tenat seemed to know no more after that.

When he thought of the strange shrines he had seen in Sika, altar bowls filled with aur, food, and flowers, Asaru wondered what had changed. The only gods he knew were the

Triumvirate, and they were less so gods than deified eresh keyel.

Tapping a claw on the rock, he followed the sun to gauge how much time had passed. And before long, Wren was picking his way back through the trees, much more cheerfully. A smile curved his face—*One that should be there more often,* flashed an intrusive thought. As Wren approached, the smell of venison wafted to Asaru's nose, and his mouth watered. Venison was rarely imported to Aedyton, and there were no animals that were not sacred to the Triumvirate on the island.

But as Wren approached, two figures appeared out of the forest behind him.

The hairs on the back of his neck rose. Wrongness swelled within him, and khetry brightened.

Asaru darted forward and shoved Wren back just in time to avoid a strike of lightning. The momentum tumbled them both down the hill. Rolling, rolling, rolling over each other. They came to a stop beyond the tree line below, at the edge of the town's major, which brimmed with merchants and common folk.

He quickly found his footing, his face wet. His nose throbbed—likely broken—and inside his mouth was a pool of blood he spat aside along with a tooth. The singed tatters of his cloak hung from his shoulders. He ripped it away with a growl, revealing his wings quick as a snap. Behind him, a human screamed, and the rest of them followed. With a glance over his shoulder, he saw the market was quickly emptying at the sight of him. *So much for staying unseen.*

Wren groaned, clutching his arm. His pain snapped through the brand, but Asaru paid it no mind as the two figures descended the hill in dogged pursuit. He made a quick mental catalog of both: gray cloaks, white hair, blue eyes on black sclera.

Wraiths, then, the human-born descendants of the dolomites who had been extinct since the Founding War. And, from the marks on their hands, Aspects too.

Heart thumping in his neck, Asaru crouched and rubbed his hands together. Fast then *faster*, building up a charge as he spun a thread of khetry between his palms like lighting a fire. The wraiths approached, one with a marked hand outstretched. The other bore two marks as they rode a rippling black wave down.

"Eșarpe save me—what are you doing?" Wren's hiss shook as he skittered behind him, face pale in terror. "Those are rogue Aspects!"

Asaru raised his arms above his head. Waiting, on a knife's edge, for the right moment.

The Aspects crossed the final span of distance.

Moments before collision, Asaru flung his hands forward and cast out the spell. Thunder shattered in his ears. Lighting cracked, tearing a line through the forest between the Aspects and forcing them apart. The pale blue bolt lashed out tendrils of electricity.

Call and response. The Aspect with their hand outstretched quickly grabbed a crackling tendril as if it were material. They spun as though guiding water and sent the bolt flying back at him.

No—not him. At *Wren.*

Asaru slid to his knees, throwing his wings up to shield them both. He gritted his teeth as the feathers pulled and his stomach ached in equal pain. No lightning stuck them; fate intervened. From the major, a third figure joined the fray in a flurry.

As if in slow motion, Asaru followed the arc of the figure's scythe as it swung down on the lightning bolt, redirecting it into the neutral earth.

The newcomer dragged the blade across the ground, a manic

grin stretching her dark lips. Rippling muscles shifted under her cape as she twirled a double-sided scythe that burned yellow with the heat of the sun. She sprinted forward and slammed her fist into a nearby tree. Instead of hitting solid wood, it melted into the white bark. She deconstructed it from the inside out, cork, heartwood, and all. Until only the ethereal structure of what was once a tree stood behind her.

The sound of a whip cracked through the air.

Asaru tensed. Drawing his hand up, he cast a spell of pure khetrical energy to block the watery chain flung from the side. The attack burst into rain, droplets flying with a hiss of steam. In his distraction, he'd almost lost sight of the second Aspect. His eyes darted around, searching—*there*. He found them by the fountain in the major.

They reached into the fountain and reared back as if tugging an invisible rope. In a quick motion, they flung another chain of water at Wren, who cowered in the shadow of Asaru's wings.

Lunging forward, he caught the watery chain and wrenched back as if it were solid. He clasped his hands, grabbing onto khetry, and swam them through the air to cast a water spell. Bit by bit, he morphed the chain into something more useful, liquid solidifying into ice from the point where he gripped it.

As he held the frozen spear aloft, the Aspect charged, a dagger tucked between two knuckles. They swung low, aiming for the middle of his chest. Asaru whirled away, the blade catching the feathers at his back. The wraith corrected and aimed to the side. Close again. Asaru ducked from the blade threatening to slice his biceps. It met his armlet in a twang of metal on metal.

He turned and pushed Wren from beneath the Aspect's next strike. Panic marred the other man's expression, and he looked moments from fainting the longer the fight went on.

This is getting tiring.

When the Aspect next struck, he overcompensated. *Let them draw in, too far, too close to stop themself.* Asaru bent back, dagger flying above his face, inches from his nose. As they readjusted, he brought up a leg and kicked, slamming them against the edge of the fountain with enough force to split a human in two.

The statue of Ariadine watched with unseeing eyes. Cracks formed in stone. Water trickled forth.

On the slope above, the newcomer fought on equal footing against her own opponent. One hand still on the fading tree, she slashed her scythe to dispel another stream of lightning. At a distance she made a frightening figure, teeth bared and pale braids fanning about her waist.

She clenched her fist and threw herself forward in between strikes. She flung the thing that was once a tree over her head and through the air. It writhed like a snake as it sailed, but the Aspect rolled to dodge.

That was their mistake.

Instantly they were trapped neck deep within a pillory of dirt. They sucked in air and blew out a large gust, but their head was snapped aside from the force of the newcomer's kick. With a swift slash, her scythe relieved them of their head. Black blood leaked from the bloody stump, pooling in the grass in a macabre puddle. The head rolled down the slope and came to a stop by the fountain.

Wren vomited.

Asaru met the eyes of the newcomer. Surprise flitted across her features as she stepped forward and froze. From a cut at her temple, viscous blood surged.

The other Aspect staggered up from the fountain. Clutching their eye, blood flowing between their fingers, they pointed downward—*sharply.* As they did, the newcomer dropped her scythe. The tendons in her arm flexed and shook as she clearly used every ounce of her strength to resist. When the Aspect twirled a finger, the newcomer began to walk. Her body moved like a puppet tangled in strings, jerking with every step, though her eyes blazed with virulent anger.

While Wren gagged pitifully, Asaru assessed. He could grab Wren—they could leave, disappear back through the trapdoor and be done with this. Let the wraiths deal with each other.

But he knew he couldn't. The voice in his mind that sounded like his brother wouldn't let him. Call and response. He had a mission, yes, but it was only right to return the help he'd been given by a fellow warrior.

The Aspect stretched out an arm. A conical spiral of blood gathered at their fist, flowing from where their eye had been, replaced by a gap in their skull, soaked in blood and liquid vitreous. A gruesome display of power formed into a blade with ridges sharper than teeth.

Asaru gathered khetry around a finger and pressed it to his earring. The act of transforming minerals into liquid, manipulating those substances—this was one of the earliest spells eresh keyel learned. He snapped and molten gold shot from his ear.

Quick, unseen, it cut through the air and both the Aspect's ankles. They screamed, collapsing as their tendons were severed clean.

The moment their concentration fell was their end.

The ground beneath the woman's feet buckled. She shook her head and glanced over to him, nodding curtly. Then she dashed at the freelancer just as they reached back toward the fountain. For the water. For one last stand.

First, she kicked them in the face with armored sandals, and then she snapped her fingers, melting the rings that formed her outer mail skirt into thin strands.

The liquid chains wrapped around the Aspect's neck in a twisted necklace. Coils rose higher until they were forced to look up at her lest the threatening edge cut their throat. Head locked in place, all they could do was spit and hiss, likely curses in the wraithian language as the woman rolled her eyes. Deft hands darted forward, thumbs pressing to both of their temples in a mockery of a tender embrace.

"Damn it, Gleissa. Almost had you—"

She pressed tighter, crowded closer. Golden light gathered where her flesh met theirs. Smoke rose from the Aspect's head, their eyes rolling back as their body went limp. They looked dead, but it seemed what the woman had done was far worse. Even from where he stood, Asaru could feel the wall of heat from the cooked corpse.

The woman slumped, her scythe the only thing keeping her standing. Through a veil of hair, a haunted expression contorted her face. Her eyes squinted shut as she panted, mumbling under her breath for a moment. It was as if all the weight of the world suddenly came crashing back down, and she was once more aware she was mortal—that she had a body that could hurt. Asaru could sympathize. The comedown was always the worst.

"There is a tunnel," he called. "Back in the forest. Quickly."

"Asaru," Wren hissed, looking to be about as close to an emotional breakdown as one could.

The woman nodded sharply and flicked her scythe. It collapsed into a staff, a faultless line of metal. Rushing over, she snatched Wren by the hood, who yelped in terror, and ran into the forest. Asaru followed close behind, claws pressed into his palm to control himself as she wrenched Wren along.

Together, the three of them slipped through the door beneath the earth. A distant clamor arose—at first a single shout, then more joined into a chorus from the town. Metal, mayhem, and many feet rushing toward the tree line. As the trapdoor shut, the sun, which shone above the white-spotted trees, was shuttered to darkness.

PALENISA

After an hour of tense, silent walking, Palenisa pulled a small bottle from her cape and downed the rest of the liquor. She patted the bottom to get the last few drops out and tossed it aside once done. Her insides began to warm pleasantly, and she clung to that sensation to keep her from falling apart into a pool of skin. As she dragged a hand across her mouth, she prayed to the Zodiac for patience. For compassion. For an end to whatever it was about these tunnels that made her temper flare and her nose dull.

The tight space was lined with some material that irritated her nose to no end. It felt stuffed with cotton, dampening even her tongue. And the scent of khetry was practically nonexistent when she pointed an accusing finger at the offending lulaik's chest.

"You!"

The terrified man flinched when she turned on him. The scent's remnants clung stubbornly to his skin, marking him as the original source. Beneath it, the iron of recently spilled blood. Distinct. Not necessarily easy to find but impossible to forget once perceived.

Part of her wanted to crush him until he understood the gravity of what he'd done. Casting a big fucking flare with his unimaginable spell. Who knew how many rogue Aspects also had his trail?

"*You.* Before I read you to filth, let's get introductions out of the way: Palenisa."

The lulaik introduced himself as Wren, and his companion—

"Asaru—I know." She waved him off. "Pretty sure everyone does at this point. I'll deal with you after, but first—" She whirled on Wren, grabbing his collar and shoving him into the wall. The intimidation worked with ease, for though he was a hair taller, there was a slightly pathetic nature to him, and Wren shook like bones in the wind. "What, by all the Zodiac, is *wrong* with you?"

"I—I—"

"How badly do you *want* to die?"

His shaking seemed to cease as he was overcome with thoughtfulness. His reply was a whisper, barely there. "More than you'd think these days, if I'm being fully honest with myself."

Palenisa blinked, looking over at the eresh keyel—Asaru, she reminded herself—as he, too, blinked, then she released Wren. It wasn't as if she *couldn't* understand him; it was just surprising to hear it said out loud.

Grasping her chin, she worked her jaw and pressed on. "Do you have *any* idea how dangerous that was? Whatever it was you did lit up the nose of damn near every Aspect from here to the badlands. And, as has been made *incredibly fucking clear*, some of the rogue ones think crusading against lulaik is a fun little national pastime."

She knew, as much as she wanted to forget, a whole coterie who thought so too.

Wren winced a bit pathetically. His hair obscured forlorn

eyes drowning in a regret that she had come to know well. It had become her. It had driven her to him. Forming a claw over her chest, Palenisa pushed it outward to cast out bad omens. He frustrated her as much as he confused her—yet, by the grace of the Zodiac, she was glad to have found him. Almost too late, and with an assassin at his side, but she found him.

And speaking of—

"Adding to that, you're with *him*." She gestured at all of Asaru, who looked mildly affronted. "One, an assassin. And two, very clearly cursed with Black Diamond."

She tilted her head and noted the black at the edges of Asaru's sclera, one of the early effects of the curse the island's warden had warned of in her message. His hands were gloves of speckled black, petering out as it went up the wrists, like blood dripped on wood. Though Wren appeared to be the same—she squinted in the dim light—his looked more like they'd been dipped in ink that faded lightly up to the elbow than coated in mineral.

"Black Diamond," Asaru said in deadpan mirth. Prominent pale scars lined his face, across his nose, at the corner of his mouth, from chin to brow, and twin fishhook marks curved under his lower lids like kohl. "Fitting."

"Haven't you heard?" she asked. "Your people's warden sent out a message, shared it all across the continent. They say the curse is spreading from a place called Saite, turning the water into tar. Sea Gate's locked down between Estyria and the island, but some nations still have passage. Fa Djain, I think."

"Saite . . ." At that, Asaru seemed not to light up so much as perk to attention. His tail flicked rapidly at their feet, and he stepped closer, searching her face. "Have you heard any news of other eresh keyel? Outside the Sea Gate, elsewhere? The badlands, even?"

Palenisa stepped back, slightly apprehensive at the way his focus had sharpened on her. Looking at him was like catching a glimpse of the sunset—seemingly harmless until its glare bit into the eyes. He'd fought like a warrior back in that town, not dissimilar to some of her former sisters. Even the slightest thought of the coterie hurt, but she held it aside for later. Asaru had been swift. Precise. Like he didn't need to expend much energy to take a life.

Shaking her head, she watched his face fall. In the moment before it flattened into impassiveness—a quick flash she almost thought she'd imagined—his eyes were somber pools. Just like with Wren, she understood that feeling too. That large nameless thing that swelled inside until the only way to release it was through a barrage of tears. Or a fit of rage. He didn't look like the type that *wanted* to cry, though.

As Asaru glanced away, she grew curious. Surely the spirits would not fault her this one small question. "Your face is plastered in every province as we speak. Why do it? Why kill the king?"

Asaru went still, dazed. A vacancy drifted across his expression like a cloud covering the sun. A furrow formed between his brows; it looked perfectly at home on his face.

"I did not want to. I was possessed." Glowering at the wall behind her, he crossed his arms and bared his teeth in a grimace. His bisected tail thumped the ground, fur raised like an agitated fox. He emitted intangible warning spikes. *Dangerous, volatile, sad.*

"Got no idea what that means."

Clearly frustrated, Asaru sighed and pressed his thumb over his lips. "My mind was vulnerable—and *something* took advantage." He tucked an auburn-tipped braid behind his shoulder and pursed his lips. "Thank you, Palenisa, but this conversation is useless. I have a task to complete and no time to waste."

As he turned to start back down the endless tunnel, Palenisa let the lethargy of the last few days crest over her in waves. With an exhale, she dropped her head, feeling the cut at her hairline throb and threaten to reopen at the sharp movement.

Clearly, the lulaik was more hollow-headed than she'd assumed, but the Zodiac had led her true. By their power she had found what she'd been looking for. A way for the coterie to take her back. It had to be—a choice she made for herself to prove her worth as a sister. Her mind shifted to how she was going to keep him alive, because she had to—keep him alive, that is. For the sake of her faith in herself, her title, and the one who had held it before her.

"Wait—just a minute, wait. I came all this way for a reason." She paused. "Please."

Asaru looked at her dispassionately as Wren tilted his head, appearing hesitantly curious.

"Wren." She turned to him, and he yelped. Her palms pressed tight together, arms out wide, elbows flat. Index fingers pointed up, eyes down, she bowed. Her voice rumbled low like a valley at night.

"I, Sister—*former* Sister Gleissa, grant you my promise. As long as I'm needed, as far as you have to go, I'll do all I can to protect you. This is a vow of great importance to my people. We don't take these words lightly."

The spirits were with her, present at this moment. She was sure of it.

"Do you accept?"

Wren stepped back, hands tight on his satchel. There was a sliver of hesitation, then he nodded.

He truly had no idea the magnitude of what she owed him.

At last, she could *breathe*. Relief escaped her mouth in a rush as hope bubbled inside her. She was so close to atoning. So very close. She could feel the approval of the spirits. And likewise, the kharess would see all she had done of her own volition and draw her back into the fold of the coterie. By the end of this, all would be as it should—she'd belong again.

"Now," Palenisa said contemplatively, "where exactly did you think you were going?"

Wren glanced at Asaru as though for approval. "Bartrom."

"Then farther south, to the badlands," Asaru cut in. "To find the Chronicler. That is where my brother should be."

South to the Desert of Burnt Glass. Which would take them back through Ilon. And Okiro if she was unlucky. Considering her recent lot, she didn't doubt she would be. Her own curse was immaterial, its consequences not so visible.

"I should warn you . . ." She searched for more polite phrasing, then quickly abandoned the attempt, as there was no point. "There's a freelancer contract on my head. I made a choice years ago that's coming back to kill me, it seems. It'd be best to avoid them as much as we can."

"And the Black Order," Wren piped up.

"Yes," Asaru deadpanned.

"No shit," Palenisa added.

If they kept a steady pace, it might take them a bit over a week to reach Bartrom with the occasional rest, not her mad, haggard dash chasing a scent while too drunk to see her own hand between her eyes.

Brushing back a braid, Palenisa slipped between the others, leading the way into the dark. A second passed and a cough drew her attention. Whipping around, she caught Wren rubbing the scarred side of his neck, avoiding her gaze.

"This, um, *this* is south," he said sheepishly, gesturing in the other direction. He tried smiling, but upon noticing her stare, the look faltered.

All right, so she made a mistake. *I can own that,* she lied. Both ends of the tunnel looked the same. How was she to even get her bearings in such low light anyway?

As they picked their way through the unchanging darkness, Wren hurried ahead to where the tunnel was more overgrown with vines that had not seen much sunlight. The walls turned to solid rock, and the floors became dirt flattened underfoot. He felt along the sides a moment, then dragged something from the wall.

"A torch?" Palenisa cocked her head, confused.

"Flintrock. The stone, it glows red in the presence of body heat."

"And we need this, *why*?"

He picked leaves out of the well of the torch and peered inside at the hunk of stone set in the middle. "As far as I know, some districts in Birinuyi are heavily populated by"—his eyes flickered over to her with a wince—"a few Norvatti clans. And, um, lulaik." He drew the torch across the wall. A thin line arced in its wake as sparks caught. The flame cast the tunnel in blue light that made it all the more cavernous. At its heart was a negligible violet tint. "When it's lit, flintrock darkens based on body heat. The more people there are, the redder the flame."

"Wonderful. Now let us *go*," Asaru said testily.

The tunnel narrowed ahead, wide enough for only one and a half full-grown wraiths to fit shoulder to shoulder, if that.

Palenisa trundled at the rear, alert. Logically, there were no clear dangers to be found. But, eyeing the pitch-black intersections as they wove through the underground maze, threading themselves farther into it, a small part of her thought otherwise.

She turned her eyes up to the ivy that crawled into hidden, secret crevices. Her mind wandered into waking dreams of the Zodiac, recalling imagined sights of untouchable spirits gathering toward her in response to fervent prayer. Her fears and nightmares walked among the living. But as long as she believed in the spirits and her promise, she knew—hope and faith—she would get through this. All would work out—it had to. She prayed and spake it so.

ASARU

Asaru felt more like a snake than a bird, yearning to shed his skin and escape the confines of Birinuyi. The tunnels contracted and expanded like a rising chest, like a swallowing throat—hours or days, without sun it was impossible to keep track. In the darker, narrower regions, the three of them were forced into a single line, blue torch as their guiding beacon.

The flintrock flame flickered eerily. Whenever red seeped into the light, they were forced to double back and make their way around what might have been a more direct route to their destination. With each new turn, redirection, shift, it felt almost like they were traveling in circles. The longer they walked, the less sure Wren looked and the lower the corners of Asaru's mouth dipped.

Almost as soon as the thought occurred, Palenisa voiced it.

"We're lost, aren't we?"

Silence stretched wide in the enclosed space, eased only by the sound of their footsteps.

"No . . ." Wren said, visibly tense.

Wonderful. Asaru's tail swished in agitation. "Then where are we?"

"That's what I'm trying to parse out." Wren frowned at the wall as they climbed a set of dirt stairs that crumbled lightly underfoot. As they ascended, he felt along the walls, marked in places with engravings, and in others with chalk. Circles within squares within circles, and so on, like spellwork. Writing in an unrecognizable tongue and scenes that evoked an ancient sentiment. At the landing, where more tunnel should have been, was the outline of an arch set against the flat jut of wall. A simple curve drawn in white and slightly recessed like a false door.

"Agaur," Wren mumbled, peering closer at the wall, eyes roving over the writing as he translated. "Estyrian arm of the Obsidian Market—often used as a . . . um, a safe haven for the Vana. Specifically."

He glanced down the stairs at Palenisa, and Asaru found himself caught between them to his utter displeasure. She had—of her own volition and quite eagerly—bound herself to Wren, if just through words. The brand pulsed as he rolled his shoulders. The world itself, khetry, had tied him to another. It was a punishment, not a promise, and it annoyed him that she'd taken something similar upon herself because Wren had been foolish. He *had* been foolish, but the fewer people that attached themselves to this unfortunate circumstance, the faster he could seek out his brother.

The phosphorescent flowers on the ceiling of the stairwell swung lazily in an unseen breeze. Asaru glanced around to discern its source. It had only been a week at most, surely, and he missed flying. He sought to ruffle his wings, the underground path too small to flex his feathers wide. They still hurt, tucked under the skin to heal. He felt every tiny fractured bone rolling as though he were swallowing them down his throat. The ache traced a finger—neither cool nor warm—from his nape to the base of his spine every time he so much as moved too quickly.

"So are we going the right way?" Palenisa folded her arms.

"We are not, are we?" Asaru narrowed his eyes as Wren slouched in miserable confirmation. "How many days more will that be? We have already lost a week. And will lose another back-tracking down here."

"We *should* be traveling aboveground," Palenisa agreed, and Asaru glanced to her, surprised by the aid. "At least we'll be able to tell where we're going if—"

The stairwell flooded with blood as red leached into the flame, bypassing purple entirely to overtake the lazy blue flickers.

The threads atop the drawn arch shifted with the manipulations of a spell being cast, and khetry shivered in Asaru's vision. A white glow expanded along the outline, then faded before the arch depressed, sinking into the wall with a solid thump.

As if of one mind, the three of them pressed themselves against the walls on either side. Asaru barely had time to take hold of the web and cast before the arch slid open. Light from the door refracted off the barrier formed by his outstretched arms, rendering them invisible at a certain angle and the stairwell seemingly empty. He prayed it would hold. It wasn't perfect and, like Sabine's cloaks, would only work in the shadows.

Through the door, a group clad in coats—woolen, embroidered—descended. As they passed, he heard Palenisa draw in and hold her breath beside him. Bringing up the rear was a hooded figure levitating crates with one hand. *Lulaik.* But Asaru's suspicious eye found no obvious spellwork, only red lines spreading from their palm into drooping sleeves. The khetry around them wove between glowing fingers with practiced ease.

The figure brushed against the tip of his tail, and he gingerly pulled it back. When they stopped, so did his heart. They doffed their hood, revealing a pair of luminescent green eyes with stars where pupils should have been. Green of a similar shade was woven into the braids at the sides of their hair. *Not just a lulaik: A Weaver.* And not just a legend either. Pitifully real. What must be a rare and lonely existence at that.

Before the Weaver could scan the stairs closer, find where the thread knotted about his fingers, their companions called their attention. They donned their hood and swept a generous arm downward to close the arch, hurrying into the dark.

As soon as they were out of sight, Palenisa sprinted up the stairs and thrust her staff into the gap, wedging it open. The earth shuddered and strained, sending a tremor down the stairwell that rumbled at Asaru's back. He dropped the spell and shook his hands, frowning when they prickled. For a moment, they felt aged, stiff.

"Coming?" Palenisa raised a brow. "I'm not about to spend another day wandering aimlessly. No arguments. Not even from you, assassin."

"Please do not call me that," he muttered. In his periphery, Wren cringed as he peeled himself from the far wall.

"What's spoken is truth. Hurry, before this thing shuts." She ducked beneath the half-closed arch.

They emerged in a storeroom, shelves full of bottles and barrels in the corners. The bottles glinted like rows of shiny-backed beetles under the thin seam of light fanning out beneath the door. *Taverna.* Asaru eyed the bottles again. *Winehouse.*

"I recognize these names." Palenisa bit a nail as she crouched by a barrel. "This is the Ruby House. We can rest a day or two and take some time to figure out where we're going—find a damn *map*, maybe."

That will not do. "A night," Asaru groused. Though rationally he knew strain worsened the exhausting mixture of poison and curse spreading inside him, he couldn't afford to rest for long. His body would betray him, as all bodies did, but before then he had duties to complete. And he would not fail the warden. Nor his brother.

Palenisa rolled her eyes. "Fine: *a night*." Standing, she passed by Wren and patted his shoulder. "Hope you have aur, because I'm flat out."

They snuck as best they could from the storeroom into the taverna painted wall to wall in red. Cherrywood tables, scarlet shutters, and varnished floors were marbled with darker crimson khetry. Chatter filled the room, which was crowded at the corners where the lanterns were the lowest and the drinks flowed the heaviest.

Ten pieces of aur later, they received a key from the barkeeper to a room furnished with two beds and a divan by the window. Through it, Asaru spied the sea, a mirror of night. Sighing, Palenisa flung herself onto the bed farthest from the window with all the grace of a newborn bird. She looked like a spilled line of paint, lying atop threadbare sheets. She turned over with a gentle grunt, seemingly asleep in an instant.

Asaru's eyes flitted over to the other bed. It sat there. Unclaimed. And its presence brightened like an accusing light the longer it went so. He crossed the room and perched tentatively on its edge, then tucked a strand of hair behind his ear and willed himself to look up. With a tilt of his head, he met Wren's eyes for only a moment before the other man averted his. A bubble of silence squeezed the room to bursting.

"You're injured. I'll take the divan and sleep in my suman," Wren said, gesturing at the woolen coat he wore.

Asaru had slept in worse places for longer. He didn't even remember the last time he had actually slept on a real, nor so soft, bed before this assignment. "We should not *be* sleeping," he muttered all the same. Not until Alvarys was in sight, not until they'd sought answers about the curse from the Chronicler. Then, perhaps, this gesture at sweet sleep would feel right, earned.

Wren fiddled with his sleeves. "You're not invincible."

"We could be making better time if we were still moving."

"It's just for the night. Even eresh keyel need rest. You're not a machine. Please."

But I am. But I am.

Despite his misgivings, lethargy settled like ash in the creases of his body, tucked itself beneath lidded eyes and threatened to drag dreams into his waking vision. He wanted to further argue, but he was caught by Wren's face as he settled on the divan. The aquiline curve of his nose formed a profile Asaru couldn't quite tear his gaze from. Wren caught his eye questioningly, and he looked away.

Once he'd settled back into bed, Asaru listened. The din of the taverna, his own heartbeat, Wren's yawn as he shrugged off the suman. For Wren, who lay with his eyes closed, covered by his coat on the slightly too small divan, sleep soon seemed to take him.

But for Asaru, sleep would not come as easily.

Restless, he rolled over, blinking away visions of gold and red and phantom hands. Killing was reserved for those who attacked first and remnants, those mindless beings of little sentience, the detritus of Oprekhet's centuries-old betrayal. Yet the king—*Zaosha,* his name had been Zaosha—clung to Asaru like the effects of the possession. He had thought he was strong; the warden had thought he was strong, she wouldn't have sent him otherwise. Yet he left his mind vulnerable to one of the rarest of offenses. Something had seen and taken hold.

Biting his cheek, he pressed a fist to his chest. *Find my brother, find the Chronicler,* he repeated the mantra to himself. *I am good, and I am here to do good.*

If that were true, what was Wren? The man who tied them together intrinsically through an affront to khetry. The man who derailed his mission. But also the man who saved his life, who bandaged his wounds without question, even after making the biggest mistake of his life. Asaru wasn't sure what he was. All he had was Alvarys to compare to, and the pair seemed worlds apart to him.

Moonlight filtered through the window over Wren's dark curls like a dusting of sugar. The scar was no less harsh in the low light, but it had to it a well-loved quality. Freckles spilled past the vee of his collar, lighter in some places and darker in others. *One, two, three, four . . .* Asaru counted those tiny dots, numerous as the stars themselves.

Celestial bodies on earth, these were the ones he could not touch.

Asaru awoke curled into a ball. He lay there a moment, shivering, though no breeze chilled him. A chant followed him—his mother's voice. And those hands. Those sleep-black hands.

Warrior, brother, son, Asaru—

His brand throbbed as he sensed its twin's approach. His eyes shot open, and he snatched Wren's wrist before it could make contact. A jolt sparked where they touched, a live wire that quickly burned the blurriness from his vision as he met Wren's surprised eyes.

"Sorry," Wren said as Asaru let go. "Didn't mean to wake you."

"You did not." Sitting up, Asaru allowed the sheets to pool at his waist, let the moment wash over him. He was an island in the midst of turbulent waters. "It was the bond."

"Right. Well, um, come on. Let's tend to your wound."

It was still dark out, that blue haze that came before the dawn misting the sky. Birdsong filtered through the bath's tiny window. There was just enough room for him and Wren to stand side by side.

Asaru sat on the lip of the wooden tub, though "tub" was a generous term for it. It was more of an oversized wash bucket. Grimacing, he removed his tunic and unwound the bandages. They were dark with blood from the fight at Anseme, which had adhered the wrappings to his wound. He bit his lip as dried fluids flaked off with each layer pulled away. His ribs ached beneath his ayashif as he stretched and unlaced the sides to loosen the binding. He then redid the black cloth that wrapped all the way up both thighs, which he wore in lieu of trousers, pulling the stray edges tight until they were secure on his legs.

Wren gently coughed to draw his attention. Asaru looked down at the man on his knees and inclined his head. Clutching the tub, splintering the wood from light twitches of pain, he watched Wren clean the injury. The irritated lines of oleander poisoning looked no more faded than the week before. His heart contracted and his stomach rolled at the thought of poison rolling through him, devastating him along with the curse before he could ever fulfill his purpose.

Back in the room, Palenisa looked up as they entered. A stray braid clung to the side of her half-asleep face. Her cape lay beside her, and Asaru noted the cache of daggers that lined her thighs under her dark patterned skirt. There was a honed muscularity to her that was familiar to him. If he hadn't already seen her fight to the death, Asaru would have easily marked her as a warrior.

"We should stock up here, so we don't have to keep stopping later," she said. "That's what you wanted, right? All nonstop?"

Sighing, Asaru rolled his eyes to the ceiling. "*Fewer* stops."

Palenisa stood, yawned, and threw on her cape. She cloaked herself in its darkness, which trailed the floor, hiding away all identifiable features, save her mouth. "That's not what it sounded like to me. But I digress."

As they made their way down to the main room of the taverna, Wren stopped him at the top of the stairs. He took off his suman and tugged on their remaining snakeskin. "Ah, wait. I'll wear the cloak; this'll cover you better."

Asaru blinked at the offered coat. The softness, the sandy shade of the fabric. He pulled off his own cloak and quickly slipped into the suman, falling into a river of wool. Well-loved, it bore a lingering floral scent he forced himself not to breathe in too deeply. Sleeves patterned in black dahlias flowed down the span of his arm, covering even his fingers. A pair of warm hands pulled the hood over his head. Shocked, he looked up as Wren smiled crookedly.

"Can't have anyone recognizing you."

He choked out a thanks and flew down the steps after Palenisa.

The layout of the city outside was strange and disorienting. The main road burrowed through the mountainside, akin to a bisected tunnel. On one side were buildings hewn from stone, and on the other was a sheer drop edged only by a low barrier. At the bottom of the cliff face, dark water crashed against stone and heaved itself onto the rocks. And everywhere people brushed too close for comfort, squeezed together on thin winding streets.

Asaru kept to the edges of the market when the road finally opened onto Agaur Major. Lingering at the edge of an alley, he kept Palenisa and Wren in the corner of his view. At the sight of a holographic screen flashing an image of his face, he dropped his head and hood lower.

Wanted: eresh keyel, regicide.

How easily one's name was tarred by false words. Well, true words—just not the entire truth. Huffing, he curled a finger at his side, snatched a thread, and twisted lightly. As he cast the spell, the screen turned to static. One had to have their petty little pleasures.

The rest of his attention returned to surveying the area. His eyes roved over every colorful thing, and his nose was assaulted by *interesting* scents. The new and the familiar. *Was that—*

A chocolate merchant sat at the mouth of the alley. Glancing from the side over their shoulder, they watched him as he watched them. The merchant stirred a cast-iron pot atop a tripod burner. Half swallowed by the shadow of a shrine bearing a sword-wielding statuette, the merchant turned back to their wares and poured an entire bottle of liquor into the pot. As if sensing his incredulity, they turned back again and winked conspiratorially.

"Want some?"

Asaru glanced aside, wary. He couldn't lie, so he spoke around it. "Apologies. I have no aur."

"I'm feeling generous today." They raised a small glass between their fingers. "And besides, someone's got to test out this batch for me."

Among the weeds of denial was a sprig of curiosity he couldn't deny. The only time he had ever tasted chocolate was—*With Alvarys.* Once, many years earlier. Hesitantly, Asaru approached to accept their offer and brought the glass to his lips, letting the taste and memory melt into him.

Fire had blazed in lamps on either side of the keep as Alvarys slung an arm over his neck. "My dearest brother! Why the serious face?"

Asaru had startled, his wings bristling. He had composed himself by pushing them against Alvarys's toothy smile and frowning at his older brother. "I am on watch," he had replied. A pause, and then: "And this is what my face always looks like?"

The confused cant of his head had turned annoyed when Alvarys cackled. He had turned his gaze upward, praying for Khertote to grant him the sweet release of death.

"Is there a reason you are not in the van?"

Light had glinted off Alvarys's halo as he steered Asaru inside Phiari Keep. The look on his face was not reassuring. That sparkle in his eyes, that particular quirk of his lips in a tricky slant only meant trouble.

"Still am." Alvarys had shrugged and taken off. "But the remnants have been less active at night lately." He had settled on the rafters, where messenger-gull cages hung like raindrops, wrapping his arrowhead tail around the beam for balance.

Asaru had stared in disbelief. *Cheeky.* Having endured the wiggling of his brother's brows for years, there was no way out but up. With a sigh, he had shot up and crouched on the thin beam.

"Now what?" He remembered swinging his feet. Remembered the ivory gulls squawking irritably at them, and the pecks he received on his soles as a result.

"Now we celebrate my promotion." A small bottle had seemed to materialize from thin air in Alvarys's signature flourish.

"What is that?"

"Liquid chocolate."

"You stole it." Asaru had stared at Alvarys, willing as much disappointment into his eyes as possible. Alvarys had always pushed like that, with his grand ideas and borderline lawbreaking. Few of those escapades ever went well, but each time, Alvarys had grinned and laughed, apologizing to the necessary parties while flashing Asaru a sly look. There was a reason he, beloved among all strategos, had been chosen to lead the Tetrarchia. Alvarys fit better in the machine; he was the light to which all gathered. Asaru himself was a cog alone, working as intended, but ill-suited to others.

"I *reappropriated* it." The older had rolled his eyes, blue as the crystal roses he so adored. "Stop being dull, and start being spontaneous." He'd twisted the bottle open and taken a sip. When his face lit up, Asaru had hesitantly—*very* hesitantly—followed. It had tasted almost too sweet, like his tongue was being bombarded with concentrated sugar. It had rolled his stomach at first. But as the initial onslaught faded, Asaru found it wasn't too bad in moderation, especially with the undertones of liqueur he was sure were there.

Asaru had passed the bottle back and wrapped his arms around his knees. He hadn't wanted his brother to know he'd liked it, thus approving of the blatant theft, so he scowled, hoping the expression was suitably disapproving.

"I will not be partaking further in your escapades tonight. But I will be sure to say 'I told you so' when our section leader does a provisions report."

Funnily enough, Asaru remembered that the section leader

already had. And, as expected, Alvarys was identified as the most likely culprit. And, also as expected, he'd gotten off with only mild disciplinary action.

Alvarys had sighed dramatically and flopped onto the beam, wings drooping over the sides as though he were melting into a blue pool of feathers. "Spoilsport."

At the time, it had sounded teasing. But in his recollection, it was almost resigned. Memories were fickle things. Half snippets, half conjuration, they were ruled by powerful emotion.

That didn't change the fact that he should have indulged Alvarys more.

As Asaru passed the glass back to the merchant, he wished the memory had as sweet an ending as the contents of the bottle. *Would that have kept him from the embassy?* He didn't know, didn't venture further down that path of wondering.

"It was . . ." He searched for a word but could only come up with "*nice*."

"Eh, it's not my best, but it's passable," the merchant shrugged, stirring a sprinkle of pepper into the pot. "You, on the other hand, might want to keep that tail of yours in check, *Asaru*. The Black Order is around every corner."

Asaru stilled, heart in his throat. Thighs tensed to run, he narrowed his eyes. The merchant looked bored, glancing lazily through one mismatched eye. They jerked their chin out across the square to where a small group of sentinels emerged. At the five corners of the major, more sentinels slid out to patrol the edges like panthers. *Not good.*

Head down and hood up, Asaru slipped through the market toward Wren. He dragged the man back to the alley by his sleeve, catching Palenisa's attention too.

"How do we get out of the city?" Asaru asked as the three of them stashed themselves quickly in an unused cave. He kept his eye on the street, glancing around, gooseflesh prickling. "If they are congregating here, they are likely to be everywhere else."

"I'm not . . ." As Wren trailed off, his gaze flitted up to the right. "Actually, I think I know *one* place." Then he sighed, looking put out by whatever thought had just popped into his mind.

Like an easily spooked bird, Wren led them through the city, navigating alleys and occasionally pressing into shrines at any unusually loud noise. The sounds of the Black Order had become somewhat noticeable to Asaru. He knew the commanding tone of their voices, the squeal of their armor and leather shifting as they ran, and he knew the way their poison felt as it spread through his system, crawling purple in his veins.

When they came to a stop at the back door of what was clearly a brothel, Asaru was quite possibly at his limit. The previous night was a waste, this morning too. He shot Wren a withering look, but the man smiled sheepishly as if it alleviated the situation at all. Wren raised a fist to the door, frowned, then rapped on the shuttered window beside it. He knocked twice, then once more, hesitantly.

The moment hung as Asaru held his breath. On a street over, he thought he could hear the march of approaching sentinels. They needed to go—*he* needed to go. Alvarys was waiting. He would be—he *must* be.

The window shutter opened, and out leaned a grumbling woman in green. Her eyes widened like two pieces of spotted amber. She stared, unblinking, as her hand rose from her necklace to her mouth. *"Wren?"*

"Rishé." Wren ducked shyly, the softness of his voice sending an uncomfortable warmth lurching through Asaru. "Been a while."

RISHÉ

Rishé blinked as though she were unsure her brain was relaying her vision correctly. But seeing was believing.

"Wren," she said dryly as she formed his sign name, three fingers tapped thrice to her cheek to imitate his freckles. He looked as he had the last day she had seen him, years earlier. His hair had grown, and his eyes seemed sunken. Though partially hidden under the hood of a snakeskin cloak, his distinguishing features were almost as she remembered. The nose they shared as fellow Norvatti, hands permanently inked black from antimony kohl—and the scar. The *scar.* Dropwort purple and wrinkled like a burn, fading into the warm brown of his face and jaw and neck, looking perfectly like it belonged there. She observed the way it splashed from the side like he'd been accidentally caught in a wave. *He had.* She hadn't seen him, nor her cousin, in the aftermath of the incident, but she knew he had.

Releasing a breath, Rishé set down her journal to collect herself and looked at his companions. At his side were two others, similarly veiled, one in a cape, the other, a suman. She could make out little of the taller one, shapeless in black, save a pair of wraith-blue eyes. But the shortest one, despite the long sleeves and thigh-length coat, had a pale scar across his nose and another that stretched from chin to brow. And slitted, hazel eyes.

"Harboring an assassin is a crime," Rishé signed, face dripping with sarcasm. *"The city is thick with sentinels, the port with the Black Fleet, and you* do *know the Justice lives up there, right?"* She gestured upward, calling to mind the highest point on the mountainside, where Governor Hadora Kaurs's manse lay ensconced.

Pursing her lips, she leveled Wren with a look. She had more than an inkling of what he was there for, but she wasn't about to let him play on her former affections. Each time she caught sight of his face, it was as if all the bitterness she didn't know she carried curdled within her. They had been friends for years, plus their entire time at the guild—she, a gemsmith's apprentice, and he, a healer in training. And then he just . . . *left,* as if he'd died. It had reminded her of her mother, leaving without warning or answers. The suddenness of it all, then the fleeting feeling in the aftermath like diving headfirst into cold waters. Rishé had only learned that he was no longer at the guild from her cousin in the guild's healing room the next day.

So maybe she was more than just a little bitter. But she didn't let it show on her face.

"Yes, I know, Rishé," Wren said weakly, fingerspelling her name. His gaze was avoidant. "But we couldn't get back to Ruby House, and I—we—need your help. Please. We're trying to reach the guild."

Rishé's brow lifted in surprise. She switched languages so the others could hear her judgment: "The guild is a neutral entity, but even they can't hide a kingslayer forever."

"I am *not* a kingslayer," the assassin, Asaru, hissed, stepping closer. Pausing, she observed his grimacing snarl. He was anxious, clearly impatient, and likely feeling overwhelmed by the *everything* that was the city of Kumadrai. From the tension in his form, she could tell he was cautious, but he might not hesitate should the Black Order come across them in the backstreets.

"Did you, or did you not, slay *the* king,*"* she signed, Wren interpreting the words for the others so she didn't have to speak. It was an old habit they fell into from their previous years speaking with people who knew little or no Eslang. Sometimes still she forgot to speak aloud. Sense memory was strong; the body didn't forget, even if the mind convinced itself so.

Asaru bristled at her question. "I was—" He shook his head and turned sharply to Wren, redirecting all that forceful energy like a sudden shock. His gaze, even shaded, was like a knife. "This is a waste of time. Let us go."

She leaned on the sill. Asaru was wound so tight. It intrigued her, his determination. She called out to him. "To the guild, for sanctuary. Right?"

"No." Asaru glanced back, hood shifting slightly to reveal twin strands of brown hair fading into auburn like dusk into night. Rishé glanced down at his black-speckled hands. The curse. When he noticed her gaze, he hid them away at his back and continued. "The guild is but a stop. I am looking to find my brother at the Chronicler's."

Recognition jolted through her. She perked up, almost falling over the sill and herself. She knew that name. At least, she'd heard rumor of it. Details were sparse, but Rishé vaguely recalled its mention in another publication, *Amanuensis,* maybe a year or so earlier. It was more speculative than most journals, well-written ramblings positing some kind of repository. Knowledge of the world that was held in either a person, a place, or a thing. To hear it confirmed as truth rather than theory reframed what she thought she knew, tended the oil flame of fascination in her heart.

She thought of Parianne's generous offer again. Though she'd sat on the fence, teetering more toward staying than accepting, this all but confirmed her resolve. There was no guarantee the University of the Commonwealth could even help answer her esoteric questions. What was this stone that seemed to lack any specific description? And, more importantly, what had her mother known about it? It couldn't have been a coincidence the necklace was Jarha's parting gift. *It couldn't.*

This was the opportunity she didn't know she'd been waiting for.

Whether it was temporary, unabashed idiocy or the most logical course of action, Rishé would come to decide later.

"Wait." She wiggled her fingers to the side in sign. "Don't go anywhere, stay out of sight," she said before shuttering the window as Asaru opened his mouth, presumably to argue. Turning to her room, she took stock of the space. How little there was, aside from the books stacked by the small bed and loose papers on her equally tiny desk. It was as though some part of her had been waiting, *waiting* for a chance like this.

She wouldn't take much. She didn't need it. All that really mattered to her in the world could be packed into a single bag. Living on the move with the Trifan clan, her family had taught her the lesson of traveling light. And her mother had always playfully joked that it made it easier to drop everything and run. This wasn't running, but it was comforting how the sentiment came in handy.

She packed her journal around her thigh, grabbed her

suman—sleeves embroidered with dancing stones—and shoved the pouches containing her remaining savings into her satchel. At her desk, Rishé lingered, fingers pausing over the pamphlets, those morsels of knowledge she'd cobbled together on her own. For a brief moment, she wondered if Erazill would miss her—in his words—"friendly face at the front desk." Most likely not—she wasn't the Screen's main attraction. The Butterflies were the stars of the show.

Decision made, Rishé penned a note—*Be back later*—and left it on the desk. Then she stuck her head out the door and called quietly to her coworker, who was busy smoking poppy at the end of the hall. "I'm going to get the laundry and do some reading. Don't bother me till closing."

"What? Wait—*Rishé*!"

"Thanks, I owe you."

She locked her door before rushing back to the window. She flung it open to find the trio still waiting, just as expected. *They* had come to *her*. Of course they wouldn't leave. Part of her preened in delight.

As Rishé climbed out the window, the wraith objected. "Whoa, no, I thought she was just going to tell us where to go, not *coming with*." The wraith had a surprisingly deep and silken voice. She adjusted her hood, revealing a hint of thick white braids, and on the backs of her hands were the suvaugrams for earth and sunlight.

An Aspect. Rishé's eyes narrowed in suspicion—*a lone Aspect traveling with a lulaik*. She hoped Wren knew what he was doing.

"Palenisa . . ." Wren mumbled, sounding pained. Sounding a bit fearful, actually.

Rishé shouldered her bag and pointed at the offending parties. "Assassin, clearly a wraith, lulaik with *very* distinct hands and tattoos," she said in a careful tone. Then she gestured to all of herself. "Human who can go unnoticed, fits well in tiny places, and knows how to act like a normal person. Anything else?"

Palenisa loomed over her, a commanding presence in all black like a vulture. Theirs was such a distinct height difference, Rishé had to tilt back slightly to meet that frigid blue gaze. She schooled her expression to neutrality.

"You know, I think we're fine to find our own way," Palenisa said coolly.

"I'm the only one who knows how to get you out of here pretty much unseen. I know the city and the secrets of Birinuyi's layout much better than Wren."

In her periphery, Wren winced, looking forlorn but mostly accepting. These were unfortunate circumstances, after all. They needed her, and she needed them if she was to find this Chronicler.

"Anything else?" No further objection arose, despite soured faces.

They took the back roads and alleys to the crumbling parts of the city deeper in the mountain, where fewer people traveled. There, the light of day barely penetrated. It wasn't dissimilar to Birinuyi in a certain way, the parts of the underground that had once been a city, at least. Much of the western cliffs of Ausre were rocky, rough-hewn, and particularly hard to traverse for those unfamiliar with its terrain. The province was the one place Queen Rhenitha hadn't made a stand against the dolomite army. It looked almost as it had in the era before Unification, or so the history books said.

At her side, Asaru kept an eager pace. She noticed as he glanced over, and he inclined his head, muttering in the most deadpan voice she'd ever heard, "Thank you."

Rishé smiled wryly. Beyond the initial friction, he seemed polite for an assassin—mostly. If they had the time, she might ask how he had roped himself to the mess that was Wren and vice versa.

Paths coalesced in her mind, lines on a map. Repeated steps and remembered passages formed a rough outline of Kumadrai, layering the image of its secrets over the city like a translucent sheet. They descended rarely used steps, caked in dust up to the ankle, and slipped into thin passageways that led to the mines in the heart of the Ausran mountains. Striated stone softened to dirt as Rishé herded them through an empty cavern long stripped of ore.

A pinprick of light shone ahead. The cavern tilted up, a strenuous vertical climb aided thankfully by stairs cut between walls. The light at the end of the shaft grew ever closer. On the other side, they emerged from a cave at the edge of the Kingswood. There, wood bled into the jewels of the Necklace, reedy islands that dotted the southern Darandell River.

As she stepped into the forest, Rishé drew in a breath. The pleasant scent of petrichor arose with each step as soil sank underfoot. The murmur of the Darandell River whispered into her ear like a long-forgotten promise. She hadn't left the Screen since she was hired, and she didn't know just how dearly she'd missed the country.

Once they were well away from the claustrophobic labyrinth of the city, Rishé fell to the back of the pack, following the others into foliage that enveloped them like a descending smog. Gazing around, taking the world in as if with new eyes, she found herself smiling. Her mother's face came to mind, framed by sunrays with the murky sea rolling behind her, and Rishé's hand rose to her pendant. She let herself wonder, illogically, if there was divine in the natural. If there *were* deities. And she was struck by the impossible thought that, if there were, perhaps her prayers had been answered.

ASARU

The curse. That smell. The smell of the curse was in the air.

Asaru wasn't losing his mind—*the chants, his mother's voice*—nor was he confused. The smell of the curse was in the air, wafting from somewhere nearby. Growing stronger the longer they walked, dampened not by the slow-moving river at their side. He wiped the back of a hand across his nose, scanning the forest. Everything felt alight—agitated nerves, a sense that he was close to *something*. Something he thought, maybe, he should have recognized.

Grunting, the same hand shot to his shoulder blade against a particularly strong pulse through the brand. The ridges of the wreath rose beneath his touch. A woven bond, unfortunately, ever more familiar to him.

"What's wrong?"

He glanced back and found Wren watching with those sad, wet eyes. Concern flooded through their bond; Asaru wanted to shy away from it, like a troglodyte from the sun. Filtering through his feelings on *that* matter was like sticking one's hand into an oil-slick pool, rummaging around, and coming up with a viscous, sloppy sludge.

"I think an eresh keyel is here. Was here," Asaru said instead. He hoped, to all end, praying to the Triumvirate—and those rare few other gods he had come to know—that it wasn't who he feared.

He jogged ahead and looked around the swampy forest. Behemoth trees towered like giants with broken backs, branches hanging low to kiss the river gently. Dotting the river were reedy spots of land, most half sunken, the rest too small to be considered islands. The water, a misty green, occasionally gave way to crystal clarity along the embankment by which they walked. Near the surface, silver-gold fish slowed as if to observe them before darting off.

A sharp crack broke the silence. Leaves rustled in the disturbed aftermath, then the swooping call of a bird. Each sound was a possible sentinel. Trailing. Watching. Waiting.

The sky faded to orange, a linen screen painted with blue and indigo following. Minutes streamed by and with them, the visibility in the woods. Thin light broke through the canopy, enough to brighten the middle distance and to guide Asaru's sight to a nearly indistinguishable lump under the leafy veil of a willow.

Gasping, he rushed ahead, the calls of the others falling behind, coming to his ears as if through spread fingers. Across the water, muck tugging at his thighs, he scrambled onto the spit of earth where the river's three tributaries merged to one.

"Khensu?" he gasped, eyes roving over the face of the missing member of the Tetrarchia.

Khensu rested against a large trunk, barely clinging to life. The curse covered her head to toe, every part of her rotting in her own filth. A gentle breeze rustled the leaves, brushed the long strand of hair away from Khensu's face as she peeled her eyes open.

The sight pained him, but Asaru couldn't look away. His pupils constricted, and his nails dug ruddy crescents into the meat of his palms. It was all he could do to keep it together.

"Ah . . . Asaru." She broke into a coughing fit. "Why are you . . . Have you c-come to, come to help us?"

Of the Tetrarchia, Khensu had always treated him, if not well, with at least a nominally detached neutrality. She acknowledged him as he was. And that had been enough.

"What happened at the embassy? What happened to *you*?" Asaru knelt, unable to focus on anything but her fluttering eyes. Splashing water burst like shadowflies in his ears as his companions crossed the river to join them.

"An eresh keyel? All the way out here?*"* Rishé signed, shutting her compass with a click.

"Alvarys."

Asaru's head shot back to Khensu at the low mutter. "Where is he? Why are you not with him?"

Khensu moved to sit up straighter, and he helped her the rest of the way. Black liquid stained her teeth as she grunted. It pooled in her lap, invisible against the same dark mineral that encased her. She wiped at her mouth but only succeeded in smearing the back of her hand with wet black.

"We w-were separated. My . . . my fault," she croaked. Her voice was the scratch of steel on stone. Clearing her throat, she rubbed her halo. Her claws brushed a misshapen ring of stones, gaping holes that stared back at Asaru as if a premonition—what could come to be for him, for every eresh keyel. "What were we . . . We were t-trying, trying to . . ."

Guilt and compassion warred within Asaru. There were two

warm presences at his back. Beside him, Rishé leaned closer, but he snarled to keep away her intrusion. Her curiosity was not of any worth. Unabashed, unashamed curiosity was not of *any* merit in this.

Gulping, he reached out to Khensu, his eyes softening, though tension tightened the line of his spine. His hand curled back in an aborted motion, before it landed on the edge of her armored shendyt near her thigh. He hated that he hesitated.

"Do you remember . . ." He clicked in their tonal language.

Khensu's face twisted. Black and graying gold spilled from under her blunt and broken fingers.

It began with a survey to Saite, she told him. For a moon, there had been no activity from the border town. Nothing in, no one out. When the Tetrarchia had investigated, they found nothing but a scar and the Phiari River tainted black. It was, at first, assumed to be an incursion of remnants. They had been spotted roaming more at night on Oprekhet's islet, sequestered on the opposite side of the mountains. The Tetrarchia brought this suspicion to the warden, and she had believed them enough to send them past the Sea Gate. *Find the Chronicler, uncover the truth of what happened, stop it from spreading.* The task should have been simple.

It wasn't.

As she recounted the story, Asaru recalled how Alvarys had spoken of his departure, voice suffused with thoughtfulness and, he realized in retrospect, apprehension. An assignment he couldn't detail. There seemed to be a lot he couldn't—hadn't shared. Such as Saite, a secret Asaru hadn't even known of.

Why hadn't the warden told him about the occurrence in Saite? Why hadn't his own brother even *mentioned* such a devastating discovery?

That struck him. Deeper than he cared to admit. Cleaved him almost in two.

"And what of the embassy?" he asked quietly. "All that blood. Those bodies."

She continued her revelations. When they arrived at the embassy, the vial had been there for a day. They could do nothing to stop it from cracking as some mechanism shattered the glass from within. It hadn't seemed consequential at first—nothing ever does. But that was the purpose of its insidious nature, foul as its assumed creator and twice as cruel in its uneven progression. The ambassadors succumbed quickly, then half the Tetrarchia. It was all she and Alvarys could do to grab the beacon and flee before the curse overcame them too.

Her face morphed into a grimace, and thick streams of saliva rolled down the sides of her mouth.

She coughed out the next part. They had flown, but the curse was merciless, ceaseless in its progression. She'd fallen from the sky, able only to watch Alvarys's wings disappear into the blue above the canopy. While she had wandered lost in the woods, he hadn't even seemed to notice she was no longer with him. Too focused on the beacon and too ravaged by the curse.

Gone.

A chill crawled up Asaru's spine. "Gone" could mean many things. He wished for her to be wrong—*knew* her to be wrong. He kept certainty in his heart that his brother *had* reached the Chronicler. There was no alternative to be considered.

A violent cough shook Khensu, and she spasmed, clutching her mouth to catch the bile and blood. Her hands—black, black up to her neck, up to the ridges of her cheekbones—bore the twilight effects of the curse.

"I—I can't see it anymore." She clutched her cheek softly,

appearing to seek what little tenderness she could, even if it came from her own touch. Her eyes widened. A milky haze settled in them, silver over a dark ocean consuming the sclera. "I can't see khetry anymore. It's gone." She sobbed, covering her mouth as a tear slipped down her cheek. "All g-gone."

Asaru tracked the wet line on her face before looking away. He did what he could, what little he could, and wiped the tears away.

Delirious, staring past him into the middle distance, Khensu devolved into incoherent mutterings, her lips forming silent words in their language. Trilling calls and avian clicks to something she could no longer see, could no longer feel. She was fading in and out of lucidity, snatches further and fewer between as she struggled for the words with a throat full of phlegm.

Was this Black Diamond at its apex? The loss of one's own self?

The khetry around her faded from bright red to a weathered gray with each passing second. A string slowly cut, a rope pulled taut as life struggled against its end. The few threads that still clung to her were but fibers. In grievous contrast, the crimson living world shone around *him*.

Asaru imagined a shadow over them both. It stood, jackal mask lowered in sorrow equal to his own, maroon eyes glowing as it slung strands of death from its arms to the veiled horizon. To a place Asaru could not yet see but feared he soon might.

"The best thing for her"—Rishé's stilted voice at his side—"is a quick death. No more suffering." She stared at him, amber eyes dripping unwanted empathy as she rubbed her pendant between two fingers.

"No," Palenisa said firmly at his back. "A natural death is better, always. No matter the cause. It's only right to let her go when she will."

On his other side, Wren remained silent. Watching. Hand over his heart, just watching.

The curse filled Asaru's nose, blotted out all sense. He and Khensu were alone in this suspended chalice of time. All he saw was Khensu. A blink, and Alvarys rested there in her place, looking at him with somber eyes that rivaled the depths of the sea. A blink, and there was Khensu again, looking nowhere, seeing nothing as the light in her eyes died in reverent silence.

Mercy.

Feeling almost possessed, he reached out.

Mercy.

He pressed a palm to her neck, her remaining colorless halo stones like raw ore beneath his touch. Blood crusted around the gaps left by the missing ones. Her fleeting heartbeat existed only in rare moments, and only if he held himself still as a corpse could he feel it.

Mercy.

Asaru's fingers spread, wrapped around her neck. And squeezed. Squeezed. *Squeezed.* Until he had given her mercy.

Then, all at once, everything was still.

It was mindless, rote work to bring his hands to his jaw and cast the spell. Flame bloomed across his tongue in sorrowful prayer. Her body went up like a pyre. Diminishing shadows raced across the ground, between the willow leaves dancing over the water like burning stars.

What was once Khensu took to ash in a matter of minutes, piled before his knees and untouched by khetry. He gathered her ashes, ducked his head, and whispered, "Your mind by Hukhetyel, your body by Chert Ouadjet, your aether by Khertote. Return home to dwell in the Red Web of Life once more."

One last time, past the unnatural end of her life, Khensu

took to the flight that had been so cruelly wrenched from her as he released her ashes to the wind. Let the sky take her. Let the world take her. She should have been in an urn, decorated with her halo stones and lovingly stored within a charnel house. She should have been with the scores of their dead kin back on Aedyton. Instead, she was here. Forever would she be here. And there was *nothing* he could do to bring her home.

For a moment, Asaru let himself sit. His throat was smoke and his eyes were sand. Lowering his head to the grass, he formed a cage, a shield, with his wings. The world was too much all at once, everywhere and unending. Everything just *persisted.*

His chest was close to bursting, held closed by the feeling of dangling from a cliff over water. A suffocating darkness filled him, cradled him, *consumed him.*

"How are you feeling?"

His shoulder blade prickled at Wren's soft voice. A nerve of pain shot through his healing wing, and the sound of shadowflies forced his mind to stagnant silence. Standing, Asaru folded his wings away and turned from the tree.

Eyes bored into his back, a haze, a silver beam, a blackened pool. Alight no longer.

"I need to keep going."

"Asaru—"

He stared blankly at the other man, quieting him. Then he looked at Rishé, who crouched, watching him like one does a wild beast. But he was not wild. He was perfectly in control of himself, a tool of singular pointed purpose.

"Someone may have seen the smoke."

Rishé nodded hesitantly and opened her compass as she ducked from beneath the willow. After Palenisa, Wren lingered.

His mismatched eyes brimmed with emotions nameless and needless.

Asaru barely registered his stare. A storm raged between his ears as he crossed the river. His hands were speckled black to the elbow, the curse in living motion. The darkness would continue to eat at him. Eat away at him until he was just like Khensu.

Like thrice-worked steel, like diamondglass, Asaru hardened himself. He would do what he was sent to. For the sake of himself, find his brother. For the sake of his brother, find the Chronicler. For the sake of Aedyton, stop the curse.

There was no other path to walk but this one alone, for time was a finite resource, and it was running out.

WREN

Wren contemplated all he knew and all he had yet to learn.

Objectively, he *knew* Asaru was a warrior who had killed remnants. Other people. The king. But seeing it framed as mercy? He squeezed his wrist to hold himself from touching his heart. Wren was a healer—*could* have been a healer—and he wasn't sure what mercy was when it came to Black Diamond. Curses were unbreakable, but was it right to not even *try*?

As they trekked through the Necklace, he found himself glancing over at Asaru occasionally, receiving flares of annoyance from the bond in response. He couldn't help the urge to peer at the black speckling under those arm wraps. The progression of the curse was unstable, unknown, and it wrapped a cord of fear around Wren's heart the longer he let himself look. The longer he let himself think and stew and overthink. The disparate parts of him longed to help, longed for absolution—longed, maybe, for further punishment.

Wren's unsteady gaze flitted over to Rishé. Her focus was locked on the horizon, she guided them on paths well-trodden from years of constant, consistent travel. Paths he had traveled maybe once, when he was very young and his mother was still part of their birth clan. Since then—and the guild—he'd lived in Sika for most his life, easily forgetting that Trinacrios was a much larger continent than a single province. The world was big. And it was full of horrors. Failures. Regrets.

Exhaling, he sped up to walk beside her. She looked different, her once waist-length hair chopped messily short. Older than him by a few years at sixty-five, though still very young for both human and lulaik, there was a sense of new maturity about Rishé. Still young, but the kind of young that knew what direction her life needed to take and was able to climb through a window to grab it by the reins. She spared him a sidelong glance before turning to her compass dismissively.

They hadn't spoken in years, and he ached at the thought of trying to fit back into her life. To slip into easy conversation like a peg in an ill-fitting hole. His mouth felt full of cobwebs and rusty from disuse.

"Why"—Rishé began, signing with a single hand—*"are you really going to the guild?"*

His thoughts already in shambles, Wren ducked his head. "It's for . . . Asaru. His, um, the poison."

Her cutting stare was an amber bolt. "You almost died there, and you're desperate to return?"

He wasn't *desperate*. But he didn't want to talk about it either. He let his mind ruminate instead on all that he'd ruined. "I didn't mean for that to happen," he said quietly as his fingers wrung themselves into nervous knots. His nails were caked with dirt. "Yes, it was my fault. I know—*I know.*"

Rishé kissed her teeth. Her jaw worked, her gaze roving over his face. It lingered on his scar a moment, and he held back from touching his cheek. Failure always left its physical marks.

"You still don't understand," she signed, pointing up by her temple. *"You never stop, never* think*—and now you've tangled yourself in a mess with a wraith and an* assassin.*"*

"Asaru's not . . ." He trailed off, truth and belief warring within him. Asaru had killed the king, and his culpability in that was clear as the cloudless Sky Court. Though another had guided the deed, his hand had committed it. A slick mass of guilt formed caverns through Wren's heart as his brand itched, an insistent, commanding presence. He weakly added, "He was possessed."

Surprisingly, or unsurprisingly, as he recalled her proclivities, Rishé perked up. A glint flashed in her gaze as she inquired lightly on the topic of possession. Her mother had been human, but her father had been lulaik, and even though that combination of heredity rendered her fully human, she'd always been fascinated by their discussions of khetry. In between training, they'd spent hours in the guild's reading room, poring over tomes and conjuring up the wildest of potential spells. They were drawn together by the simplicity of wanting to *know* more—about each other and the living threads that wove the world. Wren wanted that back. He hadn't known how desperately he wanted it until he saw how Rishé brightened, if just for this tiny moment.

Then she clamped her mouth, closing up like a tome slammed shut, and averted her gaze. The infant spark between them fizzled, as did his useless hopes.

"Never mind, it's fine." She dropped her hands and muttered, as if to make the words hurt more, "I'll ask Asaru if he's willing."

Wren was left staring after her as she moved ahead. Away from him. He shut his eyes and sighed as he squeezed to minuscule pieces whatever hurt swelled in his gut. It was only fitting. This was well due. He had left her first.

The Kingswood thinned out, though not quite disappearing. The Darandell trailed away, and they found themselves walking beside a wide road. On the far side, farmland opened into the distance, each field so vast it would take an hour to cross one's length.

Comforted by the thickness of the wood, Wren lowered his hood to take in the distant rolling hills. Valyn was second only to Romia in its mass of arable land, in sloping valleys from which the realm received its pleasurable substances.

At the rumble of approaching wheels, four pairs of startled eyes shot to the road.

Wren stilled as a cart pulled by two stumpy horses slowed to stop at the behest of its driver's curiosity. The cart was laden with baskets filled almost to overflowing with fruit and dusty red pepperstalk. A farmer, then. Common enough to stumble across in the hinterlands.

"Hail, travelers?" the farmer called, tentatively tossing out a half-formed wave that Wren found himself thoughtlessly returning. A particularly sharp elbow dug into his side, but he couldn't help that his mother had taught him human manners, couldn't help that over the years they'd become his own manners instead.

The farmer shaded his eyes and squinted. "Apologies for stopping y'all, but has anyone ever told you of your resemblance to—"

"I get that a lot," Wren said warily, stopping himself from rolling his eyes. "Apparently Rosatay and Eihron are interchangeable."

Never mind that each Norvatti tribe had its own distinctive features. Never mind that the Eihrons had long since settled in Sterrock, whereas some Rosatay clans like the one of his birth continued to travel. Never mind the constancy of such comments, hammering insecurities into his very bones. Always an outsider, throttling the balance between being not quite Norvatti anymore but neither wholly Estyrian.

Wren tugged at his curls to hide the points of his ears, itching to shroud himself in the shadows again. His cheeks warmed in a familiar flustered irritation.

"My apologies. Just been hard for many of us since the king's passing—feels like I'm seeing him 'round every corner. A good man. May he rise to Ishmer."

The platitude echoed hollowly in Wren's own mouth. Of the Estyrian afterlives, Ishmer was for the beloved dead, while the forgotten sank into Dis. Though the king may not have been universally loved, he would be remembered for centuries. Wryly, Wren wondered if the same would be said of him once his time had come. Doubtful. There was little he deserved to be remembered for.

"You know"—*Eșarpe give me strength,* Wren thought, his smile thinning as the man continued—"they're saying the order didn't even let Lady Sanawe see the body—too badly maimed. Shame for his sister, I reckon. Not even his wife's spoken out, can't imagine what Dowager Raine's going through. Poor, poor thing."

Wren's gaze darted to Rishé for help, but he found there only muted amusement. For all his want of being a healer, he didn't fare too well with the talk or sight of corpses. One could imagine any various ways the king had died, yet the cleanest was the worst: a blade through the heart. His own tightened at the thought as bile clawed up his throat. He drew the snakeskin around himself, twisting anxious patterns into the cloth. He'd rather be anywhere else.

"I'm sure they're doing well," he offered in a strained voice.

"Ah, but don't mind me yapping." The farmer waved him off

before tipping his hat back. "May I ask where y'all're headed?"

Palenisa pushed her way to the front, a menacing tower of black. "You may not," she rumbled, lifting her chin to glower, two dots of blue under her hood.

"No disrespect," the farmer said as he raised a placating hand. "It's just, evening's coming, and I was of a mind to offer y'all a place to rest your legs tonight."

At a tug on his sleeve, Wren glanced over his shoulder to meet Asaru's fierce eyes. Their bond blazed with his discontent. That accusatory gaze lit up every part of Wren, gut to gullet, with guilt. So he turned and let its fierceness burn his back instead as he accepted the offer. Rejecting the farmer would only have heightened the man's suspicion of four lone travelers, he tried to rationalize to himself.

He endured the weight of the glare as they squeezed themselves between baskets smelling of vineyards and spices. He burrowed his face against his knees all the way to the farmer's home.

The small farm was bordered by the Kingswood along two sides. Though landed, the people in the area were far from gentry, much less wealthies. Their abode was built into the base of a sloping mound with a golden field of wheat spread before it. In a way, it reminded Wren of his home, of his mother. In a garden at the rear, he noted a child about half his age tending to grafted trees heavy with nectar apples and bright quince. Wiping their brow, the child exchanged words with their father before the farmer led the four of them toward the barn.

The second level was packed tight with bales of bedstraw, sallow in the dim light. Grass and grain shoots littered the main floor, just soft enough to lie on. For a night, it would do.

A thin layer of discomfort hung in the air, thickening when the farmer's child nudged the door open, bearing a tray in their arms. They set down a helping of bread garnished with pepperstalk, honey, grapes, and slices of aromatic pink nectar apples weeping with condensation.

Far more generous than expected. But Wren's companions looked less than pleased, and though Rishé lowered both hands in thanks, her lips were thin, flat lines. The child responded in kind, signing back by scooping their arms into a curve. Before leaving, they paused at the door. Catching the look, Wren raised a brow, and they quickly scampered out.

Wren picked at a loaf of bread and braced himself. Not hard enough, unfortunately, as he came to regret the many decisions in his life that had led him there when the bickering started.

"I can't *believe* you," Rishé groused. She popped a grape between her teeth and he winced, shoulders rising. "What madness compelled you to *keep talking*? Do you have any idea how suspicious you sounded? We could've stayed in town or, better yet, the damn forest."

Well, yes, he knew he was lacking charisma tenfold, but it was *not* his fault he'd been caught in unwanted conversation unawares.

Asaru hissed. Since giving Khensu mercy, he'd been somber, as if in deep, churning thought. But once again, his voice dripped disdain. "We should not have done any of this, forest or otherwise. Time is my utmost priority, and you—all of you—are wasting mine by the day."

Rishé rolled her eyes and finished off the remaining grapes as Palenisa sat up sharply to point a claw at him. "We're all on edge—at least those of us with sense." She cast Wren a withering look and crossed her arms. "I don't trust that man. Who the fuck stops at the side of an empty road like that? We could've been bandits for all he knew. No one's that kind."

"They can be," Asaru said softly, glancing at Wren. He shook his head and touched his halo as Wren's heart sped up. "But that is not the point. This was a foolish choice, and we are leaving before those two wake. No arguments."

"I'm sorry," Wren whispered, feeling properly chastised. He set the loaf down, no longer hungry. His stomach was an ashen pit, his tongue a tasteless gravel road.

He received twin scoffs in response, Rishé having turned away to burrow inside her suman as the other two angrily finished off the remaining fruit between themselves.

Picking at the tattered hem of his cloak, Wren sighed. The snakeskin was unraveling. Something sparked in his head, and he pulled the bone needle from his pocket, knowing full well his skill held no candle to the neatness of his mother's craft. The banded fabric was beyond his capability to fix, so he focused only on what he could. He tried not to think of everything that required repair. Even as he tried to compare the work to the brand, it fell short. All the trouble he'd caused would need more than a joke of a needle and some thread. Khetry, viscous and alive, could not be untangled so easily.

In the tense respite, he let himself sink into the repetitive motion—pierce fabric, pull, flip; pierce fabric, pull, flip—as his eyes watered.

"Is that a spell?" asked a soft voice. He twitched. Blood beaded on his trembling fingertip, Palenisa too dreadfully close for his liking. She smelled of blood and cardamom and sweat, a strangely pleasant mixture that only served to worsen his anxieties. She sidled up beside him.

Sweat gathered on his palms as he gulped, shaking his head. "Ah, no. Just mending this so it, um, doesn't fall apart."

She hummed in something he dare not let himself think was intrigue. "With thread, not khetry?"

Blinking, he looked up through his hair. She watched his working hands, then, sensing his stare, rose to meet it. The blue of her eyes was less like the sky than he first thought. Colder, but not entirely frigid. Like multifaceted sapphire, many shades within the cool pools.

"I . . ." Wren gathered his thoughts. "Yes—I mean, no. I can't mend with khetry; there isn't a spell for that kind of thing. It's too . . . simple."

Cocking her head, Palenisa scrutinized him before tearing off a strip of cloth from the sleeve of her cape. When she raised an arm, it resembled an open wing, loose and feathery. "Can you turn this into a hair tie?"

Surprised, he took the cloth. It was waxy to the touch and shiny on the inside, with faint silvery stars he had to tilt it to see. Excellent craftsmanship, likely the hand of a Peskeli seamstress he was loath to wreck. But then, she had ripped it from her own cape.

Under her watchful eye, Wren deftly drew the sides of the cloth closed and passed it back, not expecting much of anything. Especially not the thanks she tossed his way, a pair of carefree words over the shoulder as she tied her hair up into a tail. He bit the inside of his cheek and looked down. Part of him remained unbalanced by her presence. But none of that stopped the smile that threatened his lips. A small thing, its fleeting existence a tiny step forward.

After some time, the barn fell silent, a featureless mass of malleable shapes broken only by steady breathing and the occasional shuffling of pages. By the wall where the moon peered between slats, Wren flipped through the primer. The nature of a curious man was not quelled so easily, much to his own shame and horrid displeasure.

Dilated eyes scanned the circle for the summoning spell, his head overfull with questions. The world had its natural laws, tending to disorder and misfortune over order and luck. How could he have been so foolish to believe there existed a spell to alter one's fate, even momentarily? Everything was set in stone. He just hoped, wished, this backlash wasn't equally as permanent.

With a sigh, Wren turned to the latter half of the primer, where the writing became more harried and frantic. He kept coming back to these pages, wrestling with himself over their validity. The notes theorized—speculated without basis, to be more accurate—about a so-called ritual required to become a Weaver. They included iterations of hypothetical spellwork and haphazard sketches of a needle imbued with blood through pure khetry. It was a fanciful wish.

But the summoning spell . . .

He frowned at the diagram. Hadn't he learned his lesson the first time? He got what he deserved for tempting khetry. But still, what if there was a path to repentance? For his mistake, his impatience, his foolishness? A way to weave back into place all he had so carelessly torn apart?

Though Weavers were pitiable creatures, lulaik who sacrificed themselves for power, if the legends were true. He thought back to the green-eyed Weaver in Birinuyi, a sight he still struggled to make sense of. *True, then.* But rarer than rare. Weavers were pitiable creatures, yes, but so too was he. A sorry bag of blood and flesh filled with failure and fatigue. If this was the least he could do, he would gladly exsanguinate himself for the mere utterance of forgiveness from Asaru's lips.

Idly, Wren touched his nose and his hand came away wet. He licked the blood coating his upper lip and wiped the rest away, red blending with the crimson of his sleeve.

Pain licked up his side, and he glanced up.

Bars of moonlight shone between the roof slats, illuminating Asaru. In the darkness, he was more shadow and highlights than a visible figure. Wren watched him bite his lip and then look up. Hazel eyes glowed, silver pupils dilated. The bond flared with a jolt as their gazes locked into place like an alignment of stars and circumstance.

Wren felt he had to say something. He opened his mouth.

Light flooded in as the barn doors flung open.

Palenisa shot awake, brandishing her staff as she bolted to her feet. Her entire body was alert in seconds. In contrast, Rishé struggled to follow, dragging herself awake with a hand over her necklace and her hair mussed at an angle.

The farmer's child hovered in the doorway. Tense with clear panic, they hurriedly glanced back as a noise grew behind them. Muffled footfalls and voices deliberately kept low.

"The Black Order," they whispered, voice tremulous. "I don't know who you people are or what exactly you're running from, but you should go. Now."

This truly had been a foolish decision, and as usual, it had come time to reap what he'd sown.

As though thinking the same, Palenisa directed a piercing glare Wren's way. He shoved the primer away and shut his eyes, bathed in regret. They slipped into the night just as the sounds of sentinels rounded on the barn. The draw of steel. The distinct mechanical cry of a tightening crossbow. Boots kicking open the doors, followed by the bark of an order. The whisper of metal and susurrating chains grew near. A bolt whistled through the air, missing them wide, though its meaning was clear.

A warning.

“Scatter,” Palenisa hissed. The edges of her caped figure melted into the black forest. Rishé donned her hood and did the same. Asaru grabbed Wren’s wrist, dragging him into the heart of the woods. With a yelp of surprise, he looked down at where they touched, his skin buzzing as his pulse jumped.

Dangerous.

Asaru wasn’t like anyone he’d ever met before. He was better. He was worse. His force was a demand, perfectly contained order only spun into chaos by Wren’s own proximal existence.

They wove carefully through the wood with Asaru as their guide and Wren trailing behind as if he were a stray note in the birdsong. His body moved faster than his mind.

This contingent was better, slicker than the ones before. They made their way through the underbrush in steady strides, calling out as they split apart to comb the forest. Warning bolts flew all around, above. Closer, closer, ever closer.

As a figure stepped from behind a tree, Asaru darted forward. His warmth was gone, and Wren’s wrist felt startlingly bare.

Asaru caught the sentinel unaware, kicking the sword from their hand. He grabbed it with one hand and pinned them against a tree with the other. Steel glinted blue as he flipped it right side up and plunged it through the sentinel’s neck before they could utter a single word. A waterfall of blood rained from the fatal injury, dying hands scrambling to snatch at life as it was quickly snuffed out.

There was barely time to breathe before a second sentinel rounded the tree.

Just as quickly, just as quietly, Asaru dispatched them too, but not before a dagger found a home in his shoulder blade, inches from his brand. Grunting, he snapped the sentinel's neck and lowered them to the greenweed as if dancing sweetly.

The bond flared with pain, Wren stifling a gasp as if it were he who'd been stabbed. His was but a phantom of the true hurt, Asaru clutching his shoulder with a pinched expression. Gold spilling between his fingers glimmered in the moonlight like spilled coins.

Wren's mouth tasted of acid. He vehemently, violently, purged the bodies from his sight and swallowed the bile with a sick grimace. "You didn't have to *murder* them," he mumbled into his collar.

"Needs must. I have a duty, and in case you forgot, I am being hunted." Asaru squeezed his shoulder with a vicious grumble to stymie the bleeding. "Take the blade, if you like. Otherwise, let me do what I do best."

"Killing?" The words were sour even as they fell out. In response, Wren received a glare. Then Asaru's tail straightened before he darted forward, slamming Wren against a tree. Wren's cry was cut off by a hand. He wriggled instinctively, trying to free himself, but Asaru's glare and the press of his hand stilled him.

Wren's breaths gained speed until he grew lightheaded. He shut his eyes, clutched Asaru's strong arm, and willed himself not to hyperventilate. Only Asaru's solid body pressed against his kept him from buckling. They slid down the tree and crouched to hide among the greenweed together. Cloth rustled as they moved. Wren gulped, hyperaware of everything. He was frozen, unable to look anywhere else as Asaru listened, ears up and alert. There was a stern set to his brow, his braid was askew, and a thin sheen of sweat glistened on the underside of his jaw.

The hand over his mouth burned as much as the brand.

The Kingswood was alive with the sounds of night. Rustling grass, the nocturnal noisemakers, the creak of a taut bowstring. Every foreign noise, a paranoia.

"Asaru, Wren."

The woods whispered. They both startled, and Asaru's furred tail grasped Wren's ankle.

No, not the woods, but Rishé. Burning eyes peered between the stalks of greenweed as she gestured insistently. A distant shout had the Black Order contingent doubling back to fan their numbers out even farther. Soon they'd notice the missing sentinels. The missing, *dead* sentinels. Following Rishé, they ducked through the greenweed to where Palenisa knelt at a trapdoor. It was hidden partially beneath a moss-carpeted log. When she pressed her palm to the dead wood, roots snaked up like vermin to push it aside.

Wren shut the door with the rustle of leaves and an exhale of dust. By the time the sentinels passed, they were gone. Lantern light shone off nearby glistening foliage, illuminating a mere empty patch of grass.

RISHÉ

The early evening was syrupy warm as Rishé dunked her face in the black mirror of the pool. She held herself beneath the surface for two beats before emerging, gulping a mouthful of air as rivulets of water cascaded down her face. The collar of her tunic darkened to the color of smeared grass, and the tentacular ends of her hair curled from the dampness.

When Birinuyi had been a prominent city, its denizens had skillfully routed groundwater into cavernous underground ponds and baths. While those waterways had long since dried up, many smaller watering holes remained, most near the tunnel entrances like the one at which she knelt.

Near the entrance, the others sat gathered around the dying embers of a fire. They hadn't made camp since that disastrous night, pushing themselves day after day until a week had passed and Rishé finally put her foot down. No person could go on forever, she had snapped at an insistent Asaru. She wondered whether the look on his face had been respect or reluctant resignation. Either way, the bags under his eyes threatened to rival Wren's.

A droplet of water fell from her braids. Ripples shattered the pool's silent surface, and Rishé was drawn to the reflection of her pendant. It always looked different near water—at least to her discerning, overly critical eyes, which made sense, considering her mother had found it by the sea.

The stone had immediately caught Jarha's eye, hidden among the pebbles strewn over the shore. Its discovery was the kind of rare happenstance the faithful so often jumped to as explanation for so-called miracles. Jarha would have called it a sign of the divinity of the natural world. Serendipity, Rishé personally believed, was the more likely explanation for such a circumstance, as detritus washed ashore all the time. Yet she couldn't help but consider the possibility of her mother's hypothetical faith.

Fingers tracing the whorls in the pendant, she found herself smiling. Not all synchronicities were so inexplicable, however. One had landed her on the path to the Chronicler, closer to understanding what it was she'd inherited. It was the closest she'd been to her mother since helping her father carve Jarha's tree ring. Despite the inevitability of her passing and many moons spent on her deathbed, they'd waited until she'd passed to carve the ring. Better to have had hope than to have prematurely mourned.

Unlike the father who abandoned her to her grief, Rishé wasn't finished mourning. Half of her was her mother, her best half. Her grip tightened around the pendant, warming the stone with her body heat. And she would never let go. She couldn't.

Her smile faded when Wren called to her, drawing her from her thoughts. Sighing, she grimaced at her distorted reflection before standing. The two of them had been elected to head to the nearest town to restock. Although "elected" implied there was choice in the matter. Two of them were as far from inconspicuous as one could get, and the third could only hide himself by virtue of well-placed hair over the ears. While this was low on the list of things she'd love to be doing, maybe her time at the Screen had spoiled her; she was not standing another day of stale bread and foraged berries. Alas, she knew herself as well as she could read others, and unfortunately, she couldn't purchase enough supplies to feed four people on her own. She was a pragmatist that way.

Rishé donned her hood and led Wren from the tunnels. They walked through the Necklace alongside the winding path of the Darandell. The late afternoon sun painted the underbellies of wispy clouds in gold, while a lovely half-moon appeared eager for nightfall.

Lips pursed, she remained determined to ignore the side glances Wren kept sending her. Their last attempt at conversation had been—well, it had been an attempt. She hoped he'd get the hint and stay quiet for the remainder of their trek to Meliste. But he had a way of burrowing himself under one's skin, settling there as though he always belonged. Rishé couldn't believe she'd forgotten that tendency of his, the reason they'd even become close in the first place.

Or perhaps she wanted to simmer in bitterness as they walked, refusing to acknowledge it. Truly a mystery.

"So, um"—Wren began, twisting his antimony kohl fingers in a manner that used to be charming—"we should talk."

"Nas." She shook her head.

If Akiki didn't register, perhaps their shared mother tongue of Nomyrs would.

Wren frowned as she sped ahead, though her efforts were for naught since he easily caught up. Because of course he did.

"I . . . It's clear how you feel about me, but, um, why are you still . . . cu-istui?" *With us?*

He winced as though her response would cut him into a

thousand tiny pieces. Had she been less dead on her feet, she might have even felt up to the task. But she was tired, with a bone-deep weariness that had no patience to spare for his endless self-flagellation and lack of either foresight or hindsight. He wanted her to get angry, to rage at him and tell him what he'd done wrong. But she couldn't. Not until he understood it himself, though Rishé was losing hope he ever would. It had been years, and he was spinning in circles around her, a spiral of endless misunderstanding.

"Ela Scrisamac." *The Chronicler.*

"Chaqu-vaneran . . . lusi?" *Is that . . . all?*

"What do you want me to say, Wren?"

"Mis ni rovnet'foms dov . . ." *I don't know.*

Sighing, she pressed her nails into her palm. One concession, nothing more, nothing intimate. Hopefully, she wouldn't regret it. *"I think this Chronicler might know something. Related to my research."*

"Your necklace?"

She lifted it. The sun glinted off its edge, turning the stone into a miniature flame of crimson-and-orange facets. The notched surface formed a tiny valley of lines, words of some kind in an esoteric language, she'd long surmised.

"And your, um, your father . . . the last time you asked him about it . . . at the guild?" The question came out half formed as Wren watched Rishé's expression darken.

She exhaled through her nose and looked away. *Why did I expect anything else?* She didn't think he purposely played on her sentimentality, but no matter how much she tried to pull away, he kept drawing her back in. It was far too easy to want to fall back into their friendship. The wounded dregs festered untouched and untended for almost a decade. Seeing him had weakened her bitter resolve. Though she was loath to let him wound her further, she couldn't afford to lose anyone else.

"That's in the past."

"Sorry." He scrambled immediately for an apology. Utter mortification flooded his cheeks with color as his hands rushed through the signs. *"That was . . . I shouldn't have brought it up, I understand better than anyone—"*

The din of a nearby market reached their ears as they crossed a bridge that curved over murky water into Meliste Major. The Kingswood melted into the swamp around the town.

"Not now." Rishé held up a hand. *"Let's just hurry so we can be back before nightfall."*

She gave him no time to respond before splitting away to roam the edge of the market.

Rising from the Necklace, Meliste was a town of middling size that sat in the shadow of an abbey resembling a gaping rib cage. For a sanctuary of faith, it was darker than any shrine Rishé had ever seen. A place of learning—and worship—for the Church of Queen Mab, an old faith that claimed an existence older than the Six. There was some merit to that claim, according to her reading, but it bore little weight with her in the face of distaste for their cataclysmic beliefs. Worse than the Six, the church was rigid, highly secretive, and incredibly hierarchical. A triad of everything she vehemently stood against. She was fascinated by them from an academic standpoint. Everything else, though, made her want to shed her skin and snatch the flesh so the church couldn't have it. Considering what they did with bodies left to rot by their sacred aetherstones—anointing them in oil, quartering them, and burying the pieces wherever the soil was stoniest—she didn't want to take the chance either.

Rishé wandered between stalls with purpose, aur slipping

from her hands to the merchants' in return for lovingly wrapped loaves of bread, sweet flag, and a small net of nectar apples pinned shut with the desert-glass gem of the Palomer family. The queen's family. Of the nobility, House Palomer was fairly well liked by their common folk—unlike House Devall, former Valynian governors who fled south in disgrace. Something about a coup against a king of centuries past. Scoffing, Rishé pushed thoughts of them aside. Nobles were of no concern to her—only Erazill had been of some use, and that was due mainly to the fact that as head of House Da'Sanjam, he was her employer.

Hefting her satchel onto her other shoulder, Rishé searched the crowd and noticed something out of place. Only slightly. As though set just so, to be seen only by keen eyes.

Tucked between a hexe to Armasin and a side street was a small stall covered in heather cloth that had been feasted upon by many moths. The stone line of Armasin's statuesque arm guided her to the table where a hunched figure shuffled a familiar deck of cards. The Weave of Fate flowed between their fingers, holographic patterns swirling on the backs of the cards like an oil-slick river. Deft hands cut the deck in half, and the figure looked up as she approached.

Their mask was the massive skull of an adderowl, bleached bone catching the light in a way that sparked familiarity in Rishé. She'd never seen a living adderowl, but she could almost swear she'd encountered this one before. The cape that fell from their shoulders was the distinctive red of dried blood.

They swept across the cards with an upturned hand. An invitation: This was the setup to a fate game. The only kind one played with the Weave of Fate.

"Did you paint those yourself?" Rishé signed, hoping the stranger knew Eslang.

Thankfully they did, and they nodded. *"A game?"* they signed, knocking their fists together and tilting their head forward.

Rishé politely shook her clasped fingers and made to find Wren, but the stranger was insistent. They held up a finger. *"Just one, for free, won't take long."*

Fate games were just that—a play of luck rather than skill. It had been a while since she'd played, so she searched her mind for the rules. A deck held twenty-one cards, half upright and the rest reversed, with three aces, three charms, and four tricky court cards. In the middle of the weave lay Eșarpe, the center of all things according to Norvatti religion, and somewhere in the deck hid the Fool, the winning card for the player lucky enough to receive it.

Eyes flicking from the stranger's mask to the cards, Rishé bit her lip. It wouldn't hurt to test her luck just this once.

Fate usually lasted several rounds, with each move, though guided by chance, a methodical process. This game lasted just one.

She plucked a card and placed it in the center of the table, biting down a laugh as the Sage stared back at her.

Hand-painted, the simple design depicted a cosmic egg bearing three pairs of eyes, around which Eșarpe the giant sky serpent coiled. A part of the world, yet the world itself. Weaver of khetry and creator of everything under the three-faced suns of Ela Prinâza, our Lady Blessed Sunnai.

Fitting that she always pulled the card that best represented scholarship, the relentless pursuit of knowledge. Years earlier, Rishé might have called it a coincidence. These days, she called it what it was. A sign.

She'd made the right choice jumping at the chance to meet the Chronicler. What perfect luck that the weave apparently thought so too. *First the gods, now fate.* She truly was blessed with mystic riches.

After she signed her thanks to the stranger, they brought a hand to their chin in response. Amid the flow of people, she watched them tend to the weave before finding herself swept away. She hadn't noticed when time resumed, but it felt as though she'd been displaced by hours. The evening market was aglow beneath tall spotlight lanterns, swaying in the cool breeze at the corners of the major, turning the town into a softly glowing mass of light.

Spotting Wren's snakeskin, Rishé picked her way through the flow of people, passing by the stairs that led up to the abbey. A small congregation of gray-clad clergy descended in perfect order. The Vesisto, she observed, the dreary sect of the church, tasked with attending to the bodies so often left at aetherstones by both followers and nonbelievers alike. They had seemed married to death the few times she'd had the "pleasure" of watching them from afar. Up close, their veiled forms discomfited her, a shiver trailing from the base of her skull to the tips of her fingers. She was all too quickly cold and lowered her head as she hurried by.

The congregation smelled of mint and ash and moonglory—to cover the inescapable scent of death. They droned a stream of chants, words she did not know and, for once, did not care to. They were in the throes of some powerful morbid prayer that rose above the canopy, too loud for as late as it was. Rishé forced her vision to blur as they passed, letting her gaze pass over them, not wanting to think of their twisted mortuary cult. Let them revel in their cataclysm. Let them preach about the end of days and whatever else their golden books prophesied. Just not near her.

Guided farther from their all-encompassing drear, she

shuddered when they finally disappeared. A heaviness that was tinged with unhealed sorrows lingered in her lungs.

She rounded the major and found Wren, pulling him from what was sure to be an unneeded purchase, like she used to during their breaks between studies at the guild. The casual sentimentality of the act tasted sour on her tongue.

Upon crossing the bridge, she released him and dutifully ignored his searching look. It had been instinct, that was all. As they retraced their steps, Rishé felt abruptly uneasy, and she glanced around as the hair along her forearms rose from a chill, though there was no breeze. She was better at watching people than her surroundings, but even she could tell there was something whose ephemeral gaze left her feeling exposed and confused.

She chanced a glance back, finding nothing on the road. That only worsened the roiling in her gut. Rishé gripped her satchel so hard her palms turned pale as they moved onto a different path. There were only so many ways to return to their campsite, but she was determined not to be entirely predictable.

"What's wrong?" Wren asked when the tension grew too thick to swallow. She blinked at him, frowning at his curls spilling from their loose half tail.

"Did you have your hood up the entire time?"

"Um." That didn't sound good. His shoulders rolled in a frustratingly sheepish half shrug. "I . . . might not have."

Rishé sprinted the rest of the way back to the campsite. Ducking under the tree that shaded the entrance, she came to a stop before the threshold. Something was very, *very* wrong. She could feel it as clear as the chattering teeth in her jaw, the pounding of her heart in her chest.

It was quiet. Too quiet. A deliberate kind of quiet. Poised and patient, like a predator lying in wait.

Nothing moved. The Kingswood held its breath.

At the mouth of the tunnel, two limp forms lay on the ground. No signs of struggle. Palenisa and Asaru, unconscious like they'd dropped where they sat without a chance to react.

Wren crept slowly around her, closer, ever closer to them.

"Don't, Wren. *Wren,*" she whispered, harsh and panicked. He didn't listen, no sense of self-preservation in that horribly curious head of his. Grass rustled. Or, she *thought* she heard grass rustle. Someone was there—someone was *still* there. A thousand warning bells rang all at once.

Before Rishé could reach out to stop him, an explosion rocked the ground.

She was knocked off her feet and flung backward into the river. She barely had time to scream before sinking like a graceless, unruly rock into the water. Pain cracked her skull in two, and her eyes slammed shut with the sudden rush of being submerged.

Water filled her nose and ears, and her lungs screamed for air. Down, down, down she sank, to the rocky river bottom, where weeds brushed her sides and curled around her ankles.

A body brushed her side, starting her eyes open. Bubbles streamed from her mouth as she held off from gasping. A pair of illuminated lake deer swam by, gills fluttering on their necks. They blinked curious black eyes at her and swam off until they were nothing more than antlers in the distance.

Moments later, Rishé swam up, desperate, struggling for the ceaseless light of a single pale eye peering down from above. As gracefully as she entered, Rishé broke through to the surface. She dragged herself ashore and vomited brackish water into the muddy grass, salt on her tongue and a belly that ached as she gasped for breath.

The moon was almost at its zenith. Acid locked her lead arm as she raised a hand. Her fingers touched the stars, brushed the painted clouds away. She gazed into the abyss of the Sky Court as her breathing settled.

After nearly coughing up a lung, she rolled onto her front and crawled to the entrance of the tunnel to Birinuyi. Her lower back twinged, her chest heaved, her throat burned. Shivers racked her head to toe, soaked into her very bones. She pushed through it all and shuffled onto her elbows.

Leading into the gaping maw of Birinuyi was a trail of hand-painted cards. The weave glimmered like wolvencat eyes, disappearing into darkness.

Rishé had swallowed half the Darandell, but filled with stone-cold resolve, she gazed down the mouth of that hungry creature, an adderowl waiting to consume her.

ASARU

The sensation of being flattened into a tiny dark space was enough to make Asaru want to writhe from his bones.

Groaning, he turned his other cheek on the slab and stared at his chains. His legs were bound, just far enough apart to be uncomfortable, the cuffs formed of mortar-gray stone. Likewise, his hands were held fast, and this created a yawning gap within him as though he'd been flayed apart and stretched unfathomably wide.

Testing the cuffs, he shoved his arms apart till they trembled. His nape throbbed as his strained shoulder ached, stab wound a burning line. The chains chafed his skin with every movement, not that he could do much in his state. Strength failed him, and for the first time, Asaru could imagine what other eresh keyel felt upon contact with black diamonds. A novel, and wholly unwelcome, experience.

His brand was a relentless prickle, insistent and persistent. Inky blackness encased him to the elbow. The curse devoured his arms, ate his scars, leaving pain wherever that night sky covered.

Worst of all these hurts, he couldn't quite see khetry. The web was hazy and indistinct, layered behind a slick film. Phantasms of faint red threads wavered in his periphery.

A trailing chant echoed in the back of Asaru's mind as he shifted. The position aggravated his abdomen. The oleander was making healing impossible, and he might have begun bleeding again. Blood-crusted bandages and the starchy shift of his aya-shif against raw skin fired across his every sensitive nerve.

Groaning, he lifted his head and set his chin on the slab to assess his surroundings.

Clearly, in the once-was city of Birinuyi, this underground room had been hollowed out from the tunnel walls and decorated with onyx carved furnishings. Upon closer inspection, the details almost reminded him of a vulgar-looking apothecary. A stone-hewn mixing bench curved to one side as rotting wood beams lined the low ceiling where plants would have hung, and the cool remains of a hearth dusted ash across the dirt. But it was rudimentary, brown and gray where Aedyton's apothecaries shone gold, glass, and sandstone in the cloud-wrought topmost ring. Different still was the sheet of obsidian spanning the width of one wall. Colors shifted in the sheet, gleaming like slick oil.

With the quiet shuffling of feet, Asaru's ears twitched, and he moved his gaze to come face-to-face with the skull of a massive creature. He jerked back, reopening the stab wound on his shoulder. Blood oozed a sluggish line of heat across his trapezius and along the side of his wing. He swallowed down the pain as the skull leaned into his face until he could hear the breath of the person within.

It was a mask, almost resembling the distortion of a remnant in a certain light. White striations radiated from a pair of large eye sockets that gave off a violet glow. The bottom of the mask was missing its lower jaw and bore only two long, serpentine teeth. Wisps of unnaturally lavender hair escaped the end of a braid slung over the crimson cape that hung from the figure's shoulders. He could see no skin in the gap between mask and collar that would indicate what they were, but his every nerve blared with disquiet.

"What is this? Who are you?"

Unfazed, the stranger silently leaned back as Asaru snarled. They lifted his chin with a finger and tilted his head to the side. In their other hand was a crooked staff engraved with patterns too dark to make out.

He wrenched his head away and snapped at their fingers, but they maintained a frustrating distance. Close enough to touch him, but not close enough that he could bite their unwanted hand.

The stranger stood and rounded the slab, tracing the powerful line of Asaru's arm to his shoulders. They tapped his armlet with a curious finger and thumbed his jaw—far too close to his halo. Revulsion slithered through him at the roughness of their gloves.

"How are you feeling?" they asked in a misty whisper. *Not their real voice,* he surmised, twisting to keep them in sight despite the protesting twinge in his stomach. They pressed on his injury, eliciting a bitten-off grunt.

"Let me go"—he seethed and his heart filled his throat in a swell of rage—"and I might give you a head start before I kill you."

A heavy cloud of pain darkened over him as the stranger pressed, then kept pressing, harder, until the wound stopped bleeding. With them behind him he was left helpless. Left to try to wriggle from their touch. He didn't want this; he didn't like this.

To his surprise, they began to clean and dress his shoulder, while they continued with their questions, despite his lack of answers. They seemed to care more for the sound of their own voice than his response.

"How long have you been cursed?"

Silence was his armor. Lips pursed, jaw tense as a spring.

"What happened to the Tetrarchia?"

Asaru's eyes widened, his head snapping to the side as he cast a blazing glare at the stranger. He bared his teeth, bloody gums, and lashing tongue. He trembled, shook, stretched the chains, even as his wounds screamed in irritation. His claws scratched divots in the rock with the force of his fury, mouth watering to rip the insolence from their audacious throat.

"What business is that of yours? Where is Alvarys?" His tone was low. The *gall* of this interloper—to hide behind a mask and tricks and strange minerals. "What did you do to my brother?"

Without hesitation, the stranger dug their knee into his stomach, and the air fell out of him in a stuttered gasp—cold, pure pain ratcheted up his side and slammed into the base of his skull with the surety of a hammer.

"I haven't even seen the Tetrarchia. I don't know." They leaned over his bandaged shoulder, glowing eyes level in his periphery as they twisted that vicious knee. "However, I do know something you might be interested in."

Helpless to stymie the jolt of pain, Asaru let out a hiss, lessened only by his wince. *"What."*

"I know where the Chronicler is. But first, all I ask is one favor, then I'll uncuff you"—they tapped the crook to his chained wrist—"and I'll release your friends."

Asaru's lips curled back. "It is not a favor if one person has the other bound," he said. "That is coercion."

They shrugged. "A matter of perspective." They sounded almost content. "It's not something *I* need necessarily—it's more of a request from the Chronicler. They allow me certain . . . liberties, as long as I retrieve what they desire."

As Asaru glanced beneath the jaw of their mask, he saw no smoke. Every slippery word was the truth, and even the amusement in their altered voice sounded genuine.

"Fine," he spat. He wanted nothing more than to open their throat but restrained himself. Alvarys was far more important. He knew little of the Chronicler aside from an approximation of their location; anything that would get him closer to his brother, the beacon, and answers was worth his own pain. Petty grudges meant little, though he simmered in disgust. "Now get your hands off me."

Satisfied, the stranger removed their knee and cupped his face. Asaru's stomach rolled, and he wished the hand belonged to another. Bracelets made of the same stone as his cuffs sent cold spots over the valleys of his face. Those hands crawled, crept, slid down to rest just above his halo. Those fingers pressed into the corners of his jaw like he was some wild beast.

Inside, he burned, utterly and thoroughly. And a growl rumbled from his chest like stones tumbling down a mountain.

It would only take a slight tilt of his head to bite into their wrist. Just one bite.

The stranger released him with a hum and slunk back to the other end of the slab. They settled down cross-legged, pulling a pouch from their cape. From it, they dumped out a mess of cards. With the practiced finesse of someone who had all the time in the world, they shuffled and fanned the cards face down.

They steepled their hands under their chin. "Pick a card."

"I am not doing that," he snapped, unable to look at the

cards. It was too strong a reminder of home. The kind of frivolous play his brother loved, which their mother used to draw him into when they were younger. A sentimentality he restrained in himself.

"You promised me one thing." The stranger cocked their head. He could almost see the grin behind their mask—maddening. To them this truly was a game. "This is my choice."

"Are you a *child*?"

"I have a feeling I'm older than you think. You're two hundred and thirty, no? That's what—fifty human years?"

Once free, Asaru was going to rip out their throat so no one else would ever be subject to them speaking again. That would be good—that would be a kindness. He tested the limits of the restraints around his ankles and found them still unyielding. Frustration calcified in his veins, spilled from the seams of his very self.

Sighing as though he was the source of all this world's woes, the stranger pulled five cards from the spread. The backs were painted gold and purple around an eye of tiny gleaming stones. *Diamondglass*—Asaru's eyes widened. He'd never seen the gem before. Ice-pale shards winked in the dim light, a rainbow of color flashing through minuscule facets like a prism.

"Pick. A. Card." They tapped each card as they spoke.

Trapped, he was an insect pinioned beneath scrutinous malintent. Nowhere to go, chained, and at their mercy. He could do nothing but sit there and accept the hand he'd been dealt.

Breathing through his nose, Asaru pointed. Anywhere. He didn't care. He just wanted this over—and this mad masked stranger dead.

They held up the card and, after a contemplative moment, set it down to reveal the reverse.

A figure of indeterminate identity danced in a field of light, one arm to the air and the other hidden at their back. Above their head was a circle of stones, a crude imitation of a halo, but where their face should have been, a mirror reflected his own confused expression.

"The Fool."

Asaru did his best to ignore the progression of the curse—the black tendrils leaking into the whites of his eyes. Just like Khensu. Just like those in the embassy. His brow furrowed. He was no fool. And he said as much, to the amusement of the stranger.

"Foolish? Not quite. Predictable? Absolutely. And lacking the sense to see what's right in front of you."

They flipped the remaining cards over one by one. A dazzling array of esoteric images.

"You don't know what you don't know, and you're scrambling in the metaphorical darkness."

"I am well aware," Asaru gritted out, "that I do not know *where* my brother is."

"Not that. I'm sure you'll find him." Waving him off—*infuriating*—they pointed to two cards. "Here's what I do know."

The first card depicted a warrior clutching a spear to her chest as she sat on an elaborate throne, an icon set at the hollow of her throat. The second, the image of a writhing serpent squeezing a cracked egg.

"Priestess and Eșarpe. The border between change and stagnation, divine transformation."

They moved to the next, a curving bloody trident piercing a black sun. Like a sentinel's sword sliding through a royal chest. Asaru averted his eyes and bit the inside of his mouth against the image of the king's dull stare, mismatched in the dying light.

"Retribution." The stranger's voice slid into his ears like the insistent hand of some possessive, indomitable presence. He shuddered, and his toes curled.

"The path to your death. And if you keep on this path, one that will be soundly deserved."

"Is that a threat?" he muttered. None had ever gone to such cryptic lengths to threaten him before. How fascinating and completely unrequested.

The stranger sighed. "Merely a prediction. You *are* cursed."

The fourth and final card was a pair of eyes, mismatched gray and gold. But as he squinted, there appeared a shadowed figure to whom the eyes belonged.

"Khetry Eye. Blood, bond, brand. Retribution is fated to keep you apart."

"Unfortunately, I highly doubt that."

"Eh, this isn't an exact prediction," the stranger said, waving their hand side to side. "It can't be, unless *I* want to break one of the cornerstones myself, but the backlash I saw on your shoulder will soon be the least of your problems. Not even the Red Web of Life can save you."

Asaru was a lonely man—he knew that. Often took comfort in it. Perhaps because he believed he deserved it. *But Wren . . . doesn't.* It was something he could only admit deep in his mind, where he could bind the thought to secrecy and never confront the way it lodged like a stone beside his heart.

He clamped his eyes shut and released a shaky breath. He couldn't compromise himself. Not for anything. Not when he had a duty. Reopening his eyes, Asaru warily watched the cards disappear back into the stranger's pouch and the pouch back into their cape.

Wariness fled to alarm when they pulled out a knife, shell

white with a jagged edge. They removed a glove, sliced the meat of their palm, and drew a bloody spell circle on the slab. *Lulaik,* his mind flashed at the foreboding sight of the spellwork.

The lulaik wiped their bleeding palm across their mask. With the other, they charged the spell, bright white around their spread fingers. In the thin net of khetry Asaru could faintly see, threads shook with the frenetic energy of life as the spell burst in a shower of sparkling light.

No . . . He drew back—as much as he could, pushing the limits of his strength and the chains—from that glowing hand.

No. A chill raced to his sore limbs. Desperate fingers reached for nothing, reached for escape. Asaru scratched at the stone and the dirt, shaking in his chains to flee, to take flight. That glowing hand reached for his face. The presence of the possessor quashed his senses as his breathing increased. He panted, harried.

"I'm just going to borrow your memories for a moment."

No!

That glowing hand pressed against his forehead and everything went white.

He still belonged to himself.

Not possession.

Something equally invasive. A psychometric spell. Reading the past. *Reliving* one's life. Even moments long forgotten, deep in the recesses of the ever-complex mind. Where possession, inescapable as it was, carried the virulent tinge of familiarity—family, home—this twisted touch was that of a stranger. An intrusive passenger to his memories as though they were their own.

Anger warred with confusion in Asaru as he struggled against the memories the lulaik viewed. The spell rendered the images murky—not a full recollection, but the emotions that came with one. More like a half-remembered dream.

Staring up at the malformed smear of Tenat's and Alvarys's faces, he was assaulted by the truth he knew—thought, believed. He was a poor son, an even poorer brother. A mismatched piece within their set of three. They loved him—they did, *they loved him*—yet there had always been some innate wrongness to him. Too cold, too angry, too different. His failure to bridge the distance between family and his place in it shamed him. None of them spoke of it; he wasn't sure they knew how.

He was a defective warrior too. Never quite enough, touched by a darkness that knew no origin and able to touch the blackness that burned in turn. Nothing but an extension of his duty, desiring to do good but bound to what he was told. A tool under the will of another. But those were his hands—hazy and indistinct in the memory—those were *his* hands that held the fatal sword.

Dead things reached for him, dragged him into oblivion with intangible hands. Hair like burning snakes and eyes like pools of night. Two who were once three—now no longer, never again to be.

Then there was nothing.

Asaru gasped as he was shoved back into his present body. Tears beaded at the corners of his eyes. All he'd tried to bury under lock and key, this lulaik had dredged violently to the surface. He didn't want this—he didn't want any of this. He drew in choked breaths, wanting to grab his halo. To pry from his nape the black shard that mired his ill-fitting existence.

"The Chronicler was right," the lulaik said, hand sliding to his cheek in false imitation of tenderness. "You are a born traitor. It's what you were *made* for."

Never had he hated anyone more than in that moment.

A deafening boom erupted through the tunnels. For a moment, Asaru couldn't breathe, couldn't think, couldn't feel.

The silence was shattered in a spray of tiny pieces of biting black raindrops.

As if it were second nature, the lulaik rolled aside to avoid the blast. Their hands slammed together to charge the spellwork stitched on their remaining glove. Blood smeared across the slab; the circle was broken. Casting off, they flung up their hands as a hail of sharpened flintrock shot toward them. The deadly shower bounced harmlessly off an invisible barrier. Blue light streamed from their fingertips, stretched out wide before them.

Through the wall where the obsidian pane once stood, Palenisa bounded. Righteous anger painted her face, and her hands hung low, chained with gray cuffs. She kicked her heel into the earth and twisted, sending obsidian pellets through his restraints. The stone cracked, split, clattered apart. As the cuffs fell, khetry threads flared as bright as the sun between clouds.

But still Asaru's head swam, unable to solidify his thoughts from the psychometric invasion that had sapped the resistance from his body. It was all he could do to blink the fog from his vision as Palenisa turned her ire to the source of their shared torment.

She looked ready to kill. Somewhere inside, past the vertiginous miasma of a reeling mind, Asaru felt the same.

PALENISA

Spirits damn these fucking tunnels.

Palenisa panted heavily, eyes darting between Asaru and the masked figure. Their captor, she surmised, inhaling sharply as she pawed the dirt.

A headache battered her temples with gale force, her vision pulsing. Her wrists throbbed from the weight of her chains. Each time the cuffs rubbed her skin, an emptiness, a disconnect from the spirits, yawned deep within her. It was already difficult to conjure sunlight, but now she couldn't even hear the clattering voices of the earth beneath her palm as it brushed the ground.

Senses dulled, she barely caught the stream of khetry beneath the bitterness of Black Diamond wafting from Asaru. He smelled of rot. The other smelled of rainfall and iron.

Lulaik. Her eyes narrowed.

She hadn't asked for this. She hadn't asked for any of this. She was trapped underground, forced to kill their captor because spirits knew she was not leaving without spilling some blood. Cheap tricks irked her, and she didn't take kindly to being knocked out.

Whoever had attacked them knew exactly what they were doing when they took her staff. It had been left just out of reach, farther back in the tunnels, in the sorry excuse for a room where she'd been chained to Wren. He would be fine. After his little human friend—*Rishé*—had melted open the chains on Palenisa's feet, she had left the two of them her scythe. They could figure out the rest on their own. She hoped. And while her hands might not have been free, she could just as easily manipulate earth with her legs. Earth Aspects couldn't manipulate marrowstone, the substance from which the suvaunoors were built, nor any other gem. But she could work with flintrock.

She kicked another spray of projectiles in Asaru's direction, and razor-sharp shards sliced through the cuffs that held his ankles. As he tugged himself free and ducked to the side of the room, their gazes met. There was a haze in his eyes. Milky, like Khensu. She scanned his body, but the black had yet to reach his biceps. That was good—for the moment, at least.

Asaru jerked back, drawing in a sudden panicked breath.

The nearly imperceptible sound of rustling cloth accompanied movement in her periphery. She inhaled sharply as she narrowly avoided a hand reaching for her.

The lulaik closed in with an open palm, glowing fingers spread wide and aimed straight for her face. As she ducked, the violet eyes set in that skull mask darted down to her. The stare burned with cool assessment.

The lulaik shifted, preparing to strike again, and Palenisa lurched away.

"Do not let them touch you," Asaru called, pressing himself

to the wall. He shook and he dropped to one knee with a wince.

She gritted her teeth and crouched beside him. "Why?"

Releasing a tremulous sigh, he clutched his shoulder. "Psychometry spell. Gets inside your head, knocks you unsteady."

Through a sidelong glance, she watched his jaw tense, sweat dripping from the tip of his nose. Worrying her lip, she reoriented. Detached from the Zodiac, she wanted to pray for their aid, but she was awfully alone. This was the dread she so desperately sought the coterie to quell. Her promise was her lodestar, and it would guide her back there, into the good graces of her sisters once more.

First—she needed to kill this damn lulaik. For the sake of her own pride. On that, she was sure Asaru, too, readily agreed.

"Together?" she muttered. He nodded tersely.

They leaped apart as the lulaik lunged.

Lilac gleamed from the massive sockets of their adderowl mask. Striated, white, scarred by a red smear along the jawbone. The lulaik reacted quickly, swinging wide to snatch at her braids. Palenisa's stomach dropped as their slate bracelets brushed her neck. She snapped her head aside, evading by an inch the same stone that weighed her wrists down.

Bloody petrichor filled her nose as the lulaik curled their fingers into the spell circle sewn onto their glove.

"You always fight the coward's way?" she shouted. "Restraining your opponents because you're a shitty warrior—is that it?"

The bracelets melted from their wrists, and Palenisa sprang back into a handstand to avoid the whip of molten rock. Her arms strained as she balanced on bound hands. The liquid cut at where she had been standing with a crack.

Carried by the momentum, Palenisa whirled her legs down and around, arcing across the ground. Dirt rose to her call. Pillars of earth rapidly sped toward the lulaik, undulating like a curved spine. Using their crooked staff like an extension of their body, they dodged, their slippered feet grazing the racing columns. Packed earth collided with the wall in a resounding boom that shook the ground and rumbled in Palenisa's chest.

A fine dusting of dirt settled over the lulaik's back. Rising, they brushed off their cape with an air of nonchalance and charged again with a glowing palm.

"Coward, and a liar too," Asaru sneered, darting forward. He brought a swift leg between them, cutting off the lulaik. Forced back, they slid into a crouch, hand planted between their knees as their mask snapped up. "You do not truly know where the Chronicler is—do you? All you know are tricks and games!"

The only response the lulaik gave their taunts was a silent shrug.

Palenisa snarled and surged, dragging up projectiles sharp as teeth. Jagged flintrock and packed earth, hardened, whittled to deadly points. From the side, Asaru lunged, hands on either side of his neck as he cast a spell. A spit of flame lashed from his mouth, red streaked with blue and ethereal white.

A gloved hand jutted out, and a translucent barrier of hard light appeared. Violet shadows and teal highlights warred across the adderowl skull.

Palenisa and Asaru pushed forward, relentless, faster and faster in tandem assaults, as though they'd been partners for ages. Each line of fire and each chunk of earth forced the lulaik back, forced them to cast up a new barrier with each landed strike. And they did so with the most infuriating ease.

This should have been easy. For her and Asaru, weaving like a spear through water, it should have been simple to cut this lulaik down. But fighting angry made one weak. Fighting angry made one susceptible to mistakes.

One thing about masks—they hid the eyes.

Haunting purple sockets shot up. Quickly, the crooked staff sliced the air directly into Asaru's stomach. Air wheezed from his chest as the impact flung him aside. His ankle slammed into the wall and his shuttered scream followed. Seizing, he crumpled to the ground. Black liquid dribbled from the corner of his mouth as he seized—eyes wide, he cried out in warning, but it came far too late.

Weakened by the stone and drained of strength, Palenisa couldn't react fast enough. She missed the figure in her periphery. When she turned, she gasped. There was a hand on her forehead and her vision went white.

Images flashed, a collection of loose meaning. Vana torn asunder, her former sisters, destruction and death and defeat. She was shoved even farther back, memories clawing their way to the surface. Her infancy was flavored with the secret sweets shared with her mother, her childhood with the fleeting whispers of a father that passed before her birth, her adolescence with the scornful lash of her grandparents' eyes across the backs of her marked hands. Time flowed into itself as the spell rooted out the worst parts of her. The depths of her immaturity, her quickness to anger, a longing for the sanctuary that had been taken from her. Not the coterie, but before that, as an impulsive child who thought she knew how the world worked.

Her body was a lightning rod of pain. Curled into a ball, she saw a spiraling blossom of red and black like plucked wings littering the bloody ground about her. Lying there, surrounded by the bodies of her mother's killers, revenge tasted bittersweet.

She could feel herself dying.

There hadn't been anything for her beyond that moment, beyond crushing Chiroyn and watching his life fade.

She hadn't expected death to take her too. All youths thought themselves immortal.

Palenisa's breaths became ragged and wet. Each inhale took effort, and with each exhale, her lids lowered. Her vision blurred to indistinct images. Slowly fading, muted by fear.

A shadow blotted out the light. Blearily, she blinked as a foot rolled her gently onto her back. The image of a woman above her clarified, and Palenisa strained against the spell.

These were *her* memories of Ada. *You have no right.*

The thought was quickly swept away as a stream of emotions overwhelmed her. Drowning—she was drowning in herself.

Sense memory was a fickle thing, the mind trying to convince itself of true touch. Palenisa imagined she felt Ada's hand in hers, leading her to the ceremony where she'd been inducted as Sister of Faith. *Faith, faith.* She pushed at the spell, crying out for the spirits as the recollection of Ada's death surfaced. *Not this*—she didn't want to relive this.

The spell persisted, and she was daggered apart once more hearing the news. A massacre at the Gladiowu estate, it had been called. Ada, gone, with the rest of her family line. Tragedy, mercenaries, accident—no one knew the truth. All that remained were star-touched shadows. Nothing but dust. Not even bodies to mourn.

She couldn't even remember her own mother's face anymore—what if she lost Ada too?

Gasping wetly, Palenisa was flung back to reality.

Her vision blurred, and her throat felt tender as though she'd been sobbing. Fatigue strained the tendons in her neck. She was a living ache. Her legs buckled as a tear slipped free. The pieces of her mind swam away too quickly to catch, too mired in oil-slick memory to call on the Zodiac.

"What . . . what the fuck did you do to me?" she asked, dazed. Her mouth tasted of ash.

The lulaik slowly lifted their hand from her forehead, staring down at her from that impassive mask.

"I only reminded you of your truth."

Hot fury flared within her. The only time she'd heard them speak, and it burned to hear their voice.

It *burned.*

She was unsteady and seeing double, but she could still move. Which meant she could still act. Her clasped hands caught the mask by the underside of the jaw, manacles cracking bone. Their head snapped back with a startled gasp. Finally—a true and honest reaction.

When they turned back, part of the skull cracked. Bone fell away to reveal tawny skin and a white scar cut through a thick brow. A loose curl of dyed hair obscured a wide violet eye.

I see you.

Huffing, they narrowed their eye. Before she could blink, their staff collided with the side of her head, and the world came apart at the seams. Darkness crept in at the edges as she collapsed. Through the fog, she reached for the Zodiac, screamed for the spirits beneath several layers of fog.

What would Ada think of me now? A familiar revenge-tainted madness cradled her, the same that almost took her life. Memories unearthed their dark and silent heads. Tear-filled eyes shut—*Forgive me.*

Where the masked lulaik once stood lay a dimming circle of swirling dust.

Then she thought of nothing more.

WREN

Wren's gaze slid over to the blazing scythe with what he thought was, frankly, a healthy amount of fear. The crescent-moon blade was a yellow inferno in Rishé's hands, like a sun restrained. He eyed the smooth edge warily, as though it would turn the room to ash at any moment. Death by accidental immolation was not the way he planned to die—currently, that is—and he wasn't any more enthused by the look of intrigue Rishé wore as she held it far too close to her face.

"You, um, plan on freeing me?" he asked, ducking beneath his curtain of hair as she turned his way. It felt as though the stone cuffs had scraped all the skin from his wrists. With each small shift, the watery blur of khetry filled his vision at the edges. It was disconcerting to see the web so faded, as though dropping suddenly into open air and falling, falling, falling, without any mind to where he would land.

Humming, Rishé lowered the scythe to his chains, and he shivered as the heat distorted the air in rippling waves of light.

"Might free you of your head instead."

Wren's head shot up and their gazes met, startled. His breath caught in his throat as they blinked wide eyes at each other. In the awkward pause his mind struggled to make sense of her words. Her tone had been almost joking. Almost . . . friendly. Close to what they used to be to each other, before he'd broken it. But not irreparably, he realized, faint petals of hope settling behind the brand over his heart. His lips twitched up crookedly, and hesitantly, Rishé returned it, her smile a cracked shade glancing over her face. That single glance drained the lingering tension from the broad slant of his shoulders. Left in its place was a tender, achingly raw wound.

Perhaps something he could heal.

Wren looked down at his wrists, biting his lips against a smile. The cuffs glowed red like the heart of a gemsmith's forge. When the heat became too much to bear, he jerked his hands away with a hiss, and Rishé yelped, dropping the scythe. It only took a flick of the wrist for the tempered stone to slip off, but the heat lingered, radiating up his arms.

For a long time, a *really* long time, Wren and Rishé stared at the scythe. Melted earth cooked around the scorching blade. *That thing is not safe for life.*

A horrid pain startled him from the thought. Wren doubled over, teeth gritting as pain stitched a line of fire up his side and dragged the vicious point of a blade up the center of his back. The brand pounded fiercely. His heart threatened to beat free from the cage of his chest.

A hand found his arm, gripped, and squeezed.

"What's wrong," Rishé asked, tracing the words against the meat of his shoulder, though he barely felt it. Her touch was solid earth to the whirlwind in his head.

"Asaru," he gasped. Asaru was doing something reckless.

Frustration buzzed beneath his skin, and he clamped his eyes shut, pressing his forehead to his knees. But he could hardly complain—not when the pain he was feeling was his fault alone.

A rumble thundered through the tunnels. Loose silt and stone tumbled free of the ceiling, then another deafening boom sent sun-starved vines swaying in the swirling dust. The tremors died slowly. Tiny needles pinched his brain, and his teeth rattled in his fragile skull as the echo reverberated through him.

"We should go," Rishé said, grabbing the scythe. Careful fingers flicked the blade shut, and once the glow disappeared, Wren felt like he could breathe again. Just barely, though, since his stomach still churned with shared pain.

Wiping a hand across his mouth, he stepped through the gash Palenisa had punched in the wall. Dirt crumbled beneath their feet as they followed her path of destruction. Birinuyi may have once been an impressive city, a sanctuary, but all that remained was a sprawl of half-formed rooms and ruins riddled with holes carved by the hand of an angry Aspect.

Crimson caught his eye through the dimness. At the end of a tunnel, a scrap of fabric—the tail end of a cape, perhaps—flashed up a set of stairs. It was almost too dark to make out, and for all the swirling dust, it could've been nothing more than the illusion of color. The denizens of the past hadn't just left the skeleton of a city, but parts of themselves as well. Wren had heard people were prone to madness in the darker parts of the tunnels, where no living thing had breathed for centuries.

He turned and squinted, but Rishé called him over before he could reason whether it was real or imagined.

A crude doorway was ringed with sharp black teeth leering down like the uneven maw of some massive, long-dead creature.

Past the threshold lay a rudimentary apothecary hewn from the earth.

A fine dust was still settling over the room when Wren crossed the threshold. The ground was littered with shards of obsidian and flintrock, over which trailed a messy golden path. He traced it with his eyes, before landing on Asaru and Palenisa sprawled in similar states of injury.

On her belly, Palenisa trembled as if caught in a violent dream. Her braids fanned loosely around her head, and several thin black cuts abraded her cheeks, fresh and bleeding.

A choked groan drew Wren's attention to where Asaru was curled beneath the cage of his wings in a small pool of blood. The mark of the curse had even attached itself to his spine, cruelly spiraling from the middle of his wings in keloidal tendrils of darkness beneath the scarred flesh.

Concern boiled through Wren as he pressed a hand to their necks and inner wrists. His fears abated only slightly when he found them still breathing.

"Get them on their backs," he said as Rishé knelt beside him. Gently, they turned them over, laying them side by side. *They'll be all right.* He watched the soft rise and fall of their chests with relief. The sight reminded him painfully of the guild, a sour realization that he forced to the base of his brain—along with an assortment of other uncomfortable truths. He was nothing even *resembling* a healer. He never would be. He'd made sure of that.

But still, he had to go on. Do what he could, what little he could, with the power he had.

Wren pulled a pinch of pungent herbs from his satchel and nicked the meat of his palm with his fangs. He drew a bloody circle of sacred geometry around the herbs, an additive to increase the spell's potency. Placing two fingers in the circle, he charged the spell. Khetry snaked his wrist in a gentle touch—and then he cast it off.

Both unconscious figures bolted awake with twin cries of alarm. Asaru's wings snapped straight with a crack of bone as Palenisa spasmed, gasps gurgling in her throat. Their panting melted into grumbles of pain as they curled away from his touch. Wren didn't let either go far, pushing them down harsher than he would have liked. Not that he could be blamed. They were a healer's worst nightmare—prone to danger, both to others and themselves. Oh, but the guild—now the guild would've liked them.

With the last of his blood, Wren painted a spell circle on Palenisa's forehead and cast it. A warming spell. Weak, but it would enliven her further since sunlight Aspects didn't do too well without, well, *sunlight*.

His brows rose as Rishé brushed a cloth across the cuts on Palenisa's cheek, and they rose exponentially higher at the violet that darkened her ebony face and the bob of her throat. Her hands clenched, unclenched, clenched in her lap. *Huh.*

He shook his head and sighed. "What happened here?"

Wincing, Asaru rolled a shoulder and tucked his wings away. Wren followed the arch of his spine, then sharply averted his gaze. His brand prickled.

"Tried to kill our captor," Palenisa said. She winced as Rishé dabbed a balm along the underside of her jaw with small, slender fingers. "They got the better of us."

"*One* person?" Rishé said, receiving a scowl for her curiosity. Unfazed, she continued working on Palenisa's wounds with deft hands for someone more suited to smithing than healing. Then again, Wren reminded himself, she'd always picked up skills quickly.

"They were lulaik." Palenisa crossed her arms, looking more

disappointed in herself than truly angry. “At least one of you knows how to protect yourself.”

“We’re not all Ignante, *oh-so-glorious war lulaik with her purple mane and golden tears,*” Wren replied thinly, shying away from her piercing glance. “Some of us are cowards.”

He glanced up at Asaru, received a nod, and began peeling away his blood-crusted wraps. Gold and gray and black. He stanched the wound, placed a poultice over bare brown skin, and lost himself in the repetition of winding the bandages back around.

“I am sure,” Asaru deadpanned, never breaking his gaze, “you can imagine how I feel about another surprise disruption to my duty.”

Irritation simmered to the surface. “And how is fighting to your own detriment supposed to help Alvarys?” Wren snapped. “Caring for your brother shouldn’t mean not caring for yourself.”

At Asaru’s cry, his mind returned to his task. He met Asaru’s wide eyes, thin rings of hazel around constricted slit pupils.

Too tight—he’d made the bandages too tight in his irritation. And now Asaru was staring at him like *that.* Like he’d done something unforgivable. In that moment his self-hatred knew no end.

A derisive snort cut through his spiral.

“Rich. Coming from you,” Rishé muttered bitterly.

Their eyes met, and she looked away quickly as if sensing the muted hurt that burned on the back of his tongue. Wren’s stomach roiled as a pained look drew across his face.

His upset was unfounded, so he dug his nails into the inside of his wrist. They were too black to leave marks, but he didn’t care as long as it hurt. After all—he deserved this. Thorns laced his arm.

Why did he always do wrong? Always tearing messes into the cloth of reality. If he were a Weaver—maybe then he could mend it. He was pathetic just for the mere thought.

"Sorry."

He didn't know whom the apology was for.

Blinking glassy eyes, Wren folded the loose edge of the bandages away—careful, *gentle*—and, once everyone was more or less in one piece, trailed after the others as they searched for a way out of the tunnels.

At the top of the stairs where he'd glimpsed the fleeing illusion was a white arch. It would have been easy for him to unlock, but Palenisa impatiently made them an exit. A gaping hole through which the sun shone in shallow streams of light.

When they emerged, they were no longer in Meliste. They were much farther south—so far south Wren could hear the sea as they walked. Waves whispered nearby. He smelled it, tasted it, wanted to see it. Instead, he was met by trees and darkness and a looming tangle of wood that made him feel like a young child again.

The Lizardwood.

Mist clung to the shadows at the bases of massive trunks in the immense primeval jungle. The source of many Norvatti nightmares, the Lizardwood was said to have spilled from the darkest whims of Furtumbér, Lord of All Shadows. The Rosatay story he knew differed from that of the Vana and Eihron. At the end of the day, they were only stories. Seeing was another matter. Walking through Furtumbér's gloom, created in the shadow of Ela Prinâza's thousand thousand suns—that, too, was very different.

They emerged from the tree line, and the Lethean Sea opened up before them. Drowned roots dipped into the water, salt crawling up the sides in a delicate frosting of white. Along the pebbled shore, salamander seals splashed in the water. Wren watched them paw at each other, their high-pitched barks breaking through the canopy. Animals were simpler creatures than people. Would that he could be one, as comfortable as Dakazna back in his mother's house.

"We should . . ." He started, but he wrapped his arms around himself and looked away when the others turned toward him. Embarrassment blanketed him. "Half of us are, um, injured. We should stop for a while. Just for a few hours, I mean."

"We cannot," Asaru said sharply. And that was that.

Except—"Actually, I agree with Wren."

Surprised, he watched Palenisa drag a hand down her face, her eyes pressed shut. She nodded as if coming to an agreement with herself, then fluttered them open. "I'm tired," she continued. "That fight took more out of me than I wanted. And I *know* for a fact it took a lot more out of you. Don't bullshit me."

"It should be fine for a night," Rishé suggested, dropping her hands to speak. The shore must have reminded her of her clan, how they used to travel by the sea. A sentimental pang coursed through Wren. "I've been here before."

Silence followed. It was as much of an agreement as they were going to get from Asaru.

A sensation of fingers pressed his brand in a quick pulse. It felt as though someone had reached into his heart and yanked. Wren drew aimless patterns along his arms as they walked along the surf.

"Hey."

"Hi," he whispered back, meeting the cold blue flash of Palenisa's eye. He found there the same tiredness he so often saw in his own reflection. A thoughtful rumble escaped her throat.

"The lulaik."

He hummed for her to continue.

"They had an adderowl skull. Purple hair. Their cape had a pattern, like this"—she drew an eye in the air vaguely resembling the tattoo on Asaru's wrist. "Wondering if you recall someone like that."

"No," he replied dryly. "Lulaik don't all know each other. Most of us aren't even Norvatti. Most of us don't even *live* in Estyria. For *obvious* reasons."

Wren would never understand that misconception. Why stay and subject oneself to rogue Aspects when prospects were better elsewhere? While *he* stayed for his mother, he often wondered why she did if not out of love for the man others called his father. Against his will, misplaced affection lingered, something he saw as a manifestation of his defective mind.

Wren expected a frown. He was surprised by her half-formed huff. Even more so by the spark of happiness that flickered to life inside him.

Chuckling, Palenisa tilted her head to the sky.

"All right, you're not all the same. Honestly, I don't know much about lulaik aside from how your spells smell." The corner of her mouth quirked up. "Tell me about *your* tribe, then."

He blinked. Once, twice. He was very much awake. "Um. Why?"

She waved away the question. "All the better to protect you with, of course."

His chest still ached, but a shy smile slid onto his face. "Of course."

Somewhere in the distance, thrushes sang in the dusk. And

along the surf, Wren shaped the story of his childhood and his clan, a place where the only merit to belonging was simply birth, as the sun sank, trailing out splendid rays of golden light.

ASARU

The water bore him like he often imagined a cloud would. Floating aimlessly, Asaru watched the Sky Court and wished he were there among the innumerable tiny stars. He shut his eyes a moment and tried to make it feel like flying. Tried to imagine it wasn't water licking at his ears, but the wind.

The tide pawed at him gently as he drifted, spinning in a sea that cared as little for him as the world seemed to. Eyes fluttering open, he gulped deep lungfuls of air. Asaru didn't free his ribs from the ayashif as often as he should have. It was as much binding as it was armor. But as someone had recently told him, he didn't care much for himself.

It was annoying because it wasn't entirely false.

How could he care for himself, though, when he'd been on this continent almost a moon's turn and was still no closer to finding his brother? Or the Chronicler. Or any semblance of an answer for what was happening to him.

All he had to show for himself so far was a mind reeling from memories unearthed. His head throbbed from the unwanted realization that he was just a tool. A weapon. An object of possession. Asaru thought again about how Wren was right—and hated it. Hated being seen both as he was and as he used to be. Though he believed they were one and the same since no one ever truly changed, they just grew around their old self, building layers like the elderly tree.

Bitter thoughts churned as he turned a cheek into the water and stared at the horizon through lidded eyes. The moon lit the night as silver starblooms unfurled to float by his face. He blew the silken flowers across the water's surface in mild interest. They bore a slight resemblance to crystal lotuses. Alvarys loved crystal lotuses.

Alvarys hadn't been in his dreams for a while. He still heard his mother, though, in Tenat's persistent chanting, her voice distorted in his slumbering mind to a low drone.

He clenched his fists. The memory of gray fetters throbbed across every limb.

Hot anger flared behind Asaru's eyes at the thought of their captor. It burned the longer he held the image of their mask—glowing eyes, cracked bone, voice layered over itself—in his head. He tipped back into the sea and screamed in a furious fit of bubbles.

The light-footed form of the lulaik dodged like they'd done it many times before. Behind his lids their mask flashed as he remembered the way they drove forward with a single-minded intensity. *And at the behest of the Chronicler.* He still found it hard to believe—he didn't *want* to believe that truth.

His hands scrambled at his shoulders, digging a claw into the skin to calm himself as he rose from the sea. His talons brushed the sandy sea floor as he found his feet.

His breathing ragged and his eyes hot with tears, Asaru

stared at his rippling reflection. It shuddered, shook, as unsteady as he felt. Everything was falling to pieces—the only semblance of control he had was over his appearance. His decisions too, he hoped, but he knew how easily those could be ripped from him.

In the water was a man he barely recognized.

He was naked from the waist up, and fat rivulets of water rolled down the curves of his breasts and bandaged abdomen. Three thin, pale scars dashed his face, and the blackness that subsumed his sclera was its own nightmare. Most striking of all was the red seeping into his hair, so bright it hurt to look at. An eyesore. He hadn't thought it would get this bad when he first noticed the auburn haunting the tip of his braid.

As he grabbed the dripping locks in a fist, Asaru wondered if it was the curse. Or some quirk of his unclear heredity reaching through the essence of his very bones to soak him in the blood he spilled. A mark for all to bear witness.

It had to be the curse. There was no doubt.

He pressed three fingers of his other hand together and swept them sharply aside. Crimson threads warped around his wrist to form an energy blade. It warmed his skin, the threads of life. He slashed, brought the remaining hair up, and slashed again until it was slightly longer in the back.

Then he dipped back into the sea. And when he emerged, he blinked at himself.

Though the slightest red remained at the fringes, his hair was mostly brown. Dark as the dirt of Deltia's forest, close in shade to his mother's and brother's, with their rich curls that turned gold when the sun banded over them.

The impulse had taken him like a fever, but not even the smallest part of him regretted it, for the choice had been *his*.

As Asaru washed stray hairs from his nape, he noted the

progression of the curse. Raised scars surrounding the triangular black diamond that marred his halo gripped the sides of his neck like a vise. Black speckled his upper arms like a mineral glove he could never remove. They would have loved him at the exclusive theaters in Aruu—had the marks not been a sign of his slow demise.

He dragged a hand through the water, watching the way the droplets rolled off his skin, the marks having made it slightly stiff, as if he were turning into rock. It was a reminder of the finite dripping of the clock that hung above him. Death. Sure as the world turned, each day that passed he felt himself grow weaker from the curse. And the progression quickened when he cast a spell. He'd seen his future in Khensu. Shuddering at the memory of his mercy, Asaru threaded his fingers through his newly shorn hair. He inhaled deeply, ignoring the strong scent of the curse. The strong scent of himself.

A scaled body brushed his ankle. He peered at dappled clayfish swimming around his feet, as they paused for a moment in base animal curiosity before darting off.

The fish were much easier to kill than catch. But Rishé had done both easily, wading into the shallows to wait patiently before snatching them up—three by the tail in a single swipe. She'd done this many times before, she'd said, as she chopped at the base of their tiny heads. It reminded Asaru of how ivory gulls dealt with crabs, pecking and pecking at the flesh between their shell and internal softness. And her triumphant smile as she'd held them up—it had reminded him of his brother.

Aedyton hadn't always been kind to him, but he missed it and the people that cared for him there. *Home.*

"Asaru!"

He turned to find Palenisa waving him over. She sat around

a fire with the others. By her side, Wren turned a makeshift spit hung with several fish salted by the sea.

Asaru sighed and went ashore. He shook his hair, and the heavy tuft of his tail, flinging water every which way. He dressed quickly—ayashif, underclothes, stirrups wrapped up his legs, and bandages over his arms. As he slid on his borrowed tunic and cinched the metal of his belt, the others noticed his hair. They didn't hesitate to comment. Not that he'd asked.

"Not too clever," Rishé said, her voice garbled between bites of fish. "A haircut is the first thing a bounty hunter will note."

Plucking a wet strand from his cheek, Asaru pursed his lips. He *really* hadn't asked.

Palenisa shrugged lazily and wiped salt from her fingers. "The red'll come back anyway. It gave you some color. Like you weren't actively dying."

"I did not do it for *you*," he grunted, wandering over to perch birdlike on a piece of driftwood. The night wind blew embers into the air, warmth kissing his cheeks.

"It, um, I think it looks nice."

Asaru looked at Wren, who ducked his head. Perhaps the comments weren't all bad. A feathery touch brushed along his shoulder blade, and he held back from reacting to the bond.

Focus.

"My hair is the least of our problems." He speared the last fish with a claw and watched the nearby tall grass sway as he ate. He chewed and swallowed before continuing. "We cannot keep sporadically camping at the edge of woods and hope the Black Order does not stumble upon us. These stops waste time that could be spent finding the Chronicler."

Rishé stared into the fire with a ponderous look. "Well, *I'm* not on the run," she said.

"I still don't know what you think you're doing, but this isn't a damn vacation." Palenisa rolled her eyes. "Lives are on the fucking line."

"You think I don't know that?" Rishé shot back. Her hands flashed quickly through some signs before she remembered to speak aloud: "You think I'm not aware what came with the decision I made to help you?"

Asaru brought his knees to his chin, eyes bouncing between the two women as they glared across the licking orange flames.

"And we're very thankful," Wren interjected, raising a placating hand. It hovered above Rishé's shoulder, pulling away quickly when she turned to him with a flat expression. But there was something raw in it. A nerve uncovered in the tunnels that Asaru knew was no business of his. Though a small—a very small—part of him wondered about the distance there. The unspoken shared past implied by how they wove around each other. He thought, for a moment, what he might do in their position. Once he found Alvarys, he promised himself, he would never again let such a distance part them.

"Yes, you should be. Do you even know *where* the Chronicler is?" Rishé directed the question at Asaru.

His lips thinned in response.

She didn't smile, but a smug expression slithered onto her face. "Look at that, my help comes in handy once again—because *I* know something."

"Which is?" He raised a skeptical brow.

"Well, I know someone who knows someone who heard *rumor* of the Chronicler."

"So you yourself know nothing," Palenisa said, jutting a claw in her direction. "That's quite literally what that means."

"Wait—" Wren suddenly whispered. "Asaru, you're . . . you're bleeding."

Thick and slimy blood dribbled from the corners of his mouth. His stomach flipped, and he emptied its contents onto the sand, the bile riddled with chunky pieces of half-digested fish. As he grasped the driftwood for balance, a shock like shattering glass doubled him over in a coughing fit. It froze Asaru in place, pain pulsing with each hack. Seizing, flexing, he was stretched too thin and squeezed too tight.

Black dripped between his fingers, filling his mouth with acid and iron. Blood spattered his hands—just as he'd seen from Khensu. The curse would steal away the parts of him he knew best until he became a husk muttering delirious nothings into nowhere.

Asaru's vision split and thinned. Through the blurred light, he saw Palenisa's look of horror, Rishé's slight worry, and Wren kneeling at his feet with a pained expression. Each hurt he received, Wren felt in turn. He wondered incredulously at the limits. What could their bodies handle? More importantly—how far would khetry push the backlash in punishment?

He nodded his permission and—*reprieve.* At the cool touch of Wren's palm against his forehead, a chill radiated down the ridge of his brow.

To his surprise, his first reaction wasn't to pull away but to lean in.

Exhaling a shaky breath, Asaru blinked watery eyes as careful fingers skirted his wounded side. He stifled a whimper. Electricity sparked everywhere they touched, and when Wren took his arms in his, they both trembled. The threads around them glowed particularly brightly. Khetry sang and strummed and shuddered with the fervid energy of life.

Their clasped hands were shaded in inky darkness. The sight reminded him of the blood that misted from the mammoth bodies of remnants. One pair healed—the other spread death. They were nothing alike—then why did they look so similar?

"Is your heart racing?" Wren murmured, leaning up to his face. He backed away—*Yes, of course it is.* "Where does it hurt?"

"You know where," Asaru gritted out.

The poison ravaged him almost as harshly as the curse. Peeling away a strip of bandage revealed the gangrenous yellow star of oleander snaking from the puckered wound. It looked alive, as though at any moment it would writhe and burst from beneath his heated skin.

"It's a miracle you've been moving so long," Wren said, placing an unfathomably gentle palm over his stomach. He looked miserable, riddled with guilt and unable to meet Asaru's gaze. "We have to get to the guild before this worsens. Please. *Please.*"

Rishé nodded, and sounding strangely shaken, Palenisa agreed.

As Wren made to move away, Asaru caught his shoulder. He searched the mismatched eyes. "Tomorrow?"

Wren nodded, softening to merely a mild concern. "Tomorrow, then." Under the starlight and the blue cast of the earrings dangling by his face, he seemed to glow. Fiddling with his hood, he looked as if he were about to continue, but he clamped his mouth shut and shook his head.

Unease coiled in the air, settling within the web as they took themselves to bed.

Asaru watched the fire snap at the air, crackling and popping in the lull. In his periphery, he watched Wren move to sit by the shoreline, cross-legged, spreading his palms face up on his knees and shutting his eyes in meditation. He watched the freckles speckling his face and the hint of a tattoo on his collarbone. He watched the rise and fall of Wren's chest when he stretched up, revealing the sliver of another piece of ink along his hip.

Asaru looked down. Between his feet, the lines he'd drawn in the sand spiraled into a tangle of madness.

Rolling his shoulders, he stood and scaled the side of a nearby behemoth tree. A whisper followed him, so quiet it was almost a figment of the breeze.

"Good night . . ."

He swung onto the low branch shaded by leaves. He curled his wings over himself, cradling the healing feathers to his chest. It was as close to the sky as he would be for a while. Shutting his eyes, he tried to let go of his desire to fly.

The rustling in the jungle faded into the chirping of crickets and the lapping waves. Dark stars twinkled at the edges of his half-mast eyes, and the moon winked at him before melting into the copious colors of sleep.

That night, he didn't see his brother in his dreams.

He opened his eyes—did he even *have* eyes?

Asaru. Asaru, warrior, brother, son.

"Tenat?"

Warrior, brother, son, come home. A mother's voice cradled his face, wiped away tears that never existed. It reached out in a distorted smear of noise and pressed against his chest. Pressed against his chest harder. And pressed through. Right into him, carving flesh like soft clay. He was malleable, made to be used, to be molded, as the voice—his mother's voice, Tenat's—desired.

Son, brother, warrior. Come back. Home, come home, Asaru.

In the cavernous black hollow within him, something glittered.

When he turned his head, it was like swimming through

molasses. Sleep thickened to a sluggish crawl, and he moved—no, he *was* moved. To look upon the oddity, distorting the darkness around it in rippling waves of a nothing color.

Two blades crossed, handles at the apex of both and a stunning gem at the point where they met. Straight, sharp edges slid against each other as the faceted oddity opened and closed like a hungry beast. Opened again. Lightning burst from the gem, flashing down the twin blades—one light as glass, one dark as jet—and up the handles, rounded like bows.

This thing—it would be the end of his world one day.

Asaru reared backward through the dense fog. His heart fell from his throat, and everything shifted, the world a kaleidoscope. Voices dripped through bright ichor, the shade of the sky when the sun crawls over the horizon as if it were rising from death. *Son.* His mother's rose through the din and lifted his face to the vision of a man who was mere bones.

The man smiled with a mouthful of rubies, spilling lifeblood down a cold chin. The tepid flesh was just beginning to rot. It sluiced away in wet, stinking pieces to reveal bone. Hollow purple sockets peered deep into him and saw the truth. They flickered out—then Asaru saw the others.

Scores upon scores of the dead melting into a distance that didn't exist. They stood in rigid rows, pitch-covered wings dripping from their shoulders. Tall unmoving obelisks of night-black diamonds. Where halos once sat, keloidal scars choked their necks.

All at once, every vacant gaze turned to him. Wind whistled through a thousand crystal dendrite trees when they opened their gaping maws.

Warrior, brother, son, come back, Asaru. Come home, home. Come back—prince—

They spoke with her voice—his mother's voice—descending upon his intangible form. Black tears streamed from their eyes, devoid of life and khetry. Where their wriggling hands touched, he bled a gray gold.

Intangible fingers rose with a controlled intent toward his neck. Toward his nape, where the black diamond—

Asaru shot awake, nearly falling from the tree.

Tears pricked his eyes. He panted, static buzzing along every part of him. Pressing a hand to his neck, he felt the jackhammering of his heart. Felt something fall away from his halo, and he caught it. When his hand rose to his face, it held a gemstone. He stilled—and stared.

Not amethyst. Not black diamond. But *diamondglass.*

It burned to the touch, similar to how he'd heard black diamond felt—was meant to feel. As he turned the clear shard over, light caught the uncut edges.

He let out a bark of wet, incredulous laughter. His body was falling apart. Gemstones he'd never seen were appearing out of nowhere. An inescapable sword point loomed above his head; he could not let that selfsame blade fall over his Aedyton kin, over his brother.

The black triangle at his nape lit his entire being on fire, a stark presence that he couldn't ignore. Asaru felt every part of it as though holding it in his hand.

With a shaky exhale, he tucked the tiny piece of diamondglass inside the fold of his tunic. Out of sight, though its luster still shone in his mind.

Wren stirred awake when Asaru descended his branch, and the others were chewing on sweet flag. Each and every movement sparked pain, lancing his back, stabbing a hot poker into his side. He could almost feel the ruinous course of the poison. His vision spun when his feet found sand, and he tipped his head back to the trunk lest he collapse.

Just a moment. He needed to let everything sink in, then he would be fine. Then they could move on, reach the guild and the Chronicler after that. *Just a moment.*

"You sleep like the dead," Palenisa said, pressing a finger to Wren's forehead as he rose to an elbow.

"Awake, I'm awake." He yawned, blearily pushing her hand away. Grass was caught in his loose hair, which stuck to the sides of his pinched face.

Near the water, Rishé idly spun her necklace between two fingers as she scanned the horizon. Under dawn's light, the murky Lethean Sea was a wrinkled white and delicate blue.

"We're closer to Porto Bierov than I thought," she said, turning to hand Asaru a sprig of sweet flag.

"Porto Bierov?" Asaru chewed the fragrant leaf, watching her swipe sand over their ashes. Swallowing, he felt his pain abate slightly.

"The guild. Sentinels might search the woods around the city since the compound itself is neutral territory—so we should go. Soon, preferably."

She rose from a crouch, dusted her knees, and popped open her compass. Of the four of them, she looked the most alert. Up with the larks in a way that niggled at the tiredness in his heavy limbs. *His* tiredness—or Wren's?

Asaru glanced sidelong at the other man. Snakeskin fell from his shoulders, recast with the spell that refracted light, swaying in and out of visibility as they trekked after Rishé.

Asaru swam within the suman Wren had adamantly insisted he keep. Chin burrowed in the warm collar, he sighed and clutched his throbbing stomach. Slow, steady beats bled into a senseless loop of pain.

Mismatched eyes found his under the fur-lined hood.

"Help me, please?" he said quietly as Wren lingered by his side. He was not too proud to admit this—he could not afford to be.

A flock of starwrens startled into flight, and their wings beat like the sound of rain, to his ears.

Through layers of wool, the supportive arm around his side was scalding. Something tugged loose within his chest, and for a vulnerable moment, Asaru didn't shy from the warmth but sank into it.

WREN

The windswept city of Porto Bierov boiled over with common folk squeezing past tiny alleys and up tinier stairs, which hugged the dwellings. Rope was drawn taut between terraces and dripped with colorful strips of cloth that swayed in the salt-heavy wind.

In simpler times, Wren might have enjoyed taking in the city. But these weren't simple times. They never were; he'd always just hidden from the difficulties.

He might even have hidden here in Bartrom, the densely packed province that acted as a gateway for others seeking anonymity. In the streets thick with bodies and smells and noises, it seemed easy to lose oneself. Fade away as one face among many. Thinking on his names—the one he claimed and the one he didn't—Wren supposed he had ample practice slipping into the background murmur of life.

Crossing the first bridge into the major, the four of them swam with the flow of people. Horses and carts and carriages trundled over the cobblestones as the city rose in tall layers, like others in the province, save the flourishing green compound that overlooked the water at the eastern end—the Hanging Gardens. The Guild of the Living Body.

Wren's lips twisted. Burning anxiety warred with the frail flame of excitement fanning inside him. With each step, he was closer to the place that was once his second home. With each step, his scar tightened at the memory of the incident that lost him that home.

An arm squeezed his waist. He glanced down as Asaru staggered, looking into a face pinched from the chronic strum of pain gnawing through their bond. Wisps of uneven hair framed Asaru's tired eyes. Where his fingers touched, heat flared across Wren's own uninjured side. Asaru wouldn't be in such pain if it weren't for him. Part of him knew that wasn't wholly the truth, but guilt reared its vicious head, flattening good sense beneath remorse.

You deserve this. But he doesn't.

Perhaps without the burden of the bond—the backlash and its biting brand—Asaru would have already found his brother. This Wren knew in his heart to be true.

A shimmer of holographic screens caught his attention, and Wren turned to find bounties for Asaru—and two accomplices—plastered on every screen they passed. Lovely—*really.*

It wasn't. But Wren clung desperately to optimism as panic threatened to cleave him apart.

Instead, he sighed, dejected at the incredible consequences of his actions, so vast they threatened the kingdom's coffers, spread across the realm as far as the sunnai touched—from Emeris to Ilon to the badlands beyond.

Wren turned away before the king's face flashed on-screen.

Another bridge rose ahead, Diwandor's Bridge. It stretched over the small bay between the mainland and the portion of the city built on stilts. Houses rose from the bay, stacked atop one another like tinderboxes shoved into an ill-fitting cupboard, against which stories-high ladders leaned precariously. Flat-bottomed boats bobbed at the bottom of stone stairs, which wound up to the side of the bridge. From them, gondoliers hollered across the water in slick-tongued Akiki.

The heavy salt of the sea mingled with the cloying scent of merchant ships docked tight together. An array of vessels from across the known world bore an assortment of sails in blue and verdigris and black.

Wren watched red-skinned figures scurry across the deck of an elaborate craft. Chilawari, he slowly realized, taking in their blended features. Human ancestry, Melarhone, was apparent in their bipedal builds, but their unusual coloring spoke to drake blood. He'd seen many of the tall and slender foreigners. They loved the sea more than land itself, and he knew they often remained in the southern waters.

South was the Veil Islands. South was another world entirely. South was an untapped chance to be someone else, somewhere else.

What would he do to be a smith, a healer, a pirate like those Chilawari there?

He wished, for a sad moment, to flee. A second of indulgence in which he forgot the wreck of his curious wanting.

The weight at his side reminded him what mattered.

An opportunity to right his wrongs. All it took was a needle—a thin, tiny blade that burned over his heart—and blood. His blood and his faith. Wren had to hold on to that. To believe that the words in the primer were true. It was pathetic, this desperate bid for a Weaver's power, which most thought was fiction, but he could do little else for Asaru beyond providing him an antidote. And there was so much more he had to atone for.

First, though, they needed to reach the guild.

The four of them split off from the crowd at the heart of the city and came upon the gates of the compound. A wall of ironwood that bore the mark of lulaik handicraft was painted with the sigil of the Guild of the Living Body. Two crossed twigs lay within a circle of creeping thorns, atop which bloomed a vibrant red eglantine.

A birdcall swept through the air, and a contingent of archers lined the wall. Arrows pointed through the crenels between spiked merlons. Mostly an intimidation tactic, but though neutral, the guild made sure they were able to protect themselves should circumstances call for it. The Chain Archers stood silent, veiled by chain mail as they drew their longbows taut.

The squeal of strings was the only sound Wren heard, as the rest of the city faded away. Breathing deeply, he doffed his hood and tugged his collar to reveal the bouquet tattooed on his clavicle. It was the same rose painted on the gate. Though he would never be a healer, the symbol of his former membership could never be erased.

Bowstrings trembled, and his face warmed as his companions glanced his way. He prayed to Eșarpe, Ela Prinâza, Furtumbér—even Sirrah, that tricksy dancer—it would still work.

At a commanding voice, the archers melted away as quickly as they had appeared. "Zalho-ouler'an'vuti!" *Open the gates.*

Ironwood gates swung inward on silent hinges, gouging well-worn curves in the dirt of the outer ward. A low clamor of noise sprang from within like smoke from an uncovered flame. The breath Wren had held came spilling out. Behind them, the silver and leather of the Black Order prowled through the crowd as the gates shut.

An attendant clad in hawking leathers from the Palace of Letters led them to the Overlook. Missing from the attendant's thick gauntlet was a gyrfalcon, used to pass correspondence between healers across the continent.

As they crossed in the shadow of the wall walk, Wren kept his head down. He didn't want to look at the compound, see how it had changed—or how it had not. He didn't want to see the journeyers, lulaik and human alike, dressed in pale gray shifts, wandering the courtyard and chatting about their studies.

Misery. Complete and utter misery.

Inside the guardhouse, the four of them settled on long benches that lined the sides of the room. They were left to stew only a short while before the door reopened, and through the air sliced a voice Wren never expected to hear again.

"Wren."

He couldn't look up from her slippered feet as she stopped before him. A knife could cut the tension.

"Look at me when I speak to you, Perseno Ingoscu." Urusy spoke with a flat characteristic firmness.

Wren lifted his head and saw the scarred mirror to his own face.

Having graduated in the decade since the dropwort incident, Urusy wore a healer's changeant. Silver threaded an eglantine at her neck. Slightly older than himself, she possessed a jade khetry eye and smooth umber hair. She was flanked on either side by the healers Geldi Zamfiru and Vair da-Len Ahndat. Masters of persons and poisons respectively.

"Sorry."

Urusy massaged her temple. The splash of a faded violet scar spidered down her neck. "I don't want your apologies. As master of the guild, I need to know why you're here."

Every second word would be an apology if he could manage it. He'd drop to his knees if he had to.

He twisted his fingers together and struggled for a smile. It came out a self-deprecating grimace.

"Mastery suits you."

"*Wren.* You have brought an assassin into my place of work seeking sanctuary, how can you expect me to be fine with that?"

"I, um, we need the antidote for oleander," he pleaded as Asaru's pain lanced his own belly. The other man trembled, his face pale from fever. "That's all, then we'll leave. I swear."

Frowning, Urusy dragged mismatched eyes to Rishé. "Pipsi vuan'tios, daj ferol danae." *Good to see you, Cousin.* "How's the Screen?"

Rishé shrugged. "Resigned. I found something better."

As the cousins contemplated each other, Geldi stepped forward. Her cane clipped the floor and her brace whirred. Above a well-lined brown face, gray-threaded braids tumbled elegantly down her slanted shoulders as she appraised them.

"Do you vouch for him, Fralino Trifan?" Geldi turned the brunt of her icy silver eyes on Rishé—no journeyer had ever been able to withstand the full force of that unrelenting stare.

Flinching, Rishé nodded.

"And what else?" Urusy folded her arms, revealing black dahlias stitched into the undersides—mourning flowers. For the king. Wren's stomach churned. "I can't trust him on words alone."

She shouldn't trust him at all. But Wren glanced sidelong at Rishé, who jutted her chin toward the master healers with a *look* in her eye.

"A . . . living sample of Black Diamond?" he tried.

Palenisa dropped her face into her hands, and even Asaru flashed him a strange look.

Why did I say that? Wren needed to shut his mouth immediately. "Just one night, and I can get you a living sample for the repository."

The guild stored all kinds of sicknesses in a repository locked deep under the compound. Access was granted only to the guild master herself and a select few healers and journeyers. Wren hadn't been so fortunate, but everyone knew it existed. It was the guild's pride, and its most dangerous joy. A curse would be an incredible boon to that archive of ailments.

Luckily for him, a glint brightened Ahndat's thick-rimmed glasses. The quiet man placed a placating hand on Urusy's shoulder, whispering in her ear. The corners of her lips lowered, and she glanced upward.

"You're a fool."

"I know."

"This doesn't mean you have a place here anymore."

"I know," he said miserably.

"On both your heads, then. Make sure no one sees *him*." Urusy pointed to Asaru before sweeping from the room in a fan of gold-warped green.

Ahndat inclined his head and followed. Before she left, Geldi tapped the bronze head of her aid, observing the four of them a swollen moment. "It's not you, Wren," she said. "She has better things to deal with than a mess you refuse to confront."

Wren's face burned with shame. "How did she . . ."

"Because she stayed. Now, try not to get into the poisons again." She patted his arm and clicked her cane down the hall.

When she was gone, Palenisa spun to him. "You never said you studied poisons."

He stared. His scar felt hot and tight and sore.

"He didn't," Rishé answered for him. She led Palenisa from the Overlook to Acorn House, the smaller of the guild's two compounds, which housed the sleeping quarters, the tearoom, and Eírtat's sacred pool.

Wren watched them a moment before guiding Asaru in the opposite direction, to Feather House, home to the training and reading rooms. As well as the room of herbs—and of poisons.

Feather House lived up to its name, slathered top to bottom in a vast plethora of feathers, long and thin and shining and dull, all in variegated shades. None, though, quite matched the spotted wings that sprouted from the back of the man beside him.

"A bit on the nose," Asaru muttered.

"I guess it is."

The rooms of herbs smelled like his mother's garden tenfold. It was twice as large as Nastradona, overflowing with an assortment of healers' implements. Fruiting plants spilled across tables, hung in bundles from the rafters, and burst in tight bouquets from every visible cabinet. Carmine milkweed preened in the sun beside pearling blossoms holding iris-sized green pearls.

"Overstuffed" was one word to describe Ahndat's abode. Many others came to mind, but Wren had no right to speak them. So he set Asaru on one of the cots behind the partition that split the room, and cleared a space on the mixing bench.

Behind him, the watchful form of Ahndat trailed his every move. Beside the master of poisons sat a jar—of water dropwort. Its mere presence sent a tremor through him. A reminder.

"Your ability to fuck things up should be studied in the

Hanging Gardens." The man's accent, slippery as the canals that wound through his home province of Emeris, was clipped and pronounced. *"An assassin,* Wren? What were you thinking?"

"I wasn't. Thinking, that is." He cringed, mixing a potion of water, pale opium, and—after Ahndat pressed a rolled pack of it to his back—gold-frilled kingsbane.

"Clearly."

"But, um, I've . . . I've been working on something . . ."

As Ahndat hummed encouragement, he inhaled, gathering his nerve. "I've been trying to distill an antidote. For dropwort poisoning, I mean." *Though ten years too late.*

He tipped the potion into Asaru's mouth. As the man drank, Wren layered a poultice over the wound and wrapped it in fresh silk. The man twitched in pain, stomach tensing and tail stiff, but remained silent. Wren smoothed the last of the bandages in place—impossibly tender—and waited with bated breath.

Ahndat waved lazily. "Oh, no matter—I developed a temporary philter a year ago."

A year ago.

Wren had wasted moons fruitlessly testing the limits of his incomplete skills as a healer, hungering desperately for a primer all the while. He brought backlash upon himself for an answer that had been found *a year ago.*

He wiped his hot eyes.

That is fine. It is fine. Everything is so fucking fine.

That just meant there was only one route left for him. A pitiful, lonely path back to the guild. Cure the curse. Convince Urusy of the depth of his commitment to atonement. Find a place, once more, among their ranks. It was all he could hope for—a reckless hope—so he gathered the tatters of himself and ventured a question.

"Master Vair . . . What do you know of Weavers?"

The room grew cold.

"That you shouldn't bother. As far as anyone knows, all who've attempted to find the so-called ritual died or disappeared," Ahndat said. He glanced over the rim of his glasses, freezing Wren in place. "Pathetic creatures senselessly seeking power."

He smiled thinly before leaving.

"I have heard being a Weaver is a lonely existence," Asaru said after a lingering silence. "Why do you ask?"

"Academic curiosity," Wren said quietly as he sought permission to take his hand. When they touched, the brand sparked his already scrambled brain.

With pumice, he gently scraped Asaru's palms onto a glass slide. Rather than flesh, the curse came away as though he'd flaked black diamond to a deadly point.

"You are lying."

He pursed his lips, staring at the living curse. It was in a constant state of change, from solid to liquid to something in between. Sublimation, condensation, freezing. Disturbing, frankly.

"I just want to help." He pressed his thumb to the center of Asaru's palm. It was smooth, unblemished stone. "Help you."

"Curses cannot truly be broken." Asaru glanced out the window as the sun completed its daily journey. "Powerful—volatile. They are branded onto khetry, bound to a cursed object with its creator's blood."

Bound.

Backlash was something of a curse, then. Irreparable, as far as he knew.

"I—"

Black fingers caught his collar and brought him close.

"Why do you have . . . these? All these . . . flowers." Asaru yawned in a husky, poppy haze. His eyes were glazed and unfocused.

"Tattoos, stitching . . . It's part of Norvatti culture . . ." he whispered, unsure what the heaviness of his tongue meant. He was on fire, turning to ash. "Sacred modification of the body . . ."

He trailed off at the sound of a light snore. Asaru was already asleep, lashes fluttering, lips parted. Suffused orange light softened the curve of his cheek. Wren dropped his head onto the edge of the cot and sighed. Then he hurried from the room. If he ignored the way his brand burned, that was no one's business but his own.

Twilight crept a crooked purple finger across the guild compound as crying gyrfalcons broke the intermittent chirping of crickets.

In the Hanging Gardens, Wren was shocked back to wakefulness as the irrigation hissed to life. As the name suggested, lush foliage fell from bars lining the glass-domed ceiling. On either side of him, the lit walking paths intersected thin waterways on which hybridized plants floated by.

He hunched over a desk illuminated under the chill of a lamp powered, to his mild awe, by khetry-infused crystals of ice. Verillium, as one of the other journeyers had called it when he asked, was a new invention from Anticarta's Court of Spares. Blinking blearily, Wren rubbed bloodshot eyes. Above him, a holographic screen scrolled through a list of glowing plants, same as at every other desk in the gardens.

He squinted at his empty hands.

Where is the slide? In the microscope, he remembered. *What was I doing again?*

He surveyed the desk covered in plant cuttings, medical swatches, the efforts of his labor, and various flasks of muddy tisanes. *Right.* He was failing to find a natural way to break the curse, on the slim hope that the speculative text he'd read about curses living off the blood of their creators held some strain of truth.

It was an aimless quest. Again: Curses couldn't be broken, much less by natural methods.

In the back of his mind, Wren had tried to convince himself Black Diamond was a sufficiently advanced programmed spell, knotted threads that a skilled lulaik could untangle. But a curse was a curse—what had he expected?

On his shoulders, stress had taken root. Dragging a hand through his half tail, Wren shoved the microscope aside with a groan. This used to be a common sight for him: working into the lean hours of morning by candlelight, sometimes with Rishé by his side.

He couldn't remember the last time he'd had a good night's sleep in his life.

A light clicked, and the gardens darkened further as the last of the journeyers turned in for the night. Their footsteps faded, and he was alone. It was time. Wren had to snatch every chance he was given by the reins.

He pulled out the primer and flipped to the sketch of Rhenei's theoretical spellwork, theories in which he was placing his entire faith. The steady drip of the irrigation system filled the quiet. Wren took a breath, then lifted his gift—the bone shaped like a needle. He pressed it to the page, charged, and let the khetrical energy flow. Blood welled bright and cheery red, pouring out of him and into the needle.

His blood, his hopes, his resolve.

This was it—this was how he would fix everything.

RISHÉ

Unlike the ceiling of her room at the Silk Screen, this one was ivory like the hair of wraiths. The flaking paint resembled unknowable constellations mapped out in meaningless lines.

Stars never held a strong place in her heart. Rishé thumbed her pendant, pressing a nail into the ridges. That place was reserved for the sea.

She stretched the tiredness from her limbs as she fully woke from her rest. The base of her spine ached from the stiff bedstraw. Furnishing was not one of the guild's prioritized expenses. At least Erazill had the sense to provide his workers with Mauriidan silk and fox-feathered beds. Or maybe he just wanted to give the Screen's patrons a comfort while they took their bodily indulgences. Butterflies were delicate creatures, after all.

She turned on her side and found her roommate prostrate on the ground.

The wraith looked to have been awake awhile. The broad planes of her back shifted beneath her haltered shirt. Many tiny braids were splayed loosely over the wide flare of her hips. Rishé's fingers twitched as she imagined how it would feel to braid. To touch. Would the tight tiny coils be soft? Or would she have to comb through them till they relaxed under her caress?

She reminded herself that she was not there to ogle women.

Tousling her own short locks, she watched Palenisa tilt her head back, revealing a long stretch of neck. Light glinted off the silver dots flanking the bridge of her nose. Palenisa mumbled a prayer in Inachie and bent once more before a rudimentary carving of the Pillars of the Gods, those monolithic obsidian suvaunoors of the wraithian religion.

Rishé scoffed at the sight. That would not do.

As if sensing her stare, Palenisa frowned over her shoulder. Their gazes met as if magnetized. Wintry eyes narrowed.

"What?"

"I heard you were excommunicated." Rishé licked the cracked scar that split her bottom lip. As they traveled, she had deduced this was Sister Gleissa, the *former* Sister Gleissa. She wasn't particularly awestruck. Frankly, Rishé found herself rather suspicious of the wraith, despite whatever "promise" had been made to Wren. Not for his sake—but for her own curiosity. No other reason, of course. "Why keep acting like some faithful sister when there's no one left to impress?"

"I'm a fucking Aspect," Palenisa snapped, sitting up quickly. The sunburst and crossed-circle suvaugrams on the backs of her clenched hands tightened, betraying a restrained strength. "Blessed by the Zodiac—it's only right to show piety for all I've done. And lost."

Rishé's eyes fluttered to the ceiling in an aborted eye roll. Why was she surrounded by self-hating fools? One was more than enough. And he was already more than her growing sentimentality could handle.

"Find the good in the bad, rather than wallowing in that misery you seem to love so much. Piety won't make the Crocodile Coterie take you back anyway."

There was a slight hitch in Palenisa's breath as though she'd been shot by a lance of carelessly cruel words. But they weren't careless or cruel—they were an honest observation.

"I . . ." *Am sorry.*

Palenisa's lips pursed to two thin brown lines. Their gazes snapped, cut by the strict slash of a scythe blazing sun bright. "When I need your opinion on the wreck of my life, *I'll ask,*" she said flatly before turning back to her orisons. The air was electric with an awkward tension.

Discomfort pressed Rishé into the mattress, the sheets tangling around her legs as her mind straggled. Mild regret welled in her like molten stone, and then she sighed and turned onto her back. Boring, bland, familiar—the ceiling stared down as though she were a meaningless speck in the cosmic Sky Court.

That went splendidly. She'd had men, women, those who ascribed to neither, in her bed—but she could speak to none of them without planting her foot in her mouth. This was why she focused only on what truly mattered. Her necklace, its pendant, their mysteries.

Frowning, Rishé got up and dressed in her olive tunic. She tied off the end of a third short braid, buckled on a fourth belt, and slipped on the bracelet her father had made for her. Back when they were still a family. One that didn't communicate through letters sent once a year, if that. Annoyed and disappointed, she gathered herself and left the wraith to her prayers and spirits.

She padded down the hall that spanned the length of Acorn House. Past the rest of the sleeping quarters and the tearoom smelling of breakfast—semolina, sausages, and burnt peppermint because not even healers knew how to make tea properly. Murmurs mingled with the faint call of firebirds that roosted above Eírtat's sacred pool to cool their ever-burning bodies.

The pool door opened, and someone stepped through, white cloth obscuring their face.

"Pipsi dahsun," Rishé signed as Urusy lowered the towel. *Good morning.*

Her cousin shut the screen door and leaned against it. Slick hair fell to her waist as Rishé's once had. She was somewhat softer in the daylight, possessed of a domineering height and commanding cheekbones.

"Dahsun," Urusy signed, raising a brow. There was a pause, and then—*"I'm sorry for last night. We're family, but I can't put my students at risk. You understand?"*

Lips quirking aside in a sheepish smile, Rishé shrugged.

"I hadn't realized you two reconnected since."

She hummed and bent her wrist in affirmation. She still didn't know how to feel, other than conflicted. Standing in the street with two unlikely companions, Wren had pulled her through the window of mundanity into the adventure she'd been craving. Torn between the tenderness that plied her heart and the bitterness she thought had petrified it, she realized her heart would never be stone. That wasn't in her nature.

Rishé came back to herself at Urusy's voice, switching languages. "What's . . . what changed? How is he, truly?"

She thought a moment. "Not *all* bad. Strangely different."

"Yet so much the same." Urusy touched her flushed olive cheek. The wrinkled scar looked like violet-fringed moonglory petals. "He thinks I'm still angry."

"You're not?" That came as a surprise, considering the cool

affect and uncompromising gaze Urusy had laid upon the nerve-scattered man.

Pressing the cloth to her chest, Urusy shut her eyes. "I let go of that a while ago. No time to hate him as guild master. I think . . . I think I'm just disappointed he lied. About something that was *both* our faults."

Wren was the world's worst martyr. He flagellated himself with sins he had no right to covet or claim alone and left her and Urusy to pick up the pieces by themselves, hurt by his melancholy.

In that moment, Rishé realized she had lied to herself. She wasn't angry. She was mostly just sad. At being left behind. Without a goodbye. Without so much as an apology. *Not,* she admitted to herself—only to herself—*that he ever really needed to apologize.*

"That's who he is," Rishé said as she turned away. *And I am loath to change him.*

Early larks filtered in and out of the reading room before the rest of the compound fully awoke. The reading room was available at all hours, and as Rishé softly opened the door, she found a few people already scattered inside. Journeyers in gray and changeant healers plucking books from tall serpentine shelves.

She was certain she'd read through the tomes pertaining to her research a decade earlier. Historical and medical records. Cover to cover. Scavenging for any mention of gems and far-fetched arcane powers in between work shifts with Brunoth. All with Wren at her side.

But it wouldn't hurt to refresh her knowledge before she met the Chronicler. Oh, the questions she had.

As she settled behind a stack of tomes taller than she, she spread her fingers on a page. Wafer-thin sheets yellowed from the many hands that had turned them through the ages. She set her pendant on the desk and flipped to a sketch of a thunderstone. While her stone looked like a red diamond, its silvery etchings had always stopped her from concluding such. Red diamonds were found mostly in the Volcanic Steps of Peskelos and farther south in Fa Djain, purely ornamental in function from what she knew.

No, this necklace was something far more special.

And besides, if it was thunderstone, her mother would have told her.

Well. Not in the last few moons of her life. In those swan song days, as the consumptive taint fevered through Jarha, she had mostly slept while Rishé wept, clinging to her mother's side, lucky enough to avoid the illness due to her youth.

The taint had come, consumed, and then Jarha was gone, and any knowledge of the stone along with her.

The page wrinkled beneath Rishé's touch. She swallowed. She was fine. She was reconnecting with her mother by pursuing understanding of the gift she'd been given and keeping the memory alive through that tenuous connection.

It was how she spoke to the dead.

The scream of a bell broke her concentration. Midday sun turned the dust in the air aflame, swathed her little corner of the reading room in harsh bands of light. The lunch bell rang again, a deep cry across the compound. How many hours had she been sitting there? Long enough that she felt a twinge of stiffness between her shoulder blades. Tangling graphite-stained fingers together, Rishé threw her arms up in a bone-cracking stretch.

The pile of tomes had slowly dwindled until all that remained was her journal, the *Encyclopedia of Minerals*, second edition, and a diagram of her necklace with obsessive notes analyzing every facet and minute feature of the unusual stone.

Progress had been minimal. The characteristics of the pendant ran in her mind as she tap, tap, tapped the desk with a dull nail. As expected, she hadn't learned anything that she didn't already know. And she knew quite a bit. Yet so little.

But—Rishé smiled as she grabbed her journal and threw on her suman—*there's someone else who might.*

Leaving Acorn House, she crossed the yard as the sun beat down on her hooded form. Bartrom sweltered with its closeness to the perpetually burning Ilon, and the workshop was so much hotter. Heat warped the air above the boxy workshop, its slanted tin roof nearly burning white. Smoke rose into the flickering haze, and steam spilled between slats of wood like a panting beast.

As she slipped inside, a gust of hot air washed over Rishé's face. Blinking away tears, she turned to the husky silhouette of Brunoth du Marinei illuminated by the blazing forge. He raised a tan arm corded with muscle and brought down a hammer to flatten a red-hot piece of metal.

The door shut and the gemsmith glanced up. Protective goggles rested on his face, black circles for eyes. "If it isn't Fralino Trifan," he said in a voice as rough as unsanded wood. "Has the life of a smith tempted you back once more? Tiny as ever, I see."

"And you're loud as ever," she signed back, sidling behind him to reach the tool table. On a shelf above the artful mess, she saw her equipment was still there. In the same place, as if she hadn't spent ten years away but had merely sat them down the day before.

The grin on Brunoth's face grew as he read her hands before chuckling. Sweat fell from the maroon tips of his hair, drenching his patchy chest. She stared, amused, wondering if he knew shirts, and not just aprons, existed.

"Did Parianne even feed you?" he asked jovially, dunking his creation—the bones of a folding fan—into water. It hissed, popped, snarled as it cooled. He set it aside, affording Rishé a closer look at the craftsmanship. The chrome-moly mount rippled like oil, with tiny, grooved blades at the end of each rib.

"As a matter of fact," she said, snapping on the gloves and adjusting her goggles, "I ate far better at the Screen than I ever did here, thank you very much. Need help?"

Brunoth jutted his bearded chin toward the forge and picked up a chunk of seafoam beryl between graying tongs. Slipping seamlessly into her past, Rishé tugged open the door to the metamorphic hearth. The smell of burning bitumen wafted to her nose alongside a cough of smoke. Sparks fell as the forge swallowed a large lungful—brightening and whitening.

Rising on her toes, she watched him twist the tongs in the hungry flame. With each rotation, the beryl burned bluer and bluer, until watery lines banded the green stone. She shut the forge, and the room cooled by several degrees. They moved to the workbench, where Brunoth sawed the beryl into tinier and tinier cubes. He sifted the shards onto a tray, creating the sound of rain on tin, then ran a hand over the cooled fan.

Tugging her goggles into her hair, Rishé planted herself on his stool—he could stand—and watched the gemsmith. In his element, Brunoth moved with graceful precision for a man built like a jackal bear. First, a pair of absurdly small pincers plucked a gem. Then, with steady hands, he lowered each shimmering stone into the blade, until he found one that fit each groove perfectly.

The pair sat silently, the roar of the fire their only companion. Firebirds and gyrfalcons sang a distant cacophony.

"Interesting fan."

"Client's a noble from Fa Djain," he replied as he swapped goggles for jeweler's lenses.

Feet swinging, Rishé worked her lips, staring into the forge. A tongue of fire snapped. Light poured from the skylight onto the workbench in rectangular streams.

"How is she, by the way?"

Rishé glanced up at him when he spoke. Somehow a toothpick had found its way between Brunoth's teeth. "The Screen or the madam?"

"Both."

"Fine, last I knew. But I no longer work there, if that's what you're really asking."

"Rishé." Brunoth shook his head, as sooty fingers pushed down his lenses. Pale lines marked the bridge of his thick nose, and the corners of his eyes crinkled in a wry smile. "This'll affect my friendship, you know. I have a reputation to maintain."

Snorting, Rishé spun the stool. "She's your sister by law—you'll be fine."

Parianne had been the sister of Brunoth's husband, Inone du Solsuqa. And though Inone had passed many years earlier, his memory persisted in the convoluted form of aggressive affection between the two that Rishé found herself at the center of. That strange relationship was the primary reason she'd landed at the Silk Screen.

She hadn't necessarily *excelled* as an apprentice. Yes, she'd been decently skilled at crafting instruments for the guild, jewelry for wealthies, and weapons for unsavory groups she chose to overlook. But it wasn't her calling. The Screen hadn't been either.

Merely a temporary passage between one life and another.

A tinkerer of minds and words, Rishé sought something *different.*

Different like the play of light through her pendant, casting orange on the walls of the workshop as she held it up. A bright flame warring with the hearth.

"Are you *still* stuck on that?" Brunoth groused. "No—I haven't seen any stone like it before. Congrats on the mineralogical anomaly. Don't forget me when you're a wealthy."

With that, he returned to his work, snorting as Rishé pouted.

As she sighed, her gaze bounced around the workshop. On the walls hung fine weapons and delicate pieces of jewelry that could only have come from the hand of a gemsmith. A half sword could be displayed beside a gold choker inlaid with lapis lazuli and moonstone, both polished to gleaming. Among the collection, some of which held her handicraft, was a mask. A jackal bear skull missing its lower jaw, with a violet handprint painted across the side.

Neither she nor Brunoth had a hand in its creation. No, those massive bone masks were the sole domain of his ward, Sagan du Costinu. Well—Inone's ward, but by virtue of marriage, it was essentially the same.

When Wren . . . *left,* Sagan replaced him in some ways. Not fully, though, as the man was incredibly flighty. His spotty appearances at the guild lasted just long enough for the construction of each new, more garish mask.

She blinked. *Damn it.*

"Where's Sagan?" Rishé drew two fingers from a claw to a fist for his sign name, as if she hadn't already surmised.

"Haven't seen him in a year." Brunoth leaned away, lips pursed. "Haven't heard from him in almost as long."

He'd never been gone longer than a few moons without at least a letter.

"Strange," she drawled. "I saw him in Meliste last week."

"How was he?"

What was she supposed to say? *He's fine—aside from the fact that he kidnapped my companions and vanished into the Lizardwood.*

"Selling fate games," she said instead. "Lucrative." Tapping the bench, she made a thoughtful noise. "Would he know anything about the Chronicler?"

"You'd have to find him again to ask." He crossed his barrel arms over his chest with a bitter laugh.

"Do *you* know anything about the Chronicler?"

Brow furrowed, Brunoth opened his mouth, closed it, then tapped his scruff in thought.

That wasn't a denial. She planted her hands on the stool between her legs, steel straightening her spine. Had she the leaf-shaped ears of a lulaik, they would have perked up.

"I heard a rumor—don't look at me like that"—a shit-eating grin widened her mouth—"from someone who knows someone in the Obsidian Market. Whispers. Of a Neyari in Ilon bragging that he'd recently come into possession of an eresh keyel artifact. Again—it was only a *rumor.*"

It might be the beacon Asaru was looking for. The same one his brother was supposed to have. Tension slithered through her. And somehow, strange to say, Rishé found herself grasping for his same rash, reckless hope that Alvarys was alive still.

"Rumors are good enough," she signed.

She hopped from her seat, coat swirling by her knees, and moved a palm from her mouth in thanks. Whatever expression painted the gemsmith's face, she was not privy to as the workshop door shut at her back, but she had the distinct feeling he was rolling his eyes.

As she hurried back to Acorn House, plans, ideas, and schemes whirled in her mind. Secrets were shed for her when she probed, worn away until answers revealed themselves from the carbon of concealment. An absent hand brushed her pendant, seeking its illusory warmth, and she smiled.

Soon, Rishé reminded herself. Soon she would uncover the greatest secret of them all.

ASARU

Asaru awoke in a jungle of herbs, twilight once more casting him in bruising shades. He unstuck bleary eyes and blinked away the black spots that flew across his vision. A moment later, he realized they were merely birds. He pulled himself from the arms of sleep, more tired than he'd ever been. The poppy fog threatened to drag him back into the darkness where his mother's voice called. He found a cold comfort in its distorted tones, imagining she was with him even when his brother was not.

A wave of fatigue took him. That wasn't *his* tiredness threatening his eyes. As if in response to the unasked question, he heard a light snore.

Groggily, he turned his head. On a quilted chair beside the cot, Wren slept fitfully. Dark circles were almost tattooed beneath his eyes, brows knit, mouth parted. Shadows stubbled his jaw, and his hair fell in a storm of curls barely restrained by a blue ribbon.

Contrary to his every whim and will, the sight sent a strange shiver through him.

Asaru watched the man sleep a few minutes more. Watched as their chests rose and fell in harmony. Then he brushed his side—healing, *healed*—and gently shook Wren. The man stiffened, eyes shooting open, darting down to where Asaru's hand rested on his knee. His throat bobbed. Around them, plants whispered with the brush of leaves on a cool, marble floor. After a moment, Asaru took his hand away.

"How long was I asleep?" Wren yawned, slumping back. Cupping the bottom half of his face, he breathed deeply through his nose as if he'd just come up for air.

"I do not know." Asaru rose to his elbows before sitting up fully against the wall. The only twinge he felt was the one between his wings at the center of his spine, and the brand that buzzed. He almost felt a new man. "I just woke up myself."

"Do you, um, do you need anything?" Stuttering over himself, Wren swayed forward, back, and forward again. His face was as open as a hound's and as bright as the sun. A yellow petal stuck in his hair, and Asaru's hand twitched. He circled his own wrist beneath the blanket.

"I need to find my brother," he deadpanned.

Wren's earnestness whimpered away as if he were a kicked pup, and his shoulders fell. Wet eyes downcast, he curled up in the chair, staring over the jut of his knees.

"Sorry"—he softened like melted gold—"I can't . . . exactly do that."

The sensitive fur of Asaru's tail brushed his skin. He shifted uncomfortably, and they both looked at the appendage wrapped tight around Wren's ankle. At a sharp intake of breath, from whom he could not quite tell, Asaru snatched his tail away. In the thin weave of silence, he toyed with it in his lap so it couldn't cause him further problems.

Wren's mismatched eyes watched his ankle with a ponderous frown as if some physical mark of Asaru's embarrassment remained there. He hadn't clung to someone like that since he was a child. And even then, rarely, considering his aversions to touch.

"I *would* like something to eat," he admitted. In his periphery, the other man sat sword straight. Pointed ears pricked up eagerly. He scrambled to his feet with a crooked smile, sleeves rolling down his kohl-dark arms at the sudden motion.

"I can—" As he backed out of the room, Wren bumped a vase of tall shoots and scrambled to grab it before it tipped over. He flashed Asaru a sheepish look and rubbed the base of his neck. "Sorry. I'll be right back."

A smile played along Asaru's lips, and he shook his head as Wren left.

Not a moment later, the door slid back open. Rishé bounded over to the cot in great excited strides, Palenisa hovering a distance behind her like a great black fist of stone. The latter crossed her arms and leaned against the mixing bench. The former took Wren's seat, folded her legs, and planted her chin in her hands, leaning forward.

"How are you doing?" Rishé asked.

Asaru looked to the right, away.

"Better."

He couldn't lie, but it was an omission of the whole truth.

A strain found life on the lowered bar of his shoulders, and his wing ached. Though he couldn't have flown either way, with the black tendrils of the curse dripping over them, devouring the dappled falcon brown. Perhaps he was not the clearest image of health. But how *he* felt didn't matter. What did was finding his brother.

Wren returned, shouldering the door open with a tray

balanced haphazardly in his hands. The scent of aloe wafted in from the hall outside. He blinked at the three of them.

Palenisa rolled her eyes and gestured as he set the tray on the end of Asaru's cot. "You have orchid in your hair," she said, plucking the petal from his messy half tail. She flicked it away, and Asaru felt a twinge of disappointment. He watched it flutter to the ground and disappear among the mesh of vines and stray cuttings.

The group descended on the tray, finding rolls of nutty bread, a samovar steaming with the scent of cloves, and nectar apples—one cracked and hollowed with honey, the rest sliced to fan around it like a sunburst, golden nectar weeping beneath the pink skins. Asaru coveted those as the others made do with bites of bread and sips of tea.

He licked the perfumed nectar from his fingers and hummed. "Thank you."

Wren's flushed smile came out crooked with a glimpse of his fangs. "No problem."

Asaru finished the last slice. He quite liked nectar apples—he thought Alvarys would too. Aedyton didn't have such fruits, since dendrites didn't grow anything on their crystal branches. He reminded himself to bring one to his brother when they met again.

Nibbling at a piece of bread, Rishé cleared her throat. "So, I learned something," she said between bites, explaining what she'd gleaned from Brunoth about the Chronicler.

"I have to ask," Palenisa interjected. "What *is* this Chronicler, actually?"

Rishé lifted her hands to reply, but Asaru cut in.

"All I know is what I was told," he admitted, recalling the circumstances of his assignment.

The warden's office was a gleaming bubble of unblemished glass in the Odeum, floating with the icy clouds that formed the topmost ring of Aruu. He'd come directly from the field, covered in remnant blood and smelling ripe. Not that the warden had cared, being a retired warrior herself. In the same homely tone that had landed her the position in the first place, Xerqet placed a hand on his shoulder and told him of his brother's fate.

Missing, embassy—*find him.*

If the beacon, she'd said, was gone, he must point himself south—and fly. To the badlands, where he would find salvation nestled at the farthest end of the desert, beyond the point of reasonable journey. That was where Khensu had been traveling. Where Alvarys likely was. The abode of the Chronicler. Hidden almost in plain sight.

"They hold the archive of our history. Aedyton, eresh keyel, khetry." Asaru clawed at the speckled smoothness of his curse-marked arms. The cloud of pain floated at the back of his mind. Sighing, he met their gazes. "And, Triumvirate willing, Black Diamond too."

There had to be some record of the curse from the eras before Unification. History, as he had so often been told, was a serpent eating itself.

"We can't go to Ilon," Palenisa said firmly.

Rishé snorted, ignoring the flat-lipped scowl sent her way—or not caring. Asaru glanced between the two.

"But we must."

"He," Palenisa said, pointing to Wren, "is under my protection. My home crawls with rogue Aspects, and while I handled *two* of them, I can't take that risk. Not before my promise has been fulfilled."

"Well, you promised to follow me to whatever end," Wren

added quietly, pressing two fingers together in an unbroken line of black. Asaru felt the tremor of his apprehension like a sharp and sudden wave. "And *I* want to go."

The candles on the windowsill flickered, a line of four, sloping in height to the smallest, which burned, scarcely there.

Palenisa twisted her lips and huffed.

"Fine." She pinched out the tallest candle. "We leave right away. Your master healers may have given us a whole night, but I don't trust the people here."

Though he hadn't seen any viridian lies, Asaru felt much the same. Alert for a threat around every corner.

Light gilded the tips of Rishé's short-cropped hair as she rose to her knees. "I agree." Palenisa shot her a look. "Bartramians may not have loved the king as much as other provinces, thanks to Governor Devall, but Asaru's bounty is worth a lot. And rising."

Asaru nodded, a wordless decision made. "An hour, then?"

"I'll steal some bread from the tearoom."

"Rishé." Wren frowned.

"Brunoth will cover for me," she said gaily as she left them to gather themselves.

Inclining her head toward the door, Palenisa asked, "Should we be worried about that?"

"Don't ask me," Wren sighed. "She was here longer than I had the chance to be."

Palenisa tossed a shrug his way. As she glanced around the room in mild interest, Wren leaned forward. His intent eyes flitted up to Asaru's face, down to his bandaged stomach, then up again, a question in those gold and brown pools.

Holding still, Asaru let the hands check over his wound. And much to his displeasure, his senseless tail was once more wrapped around the man's ankle. An abrupt rush fluttered in his belly, and a sensation he couldn't quite name prickled his brand.

What was that—what had changed? Was this strange sensation camaraderie—the likes of which Alvarys shared with the Tetrarchia? He wasn't sure. It felt like he was wading in a sea with no bottom.

After a short while, Rishé returned, woolen hood drawn, satchel bursting with supplies.

"Ready?" she chirped.

As always. Asaru swung his legs off the cot. The steady balance of the ground filled him with a renewed sense of purpose. Time was a dire, precious resource, spilling between spread black palms. In his heart he knew the path forward—it kept him moving, perpetually in motion toward the horizon of a goal just within reach.

As he stood with the others, khetry shone. Edges faded like a tense rope rising from the depths of opaque waters. He waved a hand through the red substance, twining a thread with his smallest finger. It thrummed, alive, as he tugged it.

Life—he was still alive. For as long as he had left.

WREN

Intermittent lamps burned along the perimeter of the inner ward as they made their escape. Rishé led, followed by Asaru, then Wren and Palenisa.

Beyond the wall walk, spikes jutted into the ember-strewn night.

They slunk through the shadows, avoiding the scanning eyes of the Chain Archers. Time hung suspended as an archer passed overhead, heels clicking on ironwood. The door to the Overlook shut, and Wren released a sigh that cracked loud like kindling. An elbow caught him in the side, and the flash of Asaru's brilliant eyes silenced him.

The compound was asleep, though Wren knew there would be a few healers working sleeplessly in the Hanging Gardens and journeyers milling about, passing flasks of watered-down wine between them as he once did. Alcohol never sat quite right with him, turning the gray thoughts in his head black. Flipped his stomach so his throat tasted more of bile than cloves.

A light burst to life in Acorn House—the guild master's

quarters. *Urusy.* A gauzy shadow passed the window. But they were gone before the light died, slipping through a loose slat in the unending ironwood wall. It shut behind them, Rishé smoothing the seam into place to leave no trace of their secret egress.

It was black only a second before a torch flickered, Rishé's face bobbing above flintrock blue. Wren met her eyes in the night as she passed to the front and guided them down a set of too thin, too narrow stairs onto the hidden paths and alternate ways through Birinuyi, discovered during their time together. Rishé had tried to teach him twice or thrice when they were training, but Wren was always more interested in his studies—healing. No chance at getting that now: helping people again. *At least not without*—he brushed the needle, a reminder that rested over his branded heart. He was *trying.* His hands shook, and he was thankful the antimony kohl hid the scars on his fingers.

The stairs spilled them out onto a low shoreline, dusted with chalky sand. Above, the shadow of the guild sat on spindly stilts that burrowed into a concave cliff face, stained with rogue sea spray. It looked more precarious from this angle, as if a single childish finger could knock it all over. Though Wren knew its firmament was stronger than that, as firm and unyielding as the millennia it had withstood. Since the Age of Heroes, the era in which Mator lived. Curious, the names history remembered. Gentle healers. Gentler than he.

"How did you find this place?" Wren asked, then immediately regretted the question as Rishé doused the torch in the sea. She stowed it behind two rocks and dusted the chrome-stitched hem of her suman.

"Went exploring after you left. It's called the Poisoner's Gullet." Her lips tugged upward wryly. "Fitting."

Fitting.

Wren's face burned with the memory of fresh dropwort twisting and wrinkling the flesh. The twin screams. Two forms falling away from the upturned bottle of pale liquid as it seeped into their skin, tainting brown to violet in an instant. Had it gotten into their mouths, they would have died without a single trace. Instead, it left Urusy bedridden, and him—gone halfway through the week that he should have spent healing.

A tap on his shoulder snapped him back to the present.

Palenisa cocked her head over her shoulder. Rishé and Asaru were farther down the shore. Ahead, the beach bled into Furtumbér's midnight dwelling, that thick strip of trees where primeval forest met the jungles of Mysme and Thryme.

Wind whispered through the bower of the Lizardwood as the quartet passed below and journeyed even farther beyond.

In the far distance, the rhythmic thumping of merchant ships could be heard.

Another life, somewhere else.

Night passed, then morning and another day until the sky shaded once more into evening. Wren's feet ached, and his eyes were sticky with sleep. He could only imagine what the bags beneath them looked like.

Not a thing moved in this part of the Lizardwood, the world silent and still. The worn path darkened at the edges like fading vision, and he slowly realized why.

This was the Trail of the Taken.

A treacherous trail that curled through the Lizardwood like a constricting serpent. One that had stolen many lives from the Norvatti. Some said the forest itself snatched the mind during slumber, leaving empty bodies. Others claimed it was the work of Sirrah, the tiny, winged trickster who led children away to the tune of its violin. Or maybe it was just easy to lose oneself in the gloom, so thick he could barely see a few steps ahead even during the day.

But he didn't really know. The Ingoscu clan had never traveled this far south, preferring to stick to the hinterlands. Rishé's clan had, though. And she formed a sign over her chest as a result, pushing out with clawed fingers to repel the dreary omen of the trail.

"You *do* believe in superstitions," Palenisa said, her voice dripping sarcasm.

Lowering her compass, Rishé rolled her eyes and snapped back, "I don't. It's a cultural thing."

Palenisa hummed indulgently and glanced sidelong at Wren. "Why do your people fear this place?"

Wren lifted his gaze to the dense canopy as he stifled a yawn, then told her of Sirrah and its malicious, mischievous music.

"Just a story," Rishé interjected, spinning on a heel to walk backward. Her hands slipped through the signs with a fervent passion as Wren interpreted her words. *"To explain away the pain of rogue Aspects ravaging the Vana during the Crusades."*

"That's not entirely true . . ."

"True enough." She shrugged. Wren's gaze followed Rishé's in time to glimpse Palenisa's stricken face before she ducked into the shadow of her cape.

After that, only their footfalls filled the silence with the crunch and sigh of underbrush. They trudged on quietly. They passed trees, trees—more trees—and altars sheltered beneath blankets of greenery dotted with tiny white flowers. Artifacts of centuries of countless Norvatti, followers of Nature and

Light, passing where they passed, walking where they walked. Separated by the span of a few paces, each altar was more thoroughly wreathed in plant life than the last, each one was larger than the last, older, until a strange sight sprouted from the brush.

At the end of the line of altars crouched a lone statue, so worn by the ages that the fine sculpting of its jade steel features was barely discernible. Even so, through the veil of moss Wren could make out the smooth face of a woman. From her stony back, a pair of crumbling wings protruded, and tumbling down on either side of her clasped hands was carved hair adorned with the bodies of small, writhing beasts.

It looked nothing like the shrine statues he'd seen before.

"Madib?" Asaru said, confusion lilting his tone. He reached out as if to brush the leaves from her shut eyes, paused, then pulled away. Without the poison running through his veins, he looked in better health, though the marks of the curse did their best to dampen that brightness.

"Your people's first warden?" Rishé signed. *"Queen Mab?"*

He nodded after Wren interpreted. "She never wanted to be called a queen." Asaru picked a petal from her splintered head with a hum. "Or a goddess. I do not know why humans turned her into one."

He threw the rosy petal aside and swept forward after Rishé. They left behind a goddess with many names to many cultures. *Madib, Mab, Ela Prinâza*: one gone, one myth, one whom Wren believed in.

The sky split open, and a droplet fell onto his cheek.

"Rain," Rishé said.

"Astute observation," Palenisa replied.

Rishé glowered at him—no, at *her,* but Wren felt as though her narrow eyes corroded him all the same. He shook off the stare and looked around. A crimson shadow flitted through the towering trees. Wren squinted and saw only the fluttering of red-breasted birds.

Soon they came upon the overgrown remnants of what was once a settlement, ringed with a rotting fence. Around it the Lizardwood had waned, if only temporarily, against the man-made intrusion. Yet nature had come to snatch back what it was owed. Ivy crept through dusty windows, over a once-roof hunched like Sika's rolling hills, and up fallen beams between which Wren saw only shadows.

Rain-slick hair fell into his eyes and dripped down his nape.

"We need to keep moving," Asaru said, making to walk past the ruin. "Before we lose the lead on the beacon."

Lifting a vine, Palenisa peered inside. The rough stone floors were covered in dust—thankfully dry. "Show of hands, who wants to keep going?"

Asaru stopped, turned, pursed his lips. His slackened tail went shock straight. When Wren recalled the way its fur felt, he glanced up before his ears could warm.

Smirking, Palenisa brushed the rest of the plants away with her earth Aspect abilities, coiling up her arms like gentle snakes as they slithered away. It still sent a frisson of fear through him, and Wren found himself pressing away from her when they settled in the cramped entryway.

Thunder cracked somewhere far away. Even through the foliage, a cold spark of lightning lit the forest floor aglow.

Asaru placed four fingers to the sides of his neck. Breathed in air, then khetry flared, and he breathed out flame. Broken bits of the building that had fallen into a cold ring hearth lit with a cough.

"Thanks." Rishé moved her hands over the fire like she was

casting a spell. "But you have *got* to quit worrying. Once the rain stops, we'll be that much closer to the Chronicler, and your brother."

There was little space between the four of them. Wren was close enough to hear Asaru draw in a short, tight breath.

Rain drummed the roof, a soothing sound that did little to balm the turmoil inside him, while a cool breeze crept along the floor, snarling at their fire. It snarled back when he cupped it. Sparks licked his fingers like the pinch of a needle drawing blood.

As the others rested their eyes, Wren fiddled restlessly with his sleeves, trying to count the flowers his mother had embroidered there. Pushing them back revealed the red outline of stitched dahlias. They should have been black for mourning, all things considered.

He shifted away to hide the shame of his actions and placed the primer on his knees. Khetry wrapped around his wrists as a slow, unraveling spool of blood threaded from his fingers to the bone needle. It drank the red like a thirsting beast. He held the crescent of his necklace between his teeth in concentration.

"Wren."

He looked over.

Asaru stared into the flames, his knees drawn up, his irises turned to orange islands in pools of black.

"I am sorry." Asaru's tone was husky. "For almost breaking it. Your necklace."

The pendant fell from his mouth. "It's fine; it's just a necklace."

Wren's gaze trailed over the side of his face. Down the furrow of his scarred brow, the curve of his scarred nose, vehemently past his scarred lips, to land on the scarred ring of his halo, amethysts afire.

He wondered how they would feel to touch . . . His face

warmed and his gaze shot away, chest fluttering. Where had that strange and foolish thought come from?

"Regardless, I apologize." Asaru hummed into his knees. "It was not . . . kind."

The slight sensation of fear-tinged sadness trickled thinly through their bond.

"If anyone should apologize, it's me." Wren pressed the red tip of the needle to his thumb. "For summoning you, branding you, causing the backlash."

Exhaling, Asaru shut his eyes. "I still am not happy about that."

"I know. I'm sorry."

Fire spit in the ponderous lull. The sky thundered. Petrichor wafted from the muddy ground outside.

"Do you miss him?"

Asaru tipped his head against the old, creaking wood. "More than anything. I just need to find him. The Chronicler. *Do* something about this curse. Anything."

Wren hated the pain he had caused. The faults of his own sick, selfish resolve bandied through their bond. His hurt was minuscule compared to all the rest he'd caused.

Before an apology could fall from his lips, the prick of a needle startled him out of the exhaustion. A half-formed shout caught in his throat and a hand snatched his. The touch was hot. Blazing. All too much, yet equally not enough.

In what must've been instinct, a sudden absent motion, Asaru had joined their hands. Soft, black fingers intertwined.

Wren froze and felt Asaru do the same. Face warm, the words—any words—stuck in his throat, and his chest was thick. Raising his head, he found Asaru staring wide-eyed at their single point of connection.

The man snatched his hand back as if burned, and shifted aside.

"I need to rest. Gather strength." His stilted tone allowed no room for argument.

As he caged himself behind his wings, Wren watched the shifting planes of his back. Tendrils of curse cloaked them, more black tar than feathers. He couldn't even tell where the break used to be.

He looked down, terribly aware of the living energy vibrating inside him. The pages were stained red from his efforts. More than he'd meant to spill. He felt the blood loss weakening him but steeled his resolve. Needle to a finger. Finger to a page. Blood wove through the Red Web of Life as Wren told himself this was what he was meant to do.

This was what he had to do.

PALENISA

On the first day of the Maronwuchi festival, they passed a line of boundary stones. And just like that, they were in Ilon.

And just like that, Palenisa felt sick, a thick miasma caught in her throat.

It was subtle, how the Lizardwood blended into the jungle of her home. But she knew it very well. From the dry itch of her eyes to the humidity sticking her hair to the sides of her face.

Terrace farms appeared through the trees, fields of green spilling between thin vine ladders, water gurgling down irrigation pipes buried in the trunks of those artificial palms. More signs of life that only ratcheted up the energies brewing in Palenisa's unsettled belly. She looked up at Ilon's rope bridges, strung across the canopy with colored fusion globes for the two-day festival.

The fervent hum of celebration hung in the air, an ululation rising with the symphony of talking drums.

Once, Palenisa would have delighted in the familiarity—*once*. Before that night. But now she kept her head lowered from the sights, away from the thatched-roof caravanserai climbing ribbed trunks, and the foul gutters that ran in neat lines through the middle of the street. Turbulence spread with sunlight through her warm veins. She wanted nothing more than to sink into the cool darkness underneath that knew no name or face.

They merged into the boil of bodies flowing over the wide road from Bartrom to the Ilonese subcontinent. On foot and ahorse, they descended into a bustling township.

The streets of Bolsember were thick with common folk pouring in to attend the gala, which was always held there, where the kharess's chief lived, rather than at the capital. An evening of revelry. Then, the next day, as was tradition, the hungover devotees would make the trek back to the capital to pray before the suvaunoors. The monoliths that spiraled before the kharess's manse were only replicas of the originals from Peskelos and were littered with suvaugrams in imitation of those painted by the hands of the Twelve Builders long before.

Two of those suvaugrams, she wore. A blessing from the Zodiac, to whom she was meant to give praise on this day of celebration. Instead, Palenisa hunkered beneath a hood, trying to hide from a plague of dreadful thoughts. *Wallowing*—at that, she was excellent.

In the eyes of mortals and spirits alike, her honor was filth. Disgraced. She shouldn't be there. She hadn't meant to return until she proved that she deserved to be Sister of Faith again. That she deserved her emblem—the one that was Ada's before hers.

Shame filled her at the depth of her longing for the coterie. It rent her as wide as a cavern, unending as the turn of the sun. Despite her misgivings, she longed to rush before the kharess and plead for her forgiveness. But the thought gave her pause—the kharess hadn't actually been there when her emblem was stripped away. In the memory that the damned lulaik had resurfaced, only her sisters—her *former* sisters—hissed and turned their backs.

Palenisa shook her head as the scent of spiced water rolled in on the wind.

Harsh in her nose, it reminded her of her promise. Because to speak a thing makes it thus. She had spoken it—she had to keep it. And if honesty served, a small part of her was curious about what lay at the end of this journey she'd hitched herself to.

At Rishé's behest, they split off from the main road, leaving behind the crowd and a bit of her anxieties as well. A gnarled side path descended even farther, brine wafting to her nose as the sea came into view. Dirt and sand mingled in the tiny, obscure grove hidden in the shade of a colossal leaf.

Ada. Her heart yearned. The grove didn't truly resemble their secret spit of sand. But the shattering of water into blue crystals on the shore was the same on every beach.

"Where are we?" Palenisa asked, glancing away from the glittering surf. Crossing her arms, she watched Wren and Rishé as they felt around the bases of drowned trees. They conversed in an interesting blend of Akiki, Eslang, and what she surmised was their birth tongue. Nomyrs, if she recalled correctly.

"Marrowstone Door. Birinuyi." Wren interpreted Rishé's signs before the human pointed to a shadow between two roots.

Palenisa watched as he painted a circle of seawater on the wall, placed a hand in the center, and poured himself into the spell. At least, that was what it looked like when the circle glowed white. The intricacies of the mechanics behind manipulating khetry were lost on her.

Marrowstone Door opened with the quiet rumble of a beast's

belly. Beyond the portal was a familiar, moist cavern. Behind them, Palenisa placed a hand on the sand and drew the cover of rock back over the entrance.

First, there was only black. Then a bolt of blue cast them in starlight as Wren held the flintrock flame aloft. They huddled around the flame, four disembodied heads swimming in the inky darkness.

"This leads to the Obsidian Market," Rishé said.

"Why isn't it called the Marrowstone Market?"

"I don't know," she replied dryly, "why not ask your spirits?"

"Please don't." Wren buried his face in his hands.

"How do we learn which Neyari has the beacon?" Asaru asked.

"It's hard to trace a rumor in the market," Rishé explained. "But there are runners. They move goods and secrets."

"And how," Palenisa interjected, "do we do that?"

"If you'd let me finish"—Rishé snapped her fingers between Palenisa's eyes, which crossed to follow them—"I'll tell you."

Lips pursed, Palenisa scowled. How did this small, irritating nuisance constantly niggle at her? She had respect for neither the Six, nor the Zodiac, nor whatever Wren worshipped, and she was always scribbling in her journal. Pages covered with looping handwriting and sketches of that meaningless stone on her necklace. It was only a damn stone.

Hypocrite. The spirits, all of them, she realized, seemed to press down around her as if to whisper in her ear. *You have your own lodestone.*

Rishé continued. "Runners, as I was saying, are vital. But they hide in plain sight. Save for their obsidian jewelry—one piece. Innocuous unless you're looking closely. So use your eyes, please."

The flame bobbed. Stone-spotted walls were carpeted with moss, and there was a cooling blanket of moisture. Blue flickered steadily into red the farther they walked toward whatever mass of heat lay at the end of the tunnel's maw. Packed earth floors were trod smooth underfoot, fringed by ivy and greenweed. Especially underground, the wild would not be kept out.

Light bounced off the thick bars of an open steel grate as they passed through it to the Obsidian Market.

It was as if they'd never left Bolsember.

The ruins held a flurry of life as they squeezed through the traffic. A patchwork of various stalls filled with an excess of wares tucked into alcoves. On some lay sugar elixirs, false cures sitting next to genuine healing remedies. Toss a coin, try your luck, buy a lie.

Vendors called out in many languages: Akiki, Inachie, pidgin. Reams of dyed silkwood veilari were piled high against the rubble on the side of the road, while Mauriidan silk rugs softened the steps of the masses. As Palenisa cast a critical eye around, she found a canvas painted with pastoral imagery between crumbling pillars. Cowries on strings were draped down the entrances of buildings carved from the stone walls by ancient hands. They rang when passed beneath, chittering in her ear with a million tiny legs.

Bell-shaped lights swayed above, making the space seem larger than it was. Still, Palenisa drowned. The bustle pulled her forward, submerging her in the sights and sounds and muffled smells. Sensitive nerves danced up her body, fraying at the brush of the throng. They crowded in and wrapped her tight. Each touch flayed her apart until she was running through prayers to the spirits in her head rather than searching for oily black jewelry.

Someone tugged her sleeve.

She choked on air and grabbed the hand, panting. Her frenzied gaze shot up.

"Look," Rishé's finger seemed to cry, pointing at a hunk of marrowstone resting on a soft neck. It was a choker—it was an emblem. Her vision doubled, and for a moment, the runner looked like Sister Yinka.

Palenisa blinked. Another someone tugged her other sleeve.

Over her shoulder, she met Wren's wide eyes. There was a silver sheen glimmering in the golden one as his face contorted in panic.

"Where is Asaru?"

Her ears pricked, alert. She ripped her hood back, braids tumbling free from their tie as her head whipped around.

Where *was* Asaru? He may have been short, but he wore a suman embroidered with thorns and fruit, for spirits' sake—how did she lose him? *You were wallowing,* said the imagined voices of the Zodiac, *sinking, drowning.* She was an Aspect of earth, not water. Of all that was firm and steadfast.

And yet—she had lost him.

Palenisa's guilty anxieties hadn't left. She had just told herself they had. She used the squeeze of the tunnels and its flintrock-dampened walls to pretend she was anything but a guilt-ridden mess wallowing as the imagined spirits crooned.

They suddenly rose with the contents of her stomach, threatening a retch.

Under her cape, her fingers scratched lines along her arms. A staff, a scythe, daggers. None of them could protect her. None of them could protect her charge.

Her—charge?

When had he turned from a risk to a charge in her mind?

It didn't matter. Thinking it didn't make a thing so. Regardless, she'd fucking lost him.

Forward or back. She looked between Wren and Rishé. Back to Wren, then again at Rishé cutting through the crowd after the runner.

She was a stone in the middle of an ocean, and bodies flowed around her.

Twisting her wrist, Palenisa swallowed. Ilon made her vulnerable, weak, unearthed too much—Ada, her mother, her worries.

"We'll find him," she said to Wren, pulling him along after Rishé before her past could catch up with her. "I promise."

ASARU

Asaru slipped away from the others, and the crowd surged to fill where he'd been. Not for the first time, he was glad he lacked the height of the average eresh keyel.

Something had caught his eye, and something even more interesting had caught his nose.

Ducking around the many-bodied mass, he trailed after the scent of Black Diamond, which clung heavily to the small group that filtered through the crowd ahead of him. It adorned them like a weft, embedded so deep it almost seemed for a second as though he had the vial in hand, with the curse spilling out wet and black.

Truth be told, he hadn't immediately noticed it when they entered the market. The cavern was filled with more people than he was comfortable with. Languages he didn't know rose and fell in the air. Too many people, the brush of each body niggled, writhed under the surface of his skin.

Then a group clad in feathery green gold and veils of startlingly white lace brushed past him with a scent that stuck a hook into his nose. Crooked. Snatched him until it was all he could perceive. Until the rest of Birinuyi melted away and he found himself drawn as if possessed.

Shaking the presence from his head, Asaru readjusted his hood, hiding his face well. His tail tightened anticipatorily around his wrapped arm, and a tremor pinched the marks of the curse, from shoulder to neck to foot. As he trailed from the others, the link of the bond going taut, then thin, he swallowed and reminded himself what was important. Steel laced his spine. *Alvarys.*

Woolen hem whirling by his ankles, he followed the group around a corner. Away from the throng toward sparser backstreets. The scent grew stronger as the din grew weaker. Ruin and rubble littered the sides as the market crumbled into alleys, with empty arches leading nowhere. Braziers holding blue flames flickered red as they passed, growing fewer and farther between. Darkened buildings and dry, weathered wells lined thin streets. Deeper in, clumps of climbing ivy grew over the ceilings, and the path began to resemble the tunnels that had cemented themselves in his mind. Unchanging, flowering out of hidden corners.

Asaru stayed a good distance behind, keeping to the shadows. Every so often the path widened, but it would narrow just as quick, and the group ahead turned left, right, then left again in a seemingly senseless pattern, each choice made with a swift and deliberate purpose.

They slowed, and he darted against a wall. Asaru slid into a crouch and watched as the healers—he assumed, from the green gold of their robes—stopped before a false door. The recessed niche was simpler than those of Aedyton, inscribed faintly with glyphs of winged figures beneath the eye of Chert Ouadjet.

He glanced at his wrist, where the curse had long since eaten his own wejat.

When he looked back up, the healers were disappearing into the facade. *Not so false a door, then; they must think themselves so clever.*

Once the last of them were through, Asaru scanned the street and darted forward. He grabbed the door, waited a moment, ears pricked for the sound of fading footsteps, then slipped in. It sealed shut behind him, and he cupped his mouth to stifle a gasp. Clinging to the wall, he held his breath as a large vermicular beast huffed—thankfully asleep.

Massive—*massive*—it coiled around the bottom of a tree surely as wide as it was tall. A set of stairs rose from the knot of roots, twirling around the trunk and vanishing into the darkness above. It was hard to tell where the beast ended or began when its ribbed body was composed of one endless line. Only a tapered point at one end and three puckered pink lines near the other delineated a tail and an approximation of a face.

At a rumbling snort, Asaru stiffened. The beast twitched. Then its behemoth features smoothed out. Still, he didn't relax. He crept slowly along the edges of the cavern. Pausing, waiting, listening. The scent of the curse flared as he reached the foot of the stairs. The triangle at his nape throbbed. His claws bit into his palms, and he stepped over the beast's tail. Blood rolled down his fingers. Tainted gold spotted the steps. Pain pricked him, spine to skull.

Atop the landing was a door.

Brushing a hand over the flintrock revealed a spell programmed with such tremendous skill. Its living warmth was nothing but embers of a flame flickering in the living substance around him.

He pushed it open.

And found the embassy.

No. Asaru blinked the glassiness from his vision. Not the embassy. A room resembling it.

Whatever this place had been before, it was a sick house.

The bittersweetness of the curse assaulted his senses. His head filled to the brim with its sour, pervasive scent, a rot that peeled everything away inside him.

A carved niche resembling a false door with an altar sat recessed in the far wall. Columns marked the perimeter of a mosaic resembling the sun being shattered with a lance of lightning. Over the piercing rose a lone slab, blanketed with a shroud white as snow. White as the moon reflecting off the sea. White as the dappling on wings that had once spread proud.

At the edges of his foggy awareness came murmuring from another room nearby. The voices were muddled in a watery blend beneath the beat of his heart in his eardrums. The unmovable web that wove all things thrummed.

It was life, yet there was none in this room.

Asaru doffed his hood and walked forward. Dread filled each step; pure gray dread that dragged him into nothingness.

Come, his mother's voice whispered in the tatters of his mind. *Warrior, brother, son—prince.* The words bounced in his skull. *Come.*

A whine rose, a reedy, quavering sort of sound.

Faster than he could blink, he was there. Hope dried up and died a slow, bitter death. The indistinct silhouette of a jackal's head lingered in his periphery.

An arm in a familiar gauntlet hung from the white sheet. Black fingers dripped bloody spots across the scalloped mosaic. Unlike the web, there was no pattern in sight. No meaning.

Outside his body, Asaru watched himself pull away the cloth. Heat choked his lungs.

Cornflower-blue eyes that once crinkled in amusement, narrowed in jest, and softened in quiet moments—lay wide, drowned in a sea of curse black.

The world fell out from under him.

Asaru was back in that oppressive darkness, the intangible colors of sleep. He hadn't felt his knees hit the floor. A hand fell before him. *Brother.* He grasped it. *Brother.* He clutched it to his lips. *Alvarys.* He sobbed.

From the stiff fingers, he thought he felt dregs of warmth. A foolish hope his mind grasped helplessly for as his tears gouged rivers of remorse down his face. He would drown without an anchor.

What use was he?

His brother was dead. He had failed.

Did he ever really have a chance?

Years spent doing what had to be done—what he was *commanded* to do, no reprieve to dwell in the experience that was himself. What did any of it matter when *his brother was dead*? Perhaps if he had been faster. Perhaps if he hadn't spent as long dallying to the whims of a brand that sapped any semblance of self from him. Perhaps, perhaps. *Perhaps.*

Death is a commonplace of life. But it should have been him.

And their mother—what would he say to Tenat?

Already he could hear her gut-wrenching caterwaul, born of inconsolable loss. As it drew higher into a deafening whine, Asaru shattered beyond the shell of himself.

His shoulders jumped with sorrowful tremors. Hot tears leaked from the corners of his tightly shut eyes. What remained of his blackened wings dripped listlessly at his back.

Minutes passed, maybe hours, maybe no time at all.

How long had he knelt there, hand in cadaverous hand? It must have been forever.

There was a grounding touch to his shoulder.

He started, a sob catching in his throat. Through blurry tears, Asaru looked up and saw a woman. The wraith wore a wrap of undyed cloth stamped in a motif of silver scales and golden cowries. One long end was thrown over her shoulder while the rest of the raiment trailed like smoke over slippered feet. Bronze bangles lined her arms, clattering as she moved, and around her head was a tight band from which white curls fanned in a cloud. Her face was a carefully blank veneer.

"I had not thought to find you here," she said in a meandering tone. "I didn't think you had the time to ask Zaosha—Zodiac damn his spirit—if there was a second embassy. Before you stabbed him in the heart, obviously."

Creases wrinkled the corners of her eyes as she smiled. As though there were any jest to be found in her words.

Anger curdled in Asaru's chest, tangling venomous roots through his heart.

"Fuck you," he spat, scrubbing at frustrated tears.

"Crude."

Her skirts whisked the floor as she glided as if on water, taking him in with deep blue eyes. Pinned to the spot, Asaru felt her shrewd inspection split and bare the pieces of him wide open.

"I am Chiwatel Dust. Kharess of Ilon. And I know that you"—she tapped his forehead, which earned her a snarl—"are Asaru. The *assassin.*"

"Fuck off."

"Honestly." She tutted, brushing back his crimson-dipped fringe. He jerked away in a rage but was too exhausted to do much else, luckily for the kharess. "I'm trying to help you, Asaru."

The fur on his tail stood on end. He cast her a sidelong glare.

Chiwatel rounded the slab and traced a finger down the

profile of Alvarys's face. Indignant, heavy tears welled in Asaru's eyes. What little he cared for in the world was lying on this cold slab, and he couldn't even be afforded respect in death.

"You've found yourself in the Aerie, much to my surprise," Chiwatel said. "This is, or perhaps *was*, the Ilonese embassy—a joint creation devised between Zaosha and I after your warden informed us of the Tetrarchia's mission. It was meant as a temporary stop to gather themselves before their journey to the badlands—but only one warrior arrived."

She leaned forward, her eyes a pair of coins.

"Now it's his tomb."

Her voice warped in Asaru's ears, and fat teardrops spilled down his cheeks, splashing at his feet.

"*He* was Alvarys," he muttered wetly, "and *he* was my brother."

"I know," she sighed. A hand found his head—he hadn't realized she'd moved—and she brushed through his hair in a mocking reminder of his mother's embrace. "I'm sorry to hear that."

Asaru was reminded of who she was—where he was—when that hand took him by the chin and forced him to look upward. His vision doubled. The world was a smear of colors as his mind came undone.

"I'm going to tell you something now. All right?"

He nodded—or he thought he nodded. Everything had a slow, sluggish quality to it.

"Good." She squeezed his cheeks. "The person I gave your Chronicler's beacon to placed it in a chest enchanted by a ward Aspect. This chest can only be opened by the blood of the person who locked it."

She cocked her head.

"Do you understand?"

Unflinching eyes assessed him. When it seemed she had

found what she was looking for, she smiled. Calm and pleasant, tinted with a cool air.

"This is a *fine* opportunity." She hummed, patting his cheek. "You get your beacon back, and I get a nuisance dealt with. Reciprocity is so sweet a gift."

Through the altered haze, a slip of sense returned. The meaning behind her words tugged free something. A tool, a weapon. It was all he was. Made to be used. The kharess of Ilon was merely doing as his existence demanded.

Murder was easy, as he well knew. And his hands were already drenched gold, black, and red.

III

CUTTING CLARITY

WREN

There was a torrent in Wren's skull, turmoil brewing in his stomach—boiling up his throat—and the wreath over his heart would not stop burning with grief.

It had been hours, and they still hadn't found Asaru.

Not back down near Marrowstone Door. Not in the main hub, where the flow of traffic was thickest, though they most certainly tried. Not in this side tunnel where Wren clutched his head between his knees.

He was useless, a wreck of overwhelmed nerves and over-stimulated senses.

"Hey." Wren looked up at Palenisa, and her lips flattened. "If he'd been captured, we'd know. All things considered."

That was not as reassuring as she thought. That was not reassuring *at all*. Even she had unraveled, working the chains of her skirt into undulating liquid beneath restless fingers. She paced before she paused and leaned against the opposite wall, tapping an impatient foot. Her nerves bled into Wren's like the world's most vicious cycle of dread. Feeding off her freneticism, his mind spiraled. A whirl around a single central repetition of *your fault, your fault, your fault.*

A high squeal of a whine escaped the back of his throat as he rocked back on his heels. Master Vair was right—his propensity for fucking up due to his neuroses was its own phenomenon. Like the three cornerstones themselves. Really, it should be studied. Maybe the academics of Fa Djain would like to crack his skull open and examine the mechanisms that ran him.

Wren had lost him—lost Asaru. Nearly as offensive an insult as summoning him in the first place. He wondered, in a moment of mad hilarity, if this deserved backlash too—what would his new brand look like? A fucking question mark?

All the blood he'd spilled into bone would be for naught. If he could not undo this error, he wouldn't be able to help Asaru or prove to the guild he was worthy of being more than a failed student. Truthfully, Wren thought he was worth less than half an aur. If that.

Grief swelled through the bond, evincing a wince. Reeled out across a crevasse so deep that to acknowledge it struck an unbearable chord through his bones. A tear fell from his eye, and when Wren wiped it away, another soon took its place.

The clamor of the market was still too close. Thunder rang in his ears in a blare of panic as his breaths came short. Quick. Abrupt.

Then a hand wrapped around his.

His head shot up to find Rishé, concern lining her face as she squeezed his hand. Between their hands was her necklace. As she ran his fingers over the textured facets, over each bump and silvery whorl, the imperfections inherent to rock—Wren's anxious energies were quelled, and slowly, he calmed.

Once his vision cleared, Rishé's face came into focus like a cloudless sky. There was the scar on her lip. There was the spray of freckles on her cheeks, so light one had to be inches from her nose to see them. And there were her almond eyes, big and wide and orange.

She held his gaze unwaveringly. "Palenisa."

The rattling paused, and the wraith hummed in acknowledgment.

"Can you track Asaru by scent?"

Palenisa shook her head, chains clicking like the snap of a razor-billed starwren. "Not if he hasn't cast a spell recently, and not here. The walls. This flintrock."

Rishé pushed their clasped hands toward him. Against his chest, the unnatural heat of her pendant seemed to burn as red as the stone itself.

"Can *you* use your bond?"

Wren . . . hadn't thought of that. His tears dried up. *Why didn't I think of that?* Sitting up, ignoring the twinge that laced down his spine, he blinked, and khetry flared to life. One strand shone brighter, loosely braided threadlike hands that reached into the wreath over his heart and stretched out into the rest of that glimmering web.

Life to life, Asaru to him.

He felt the buzz of the curse. A flood of sadness and anger-tinged grief. And a strange, broiling feeling he knew was Asaru.

"You hadn't thought of that?" Palenisa asked incredulously. "Well, does it work?"

"I—I think it does?" Wren sounded confused, even to himself.

There was a bright cast to Rishé's eyes as she cocked her head. She'd already assumed as much, hadn't she—with her scholar's mind, tumbling over theories and possibilities the moment he'd confessed to the backlash. Drawing conclusions from instances in legend, legacy, and lore. Neither of them smiled, but something shifted. Ever further into place, not as it once was—but as it could be.

"Come on, then." Rishé signed for him to stand. *"Let's go find him."*

Wren's resolve was a watery thing. He grabbed for it, tried to form it into something more solid, though it would never quite resemble steel. His will was weak, so he let Rishé pull him up. Their connection never broke.

Wren let instinct guide him. He felt past the numb grief tempering the edges of the bond like glass. So fragile that it felt as if a mere wrong move would shatter him to pieces. Pressing his free hand over his heart, he followed the tug, led his companions through the backstreets. Left, right, then left again to the end of a dusty path where two side streets crossed.

Set into the wall was a niche sculpted in the shape of doors. He pressed the raised relief of an eye, but it was Palenisa who slipped a palm into the imagined gap between the doors and pried open the earth. It was a bit unnerving, but Wren was far more enthralled by the twirl of that one shining red strand.

Palenisa sealed the secret door, and they held their gathered breaths as a guard wurm snuffled in its sleep. The pink beast wriggled when they stepped over its pointed tail, shifting as they ascended the winding stairs. It was doing a poor job of protecting.

There was a door on the landing. It was etched with white spellwork and recklessly knotted in a programmed spell. Someone was trying to hide something. And it had his worries rising.

The sensation nudged him forward.

They pushed the door open, and when it shut, all Wren could

see was a slab and a hunched form holding somber vigil over it.

"Asaru," he breathed, dropping Rishé's grip and taking a step forward. Then another and another, sliding to his knees by the white slab. Beneath the shroud was a body. He had never met them, but he already knew who it was.

Asaru slumped against the side of the diorite slab, staring at nothing. He barely registered the three of them, save a flicker of a glance. Silver slits had dimmed to a matte gray. His wings dripped from his shoulder blades, black miring the spotted brown. It was hard to tell where the broken feathers had been under the curse's slick.

Wren held his hands aloft, uncertain if his touch would be welcome.

Dull hazel eyes turned to him, two pearlescent drops hovering at the corners.

There was a heavy pause as they stared at each other. It felt like he wasn't breathing; it felt like no one was breathing.

Salt tracked Asaru's cheek as he moved a hand from the corpse's grip to wipe bile from the corner of his mouth. "My brother's dead."

Wren's heart shook the bars of his ribs. He didn't know what to say. The others were in similar states of shock, confusion, and disbelief. Rishé stood beside one column, eyes large and haunted and never moving from the veiled body. She squeezed at her necklace as if it might spill between those small fingers.

"What happened?" Palenisa asked, padding carefully closer. She gazed around the room in shaken awe. "What is this place?"

With great effort, Asaru rolled a shoulder, and Wren felt the shared twinge in his.

"Kharess Dust told me where the beacon will be tonight." He sounded so very tired.

Crouching, Palenisa trailed a hand over the scaled mosaic and cupped her mouth. He caught snippets of her mutterings—*How could I not have known? How could the coterie not have known? What else did—*

"You should go." Sighing, Asaru brought his brother's hand to his forehead. Dark lashes trembled. "You don't need to entangle yourselves further in my . . . my issues. I can do this alone."

Wren started at that. They could help—*he* could help. He *would* help. He had come too far not to. The needle burned a hole in his pocket, searing through to his skin, painting him red. "No, you can't," he said, surprising himself at the firmness of his voice. Asaru's gaze rose, a curious flash of light seeping in. "And no, we won't. Go, that is."

Wren looked at Palenisa, and despite her shakiness, she nodded. When he looked at Rishé, she pressed the silver-crimson stone to her lips, turned away from the slab, and nodded too. Tentatively, he reached out.

One, two, three, four, five.

His hand found Asaru's shoulder, and tension bandied between them.

"We *are* with you—you know that, right?"

Asaru's face shuttered closed. Hazel eyes peered into Wren's, daggering him apart. He felt raw at the edges, open in a way that hurt—but also didn't. Thickness at the back of his throat stilled his breathing. *One, two, three, four, five.* A palm covered his, and Asaru squeezed, though the flat expression he wore never wavered.

Wren froze when Asaru leaned in. Tensed when Asaru's head fell onto his shoulder. Choked on air when Asaru pressed his nose—*bare*—against the side of his neck—*also very much bare.*

"Thanks."

But Wren scarcely heard it over the rush of blood in his ears; the warm, steady breaths prickling across his skin; the burning throb of his brand, double time—like a heartbeat.

ASARU

Asaru.

Warrior, son, brother.

Brother, son, warrior—prince.

Chanting. *Come back.* His mother's voice was chanting. *Come home.* His mother's chant dragged through his ear, twisting with all the rest of them—that droning chorus who watched with dead, unseeing eyes. Phantom hands squeezed his throat with hundreds of fingers.

"Asaru."

He started as a hand snapped before him.

Rishé tapped two fingers together by her mouth like a beak, formed a fist to sign his name. The call pulled him back to the present, but as Asaru stared at the night sky, he felt disconnected from everything. The world was crimson at the edges. He was back *in* reality but not back *with* reality.

He remembered where he was when the swaying of the wagon tumbled him into Wren's side. A hesitant arm hovered over his waist, and he glanced up, nodding. The hand settled where Asaru's wound had healed yellow green around the puckered purple starburst. Still, he was forced, albeit gently, to keep silk tightly wrapped around it.

Absently thumbing his hidden wejat, Asaru recalled how the leader of his contingent had inked the tattoo. The day he became a warrior was a good memory, untainted.

As the intangible hands of his grief-stained daydreams settled around his throat, he couldn't help but dwell silently on how disappointed Alvarys would be in him.

One of the only people who'd cared for him was dead, never to return. People didn't come back from the dead. Once they were gone, they were gone.

The phantom of loss echoed through him.

His nape throbbed.

The night wagon trundled over the stony road to the chief's estate, brimming with passengers. Their eager energy washed over and past him as he sidled closer to his companions in their little corner at the back. The four of them wore cloaks with a verdant shimmer that warped the fabric like a lie, falling to sweep their feet. "Enchanted," Palenisa had said after Rishé purchased them, "by ward Aspects." It was similar, he assumed, to the spell cast over the snakeskins. It hid his halo and face but had no slits through which to free his slick wings. Better to be protected than free; better alive than dead too—but he wouldn't have that luxury much longer.

Against his better judgment, Asaru had let them join him. It was a foolish decision, but one his raw heart had no strength to counter. He held himself together as if by gutstring, because the moment he released his resolve, grief—with its wretched, pitying faces—would grab him and never let go.

Embers chased the clamor of music into the Sky Court. From

somewhere in the distance, a drum rang like a bell around his head. The scent of cloves and fragrant flowers blew in with spices on the wind as the wagon rolled into the gated estate. While the road had been dimly lit by fusion globes swaying from palm leaves, the manse was a brilliant bouquet of lights buzzing like shadowflies.

The courtyard was overfull with all manner of transport and the crowd trickling in. Open to common folk and nobility alike, the gala was awash with sounds and sights. The mass swarmed into the manse through the hulking mouth of a door. The frame was wrought into a serpent that wound along the edge toward the center, a pair of bloody garnets resting in the hollows of its titanium head.

Everywhere Asaru looked, there was life and revelry. He wanted to hate it. Why couldn't it let him mourn in peace?

His claws pressed dots into his palms as Asaru slid from the wagon. It was horribly easy for them to blend in with the crowd. Just four more faces among many, they disappeared through an entrance hidden in the panels of the walls. The gala faded into the background, and a little of the tense tangle in his chest loosened.

At best, Palenisa had a vague idea of the configuration of the manse, since most were built to the same specifications with few variations, and she led them through the skeleton of the estate by way of the servants' corridors. Passing a kitchen bustling with noisy cooks, they came upon a bolted door. It looked expensive, but then again, it all looked expensive.

"This it?" Asaru asked as Palenisa knelt to examine the keyhole.

"Should be." She stuck a claw in the lock and twisted it to pieces, with a crack like breaking tiny bones.

When the door clicked shut behind them, Asaru took in the showcase before him—a cylindrical room with a golden crocodile mosaic scalloped in the floor tiles, a crystal pendant dripping moonlight from above, and a much larger door between two monumental columns. Alcoves were cut from the walls, and in each rose-petal arch was a pedestal, atop which sat the chief's most prized possessions. Trinkets the wealthy few had little use for, save to hoard, content in the knowledge that they owned more than anyone else.

He trailed the margins of the room, walked a circle through his own mind. He found obsidian bowls overflowing with red diamonds, tablets of solid gold, carved hunks of minerals that writhed like flame. He touched the treasures, and some of them even touched him back.

Nothing remotely resembled what he was searching for, though. Just the artifacts of a rich man.

It's not here. Before he even realized what he was doing, his leg came down on a plinth and shattered it apart. Thunderstones spilled in a red wave. Fragments of obsidian fell around him as though the curse had somehow been sluiced away in chunks of hard, mineral flesh.

"Throwing a tantrum is extremely helpful," Palenisa said, snatching the back of his cloak and pulling him away. He shoved away from her and began pacing. Irritation fluttered on his tongue, curling down to his tremulous fingers. He pressed them to his forearms, grounding himself—he hated this new world and his place in it.

"It's a healthy expression of emotion," Rishé called with an amused lilt. Palenisa sneered back.

A growl rumbled in his chest. He needed them to shut up.

Approaching footsteps cut through his thoughts. On

instinct, three of them fled into the arches. They were decently well trained at that—*hiding.*

Pressed against the curved wall opposite a noseless bust, Asaru watched Rishé intercept the servants at the columned door. She lifted an arm to the frame and held it shut as best she could.

"What are you doing here?" A faceless voice spoke up.

"Wanted to see the relics. Fascinating stuff," she said, high-pitched and saccharine. "But one seems to be missing. You know, *that* one."

In the beat, Asaru blew crimson-tipped strands out of his eyes and tried to quell the nerves skittering down his useless limbs. Couldn't save his brother, couldn't find a damn beacon. He had no one left to disappoint, and still it slung across his branded shoulders like bars of lead.

"Unfortunately"—the dry response, in a different voice this time, was faintly amused—"Chief's planning a whole function for its display, if you can believe. Surprise, surprise."

"Hmm."

"He carries that fucking box around like a damn baby," the first voice said.

"Uh-huh."

"Been telling everyone—*everyone*—it's got a *gen-you-wine* eresh keyel artifact inside," added the second with a pronounced emphasis.

"Wild."

"I'll believe it when I see it," the first said with a snort. "You know what I mean?"

"He always has it on him?"

"Always," the disembodied pair agreed.

Good to know.

Once Rishé, after several banal minutes, talked the servants away, they waited until the footsteps faded before returning to the corridor with the door and the noise of the gala.

Leaving the mouth of the corridor, they came upon the ballroom.

Tucking a strand of hair behind his ear, Asaru glided into the mass, avoiding contact where he could. Guests moved in undulating waves of color, like fish flitting through the depths. Dotting the room was an array of carpets and comfortable chairs where others lounged in loose, languid states. Masked servants swanned the floor, trays of glasses held aloft. The air tasted of fruit wine and burnt wood, the latter particularly acrid.

Asaru covered his nose. It smelled like a taverna.

The extravagance reminded him of Aedyton, which was prone to similar indulgences, especially high in Aruu and deep in the underbelly of Deltia. Despite the Sea Gate, eresh keyel were a proud people. They liked to ornament themselves in gold and metal. He'd lost his own proud gold in Anseme—and it hurt too much to take Alvarys's. Though he should have.

Before burning the body. Saying the rites.

Focus.

He exhaled, disgusted by the audacity of the gala, and rose to the balls of his feet. To his surprise, the chief was right where the kharess had said he would be, on an altar to his own ego. Asaru didn't know why he was surprised—nothing she'd said had been a lie.

At the center of the room rose a dais, illuminating the man in the seat of honor. Among cushions of navy and gold, Idris Tengwe slouched on his garish imitation of a throne. His ebony face flushed violet as he grabbed a flute from a passing tray. Perched on his lap was a human in a skirt slit all the way up their tawny thigh, their arms painted with flowers and wrapped around his neck.

"What *is* that?" Rishé muttered from his right.

"A gaudy throne," Wren whispered at his back.

"An ego trip," Palenisa said caustically to his left.

A mark.

Asaru paced around the curve of the room with Rishé as the other two did the same on the other side. From all angles, Idris appeared guarded. Some bodyguards stood, others perched on the steps, all grasped steel-tipped spears.

When Asaru blinked, a different man sat there—gleaming crown and silver sword. Blinking again, Asaru lowered his gaze. And there it was.

Between the paws of that ridiculous throne, a small chest glowed like a lie. The green enchantment brightened and waned, then the crowd swarmed, erasing it from sight. Humming, he looked up at the glittering mesh that hung from the walls in heavy drapes of translucent cloth. He needed something fast, something quick—something *big.*

His shoulders ached—his entire *being* ached—as khetry blinked to life in his vision.

As if sensing his intentions, Rishé snatched at his sleeve with a hiss. "No, don't."

Asaru ignored her, pressing four fingers to the sides of his neck, and the web grew taut, heat gathering on his tongue. Rumbling up from his belly like a hearth. Spilling from his mouth to lick at the drapery. And he didn't stop at one. Orange and crimson and lightning-blue flames rushed along the walls in an angry mingling of color. He was furious with impatience.

Panic in the room started with a single scream, as most things concerning him did.

The commotion swirled the gala into a miasma of shock and fear—and maybe even a little excitement. Smoke receded as guests scattered in a fray. And shrugging away the withering amber scowl aimed at the side of his face, Asaru twirled with them.

His gaze locked onto Idris's back. Though guards surged around the chief, they fanned more to his front to block the fiery tongues from encroaching. From the rear, Asaru picked his way up the stairs to the top of the dais. *This is familiar.*

Over distressed heads, he found Palenisa, met her eyes, and dropped his own. Then, in a split second, he kicked the box through the crowd. In a smooth action, she caught it with a foot, dragged it beneath her cloak, and subtly bent to pick it up as though adjusting her sandals. She jutted her chin in a nod.

As the ballroom cleared, Asaru watched the others flee. He, on the other hand, was not done. A tool had not realized its use merely because a single cut had been made.

Come, his mother called. Asaru stepped behind the throne, hidden by a refraction spell layered atop his cloak.

Come, his mother called. Leaning over the spine, he ran a claw across the bloodstone ornaments.

Come, his mother called. Shadows played across his wavering form as he watched Idris's chest rise and fall with rapid breaths. The man curled up in his ostentatious seat, spitting guttural curses at his guards.

Darkness rushed into Asaru's vision. He snatched the chief by the neck. Looming unseen, save flashes when gouts of fire raged, he held Idris's life in his hands. Terrified blue eyes shot to the side before freezing. He had nothing to say to the garbled whimpering—this man was nothing to him. Less than nothing.

A clawed fist erupted through the front of Idris's gold-ringed throat.

This is very familiar.

Skin parted roughly. Bones cracked like the whip of a bolt through air. Like lightning on stone. Asaru pulled his hand back, leaving a gap in its place. Violet blood coated his hand and stained the dead man's fine, expensive clothing. Dripped down the false throne as though someone had drunkenly tipped paint across the scene with not a care in the world.

Red, gold, violet. He had them all.

"Your mind by Hukhetyel, your body by Chert Ouadjet, your aether by Khertote. Return home to dwell in the Red Web of Life once more."

Asaru melted back into the crowd, cloak and spell rendering him insignificant, with a warping of light the only sign he was ever there.

His mind floated away.

Warmth prickled his arms. When he came back to himself, he was outside. He hadn't realized where his feet were taking him. Hadn't realized that he still belonged to himself—not possessed by anything other than a dazed fog.

But he *was* possessed, wasn't he? Not by anything khetrical, no. Instead, by the will of another's words. Just as powerful.

A whistle swooped into his ear.

Still dazed, Asaru followed it and saw his companions—his reckless, foolish companions—astride a pair of mahogany palfreys they had unhitched from a night wagon. Wren called for him, reaching back as the horses began to speed away. Sprinting forward, he caught Wren's hand and used it to hoist himself onto the back of the palfrey, before catching the chest Palenisa tossed his way.

It was smaller than he'd thought, barely bigger than two fists side-by-side. Uglier too—excessively embellished with raised ringlets of obsidian and jade steel studs. The emerald hue of the enchantment bubbled around it in a thin sheen.

"Asaru," Rishé called from the other horse. She was not looking at his face, but at his hands. His red, gold—violet hands. "What did you *do*?"

He placed blood that was not his own atop the chest, where there would usually be a lock. The enchantment popped, then fizzled in a spark of olive stars, and the lid simply popped open.

Inside, there *was* a genuine eresh keyel artifact.

"It does not matter what I did," he said, lifting the beacon. "Because now we know where the Chronicler is."

He cracked open the geode, and the crystal innards lit him from below in cool incandescence. Under the wide eye of the night, a hologram flickered to life. A single destination floated, spinning in the tangle of light like an insect caught. There—the Nest. There—the Chronicler.

In the silence, the only sound was the panting of horses and his own breathing. Beasts, the three of them. Beasts.

PALENISA

As the rhythmic strides of the palfreys pounded into the desert, Palenisa looked back to try to find the glow of fire brightening the night. She saw only the distant sprawl of jungle as Ilon faded to a speck.

Spirits watch over me, she pleaded. *Zodiac watch over us all.*

Conflict warred within her as she prayed. For solace, strength, knowledge. For decades, the coterie had been her entire life. In place of a mother who was dead, a father she never knew, and maternal grandkin who wanted nothing to do with her—her fellow sisters had been like family. And the kharess had been—well, not a mother, but *something.* They had been solely dedicated to the kharess above all else, and that *something* had kept secrets from them.

What other secrets had Kharess Dust kept beyond the Aerie?

What other secrets, she wondered as she glanced sidelong at the second horse as it kept pace, *do we keep among ourselves?*

At the rapid, steady clomp of hooves on glass, Palenisa turned to the desert. Desert, badlands, either way—as far as the eye could see, in every direction, was a plain of glass. An inky mirror reflecting the Sky Court in its smooth, polished surface.

It wasn't just black glass—it was marrowstone.

"What . . . is all this?" Asaru's murmured question crested over the breeze as the horses pushed on.

"The Desert of Burnt Glass."

"Nothing burns here, though."

She didn't need to touch the scarred earth to hear its desperate wail. The sand had burned and boiled and fused—a grave for humans and her dolomite ancestors. All the same in death. Charred to glass by the murderess Oprekhet. That name was a foul omen—whether spoken or thought—so she pushed it out of her mind, pushed it far away.

Stricken, Palenisa leaned forward and flicked the reins, urging the horse faster.

"It did. A thousand years ago."

On the backs of the two swift palfreys, they rode hard from sunrise, before pink fingers of light touched the sky, to midday. And from afternoon to the early hours of morning, they rested, slept, watered themselves and the horses. For two more days, they traveled like this.

As dawn overtook the third evening, an incessant ache began to crawl throughout Palenisa's body. It just kept aching and *aching*. It blanketed her in a dense layer of fog. A trick to hide the rising pulse at the backs of her eyes, which she knew went before the clattering headache that would soon ring a drum inside her head.

Grunting, she sent up a prayer, asking the water spirit to bless the sky with rain. Or her with the sweet, sweet release of death.

Her hand tightened around the unassuming gray geode, the Nest swimming as it floated above the iridescent crystal. When she swept her fingers through the holographic castle, it faded like water. Her vision doubled, and she glowered at the beacon, trying to sew it back together.

There was vomit bubbling out of her mouth before she realized her stomach had upended itself. Tightening her knees and her grip on the reins, she jerked to a stop, leaped off, and threw back her hood to vomit a vile green-brown sludge onto the glass.

"We're stopping," Wren said, halting his and Asaru's palfrey beside her.

"I'm fine," she heaved. "I can keep going."

"Even wraiths need to rest, right?" Asaru said wryly as he dismounted, landing on elegant feet. He didn't wear any shoes—she hadn't fully noted before that he hadn't worn any shoes. Oh, she was definitely delirious. As well as thirsty and nauseated and dizzy—but she was fine. This was fine.

Palenisa emptied the rest of her stomach in a violent retch.

This was not fine.

Can guilt manifest physically? Push sickness through the body of the contrite? It certainly fucking felt so as she huddled in the scattered ruin they were camped in. Leaning between her knees, Palenisa cupped her forehead and groaned. The world needed to stop spinning. Just for a moment so she could gather herself.

"Here." Glancing through the ivory waterfall of her hair, she watched Rishé spread her coat across the ground. Patting it flat, Rishé held an unreadable expression. "Lie down, catch your breath until you're *actually* fine," she said emphatically, turning away before Palenisa could respond.

She didn't need sympathy from a nuisance. But as she burrowed her face in the fur, she grumbled. *Damn it.* The wool was soft.

Minutes passed, then hours. And when she looked up, the

Sky Court was shaded lavender with dusk, and the horizon had swallowed the sun. The desert—any desert—at night was death without a way to keep warm. Outside the mouth of their shelter, a trade wind tore through the air. It raised bumps along her nape. Chain mail rattled over her skirt as she shifted beneath the protective circle of her cape.

Flames crackled suddenly, and she glanced sidelong as Asaru coughed away the smoke of his spell. The fire spilled a golden pool of light in the middle of their loose ring of four.

Shivering, Palenisa shifted closer. She barely had it in her to muffle the endless cry of the earth, much less warm herself with the lingering dregs of sunlight.

She and Asaru were the only two still awake. The Norvatti pair slumbered beside each other, an arm's length of space between them.

Turning on her side, she unbound her braids, lifting one to her face. They were knit with frizz and would need to be remade soon. A bout of fatigue ran through her at the thought of spending hours braiding her hair. Perhaps it could do with a trim instead.

Chancing a glance at Asaru, she considered him.

He was perched on a piece of rubble, coat flowing down his back like a tail. Scarlet stained his choppily cut locks nearly to the root. It must have been the curse, for they mimicked the red streaks that she'd sometimes seen scoring black gems. Tension corded his neck as he swiveled his head owl-like over the flat, featureless span around them. If anything approached, it would be seen long before it could cross the great distance.

The silver slits of his eyes blinked slowly at her. His eyes glowed as though there were a moonlit reflector behind them.

For a flash, Palenisa could see it. Could see why the southern drakes, against the condemnation of the wraiths, had urged Rhenitha to raise the Sea Gate a thousand years earlier. *Eresh keyel are dangerous.* Oprekhet had set that precedent. She had ensured the continuation of the dolomites through their wraithian progeny—but it began with the betrayal of her sibling and her own kind.

Do you not see yourself in her, chimed the conjured twelve voices of the Zodiac in the waters of her mind. *Did you not betray your own leader's commands?*

But it wasn't the same. Palenisa hugged her squirming middle. That was a different kind of transgression. At the rustle of fabric, she dragged her gaze back up.

Asaru had drawn his knees up to set his chin on them. As far as she could see, he was speckled from talon to claw in black markings that glinted like the desert. The only difference between marrowstone and Black Diamond—the latter was unbreakable. He'd been quieter since the gala. Since he'd wiped his hands coated in violet on the sides of his legs. The shades blended well together, deep purple on black.

"Why did you make that promise to Wren?" Asaru turned his head to face her.

The reminder of her disobedience and dishonor slathered her in shame.

"There was a choice to make," she muttered sourly. "Apparently, I made the wrong one. And I keep making the wrong ones, no matter how much I pray, and I *do pray,* for guidance. I don't . . . I don't know what choices are right anymore. But I know Wren is one of them."

"Why?"

As she was mesmerized by the dance of the fire, her words

came from outside herself. "He's my path back to the coterie. Redemption. Absolution."

"You find absolution in another?"

"By *helping* another." She corrected him. "I was the Sister of Faith—I broke that faith. I need to prove to . . ." Trailing off, she frowned at the thought of the kharess and shook it away. "Anyway—" She rolled onto her back, hands clasped over her chest. "What about you?"

"What *about* me?" His voice thinned.

"Have you ever made a wrong choice?"

Asaru frowned at the fire. It burned low, and she had to peer through the dimness to see him as more than two glinting dots for eyes. He released a breath. "I don't get to make choices. I'm a warrior. I do what I'm told."

"We're warriors," she agreed. "We let brighter minds make the choices that matter for us."

Asaru raised a shoulder, clicking his claws together with a tap, tap. "They're not always brighter. Some of them, I wonder if they even have minds."

Palenisa's upper lip curled back. "You kind of have a horrible personality."

"I am in no position to entertain fools."

"Didn't say it was a bad thing. You've met me, after all. I am a bitch."

Humming, he arched a scarred brow. "And *you've* met *me*."

She snorted and he huffed, amused. After a moment, a somber look slid back onto his face as he grew quiet once more. In the lull, he tugged his coat closed as though shielding himself, in the same way she'd seen him fold his wings around himself. The colorless air that pressed him down bore a familiar tint. *Sorrow.*

"I'm sorry about your brother," Palenisa said to the ceiling, which she imagined was once sand. In her periphery, Asaru stilled. "I can only pray the Zodiac will guide him peacefully back into the aspects of life."

A pained look tainted with a hint of bitterness shuttered his eyes. But it fled quickly—like a flash of sunlight through trees—and he turned from her. The way he hunched made him look like a clenched fist atop which welled a single drop of crimson blood.

"I'm sure he appreciates it, wherever he is beyond the veil."

His breathing slowed, but Palenisa could tell he wasn't asleep.

The desert screamed with dry wind.

She couldn't sleep either. Her mind was a restless tumble. Rolling her shoulders, she stood. The ground swayed dizzily as she waited for her stomach to settle, panting.

A sharp exhale, inhale. And she found herself.

Donning her hood, she walked farther into the shelter through burned remains. The glass ruins, she realized mildly, had been a caravanserai. Once these collapsed walls may have formed a reception room, these columns a hypostyle hall, these arches the entrance to a long, elaborate processional passage.

Her suvaugrams felt strangely charged. She could almost sense the spirits—earth and sunlight. And ten others flocking nearby like birds along a string. *All twelve of them?*

That wasn't quite . . . right.

Before she knew it, she emerged in what she first assumed was a courtyard. Open to the sky, the ruins cut a clear expanse of black around a hulking monument at the center. Where in any other caravanserai would be a well was what looked like a suvaunoor.

Wait. Not a suvaunoor. Much too wide.

Moving closer, Palenisa found herself face-to-face with her

reflection in stone. The hooded face cloaked by shadows stared back with carved half-lidded eyes. The thing was a statue. A statue that so resembled a suvaunoor from afar that it had confused her eyes until she leaned close. Carved onto its cheeks were three distinct suvaugrams. Chaos with its diamond spiked ring; blood with its firework pulse framed by three dots and frilled by four curves at the bottom; and starlight. Her intrinsic opposite. A solid circle from which four cardinal lines spread between short, jagged arches.

The interruption in the landscape punched from surrounding glass like a crumbling fist. Only its upper torso was visible, and though it must have been white in the past, it had turned marrowstone black over time. It hadn't been transformed into glass like the rest of the desert. It was out of place and time.

Enthralled, Palenisa reached out to the starlight suvaugram.

A hand that shouldn't exist snatched her wrist, and a voice that was not the desperate earth crooned, "You're not an initiate."

From the shadows behind the statue stepped a figure made of night.

They bent her wrist to her chest and moved closer. With their other hand, they doffed their hood to reveal a Peskeli wraith with hair the color of ripened mulberries. They wore a cloak of midnight with innumerable strips of cloth that flowed loosely around their legs.

Palenisa recognized the checkered mask on their face—the Shadows of Anajera.

Only bad omens could come from a shadow. They blasphemed the animant resplendence of the Zodiac with their corruption of the spirits and their profane, ill-gotten powers.

She ripped herself free, sliding back from the cult member. Forming a claw over her chest, she pushed it out.

She reached for her staff, but it wasn't there. Neither were her daggers. She'd removed them earlier in her attempt at sleep. It was midnight and the earth was burnt. She cursed, for she was at every disadvantage.

"You do not follow the Shaded One," the shadow said, "but were drawn to its totem, nonetheless." They cocked their head. Wind roared, and she bristled as their cool gaze flickered over her. "There is something metamorphic inside you." Before her narrowed eyes, they glided around the totem, slipping into one shadow and out another like tar. "You are more than—"

"I'm not listening to your heresies."

Sighing, the shadow slouched against the totem. There was nothing casual about the sleek, sensual motion. It reminded her of a figure masked in bone, limber as a wolvencat.

"You may call me the Greywall, Azubike." Their sensuous voice rippled under her skin uncomfortably. It was too precise, too much like the hiss of silk. "And they are not heresies. But the truth behind the making of this world."

They melted into the darkness at their feet and reappeared closer to her. She took a step back, lowering into a crouch. Her eyes darted to the sides—but there was shadow everywhere.

"Can you not see its geometric pattern?" Heels clicked on glass. "Do you not want to know what germinates inside you?"

"All I *need* to know is the people you steal. Their blood you drink. It's an insult to Suvaun."

"There is more than Suvaun," Azubike said. They fell into the shadow of the totem, and their voice seemed to come from everywhere all at once. "Not twelve separate aspects, but one. That same wide tangle, active and living and changing."

What? They couldn't mean—no. *No.*

Far down, a very small part of her wondered—could there

be, at the heart of all things, more to the Zodiac than just twelve aspects? But this was a lie, a trick of the light. She would not falter in her faith. Blessed—she was an Aspect, blessed. She was cradled in the power of the Zodiac, and piety was a steel sword lining her heart.

Crimson clouded the edges of her vision. A net of anger misted her eyes.

A presence drew up behind Palenisa, and she whirled, swiping her arm wide. Her hand curled around a weak ball of sunlight in the center of her palm.

She'd struck first. But Azubike was faster.

They grabbed her wrist and blocked a punch. Twisting her arm behind her back, Azubike pulled her close. With a hand gloved in red as if dipped in a cistern of blood, they pinned her glowing hand against her chest. The sunlight fizzled out and she snarled, writhing like a feral beast.

"I see you, Ojujevé." They gripped her forehead, velvet voice caressing her ear. *Ojujevé?* She didn't understand, confusion seeping like malady into her bones. Focusing for a moment, she felt a slight slackening. A chance. "And you will see it too."

Palenisa clenched her teeth. "Screw you, heretic."

Taking advantage of the loose arm, she ducked. Wrenching the grasped hand from her chest, she shoved her palm against Azubike's chin.

They staggered with a grunt. But their vise grip still pinned her other arm. She slammed a foot down and threw an elbow out blindly. It connected as she twisted the limb painfully in its socket. Throwing an arm around Azubike's neck, she pressed their head against her hip in a serpent-tight lock. As her knee came up, an arm wrapped around her thigh. Palenisa found herself being tipped over backward.

Her spine connected hard with the glass, forcing the air from her body. Cracks bloomed out from her head. The beginnings of a headache throbbed in her skull. Her vision swam into two, into three. Azubike fell above her, blotting out the moon. Strips of their cloak brushed her sides. With satisfaction, she noted that their checkered mask sat askew.

Palenisa drew a hand to her collarbone. She collected small spheres of light on the tips of her fingers. It wouldn't be as strong. But as she swirled into the movement, she hoped it would hurt. The light was blue, but there was no time for surprise, even comprehension, because Azubike swiped their claws at her face. She aimed her smallest and index fingers upward only to encounter empty air as the shadow swayed away. Silent as death, they sank into the liquid dark her body formed on the glass.

The last thing she saw was violet flowing from their nose.

The last thing she heard was a quiet whisper. "You will understand—*everything.*"

Once the shadow disappeared, the world grew still. The Shaded One loomed. Its broken beckoning hands seemed to mock her.

Adrenaline faded. Pinpricks of blood welled where the shadow had gently, *oh so gently* held her.

Her mind ran circles around itself. Wide-eyed, she stared at the moon as it stared back unblinkingly. Sunlight was not blue. Sunlight was *not* blue. Sunlight was not *blue.*

The words of the shadow scratched through her with a stinging energy. To speak a thing made it so. To say a thing out loud brought it to life.

It was a trick of the light. It had to be.

But sunlight was not blue.

There was a simple explanation. At night, the world was

tinted blue because of the moon—that was why. Yes. The Sister of Faith had to keep hers beyond all others' doubt. Ada's legacy would not be tarnished by the rusted words of some cultist.

The sunlight was blue because it was dark, and she was bleeding. The tired mind concocted the most interesting mirages.

As Palenisa lay there panting, stars twinkled in the Sky Court. Constellations netted the night—Ada used to draw the suvaugrams there. Telling her that in other places, those images had names. She did not remember their names anymore. Nor what they looked like.

First to last, she mumbled the names of the Zodiac to herself instead. Then last to first, as if hidden somewhere in that list of twelve was an epiphany.

Her lids lowered, shut. Hopefully the totem wasn't too far from the fire. She was cold. So unbearably cold.

Shadows trembled around her, starlight in the glass.

ASARU

Chanting followed him to the waking world as he tugged free of the viscous arms of sleep. Ever present was the haunting choir of his mother—*warrior, brother, son.* Always chanting. Those dark red words at the center of which lived a lie.

How could he be a brother when Alvarys was ashes?

Groggily, Asaru blinked teary eyes as the afternoon sun glinted sharply off obsidian.

The mirrored surface of the badlands was a frozen pool that boiled his blood. Overwarm and lethargic, he examined himself—pitch wings, tail, mineralizing limbs, off-tempo pounding in his tender head. He wondered if the ruddy haze blanketing him was sun poisoning, a mild sickness born from too much exposure.

They tried to avoid the worst hours, when the bite of the sun gripped the hardest and obsidian burned the hottest. The sides of their palfreys heaved, and so too did their chests from exhaustion, even after cooling themselves with dabs of water. And at night, the winds howled, too cold to travel. So they rode, rested, repeated.

One of those rests found them in the ruin of a collapsed tower. The desert might once have been filled with such structures, rising from the ground in commanding pillars. Now they were hard pressed to find notable interruptions in the featureless span, much less depressions in the glass where water could collect from the infrequent rains.

A groan escaped Asaru as he fully woke. There was a cool cloth on his forehead. This wasn't the worst way he'd risen so far. Leagues more pleasant than the first time, the phantom pain of which throbbed through his stomach. Vertigo spun through him when he tried to rise, limbs aching. It felt like he was pushing through molasses to move under the smear of sun poisoning.

"Slow, slow." A gentle touch cupped the base of his spine, just above his tail. "You almost fell off the horse this morning. Are you *sure* the wound's healing well?"

Asaru allowed Wren to help him sit up. Strain at the back of his shoulder blade caused protests from the cicatrix. On the other, the wreath pulsed continuously the longer they remained connected. His skin prickled, and he released a disgruntled sigh, looking up as Wren formed a shadow over him in concern. A hand hovered at his side. Always so attentive. To the point that sometimes, he just didn't know what to do with all that care.

"Tired." Asaru unstuck the dry word. The wheels in his mind must not have been turning fully, for he found himself reaching out before he realized. He brushed the stars on Wren's cheek. It warmed beneath his palm as he tugged on the stray fringe that obscured a pair of dilated eyes.

Soft.

Pulling his arm quickly to his chest, Asaru put space between them. *Why did I do that?*

"Fine now. Awake. You don't need to worry about me," he

murmured, lightheaded. *Comforting a companion. Right, yes.*

Wren's gaze dropped to his hands before being averted. Probably to spare him further shame. Asaru locked his tail under his leg to keep the appendage in place and peeled the cool cloth from his head. Setting it on his lap, he took the chance to examine their shelter.

By the wreck of a door, Palenisa leaned on the frame as the beacon lit her chin. Her face was long, as though she'd spent the better part of the day crying. Since the night she had returned bleeding, she'd been in a bit of a daze, occasionally mumbling prayers under her breath.

Behind him, someone chewed rather loudly. From her seat on a broken mound, Rishé spared a glance over when he looked at her and the half-eaten nectar apple in her grasp, his ears pressed to the sides of his head. Her gaze flitted to them, and she snorted, reaching into her satchel to toss him another. The blushing fruit cracked like an egg when he split it apart, spilling yolky nectar into his mouth. It was gone in five bites, and he licked gold from his fingers to savor the rest.

Chest rumbling, Asaru pulled his knees to his chin and peered out. Late afternoon was bleeding into lavender-tinged evening. He looked at the consumptive path of the curse and shut his eyes. Each time he did, part of him feared it would be the last. Feared the many-colored darkness would drag him beyond the veil, and the last thing he would know was the distorted call of his mother's voice in his final moments. In a ghoulish way, at least he would have that one lingering memory of her unstained by the curse. Not like Alvarys. Not like those wide terrified eyes, long dead.

Black Diamond hung a perilous, heavy sword over him. As its skittering hands reached up, threatening to drag him beyond the veil, he ducked his head to keep the tears at bay. Asaru found himself starved for breath, lest he drown in the mire where scores of aetherless dead watched with empty skulls. Waiting. Hungering.

His duty had led to a white-shrouded vision of the future. If he did not force himself to move forward, move past it, the end would devour him whole.

Just like the king. Just like the chief. Just like his brother.

They made their final stop at midday.

According to the size of the floating icon, the Nest shouldn't be far. Though from the landscape, one would be hard pressed to tell if they were any closer to their destination than the day before.

Asaru dismounted after Wren, landed on slightly shaky feet, and led their palfrey beside the other mount. Palenisa took the reins from him and fed the panting horses the last of the stolen fodder. In a secret moment, he saw her trail a finger through their dusted manes as they drank rainwater from a recess in the glass when she thought no one else was watching.

The four of them formed a loose circle in the mouth of a malformed structure. Even in the shade, heat shimmered in the air, rippling like the crystal water of Aedyton's lagoon. The flat expanse was a mirror that cut the world in half. Where upper portions were lightened with a cloudless dayglow, everything else looked the same. Black to the left, right, and straight ahead, reflecting the burning eye above in its unnatural smoothness. This was no desert. This was, as Palenisa had said, a grave. Truly "bad" lands. Nothing still burned, but Asaru had a lingering sense of Oprekhet's murderous rage.

Stomach roiling, he slid a talon across the glass with a thin screech, gouging a thin, pale line. Her name was almost a curse in and of itself; it shuddered discomfort through him. He'd spent forty years killing worse things than men beyond the mountains of Oprekhet's islet. A thousand years later, his people were *still* beset with the consequences of her choices. The Sea Gate, the remnants. Centuries of warriors quelling the treacherous boil of her mutated experiments with the hope that one day the last of them would be struck down and then sunk into the Sea of Tranquility, to rest alongside the weapons that had initiated her betrayal.

The sound of the beacon clicking shut snapped Asaru back to the present.

A frisson crossed his skin like needles as he watched Palenisa roll the geode between restless fingers. She lay on her cape, which she had folded into a makeshift cushion.

Noticing him, she sat up and cleared her throat. "I've been wondering for a while, but what are you going to do if the Chronicler isn't there at the end of all this?"

"They will be." *They had to be.* He'd already failed once—*twice*, he reminded himself, thinking of Khensu. He dreaded imagining how much worse the island was.

"OK . . ." She leaned forward, clutching the hem of her skirt. "But *what if* they aren't?"

They will be. The desperate hope held tight in the hollow of Asaru's chest. He told himself it was the truth. Eresh keyel could not lie—omit facts, trim the details, yes. But lie to others, they could not.

To themselves, though?

Scowling, Asaru picked forcefully at the wraps on his calves. Static buzzed under the surface of his skin.

"Then we'll still find their archive," Rishé said, tapping a nail on the polished glass like the clinking of coins. Tapping, tapping, like a reminder. Like the endless drip of a spinning clock. "A castle like that doesn't just grow legs and disappear."

The reassurance calmed the sensitive thrum of energies in him ever so slightly. Numbness fled from his fingers as he drummed them along the back of his leg. Drawing in a breath, Asaru held it a moment before exhaling.

There would still be the records. In them, hopefully, some past knowledge of the curse. Its creator. Any answers that would make the pain worth it. More than a duty bestowed by the warden, he had to do this for Alvarys.

He shook loose the memory of an incinerated body made black as a burnt desert.

Still wearing a thoughtful frown, Palenisa hummed. She twisted her staff apart, setting the inner crystal tube outside to soak up the sun, while Rishé sent a nod his way before she went back to scribbling furiously in her journal. And that was that.

As they settled in for the rest of the day, Asaru noted a telling silence beside him.

Wren leaned against a ruined half wall, the remaining snakeskin draped over him like a blanket. They'd abandoned the shimmering green cloaks in Ilon to avoid detection—whether it had worked remained to be seen, but they were left with a few scant coverings for the chilly nights, including the thin snakeskin. Well worn, the gray scaled fabric had been torn, mended, ripped, and re-mended. While it had started as Sabine's sole creation, it had become something more, the mark of another's hand visible in crimson thread stitched not quite as neatly. A physical representation of both mother and child. Wren fiddled with the hem with an intense expression, looking nowhere in particular as his jaw worked.

Something jolted through the bond, and mismatched eyes darted to meet his. At first, Asaru wanted to look away, but as he stared, his will weakened. He felt warm—distinct from the heat of the desert. A hummingbird heartbeat hammered in his throat, and he swallowed it down.

His brand fluttered as though brushed by a feather, falling to settle in his gut.

"I'm sorry. Again." The apology spilled unbidden from Wren's mouth, and Asaru frowned. The memory of rain on a crumbled roof as a hand snatched another. He didn't want to linger on what had already been done. Something overwhelming swelled up his throat, and he made sure the others were well distracted before setting it free.

"What for this time?"

Wren ducked his head, rubbing his nape. Dropping the hem of his cloak, he placed a hand palm up on the inside of his crossed knee, like he was meditating. "Just, um, everything. What I did . . ." His voice was wet, and Asaru smelled salt, felt gathering tears but did not feel them fall. "If I hadn't caused a backlash—you might have gotten to your brother, um, before . . ."

Asaru shut his eyes, sighed, then opened them. The flutter soured to irritation, which he showed by clapping a hand over Wren's mouth. He sent the man a hard stare.

"I don't give a shit anymore. What's done is done. We're bound. Alvarys is dead."

Dark brows drew together in confusion, then drooped to sadness. The tips of freckled ears darkened, peeking through a sheaf of curls.

"All I can do now is learn what, if anything, can be done to stop the curse and help Aedyton." Pausing, Asaru breathed out from his nose and looked back up, tempering himself with resolve. "If the creator can be found."

Behind his palm, Wren sighed, a light puff of air that fanned the underside of Asaru's wrist and sent a curious shiver racing up his spine. "And, um, if you do?"

Lowering his hand, Asaru thought of the malevolent presence who had thrown a noose of dark stone around his halo. Tightening it more each day, each time he cast a spell, each time he tried to merely breathe.

His mind wandered to the murderess. Her well-deserved death at the hand of her missing sibling, Niekthe. In one fell swoop, it had quelled further bloodshed and cast Niekthe as a kinslayer. An unimaginable act. Reprehensible. Yet it had done good for the rest of the known world. A dark blot on history—a necessary transgression.

Asaru understood necessary transgressions as a sword understands the soft give of flesh beneath its blade.

The phantom of violet blood dripped from his fingers, clinging like a second skin as he recalled the way that hand had slid seamlessly through flesh and rent the chief's neck apart, leaving in its place a ragged hole. Revulsion coiled around Asaru's heart. He shoved aside the fleeting thought that he'd enjoyed it, though he didn't deny it.

"When I learn who created this curse, I will kill them," Asaru said simply. He felt more than saw Wren shudder. His eyes shot to the ceiling as he gritted his teeth. "*What* should I do if killing is so distasteful, then?" He continued, grabbing Wren's hand, almost forgetting the sparks that danced where they joined. "Wouldn't you forsake yourself, do anything, if it meant making amends?"

The tension that charged the air was its own answer.

A second later, guilt seeped into the bond and ran cool fingers along Asaru's back, tugging him closer to that strange, wriggling feeling he sensed within the bond as—*Wren*.

Sighing, Asaru lowered his forehead to where the man's neck met his shoulder. They pressed side by side in a line of warmth that seeped in where their shoulders touched. For a terrifying moment, he wanted to crawl inside Wren's bones, settle in the hollow between muscle and marrow, just to feel something other than numbness. He tangled their fingers together, thumbing scar-calloused knuckles. Wren's curls brushed the side of his face as water filled his eyes. He'd cried enough to last a thousand years.

The grief Asaru carried within, this hoary burden, hatched anew, spilled sorrow into a river overflowing. He wanted his brother back; he wanted to go home; he wanted to stay right there in the warmth of Wren's side—though he didn't know why. He wanted to bring back the dead—but he couldn't, no matter how much he wished it.

A breeze lightly skimmed the obsidian plain with a faint wail, as grief darkened to a black seed of vengeance.

Only forward.

RISHÉ

They arrived at the Nest just before midday, when the sun sat in the middle of the great blue expanse, splintering light in all directions across the desert. The last leg of the journey took them up an incline beside a sheer drop into the Lethean Sea.

High in the painted sky, two sailbirds took flight, and Rishé's heart threatened to go with them. She was, to put it mildly, thrilled. Exhilaration warmed her chest where her necklace fell. When she squeezed the scarlet stone, she felt closer to her mother than she had since Jarha's passing.

Dismounting, they walked the horses up the last bit of incline and came upon the castle.

The Nest rose stark white from melted earth, a low construction with a tower at the rear and a short set of stairs framed by waist-high palings that led to the castle proper. Amethysts formed the lidded eye of a stained-glass window set near the tower's peak. She thought it was surprisingly small, until she glanced over the precarious edge and saw a massive portion of the edifice carved into the cliff face like the quartz cavity of a geode. Below, the murky sea thrashed against glossy stone, and it reminded her of Ausre.

"Is that a fucking ward?" Palenisa's voice broke through Rishé's admiration.

As Palenisa dropped the reins, Rishé squinted. Alas, she had been right—there was a green bubble of a ward around the castle. When she tilted her head, light caught the barrier, and geometric patterns came into view. It bowed beneath Rishé's palm when she pressed inward, but it did not give.

"Whose blood do we need?" Asaru peered through the green net. Unlike khetry, Aspect enchantments were visible to all.

Rishé frowned at his bloodless hands, then at the Nest. One life for a chest—how many for a castle? She hadn't seen him kill before, but did he even care?

Palenisa stepped forward. "Hopefully no one's."

Flicking the blade from her scythe, she traced the ward with overly suspicious eyes. She reached out. Rather than stopping at the semisolid spiritual energy as Rishé's had, her hand slipped in—past—*through* the ward. A rectangle of the green peeled upward before her. Wide blue eyes met amber as Palenisa jerked her hand away. But the slit in the ward did not mend and instead remained open as though it were a drape pinned in place. The edges were flecked with white like striated stone.

Rishé squinted at the suvaugrams on the Aspect's hands—only earth and sunlight. Nothing else. *Interesting.*

"Is that, um, supposed to—" Wren was interrupted by Palenisa's panicked screech of denial.

"I don't want to talk about it!" She flicked her scythe into a staff, grabbed the reins, and stalked through the gap before anyone could respond.

The three of them glanced at each other and followed.

Behind them the ward sewed itself closed, resealing the viridian dome. It felt no different inside from outside, but the sky was tinted a sickly green due to the faint filter.

Rishé picked her way up the steps and reached the grand doors first. More than thrice as tall as she was, they were made from indigo stones with an eye down the center. The gap split it as if the iris had two pupils. She ran a palm across the bottom, and her hand came back covered in dust. Well, that wasn't encouraging. If the Chronicler wasn't there, she hoped their records remained untouched. She looked back to the others before pushing open one of the doors.

Despite its size, it slid open effortlessly, like a prow parting water. And once it shut with a resounding thud, they were plunged into a sudden and complete stillness. Noise and movement vanished as if it had never existed. A distinct nothing hummed in her ears.

At first, upon entering the abode of the Chronicler, Rishé was certain they were alone.

Dust floated in the air. Motes flitted away as they spread out along the sides of a blue pool set in the middle of the glass-ceilinged atrium. The castle spread out before them in an unbroken hall with a set of winding stairs at the end, which she assumed led up to the tower. On either side were doors to rooms she imagined made the Nest look like a many-legged insect from above.

Asaru called out as though he were scared to break the woven silence that blanketed the halls.

"So," Palenisa said, "is the Chronicler here?"

Asaru brushed his keloid-wreathed halo stones, frowning more deeply than usual.

"They have to be." His reply was curt. Beneath his

determination, Rishé saw the glimmer of desperation that he seemed to cling to, appearing to think it better than being left with nothing.

She admired his resolve and its resemblance to her own staunch hopes.

A three-ringed mosaic stared back from the bottom of the pool. Awe sparkling in her eyes, Rishé crouched, heels flat to the floor as she peered into the water. A carmine fish darted across the turquoise stone, then two others. They looked well fed. She frowned, no longer as certain that they *were* alone.

Glancing around with new eyes, she expected to see gray cobwebs in the ceiling pendants, rust crusting the inner edges of the pool, or maybe even grime grouting the marble tiles. It was all too neat, as if it had been frozen in time the day the Chronicler left.

"Someone was here recently," she whispered. "Or is here still."

Asaru's calling ceased, and a rustling cracked the yolk of silence. Was it the shiver of leaves? The whisk of silk curtains? The click of stone on wood?

Slowly, Rishé stood. Ducking past a curtain, she entered a study and froze.

"Sagan?" she cried incredulously.

An adderowl turned to her, strands of purple hair peeking from an embroidered suman. The figure lowered a stone to the desk in front of them, atop reams of paper—desert glass. The jewel of the Palomers, the queen's family.

Damn it, Sagan. What have you been doing?

He pulled the mask back to hang from his neck, mismatched eyes coming into view. The left a vibrant purple and the right a deep brown. Unpigmented patches dotted his skin like islands on a light olive sea, the largest halving his face, and a cut split one of his brows. He cocked his head, and his lips broke into a slick little smile.

"Rishé."

She made to move forward, but the curtain was flung wide behind her. *Oh no.*

"You!" Palenisa and Asaru seethed in tandem, acrimony lacing their tones. *Oh no.*

Before Sagan could grab his crook, Palenisa surged forward and launched a fist drenched in sunlight directly into his stomach. Sagan slammed against a window. Bleached bone cracked on glass. The air in him came out in a wheeze as Asaru's foot knocked his head into the bookshelf at his side. His body slackened, dropping to the ground. The crook came tumbling after him. *Oh fucking no.*

The four of them stared. The moment held as they kept staring. Until some modicum of sense returned.

"Why would you *do* that?" Wren asked in a defeated tone. He tugged at his hair, leaking frustration and anxiety. So much anxiety. "Are you *trying* to kill him?"

The indignant two looked at each other: Asaru had a foot on Sagan's nape, while Palenisa was half finished binding his arms with liquid metal from her mail skirt. Then they looked at Wren like he was a fool.

"Yes," they answered together.

Rubbing a hand over her face, Rishé groaned. It wasn't that hard to think ahead a little, maybe sit for a cup of tea and calm down while they were at it. But no—of course not.

"Please don't kill him," she signed as she spoke, deliberately and emphatically in two languages so perhaps they might stop trying to wring the life from Sagan.

"This is the lulaik who chained us in the tunnels," Palenisa retorted, tugging his head up. Blood streamed from his surely broken nose. *Wonderful.*

"Good point," Wren said in a tone that indicated that was *not* a good point. Not even on the same continent as a good point. "How about we do anything but *that,* specifically! Please, I mean."

Rolling her eyes, Palenisa twisted her fist, and the metal tightened on Sagan's wrists. "He smells as much like a snake as he acted down there. Damn stone cuffs."

"For what other reason could he possibly be here than a trick?" Asaru said, rolling Sagan onto his back and wrapping his tail around the man's neck. "A trick doesn't have to be a lie." His ears flicked. He looked wired, impatient—volatile. They'd found the Nest empty—Rishé could only imagine how he felt having his worst fear, the one he never once admitted to them, yet she had always seen in his eyes, confirmed.

"We don't know that." Wren sighed.

"We know that he is here and the Chronicler is not."

Rishé lifted a hand, snapped, and drew three pairs of eyes to her. Just like hounds, the lot of them. She was pleased to have them finally listening, and the corner of her lips twitched upward. There must be something about this castle that empowered her. She gestured to the unconscious captive and deadpanned, "Here's a neat idea. Why don't we interrogate him first?"

After a lull, they relented, awkwardly dragging Sagan to a brocade chair. Fist clenched tight to the point of paling, Palenisa wound the metal tighter until his wrists bruised. The sneer never left her face, elegant features pinching in anger. While Wren dithered nervously at the desk, tapping a tuneless pattern onto the wood, Rishé sat before Sagan.

Maroon blood flecked his nose. The broken bone was

purpling fast, and fatigue dusted his lower lids. Whatever he'd been doing this past year, it hadn't been easy.

Brushing braids behind her ear, Rishé crossed her legs, then fanned back her suman, nodding at Asaru.

Asaru clambered onto the chair and brought a fist down on the man's skull with a swift, painful-sounding knock.

With a gasp like the drowned coming up for air, Sagan caught his breath. Bloody saliva dripped from his mouth, and he spat out a cracked fang, licking his lower lip, which was scarred similarly to hers.

"Sati."

"Hello to you too," Sagan said, tipping his head to her.

In her periphery, Palenisa stepped forward. Rishé pressed on and switched to the Peskelos dialect of Nomyrs—*his* birth tongue, which she knew less of than she'd have liked. Most of what she did know had been taught by him during his previous stints at the guild; the rest came from her mother, to quell the curious nature of her child's mind. Over languages, they'd bonded, and over gems too. They were crows like that, collecting tongues and stones.

"I'm disappointed," she said in Nomyrs, "that we had to meet again like this."

"Had to be done." He rolled a shoulder. Then in Akiki he coyly added: "My sincerest apologies it had to happen in such a barbaric manner."

"The barbarian here is you!" Palenisa interjected, snarling.

A small braid fell over his shoulder, and Sagan huffed lightly, as if he weren't being forced to bend by angry metal strings. His amusement seemed to stoke the flames of fury in her companions. Sighing for patience, Rishé shut her eyes. Did she need to pray to the spirits of the gods or whatever natural powers Wren believed in for this to go smoothly?

"Please ignore my friends' anger." She pushed on. "They can be a bit temperamental."

"I did only as the Chronicler wanted. Well, not exactly. But the sketch of it."

"What about what Brunoth wants? He misses your letters, you know."

Asaru wrenched Sagan back by the tail of his small braid, until the line of his neck formed a curve. He stared directly down, and Sagan stared back, lips quirking, then going coolly flat.

"Straight answers. Now."

"All I have are queer answers. Sorry."

"Please," Rishé sighed, pinching the bridge of her nose.

"I will murder you." Their noses were inches apart, Asaru's scowl meeting Sagan's grin.

"How's the curse?"

Asaru's blackened hand touched his unpigmented cheek. Sword-sharp, his claws trailed the jut of Sagan's jaw to his neck and pressed into the tender flesh, red dots welling. His hand was a scarred choke collar, like slavering jaws around the neck of a rabbit.

"Nibon aebran'tios-kinir." *Stop angering him.*

Sagan worked his lower lip. His purple and brown eyes danced between her and Asaru, giving little away even for her to read. History had shown that of the two of them, she caved first, quicker, easier. A splash came from the atrium as well-fed fish leaped in the pool.

"Why isn't the Chronicler here?" Asaru asked. "What do they know of the curse? What do *you* know of the curse?"

"Neck," Wren said.

As if suddenly realizing his own strength, Asaru released his grip, and Sagan inhaled.

"The Chronicler"—he coughed—"was never here."

Palms on her knees, Rishé sat up. If her ears could perk, they would have.

"There is a spell on the Nest, programmed to record. To archive. Not just your people—but *every* observable event in the known world."

Shock rattled her as Sagan's voice wafted into the air, low and silken like the shear of beryl into thin blue-green wafers.

"Every event, including when black vials began turning up in Saite. Contaminating the river, then the people, then the embassy. And your brother—"

"Sagan."

"Scavite," he apologized, sounding not the least bit like he meant it. "When the Chronicler learned what happened in Saite, they realized it was a curse. One with the potential to decimate Aedyton. So they traveled the world, perfecting a ritual."

"To break the curse?" Asaru released the violet-dyed braid.

"No." Sagan shook his head as best he could. "Curses *are* unbreakable. All the ritual can do is nullify the curse. Black Diamond will never be truly eradicated from this world."

There was a painful finality to that truth. Black Diamond was as persistent as the stars in the Sky Court. The death of a brother. The death of a mother.

The blue crescent of his pendant fell from Wren's teeth. A familiar curiosity blazed in his eyes, taking Rishé back to their days at the guild. They were ten years younger, and Rishé saw, for a moment, the friend that was once like a brother.

"This . . . um, ritual, is it a spell?" Hands planted on the desk, he swayed forward, practically drenched in intrigue. "Does it need an additive? What kind, how much?"

Sagan shuffled side to side. The adderowl mask shifted to rest in the furred cradle of his hood, hung from the cord around his neck, pressing the skin above and below it.

"Diamondglass," he said. "In addition to an ancient primer—"

At that, Wren shuddered, his shoulders jumping.

"One of the things I was sent here to find was a store of diamondglass large enough to cast the ritual over every person on the island."

"You want to rob Anticarta?" Palenisa scoffed. "More than a bastard, you're brainless, aren't you?"

Rishé tapped her lip, part of her inclined to agree. The land of Neverdawn fiercely guarded diamondglass from the rest of the known world. Sharp enough to sever both steel and bone in a single slash, it was one of the strongest minerals in existence—second only to black diamond. As far as she had read, diamondglass didn't even occur anywhere outside the north pole.

"There are other places besides Anticarta where it can be found."

"Oh, do please fucking enlighten me."

"Well, *I* don't know." Sagan raised a brow. "That's why I've come to search the Great Memories below."

The Great Memories.

The records of the known world's true history were right beneath them. Rishé cupped the lower half of her face to hide a grin. Even her toes trilled with excitement, curling and uncurling in her boots.

There was a pause, and Asaru pulled something from his tunic. Her eyes narrowed, then widened as the room was cast in rainbows, light from the window glinting through the crystalline diamondglass. This tiny shard was as bright as a fusion globe, a star coalesced.

"Like this?"

"Oh, perfect." Sagan reached out and plucked it from Asaru's hand. *When did he escape the bonds?* Rishé's head whipped to Palenisa's startled mask of annoyance as she glared at her flexed hand like it betrayed her.

Sagan held the shard up to his khetry eye. The iris ballooned in the stone. "Yes, just like this." As he examined the stone, he waved lazily toward Wren. "And the Chronicler needs you too."

Rishé had anticipated the twin cries of protest, but not the voice that cut through them.

"Whatever it is, I'll do it," Wren said adamantly.

She met his eyes. They shone with purpose and promise.

Blinking, she turned back to Sagan. *"We need time to think,"* she signed, tapping a finger to her temple.

"As you like." Sagan shrugged, then slinked to his feet like a wolvencat stretching its languid, sinewy body. He wore a crimson suman, sleeveless, hem embroidered with scenes of a hunt in thread the color of moonlight. "And when you're done *thinking,* there are rooms in the tower, if you wish to stay the night." He stopped at the door. "I do hope you enjoy the Nest. You've been traveling *such* a long time."

He definitely wasn't this irritating a decade ago.

They waited for his footfalls to fade.

"We aren't thinking of going along with this." Palenisa threw an indignant hand out. "You aren't actually going to do this. It's obviously a trick!"

Turning, Wren crossed his arms. Hidden in the shadow of his hood, he spoke. "I am, and I will. I . . . have to."

Conflict carved Palenisa's face when she glanced from Rishé to Asaru, as if she would find some solution to the conundrum that was Wren du Ingoscu. There was no answer to that conundrum—he burrowed his way into the mind and settled in the heart, no matter how much one tried to calcify it.

"A trick perhaps, but nothing he said was a lie," Asaru muttered, clasping his hands over his mouth. "Unfortunately."

"Sagan is cryptic, evasive, and chronically unreliable," Rishé replied, "but he's not a liar."

"We're scrambling in the dark. Have been for nearly two moons," Wren added, turning on a heel. "He just offered us a light. It wouldn't hurt to take it." Uncharacteristic steel silvered his gaze as it alighted on Rishé. His words sounded like an apology. "This could fix everything."

Whether it had happened the year he left the guild, or during their moon's long journey—Wren had changed. Thinking on the friendship they used to share stripped her to a husk of sentimentality. But the bitterness—she clutched her tunic over her heart as she realized there *was* no lingering bitterness. There was only a raw nerve, perhaps ready to heal over.

An opportunity for something different. Something new.

Her absent hand found her necklace and thumbed the whorls, seeking its false warmth. "I agree, we should do it."

Agreement crept in like a snail. First Asaru, jutting his chin sharply. Then Palenisa, though it clearly seemed to pain her, and she mumbled inane prayers under her breath afterward.

As the others trailed from the study, Rishé remained seated, meditative. Gazing in a half daze through the window above the gilded chair, she twirled the pendant between her fingers and thought of the Great Memories. It was within reach—so close she could almost taste it. She had joined them for the Chronicler's knowledge. To learn what her mother must have known and to keep her memory alive in the world just one day, year, *decade* longer.

PALENISA

Palenisa stood before a mirror with a clean line wiped through its dusty surface, gazing at the cloud of hair she was binding with the tie Wren had sewn from her skirt. She'd ripped the stitches to better handle the mass of freed curls that were flowing around her head. As she wound it once, twice, her eyes lowered, then widened.

The damned shadow had scarred her.

On her temple lay a nicely healing line—but on her neck were the imprints of *one, two, three, four* fingers. Shock ran through her and froze her feet to the floor, chasing the warmth from the room like desert winds. The shadow's blasphemous caress on her cheek felt like vermin wriggling under umber skin, gooseflesh prickling her nape.

Suddenly it was night, suddenly the gauzy voice of Azubike whispered falsehoods into her ear. Tricks. Like the play of light across the crumbling cheek of a totem.

Sunlight was not blue.

And she was perfectly fine.

Shuddering, Palenisa turned from her marred reflection. She brushed her hairline and shut her eyes with a shaky sigh that trembled like mist rolling across marrowstone. The backless veilari top she wore was tied at the neck and cinched with a thin leather corset at her middle, and the platinum links of her chain skirt rattled beneath the wrapper that swayed over her hips.

Setting a resolute mask on her face, she donned her hood, cloaking herself in darkness to hide the mark. Cracks revealed doubts that, if she did not quash them with prayer, would bloom into horrid beasts of heresy.

Her stomach turned at the thought that somewhere in the shadows lingered those who believed Suvaun was entangled with khetry like some . . . some wide net of mired energies. But she knew what she knew, and she *knew* the way the world worked. Both powers had distinct foundations that in no way overlapped. While blood or spirit Aspects might be able to heal, same as lulaik and eresh keyel, there was nothing similar about the core mechanisms of the act. This was how she knew the Greywall's words had been lies. Only lies. An attempt to shake her from the path that led out of the cloak of shame and to honor.

Thinking it was one thing, to speak it made it so. This Palenisa repeated to herself, over and over and over. Until she had confirmed that her faith was steadfast.

Green shone behind her lids. Eyes fluttering open, she was met with the bloom of the ward outside the window. Geometric patterns swam on the surface of an emerald haze, casting the Nest in a sickly hue. That fucking ward. The sight unsettled her no matter how hard she'd tried to rationalize its presence. The disconnect warred with the stability she had just held. Against her better judgment, it also spurred questions.

Had the kharess known? She had to.

What other secrets had she kept? More than Palenisa realized.

Why, why, why? For that, she had no illusion of an answer.

An Aspect's ward was concealing and protecting the castle of an eresh keyel. *That was a fucking absurd combination.* After the extinction of the dolomites, relations between the wraiths and eresh keyel were strained, considering the latter had been sequestered behind the Sea Gate in perpetuity for the crimes of one among them. But they had been close before human envy plunged the continent into war. Once too, her people had mated with humans. After all, wraiths were the mutant fruit of dolomite coupling.

Palenisa was no scholar, but it seemed history had an odd way of shading itself, much like viridian light, depending on the angle at which it was seen. A wraith, a lulaik, a human, and one eresh keyel warrior. Missing two, maybe three peoples, perhaps—but they were history made flesh. They played out the silhouettes of a story that had occurred a millennium earlier.

Palenisa wasn't quite sure she liked it.

Staff in hand, she descended the tower steps. A restless ball of sunlight, she wandered the halls.

She was more energized than she had been in weeks, but nausea still rolled lightly through her as she picked her way through the castle. From the tower, the castle spread out in a single line, rooms spidering on either side. At intervals along the walls were reliefs of wide unblinking eyes. Each had minute differences, she noted, a mark curving from the bottom or a red jewel in the center of an amethyst pupil. The stones were strangely slick beneath her fingers, and she wondered whether she might be able to press through them, as she had with the ward.

No, you didn't, she told herself.

Then it came to her. That smell.

Not khetry, *thank the spirits*—something sweeter. Fragrant like spring air before the superbloom.

Following it through a silk-framed doorway, Palenisa entered a kitchen and found Wren.

Well, the top of his head. He was crouched behind a table, heels pressed to the floor as he peered into the orange hearth. His black curls were tied in a tight tail that he brushed back with one hand, reaching the other inside the squat oven's brick mouth.

Gliding over to the table, she watched a moment as he tended the charcoal. Sparks trailed his fingers like stars chasing the night. He wore stars on his face and neck and body—even his hands, inked as richly as they were.

"Good morning."

"Morning." She planted her elbows on the table, her chin on her palm, and twirled one of her wispy white coils. The snapping of the fire in the oven quieted when he shut the door, the heat in the room dissipating. In the lull, she heard his breathing, hers, and the ripple of water from the atrium.

"I've, um, I've been wondering . . ." Wren trailed off. His hands fell to his thighs, and he rolled his shoulders. "Of all people, why grant me a promise?"

Palenisa flung her mind back to that starlit night and the hazel eyes watching her from across a dancing fire. A shadow stuck its hand down her throat and pulled up uncomfortable memories. Of every emotion, every tear, the aftertaste of palm wine on her tongue and a dagger twisting her apart. Her neck was lighter without her emblem. Though not as light as it had been the night after and the first weeks following her excommunication.

"I need to regain my title as Sister of Faith," she said simply.

"Why?" His question was a rustle of air, an echo of an echo she'd heard before.

Because she may have been an ill-fitting piece in the circle of twelve, but it was the only place she'd felt the least bit like a person since nearly losing her life.

"Because someone I loved saved my life. She made me pious." She met Wren's curious glance with a sad smile. "And I have to honor that."

Tipping his head against the legs of the table, he returned her morose expression. His hand rose to his chest and clutched his collar, as if his heart would fly free without grounding it.

"I think I understand." He nodded. "It's the same with the guild."

Scoffing, Palenisa swayed back on her heels and rolled her eyes. "You don't need some shitty feather robe—you *are* a healer," she declared. "A helper."

"You know too well that's not really true. Look where my help has gotten us. Everyone would be better off without me breathing misfortune everywhere." He huffed mirthlessly and sat back. "I'm just confused why *you*, in particular, stuck it out so long. In case you haven't noticed, I'm a mess."

She sniffed, lifting her nose to the air. "I keep my promises. What is a person without integrity? Honor?"

Wren's mismatched eyes softened, gold turning to nectar and brown to chocolate, and he brought his knees to his chin. He tipped a cheek to rest on one of them and sent her a secret little smile. The bags beneath his lower lids were deep and purple, and though it seemed sleeping in an actual bed hadn't done him much good, the air around him felt airy as dawn. "Glad you kept it," he said quietly. "Even if I've been a monumental mess. Sorry you couldn't have found a better charge."

With no braids left to hide behind, Palenisa covered her mouth at a sudden bubble of incredulous laughter. "Makes two of us—messes, that is."

Wren ducked his head between his knees and laughed. It was not a particularly happy sound—then again, neither was hers. They had precious little to *be* happy about, other than their being alive. And there was a grim sort of humor to sharing one's self-made mire with another.

As they giggled morbidly, she tried to remember if there had been any laughter within the coterie. Or was it just duty and the will of the kharess?

And why did she not feel hollow anymore?

Granted, her neck felt exposed without the emblem, and she yearned just as much for her title. Still, a hearth flared in her belly. Her face warmed, her ears twitched, her smile was no longer as sad, and—"Do you smell burning?"

Wren started, eyes constricting. "Shit!"

Laughter bent her in half as he scrambled to pull a large round loaf from the oven. She doubled over when he burned himself, dropped it, and had to use his shirt to pick it up again. Palenisa wiped the gloss of amusement from the corners of her eyes as Wren set the wooden board on the table. On it sat a . . . thing. It looked like a braided wreath decorated with small protrusions resembling what she thought to be a leaf—or maybe a flower, she wasn't sure.

"What was it supposed to be?" She chuckled, rapping a knuckle atop the blackened mess. It sounded like heels on marrowstone.

Dragging a hand down his face, Wren groaned. "A Norvatti food, panmi."

"You failed." She pointed, wearing a most helpful shit-eating grin.

"Thank you *so much*."

Silently, she rounded the table and casually knocked their

shoulders together, glancing sidelong when he jerked in surprise. Skittish as a wolvencat, with his wide wet eyes and anxious hands. Palenisa grinned and poked at his failed efforts.

"So, how are we going to fix this?"

He stared at her in shock. Then at the burned rock of panmi.

"Wait, really?"

She sent him a flat look. "No." She flicked his temple, ignoring his feline hiss as she rested her arms on the table and raised a brow. "You want to fix things? Start with this and tell me how I can help."

Toying with his fingers, Wren shyly looked back at the burned rock of panmi. He paused, throat bobbing as if working through the words as they formed.

"Um, right, then. Shall we?"

Palenisa stretched her hands out before her, interlacing her fingers. "We shall."

Braiding dough into a circle didn't fill the ache in her chest. Nor did cutting petals from pastry absolve the dishonor that still stained her. But she hoped the Zodiac were pleased with her choice. That it had been a good one. They called to her—*all* the spirits—when she prayed these days. *Yes,* they said, a dozen imagined voices sounding a chorus in her ears, *you are good, you are right, and once you see this to the end, your honor will be as whole as your faith again.*

RISHÉ

The Great Memories felt like an endless gift to Rishé as she sauntered through the aisles, piling her arms high with bismuth slates. It was quite possibly the grandest library in the world. A chronicle of the past, the era before Unification—everything that had ever happened, a thousand thousand years ago. A record of the present, the era after Unification—everything that was still happening, expanding constantly as time dripped.

The archive in the belly of the Nest was filled with a million gray tablets covered top to bottom and back to front with tightly packed inscriptions. At first, the symbols had appeared as strange glyphs, but the longer she looked, angling them in the unnatural light, which seemed to have no source, the more they glimmered to intelligibility. Someone from Anticarta might see Vulgar Antic where someone from Fa Djain would see Pshan.

It was among the most wonderful things Rishé had seen in her life. Easily top three, if not the first.

At the bottom of a winding set of stairs, the Great Memories radiated outward like a wheel into thirteen aisles of shelves that shot to the high ceiling. Down one aisle, Rishé walked with awe-stricken eyes and arms laden with slates, her head tilted back to gaze at the glittering vaulted columns.

Half spheres scooped the aisles in place of traditional shelves. The rim of the basins glowed lightning blue with slates set into the circles like frames in a hive. They bubbled lengthwise along the span of a marbled wall. And everything was lit in white and silver and drenched in crystal-clear hues.

Rishé imagined it was easy to get lost wandering.

Pausing, she juggled the slates she carried into the crook of one arm to pull another from the shelf and skimmed it. On it was mention of a strange stone with unusual properties—*perfect.*

The number of bismuth tablets in Rishé's arms grew as she wound through pale serpentiform halls, as if it had become second nature.

Then she took a step, and her foot found open air.

A scream caught in her throat as someone yanked her back by three of her belts. She fell into the arms of Sagan with a half-born cry on her tongue. More importantly, the slates had almost toppled out of her arms. What a horrible thought: bismuth cracking, shattering to pieces on the pristine floors.

"Watch your step," Sagan said coyly, setting her back on her feet and tucking a braid behind her ear. He raised a thick, split brow when she squirmed from his grasp. "There's a hole."

"Bastard," she grumbled, reshuffling the slates so she could press the side of a palm to her forehead.

Humming, Sagan swanned around her. He hadn't put his mask back on, so she saw his cool scrutiny. Wisps of dyed hair flew free around his face. Brown had crept in at the roots, marking the time he hadn't been back to the guild. She remembered once helping him paint it—that time they'd done him up in bright red. With the patches on his skin, it had made him look northern, Antorcan.

She rolled her eyes and moved carefully to the edge where she'd nearly fallen.

It was a massive borehole. More accurately, *a chasm*. Deeper than the ceiling above was high, and so dark that she couldn't even see the bottom—if there was one. It was as if a giant fist had punched its way through the floor. And there was not even a barrier around the margin to denote the danger, just a sudden sharp drop into nothingness. Her inquisitive eyes roved over walls made of unblemished stone. Well, not entirely. Gouged deep into the circumference of the well were unfathomably long scratches, harsh and jagged. There was a desperate quality to them, several forming a lattice of black that wept into the unseen abyss.

She squinted, unsure, but it looked almost like the cursed bile that seeped from Asaru's mouth during his worst spells.

The Chronicler was never here. She didn't believe that for a second.

"What is this, Sagan?"

Freeing a hand from her burden, Rishé gestured to the bleeding lines and turned to meet the glowing sockets of an adderowl. The violet of Sagan's eyes trailed in an afterimage of light as he moved, bobbing his head over the side of the chasm like a drinking bird.

"I don't know." Mask back on, his voice doubled, a high tone melding with his velvet timbre. Without looking into his eyes, she couldn't tell if his words were genuine or more distortions of a somewhat truth. As Asaru had told them, he didn't lie. But it felt like the last year had taught Sagan strange new ways of twisting speech into a net that concealed his intentions.

"Is it your mission in life to be infuriating? Is that what you learned while you were away?" she asked, taking a step from the chasm. Then another. Sagan followed. Until they were both in the arched mouth of an aisle, more secure in their footing.

"Perhaps."

Yes, it is, she heard.

Sighing, Rishé readjusted her stack of tablets, feeling their words graze lightly over the skin of her arms. "You know Asaru and Palenisa are furious with you."

Sagan smoothed a finger over the cracks in the skull and said, "I know perfectly well what your friends think of me. Can still feel it in my nose."

"You used a *psychometry* spell on them," she pressed, rising to her toes until their eyes were level. "Something tells me that isn't exactly what the Chronicler asked you to do. You went too far."

He swayed forward so suddenly that she stumbled, her back connecting with a shelf. The coolness of the stone bled through her tunic and raised the hair on her arms. Heat fanned out from the mask's twin-fanged jaw, as the shadows that hid Sagan's neck darkened. "But are *you* going far enough?" His gaze fell to her overfull hands, then rose to her necklace. "Those don't look like they'll help us find any diamondglass."

Rishé's lips twitched to a frown, and she lifted the slates, tucking them closer to her chest as she leaned aside.

"I wonder," Sagan said as he spun on a slippery foot. His suman flared out around his baggy trouser legs. "Are you here to resolve the curse—or satisfy your own curiosity?"

He assessed her over his shoulder before he glided down the hall and disappeared around a corner. When he was gone, Rishé dropped her head onto the tablets. Not because he was right, but because he read her so easily. He had a particular talent that was even more lancing than hers: to see people and to *know* what made them tick almost instantly.

Warmth burned over her breast. The unnatural heat of the pendant reminded Rishé what was important. The curse, yes, but *her* aims too. She'd climbed through that window because she needed to find this place. For herself and, most importantly, for the memory of her mother.

This was how she kept some part of her mother alive, after her father had left her to bear the loss alone. She wondered, fleetingly, where the Trifan clan was—if he still traveled with them. From Isile Dandar, she had a bracelet as a scarce reminder of a living parent. From Jarha, she had a pendant. Rishé's face was half a woman she yearned to remember, and half a man she didn't care to. And her resolve renewed.

There were four—*five*—of them working together; she had time to be a little selfish in her research.

Straightening her spine, Rishé huffed and tracked back through the aisles to the others. As she walked, the white of the tile grayed like clouds shuttering a winter sky. Polished marble walls soon gave way to what looked to be dust. *Ash.* Thick ash that covered the floor in a generous layer lapping at her heels.

As she moved on, the basins began to flicker with dying breaths, and the bottoms of the shelves became singed, growing ever more ravaged until she came across the source of destruction. A scar of black spread before her. The shelves had melted, crumpled under their own weight before falling across the aisle like spent matchsticks. The span of the hall appeared coated in obsidian, dusted with fine gray-black ash and crumbling stone.

A crunch came from underfoot. Glancing down, Rishé found a charred scrap of paper, and her heart rose to her throat.

It can't be.

But it seemed it was.

Unlike the rest of the Great Memories, the records in this aisle were *paper.* And as far as she could see, every single parchment had been scorched. Fragments littered the ruin, tinted the entire span of records black or smoky gray.

Rishé picked her way past a damaged plaque, half broken and melted. She knelt and cocked her head at it, only the words "d-rk" and "-ef-re" remaining visible. Staring at the cinders, she pondered the depth of what had been lost. Precious early memories of a time before anything she understood of the world—erased. *The dark before.*

It was eerily quiet, a nothing noise, like being submerged underwater. Her breath came out in puffs that stagnated, dissipated.

From the middle of the burnt remnants, a glint caught her eye. Rishé set her precious tablets aside and peeked down. In the seam between two half-incinerated shelves was a disruption in the ash. Digging her finger along the crack, she searched for purchase and pulled. As black stained her hand, a square panel came away easily to reveal a hidden cache. Inside was an untarnished crevice built to resemble an ornamented chest. At the center sat weathered scrolls waxed shut and a tome.

Surprise shot through her. *An actual paper-and-ink book.*

On the rugged cover was a series of concentric geometric patterns that bore a deliberate unfamiliarity to spellwork. The lines resembled larimac trees, thin limbs and thinner branches, dotted intermittently with dark jewel circles. When she turned it over, the tome felt heavy . . . and oddly waterlogged, as if it had just been rescued from the atrium's pool.

Rishé wiped a wet hand on her thigh and peeled open the front cover, wincing when the pages stuck together. Ash footprints trailed her as she shifted into better light.

On the sepia-tinted endpaper, in distinctly different hands, were three—words? Names?

Iosanne . . . Anad . . . The last had been scratched out so thoroughly, it was nearly unreadable. She squinted and was finally able to make out *the scar.* A story from Fa Djain of an assassin—*thief.* She corrected herself. False at the end of the day, merely a myth.

As Rishé turned the pages with great care, her eyes widened in wonder.

Diagrams of gems, gray and red ink shading the sketches of stones that looked exactly like her pendant.

This is it. She blinked in disbelief. *This is really it.*

She didn't have the words to convey the enormity of what this meant to her. It made her want to climb out of her skin and wave the loose flesh like a madwoman, run through the streets, and maybe even desecrate an aetherstone. She felt like flying. Like she was both living life to the fullest and dying.

Rishé snapped the tome shut and tipped back, searching the aisles for an adderowl. Let it be known: She was not a suspicious person. Usually. Sagan's *interesting* new mannerisms had just put her on edge. That was all.

Leaving behind the tablets amid ash and burnt ruin, she paged through the tome as she walked through the archives. Before she knew it, she was back in the teardrop alcove where her companions were sprawled on cushions dragged from the castle above, towers of bismuth slates spilling around them. In the center of their lazy circle was a candle crying wax and a hunk of half-eaten panmi. Pastry petals and stars decorated the slightly burnt bread—a valiant attempt.

At least someone was enjoying the dessert. "Enjoying" wasn't exactly the right word—"tolerating," perhaps. Asaru and Palenisa pulled chunks from the panmi. Asaru chewed and swallowed with an expressionless focus on the tablet against his knees. Palenisa grimaced as she lazed on her back, blue eyes roving over hers.

"Is that . . . an actual tome?" Wren asked when Rishé sat in a cross-legged meditation. He rested against the back wall, hooded by the suman that he and Asaru seemed to share custody of. There were two tablets in his lap and faded rings beneath his incredulous eyes.

"What does it look like?" she signed, pointing to her face then his. She pressed her foot against the side of his thigh until he rolled it away from her with a huff.

"A tome." His hint of a smile was sheepish.

"Good job."

The tips of his ears flushed and flicked. Rishé snorted and returned to the tome.

Surrounding the sketches, the sodden pages were covered in a faded script that floated before her eyes. Tracing the elegant writing, she found herself mouthing the words in an orthography she at least knew. Something sparked in her brain, and she realized they were incantations. They didn't morph into understanding; the language was too unfamiliar and, from appearances, much too ancient. Bewildered, she flipped to a drawing of a monolith done in a haphazard hand.

Pillar of the Gods, she thought in delirious delight, wondering just what in the world this meant. None of it made full sense, yet she read on, intent to find out.

Warmth radiated from the striated stone on her necklace. Grasping it, she felt the phantom of her mother's hand in hers. Jarha was almost as present as the ground beneath her. Both alive and a shadow on the wall. An illusion.

A tap on her thigh snapped her head up, and Rishé locked gazes with Palenisa.

"What?" Rishé asked guardedly, eyeing the fingers on her knee and holding down the urge to shuffle away from their startling warmth. The tome burned in her lap as well, waiting. Waiting.

"I need your opinion. I think I found something."

"Why?" *Well, I'm eloquent today.*

"It should be obvious." Palenisa rolled onto her side, wearing a thin sheen of annoyance. "You're good with navigation and shit."

The wheel in her brain caught, reeled, and stuttered to a stop. For a moment, all Rishé could do was blink as the other woman stared at her, shockingly expectant. The bismuth slate hovered between them. In a rare flustered moment, Rishé's cheeks warmed. She wasn't a beacon of faith, but it felt like a sacred offering.

"Lost in my mind a second," she signed, too embarrassed to speak Akiki as she scrambled to put her mind straight. Palenisa tilted her head, frowning at Rishé's hands.

Rishé opened her mouth but thought better of it and shook her head instead.

Taking the tablet from Palenisa, she inhaled, exhaled, and forcefully reorganized her thoughts. *Not an entirely unwelcome surprise,* Rishé admitted to herself, watching the woman in her periphery. Ivory coils billowed around Palenisa's head, softening her features. The canary yellow of her blouse brightened her countenance such that she actually looked like she matched the title of sunlight Aspect.

Rishé would have examined her further, but the content of the tablet drew her attention.

Oh, Palenisa *had* found something.

The tablet described a series of excursions to an island in the Broken Spine. It claimed, she read, intrigued, that according to the geographical features, the Spine had once been part of Anticarta, an apt name for the treacherous jag of rock. So the northern continent laid claim to the sole island in the Spine that was fit for mooring, as well as any deposits of diamondglass found there.

"Treveyna." She mouthed the island's name to herself.

And her horrible thoughts came true. The sound of bismuth shattered in the air, cracking with the wail of a claw scratching glass. Three heads jumped up. Up to Asaru. Asaru, who was staring at Wren. His haunted eyes shone like wet black stones, at the center of which sat wide rings of hazel with tiny silver pinpricks. Shock painted the scarred canvas of his pallid features.

He whispered brokenly, but they all heard.

"The king . . . Was Zaosha your father?"

The wheel in Rishé's head crashed, burst into flames. Both the tome and tablet in her hands lay forgotten, because *what*? The silence was its own answer. But he had never been one to mildly upend her world in a single move alone. Stunned, she looked at Wren. He met her gaze before averting his own. With unnerving calm, he brushed his scarred jaw and let out a breath through his nose.

"Yes," he said with a shrug. "My father was Zaosha du Velanescu. And I'm a bastard."

It couldn't be possible. But as she thought, she decided it was probable—more than. It was the truth. Velanescu blood was strong, yet Tilde and Wilars Palomer, the princess and prince, were said to favor their mother, with lighter skin and pale red curtains of hair. Not to mention, they hadn't taken their father's name—if he even *was* their father.

And by the same logic of heredity, Zaosha had been lulaik. As had his mother and his father and all the rest of the Velanescu line a thousand years back to Rhenitha of the Vale. The founding queen, who had hidden her identity to unite the domain of Munryvos into what would become Estyria.

Rishé didn't need to read a slate to know it was true.

Why hadn't he told her?

More importantly: Why hadn't she *seen*?

Surprise bled into regret, which bled into guilt, miring her gut. Her pendant was warm, but her heart ached. As Wren turned, she saw it. For a second, the light caught him there, and she could almost imagine him crowned in gold. Crowned in opal.

ASARU

He liked the hearth room. It was warm and quiet, lit amber by the perpetually burning brick hearth set into the wall. Good for thinking. Grieving. Wallowing.

Asaru sat by a window overlooking the sea, arms wrapped around his knees, and a halo of bismuth slates around him. The glyphs wavered to intelligible symbols—*and King Drakar ended the Devall Rebellion in—and King Drakar ended the Devall Rebellion in—and King Drakar ended the Devall Rebellion in—* and nothing. Because he did not care about fucking King Drakar. Nor any of the rest of them.

He turned his cheek aside and blinked at the man in the window. Twilight touched the sky with a kiss of lavender fire as his face swam, misshapen, in the glass. Pale scars and fire—bright, bright, bloody. He didn't know whether to laugh or cry at the red of his hair, which had taken roost all the way to the root, leaving a band of quickly fading brown. Cutting it had been useless, and yet—

It, um, I think it looks nice.

And yet.

There was a chisel scraping at the insides of his skull. As the wreath on the back of his shoulder throbbed, Asaru buried his face in his knees. On the backs of his lids, kohl fingers found the once soft insides of his elbows, the small of his back above his tail, his wounded side.

I think it looks nice.

Something nameless flowed up his throat, threatening to choke him. What kind of warrior was he? He had strength enough to kill remnants but not to battle the swell of a lamentation song. As a hummingbird beat behind the fading jewels of his halo, that unknown feeling curdled in the gray depths within him.

That strange, hot feeling of friendship. Yes. Of course.

Facing remnants had never been as hard as facing these . . . feelings. Feelings for friends.

And what a wonderful friend he was. After all, Asaru had killed a king, lulaik, the father of the man he was bound to. The man he had feelings—of friendship—for. The thread that connected them pulled tight, *tighter.* A taut line from him to—

"*Wren*," he mouthed.

Stars winked into sight in the Sky Court as the sun glinted beneath the horizon. Wine-dark water rippled, warping his frowning reflection.

For a night and a day, Asaru had sequestered himself inside the hearth room, leaving only to grab more tablets before skittering back to avoid the source of his confusion. How was he supposed to meet that gold-brown gaze, knowing the weight of the sword that had slipped into Zaosha's heart was still heavy in his hands?

The memory of possession hovered at the corners of his mind. Static snatches of an overpowering presence radiated to his extremities. Pained, he curled them. He was still his own. He still belonged to himself.

Possession was an explanation. Not an excuse.

He never claimed to be just. He never claimed to be nice. But he tried to be kind. Worthy of the wejat hidden on his wrist. But he was the worst person in the world. *That* wasn't a lie, spoken or thought. Not for the first time, Asaru pondered the circle emblazoned in raised flesh. Eternity, too, was a wreath, a self-consuming ring. He wasn't ready for the next day, much less eternity; he wasn't sure if he would make it.

Several heartbeats passed, and he closed his eyes. His ears flickered at the swish of silk, then steps padding over the striated wood, approaching him.

"Asaru."

Opening them, he was met with Rishé's small form. She tapped an erratic pattern along the top of the hearth's uneven bricks, purple and white like the rest of the Nest. He looked at her dully as she stood before him. Against her cocked hip, she held that waterlogged tome that never seemed to dry.

"This is ridiculous," she said, unamused. He was not trying to be amusing.

Dropping to a crouch, Rishé set the tome across her thighs and peered up like an angry little bird. Her narrow amber eyes scrutinized him.

"Being in this castle is stifling—*you* are being stifling."

"I haven't left this room. What could I possibly have done to you?" His hands twirled fur, loosened, twirled again. Agitation prickled his nape where crimson hair brushed black diamond.

"It's what you haven't done that's getting on my nerves. So"—Rishé clasped her hands, heels pressed to the ground—"for the love of all of us, before someone immolates, *go talk to him.*"

Asaru sent her a flat stare, wanting desperately to be left alone to wallow. To *keep* wallowing. "I do not know what you mean. And even if I did, that's not your concern," he said, voice rasping like rocks drawn against each other. "Why do you care? I thought you two hadn't been friends in a long time."

"We're working on it." She waved a hand by her head. A sigh later, she shook her head and added slyly, "Besides. I've seen the way he looks at you."

"I . . . am not exactly sure what you mean."

Rishé returned his flat stare with her own, scoffing. "Don't insult my intelligence. Or my eyes." Rising, she muttered something in Nomyrs and pointed. The accusing finger maintained a respectful distance from his forehead. He scowled at it, a spark alighting from between his wings to the tip of his tail. "Against his better judgment—because he is a fool with no sense of self-preservation—he'll forgive you."

"I killed his father."

Rishé rolled her eyes. "Just go to him. He's on the tower."

This is ridiculous, I'm not a child. Asaru pursed his lips as she pointed one last time before leaving him to the pop of the hearth. *Then why do I feel scolded like one?*

For a moment, he thought of Tenat and the rare scoldings he'd received as a child. It brought a bitter twist to his mouth. Once, trouble had been a difficult thing for him to come by; he'd always done what he'd been told, commanded, *possessed* to do.

Outside the window, the night sparkled. These were the hours during which nocturnal creatures thrived, kept their secrets with their many biting teeth. Dark, amorphous shadows rose, room aglow under the soft yellow lanterns that sat in the corners and atop tables and shelves. Asaru exhaled. Before he could overthink it, he gathered his hesitations, shoved them aside, and went to the tower.

The stairs spiraled around a thick central column, which was interrupted every twenty steps by an off-white door leading to one of many rooms. At the very top, where the column met the flat of the ceiling, was a trapdoor. It was slightly ajar, a rope ladder crawling up the wall and out the opening. Through it was a glimpse of night.

Ascending, he found Wren hunched over, staring at something in his lap. The cracked tablet with his paternal lineage, the secret etched there, unbound.

Rhenitha, Zuzandra, Tondis, Drakar, Rhenei, Cozimar, Zuminta, Zaosha—and Wren.

Closing his eyes, Asaru steeled himself, waiting a tremulous moment before opening them. A sprinkle of pale leaves tickled the pads of his feet as he crept closer. Gently knelt. His tongue felt too thick to speak. Not that he knew what to say other than an apology—he was getting good at those. He wondered, at the end of all this—if there was an end—who would have apologized more.

"I am sorry."

Wren set the slate aside. A tragic weight burdened his slumped shoulders. Moonlight sculpted his profile as he stared across the shivering sea. His shirt was buttoned to the neck, rolled sleeves revealing a swath of black-stained skin and stitched flowers. Curls kissed his shoulders, the blue ribbon wound twice around his wrist. Releasing a breath, Wren sprawled back onto the leaves and flung an arm over his eyes.

"I should feel worse about it, shouldn't I?" Wren muttered. "But I don't know. I don't really feel anything at all."

Asaru had no answer. He moved closer, folded his legs beneath himself as a tremor made itself known from the brand. Guilt, sadness, and a conflicted miasma of unnamable—untouchable, unspeakable, uncountable—emotions. Grief was a prism through which the light of sorrow shone differently for all who gazed upon it. For himself, it was tears, hours spent sobbing at the altar of his own failures. And through the bond, Asaru sensed a deliberate blanket of numb nothingness.

As they sat in the windy lull, Asaru's eyes traced the downward curve of Wren's nose, the scatter of freckles, and the lilac splash of his scar. Traced the lines of hard and soft, the barest hint of stubble, and the shadow of overlong hair.

Beautiful, came the unbidden thought.

Asaru's tail spasmed against his leg, and he grasped it firmly in his lap. "He was your father."

"'Father' . . . is being generous."

"But you're family."

Wren lowered his arm, and a notch appeared between his narrowed brows. "He never joined our clan, he wasn't even there when I was born—he was *not* family."

"Still, I killed him." Asaru absently touched his halo, which leeched warmth from his fingers. "My body, my hands."

"No." Wren sat up suddenly. "You were possessed."

Asaru swallowed at the determination in Wren's gaze. Heat lapped at his skin, the heavy air so charged he could taste it. Lost for words, he gathered the remains of himself and nodded. "I was, but—"

"What does it matter anyway?"

Wren moved to his knees, intently passionate. He looked a mess in his rumpled shirt, with purple valleys beneath his drowsy eyes, and more scars than he had left home with.

Asaru couldn't look away.

"I didn't know him. I only ever met his sister, Sanawe. I don't *care* about him. I only care about my mother. I only care about . . ."

As he trailed off, darkness spread over his freckled cheeks, and Asaru watched, enraptured, as his throat bobbed. "You."

Asaru's breath hitched, and his face warmed. He looked down to hide it.

Khetry shimmered at the edges of his vision, the brightest it had been in a long while. Their braided connection pulsed, and the entire web trembled, vibrating with the rich vivacity of life. It was the most alive Asaru had felt since being cursed. It was the most alive he'd felt . . . *ever.*

Oh.

Perhaps this strange, hot feeling wasn't *only* friendship.

Oh.

He'd had no frame of reference for this. He didn't know what the tangle gnawing in his chest could mean.

Something sparked across his upper back, and he bit his lip. He shifted closer until he could see flecks of copper in a golden eye. Slowly Asaru twined their fingers together in black communion. Stone and skin, to harm and to heal.

The hand froze in his as Wren spooked. Glancing sidelong, Asaru found himself breathless at the sight of this man bathed in stars. Rather than pull away, he moved until their bodies were pressed in a burning line from arm to thigh. He craved that warmth the same as a lulaik craved touch.

"Are we friends?"

A heavy pause. Wren gulped loudly in the quiet before responding "Despite my . . . summoning you, I hope we've found some sort of, um, bond. Beyond the one that's, um, branded on us, that is."

"Then, a different . . . kind of friend?" Asaru asked quietly. As he locked onto mismatched eyes, he realized what that look he'd been wondering about was. The one that scorched him top to talon like an inferno.

Affection.

Asaru's chest ached in a shameless happiness, bared amid an endless waterfall of sorrow and misery. Why would that gaze carry such deep and overwhelming affection?

A furiously warm forehead pressed to his, and he was unmade. He shuddered, eyes fluttering at the sensation of being undone so simply. So easily. The curse had weakened him—but the bond was flaying him apart.

Asaru whispered so as not to shatter the silence.

"Is this all right?"

As if through thick molasses, Asaru reached out, fingers brushing a flaming cheek.

"Um, I . . ."

The corner of Asaru's lips twitched down, and he went to pull back. But a strong grasp snatched his arm wraps. A gasp stuttered half formed in his throat.

"No, wait."

His gaze flicked to Wren's darkened face.

"I mean, yes. Please."

His hand was guided to rest on the curve of Wren's golden-brown jaw. Inside, he'd been upturned, that feeling—*friendship, but different*—swooping through his belly. Entranced, half-mast eyes watched as Wren teased a lock of deep crimson hair between his fingers. Black and red like bloodstone. Asaru held his breath as Wren tucked the strand behind his ear and slid that hand to rest at his nape. Gentler than anything he had ever felt before. Purring, Asaru leaned into the touch. He curled his grip around Wren's wrist, pressed his hand more firmly against Wren's skin. A touch he wanted to drown in rather than jump from.

Wren broke into a shy smile. A tender thing, hesitant at first, before slipping seamlessly into overflowing affection. Asaru found himself returning it. The sound of the wind faded away, and it was just the two of them. They were the only two people that existed. Just the stars above and the space between them.

The trapdoor flung open, and the moment was over like light breaking through the cloud of night.

"Are you two up there?" An unwelcome voice called from below. "We found something, if you'd care to join us."

Warmth receded as Wren drew back, dropping his hands as if burned.

Asaru slid away with a guttural growl, but before his glare could land upon that adderowl visage, Sagan had fled below, a gloved hand beckoning for them to follow. Leaving him to stew in the tightness lining his stomach and the speeding of his heart. He felt it would beat right out of his mouth.

Clenching his eyes shut, he dropped his forehead to the crook of Wren's neck. A cool breeze blew his hair, but he was warm from head to toe. "I swear to the Triumvirate, I am going to murder that man."

The faint pressure of a pair of lips lingered along his hairline. His face bloomed, and Asaru sank into the honeyed laugh he received in response.

On the desk was an ancient tome, thick and bound in what he hoped was leather. It sat unassuming, borders gilded, older than anything Asaru had ever seen before. In fact, it looked as though a sudden harsh glance would send it falling apart. Though it was no ordinary tome. It was—

"The primer I was sent to find." Sagan rapped it with a knuckle.

"Where?" Asaru asked.

"Where what?" Sagan tilted his masked head, which irritated Asaru all the more. His upper lip curled back, and he took a step forward. But Rishé, clearheaded, threw a hand between them before fists or feet could fly.

"Don't," her eyes seemed to warn.

"Fine," his crossed arms said in response. "Where," he bit out. "Did you find this primer?"

"The chasm in the Great Memories."

Mouth agape, Rishé sent Sagan an alarmed look. "At the bottom"—she began as if speaking to a child—"of that massive borehole?"

Sagan nodded. "Mmm. But not at the bottom." He ran a hand over the puckered ridges of leather, and the back of his glove came away covered in gold dust. At the center of the cover was a trident spearing a black sun.

"Sword of Light," Wren murmured.

Wren locked gazes with him, and heat spotted Asaru's cheeks. The corners of Wren's dewy eyes crinkled. Clearing his throat, Asaru took a discreet step aside and shook the thoughts back into his head.

Focus.

"Why does the Chronicler even want this in the first place?" Palenisa groused, drumming her fingers along her staff as she glowered at Sagan, the tension on her face matching what Asaru felt inside.

"I don't know." Sagan shrugged. "There's a lot I don't know."

"So you've been feeding us bullshit?"

As they quarreled—one-sided, since the masked party responded with vague answers—Asaru flipped the tome open. The brittle pages were covered in glyphs of the eresh keyel language.

Not the kind of writing they'd found on the bismuth slates, these flowed in a tiny, spidery script looping into itself, as though the author had thought faster than they could write and was rushing to catch up. The ink started out red and neat, but as he turned the pages, it bled to black and grayed gold and the hand became harried. Frenzied. Mad.

A stone dropped in the pit of his stomach as familiar images appeared. Drawings of remnants and black diamond weapons done in cursed blood—a sketch of the same vial he had found at the embassy, shaded entirely black.

This tome belonged to the creator of the curse.

Asaru turned a page and found a diagram depicting a device of science. *Protoscience.* The profane manipulation of organic matter to splice multiple organisms together with khetry. The banned art from which remnants were born, contaminated effluent of the experiments of its creator.

Oprekhet, the evolutionary. Oprekhet, the betrayer. Oprekhet, who was *dead.*

A horrid sensation blossomed in his chest at the very thought of her, intangible fingers pressing malice into every inch of his skin. There were two sides to the woman who incited the Founding War. Her name, an omen. She'd urged the wraiths and dolomites to attack Rhenitha's clan, and after that—war. Deserts of burning glass and fields of fire, all leading to that fateful day the Sea Gate was erected. Oprekhet murdered thousands in her pointless war. And she died a pointless death for it. Or she should have. That was what history told.

Asaru swallowed down both disgust and horror as his mother's voice curled along his ears. *Warrior, brother, son. Come back.* The brush of gentle, intangible lips. *Come home, son, brother, warrior.*

He slammed the tome on the table, silencing his companions. Four pairs of eyes shot to Asaru as his mind whirled to fit this revelation into the puzzle of what he knew. An inferno blazed within as he scowled at the diagram of a centrifuge, six black tubes spinning in a ring. The page was torn almost in half under his fingers. There were no words that were quite apt to describe how he felt. Steely eyed, Asaru lifted his head. Secrets had come to bite and left him bloody with the revelations.

"This belonged to Oprekhet. She is alive." *And she killed my brother.*

She was killing him too. Killing Aedyton as they spoke.

The room burst into a cacophony of shouts as everyone spoke at once.

Pursing his lips, Asaru ducked to wipe bile from his chin. The viscous liquid stained his neck, a vulgar smear across his halo. Violet, crimson, ink black—he was drenched in blood down to his feet.

Palenisa flipped through the pages. "How? *How* is that possible? Even *I* know how she died."

Pulling the tome from her, Asaru turned back to the tight scrawl of words—Oprekhet's words. Utter agony squirmed under his fingertips, touching the raised markings. "She cursed herself as the index case." He read and was repulsed by the rigorous order of her experiment logs. Every day and every symptom accounted for—almost four hundred years. "From her affliction, two strains of Black Diamond were extracted. The first she seeded into the waters of Aedyton, using Saite as a testing ground. That accounts for the decrease in remnant sightings near the mountains over the last year."

He turned the page. Drawn on the next was a remnant, its

body bent at an unnatural angle, with dripping limbs askew and a dozen bulbous eyes littering its misty form.

"And the second strain—"

"She sent to the embassy," Sagan finished.

The air grew cold.

"Did you know?" Asaru breathed, the image of a grotesque remnant swimming in his vision. His blank face rose to meet the adderowl. "Did. You. Know?"

"I didn't, I swear." Even through the distortion, Sagan sounded equally stunned. It was the truth. That almost hurt worse than if it weren't.

"The Chronicler?"

Sagan shook his head.

Asaru blinked the fog from his eyes and thumbed the depiction of Oprekhet's *fine* work. He understood the numbness that tempered Wren's emotions through their bond. Anything was better than this. Perhaps even the all-encompassing haze of possession.

"But they will be pleased to hear of this, for the ritual," Sagan ventured, taking a tentative step closer. He was careful. *Good, he should be.* At that moment, Asaru felt he would shatter apart at a single wrong move, a misplaced word.

A hand pressed between his hidden wings, and he cast emotionless eyes up to Wren. Surprise sparked faintly at the edge of his awareness, but he remained mostly empty inside. A yawning cavern left him a gutless husk.

"But how did she cast the curse in the first place?" Wren asked, looking at the tome over his shoulder. "The cursed object is black diamond, but didn't the warden at the time dispose of every last diamond in the Sea of Tranquility?"

"It seems she managed to find more," Asaru said flatly, turning to a diagram of the gem. Every quality and important feature was noted—its use as a weapon, its use as a curse.

Palenisa slouched against the desk with a frustrated huff, tugging her snowy curls. "She also managed to come back to life."

With a thoughtful expression, Rishé pulled a bismuth slate from the deep pockets of her tunic. She set it on the desk with a light thunk. "But if this ritual works, then we know how to stop her." She inclined her head. "And we know where to find that diamondglass."

Asaru shut the tome. Dust and flecks of dried blood puffed into the air. "Where?"

"It was all her," she said, lightly checking Palenisa's hip. Shying away, the taller woman crossed her arms. "Treveyna. The island used to be part of Anticarta, and research excursions there found traces of the gem. Maybe there's more."

He frowned. "Is that for certain?"

She lifted a shoulder in a shrug. "Better than nothing."

If bone could smile, Asaru was certain the adderowl skull would be wearing a rictus grin. His hands itched to wrap themselves around that pale neck and squeeze and squeeze until there was blessed quiet. "You already knew."

"Perhaps. Perhaps not." Sagan swayed, shifting on his toes. "Your luck is finally turning."

"You were the reason for at least a tenth of that bad luck," Rishé snarked, waving a hand by his face.

Sagan pushed her hands down and continued as if she hadn't spoken. He would have made an excellent snake in another life, moving around the room in that infuriating manner of his. "You might be able to stop Oprekhet before she can curse all of Aedyton," he said. "Take heart. Have hope."

Where had hope gotten Asaru? He had made himself believe his brother was waiting for him. Instead, he had received a dreadful taste in his mouth that lingered when he set the tome down. The thump of it was decisive. This was it. Soon, he would go home. Soon, he would return to his kin, beset by the curse. To his mother, who called him. The feeling was tinged with a bittersweetness. After all, what kind of gift was ash and the death of a firstborn son?

From its placement at the center of his spine, Wren's hand slid down to the inside of his arm. Their index fingers hooked together in the tiniest connection. Then tightened. The rest followed until their hands were joined. A seamless clasp of black. Asaru caught a glimpse of the affection sent his way, terrified to bear the enormity of its meaning. It spread over every inch of his skin. Like honey. Like blood spiraling into water.

Take heart. Have hope.

There was an end in sight, and a cursed sword at his neck. But one could only do so much; and hope was so fleeting.

WREN

The needle was red. Almost entirely red.

As he drew his blood into the bone, khetry whirling in a weave around his wrists, Wren wondered if this was what exsanguination felt like.

Starwrens whistled past in the late-morning sky. A gentle blue across which thin clouds floated, obscuring the sun a moment before casting him back under its unbearable gaze, giving him the sensation of being watched. But even more so by a single bird that decided to settle on the tower's edge, staring. Its razor beak released a trill as it puffed its chest, and there was a judgmental cast to those beady little eyes. Wren could feel it gnawing at him.

"I know what I'm doing," he muttered darkly. *And I know it's not right.*

But he *had* to.

Determination surged through him, and he pressed his hand firmer to the bloody page of the primer, repeating the refrain. Khetry tightened. His palms wept blood through the spell circle, and the needle drank it deeply, drank gluttonously like this had been its entire purpose. As Wren drained himself of his vigor in pursuit of piteous power, he didn't know what lay at the end, what the lived experience of a Weaver truly was or what the title meant, but he believed—*he had to*—the ritual sketched in the primer. It was a foolhardy venture. Still, what else could he do, drained as he was and in search of absolution?

Sometimes Wren imagined kneeling at Asaru's feet, presenting him this thin red blade with a waterfall of apologies. *See,* he would say, *I did this for you.*

The senseless thought fanned heat across his cheeks. Whether that rapid pulse in his chest was his heart or the brand, it rushed to his ears, smoothing them flat against the sides of his head. The phantom sensation of another forehead against his bloomed, the tender brush of a hand along the jut of his chin. Blackened fingers curled around his wrist.

By Eșarpe, he *was* a fool. He and his feelings for the man he'd summoned and bound to himself. It was khetry's worst joke, branding them both with the wreath of acorns. The fourth card in the Weave of Fate, whose other name was . . . the Lovers.

Wren shut his eyes, flustered. Told himself not to think about it, because there was nothing to be *thought* about there. He and Asaru were *friends.* When he opened his eyes, he watched, lightheaded, as the starwren took flight. He stared after it for a melancholy moment.

Catching himself, he shook his head to refocus, but the world swam in an oil-slick haze as his fingers numbed. His eyes fell to his other arm and the pattern stitched onto it. Delicate red stitching formed a single black dahlia, petals blooming in a burst like tiny scales. There was one reason the Rosatay sewed these flowers into their flesh. Tradition compelled, though he did not think this particular departed had been deserving.

Wren hadn't lied that night: Zaosha was *not* his family. He bore no love nor memory of the man who broke his mother's heart and made them outsiders to their clan in a single careless act.

Truthfully, he'd done the stitching only because sewing the thread through his skin had quelled the conflict within him to a low-grade rumble he was more than happy to ignore.

The corners of his vision darkened from blood loss, while his fingers numbed further, sending a shiver through him. At that, he knew he'd spent enough of himself for the day. All who sought a Weaver ritual had disappeared or were dead, Ahndat had said. That couldn't be him. Not when he was so close.

The needle, which he tucked back into the pocket over his heart, was almost entirely red.

Sighing, Wren tugged the string tassels at his veilari collar in an absent habit. He ran a hand through his hair and bound it in a loose half tail that reached the middle of his back. For a second, he let himself preen in the viridian sunlight. For a second, it seemed as if the world was at peace.

He made his way down the tower to the rear of the castle, where the palings formed a terrace overlooking the peaceful sea. The tower cast a long, dark finger of shadow behind Wren when he stepped out to join the others. Perched on the banister, Sagan sat, legs dangling precariously over the cliff, with little regard for the sheer drop. There was something about him that seemed to drink in risk and provocation like amber wine.

At the sound of the door sliding closed, a pair of eerily glowing eyes met Wren's. The adderowl acknowledged him with a nod. By habit of manners, Wren raised his hand, but the skull had already turned, and he was left feeling just slightly awkward.

Ducking his head, he moved to join the others spread out along the banister. They watched the empty horizon, waiting. Anticipating.

Beside him, Asaru glanced up. They perceived each other through the bond in an instant, like a bell chiming at the base of his brain. Drawn to each other like a pair of glass moths circling a khetrical flame. Threads braided taut, tightening as a noose that pulled them closer to an inevitably horrible end. This should have been his punishment alone—he wished he hadn't had to drag Asaru along with him.

The curse was devouring Asaru, fastening a dark circlet of keloids around his jeweled neck. The amethysts of his halo had lost much of their luster. His eyes were drowning in black, and the markings hooked beneath them blended into the tendrils snaking from their corners. The remaining snakeskin was draped over his shoulders, and beneath it, he, too, wore a cooling veilari garment: a black high-necked tunic open to reveal the pleated backplate of his binder, sleeves bunched at his elbows.

Wren found himself reaching out. And Asaru intertwined their hands. In one unbroken black line, they looked like they belonged together. Fated. *Just as false as luck spells.* Wren received a gentle glance from beneath dark lashes, affection flowing through the bond in gentle waves.

A very small, very ravenous part of him wanted to sink into the sensation. Into the other half of the bond until they merged in rippling waves of flesh pouring into a single chalice. Beyond sex—an attraction that he did not feel—this was something far more base. His eye throbbed in a wince—this was something far more *khetrical.*

"What are we waiting for?" Rishé asked with a yawn,

dragging him to the present. She stood to his left, rocking back on her heels so that the layers of her tunic swayed from her absurd collection of belts.

"A sign," Sagan answered.

The sign came in the form of a sailbird. Wings spotted silver spread wide like eponymous sails, gliding on wind streams.

Sagan crossed his legs and laid his staff across his lap. He held out an arm wrapped in thick brown cloth for the white bird. It landed seamlessly, twitching its silver-crowned head as its talons dug for purchase.

As he removed and scanned the parchment attached to its leg, Wren appraised him. With the mask, he was a mystery. His body was a slender line, every cryptic act deliberate.

He recalled how, a few nights after they'd found him handling the jewels belonging to Dowager Queen Raine and her children, Sagan had told them they needed to part ways. While the others sailed to Treveyna, he would take Wren to the Chronicler. Again, Palenisa had protested, as had Asaru. But Sagan had held fast—the Chronicler would meet only Wren. The ritual had no chance without diamondglass. Enough to save an island drowning beneath a cursed tide. And when Rishé had asked how he planned for them to reach Treveyna—Sagan had shrugged, slipped on his mask, and said he knew someone.

"Oh," Rishé gasped, pointing over the banister. "Is that it?"

Wren followed her finger to the horizon, no longer empty.

Amid the vast blue, a dot grew into a ship larger than any merchant vessel he'd seen before. As the sea bore it closer, the black pennant trailing from the main mast came into view. On the flowing fabric, he could make out decaying flowers cradled in a mass of bones. Crimson-skinned Chilawari flashed in his mind's eye—the impossible thought of sailing somewhere else, sailing somewhere south.

"Pirates," Wren said flatly. "When you said you knew someone, you meant pirates."

He was sure that beneath the mask, Sagan was smiling as the man tossed him a loose shrug.

The Nest was meant to be a secret—Aedyton's greatest-kept secret. Unfortunately, secrets seemed to have a way of crawling free.

"Looks like another ego trip to me." Palenisa rolled her eyes, leaning back on her elbow against the banister.

"She's a pirate. They tend toward—" Sagan stiffened and shot up. He leaped from the banister, head tilted to the air like a bloodhound. Like an adderowl. Under his breath, he cursed in a dialect that Wren couldn't fully catch. "Someone's coming."

That was when the earth rumbled. The castle shook like loose teeth in a bleached skull, and the castle's ward flickered to life. It felt as though the world would never stop shaking. But it did, and Sagan sprinted inside in a panicked sweep of cloth. The four of them looked at each other and hurried after.

"How did I not notice," Sagan said to himself, shoving down his mask as he swung the grand doors open. The words fell from his lips, stacked atop one another. His eyes were wide as bowls, laden, for once, with obvious emotion—concern. "Freelancers."

Approaching quickly from the base of the incline were five figures, all dark, save for the white of their hair stark against the desert.

Palenisa swore. "They tracked me here."

"Not you." Sagan stepped outside, leaving them to peer

around the door from within the castle's protection. Sun fell over him in bars of green light. "More likely, the chief's family put up a kill contract after Asaru assassinated him."

Aghast, Wren looked at Asaru. Mildly, he registered they were still holding hands, and his heart fluttered foolishly. He recalled the sensation of them wrapped around his middle and coated in blood. He remembered how no one had spoken of it, the truth that hung unacknowledged as they fled from Ilon.

As if he were confirming the weather, Asaru shrugged.

Clutching at her hair, Palenisa groaned. "Zodiac give me *fucking* strength!"

As if in response, the ground groaned like a starved belly. The ward shuddered and faded, granting clearer sight of the Aspects below. Fire wreathed the arms of four of them. The fifth trailed after the others at a terrifying, unaffected pace. He had an inkling of what kind of Aspect they were but wanted to neither say nor think it.

"Chaos Aspect." Palenisa hissed as though burned, bringing his fears to life. "Shit!"

The most powerful of the twelve, not only could they counteract other Aspects, but rumor had it, they could do so with spells as well. *Only rumors,* Wren told himself. But, just the same, the prospect froze him to the floor.

During her rare visits, his Aunt Sanawe had spun tales of the Crusades, when rogue Aspects openly hunted lulaik and Weavers. She'd said chaos was a Weaver's worst nightmare. She'd said they were the reason the Weavers had died out. Though just stories, she probably shouldn't have been telling all that to a child.

"Shit, indeed," Sagan said, turning to her. He reached into the folds of his suman and pulled out an alexandrite token. Pink, blue, and green streaked the glossy coin, a single dark line banding the center—*cat's-eye* alexandrite. The kind found only on Anticarta.

"Give this to the captain, Yuri—do *not* call her that, by the way. Beneath the stairs in the tower, you'll find a trapdoor and tunnels leading to a cove. They'll meet you there."

Sagan pressed the cat's-eye into Palenisa's hand, appearing to ignore the agitation his touch elicited. The pause was palpable. It burrowed as deep as a well. She stared at the gem, then at him. Lips thin, he raised his brows. *"Go."*

As if drawn back to the situation, Palenisa started. She jutted her chin sharply, and before she left, she locked worried eyes with Wren.

"Don't die?"

A weak grin painted his lips. "I'll . . . do my best."

Behind her, Rishé's eyes rolled so far back they almost disappeared. She pushed the other woman down the hall, almost tumbling them both into the atrium's pool. "Wonderful, no one will die—let's *move it.*" Rishé peered up through her choppy fringe. A wordless moment passed between them. An apology from him, and what he hoped was acceptance from her. A decade had degraded his ability to read her as he once could. They would never be as they once were—but he hoped they could be something new.

"Take care of yourself," she mumbled in a raw tone, leaving him with more of her heart than he expected.

They left him and Asaru standing by the door as the world closed in, their time together drawing thin, though he still had so much left to say.

The hand in his tightened.

"Wren."

He took a breath, tried to wrestle his feelings into submission, and failed. Another gentle hand took his jaw, guiding his face down to meet Asaru's forehead. He gulped as those fingers moved to the crook of his neck. Their breaths warmed the air between them, a bubble that contained no one else.

Asaru lifted their connected hands, pressed them over Wren's wreath. Their bond—their own special brand of curse.

"A different kind of friend?" Asaru whispered. The smile he wore was lopsided, as if he didn't do it often, soft as the suffused pink of dawn. It looked like the kind of smile about which poets waxed, scribes eulogized, painters spent lifetimes replicating. Wren scanned his face, committing to memory that smile in the clay of his mind.

"A different kind of friend," he replied. From his shirt pocket, Wren pulled out the paper flower he'd crafted the night before during his most embarrassing emotional turmoil, utterly agonizing in his tower room.

Fetching eyes widened, as big and bright as the thousand thousand suns. "A crystal lotus."

"I, um, searched the Great Memories for accounts of what they looked like . . ." Wren said, tucking the twisted stem behind Asaru's ear among mussed tresses, lingering a moment before drawing away. "Hope I got it right."

The bloom was crafted of folded graphite-smeared paper torn from his primer, too limp to stand straight when held by the stem, lacking both the minty scent and shimmering moonlight petals the accounts described of a real blossom.

"Not really," Asaru said, cupping Wren's cheek and releasing an exhale that sounded almost like a laugh.

Desperation bled into Wren's sword-impaled heart, stealing the air from his lungs. He licked his lips like a man dying of thirst as the words stumbled free. More than anything, he needed to know. "Can you promise we'll see each other again?"

They were wrenched apart before he could hear Asaru's response. If there even was one.

"We have to leave. Now." Sagan hauled him outside, his grip surprisingly strong for his stature.

"Asaru!" Palenisa tugged the man down the hall, deep into the castle and away from Wren.

Blackened fingers lingered as they parted, the sun kissing the horizon goodbye. Only hope held that it would rise again from its temporary death the next day.

As the Nest door was closing, Wren watched Asaru disappear beneath the floor, his gaze filled with the same keen yearning emanating through their bond. The door shut, and he was unsure it would ever open again.

He blinked a sheen from his eyes as the ward trembled again under a barrage of fire. Red and white rebounded violently off sparkling green. Midnight sludge pooled at the border of the ward where they fell, a writhing dark ring. Boulders of flame struck the incline below, shaking through the earth. Black glass gave a serpent's hiss as it ran like tears. The desert was crying.

"Damn it," Sagan muttered at his side. "This wasn't supposed to happen."

The man slid his mask back on, violet blazing to life in the sockets. Expression hidden, his body language betrayed nothing as he undid his wraps and shoved up his sleeves. One forearm bore the image of Eșarpe coiled around an egg. A spellwork mural was stitched across the olive flesh of the other.

War lulaik. The thought rose to the surface of the tangled emotions within Wren, recalling tales of the lulaik who fought in the Founding War. Nothing like him, failed healer that he was.

Crouching, Sagan folded his arms one over the other in a line, fingers pressed into multiple spell circles to charge. The red glow of khetry hung from his wrists, flicking and spinning as the living substance strummed. Then he swung them out in a spiral and cast a spell that the ward echoed in turn.

Geometric patterns whirled to life, flaring on the virulent green dome. The same shapes shone on Sagan's gloves as he held his arms out, stepping forward as if pushing against the torrent of a sandstorm. The patterns flashed, shifting forms quickly. Concentric, looping, endlessly changing.

Sweat trickled down the side of Sagan's neck. His arms shook from the effort of maintaining his reinforcements on the ward. It was an honest effort; it wouldn't hold. The green shield shuddered, the gaps in the barrier growing larger and longer.

"Sagan," Wren said. "It won't hold."

"This is the Chronicler's life's work." Sagan's distorted voice wavered with strain.

A wispy arm of darkness slammed into the ward with a deafening boom, and spiritual energy shattered like soundless glass. From the uneven hole in the ward, gray lines splintered outward. An infection eating at the green.

Wren recognized it instantly—*chaos.*

Under his mask, Sagan gasped.

He and Sagan lowered their gazes to where the lone figure stood flanked by fire. The Aspect's face was hidden by a collar of silver fur, but from their arms dripped a hoary mist, warping the air. The mist doubled in Wren's vision, and his eyes refused to settle, constantly drawn upward to the chaos Aspect's unseen eyes.

The gray kept creeping, eating the ward into nothingness.

Slowly, as if moving through molasses, the freelancer raised an arm. They framed their face with their other hand, palm flat.

Wren's breath caught.

There was a tense pause. The freelancer snapped. And the ward shattered.

All the air was sucked inward to a single point of impact. A high, piercing screech accompanied the torrential winds billowing in every direction. Across the desert echoed the shattering of a hundred thousand crystals. Fragmented, innumerable. Irrecoverable.

A pair of arms wrapped around Wren's waist, and his eyes slammed shut as he was thrown aside. The ward spared them from the worst of the gale. But as he peeled his eyes open and squinted over Sagan's shoulder, he watched the rest of it fall apart until nothing remained of the proud ward but green slivers woven through with gray chaos like a fraying net.

One of the fire Aspects snapped, sending a firestorm raining down upon the castle. Bolts of lightning accompanied the blinding blasts as the air thinned of water.

When Wren turned, the Nest was crumbling.

White boiled and popped to reveal nightmarish black innards where the desert merged with the stone as it dripped waxen down the dark candle of the cliff face. Giant burns scarred the previously unblemished surface. What sounded like a million snakes hissed from the interior, consuming everything in its path, as fire was wont to do.

"It's gone." Barely audible, there was a tremor to Sagan's distorted double voice. "Now we are alone."

One of his gloves fluttered to the glass in tatters, stray sparks sizzling across his swollen fingers. The thin black lines tattooed around the index and middle fingers were hidden by purple and covered in thin cuts Sagan tried to hide from Wren. Their eyes met and he offered his hand. Wren took it, letting Sagan tug him upward. He wished he could see the man's true eyes. See if the emotion that welled there was the same as what slumped his shoulders.

Breaking his gaze, Sagan took a cracked shard of obsidian and carved a spell into his palms before clapping them together. Feathery light streamed from his fingertips. Blue lines branched into the veins of a leaf, forming a convex shield to protect the front of the Nest. What little it could protect.

Still, the Nest burst into flames, an explosion of ethereal light coloring the distant, flat expanse with a sickening green. The smoke provided them cover as Sagan took Wren's hand again, and they hurried around the castle.

"This wasn't supposed to happen." Wren heard Sagan mumbling. He tried not to listen, but he heard it repeated. "This wasn't supposed to happen."

The ground split to reveal a set of perilous steps carved from the cliff face that disappeared behind them as they gingerly descended, sliding seamlessly back into the wall like dresser drawers being shut. At the bottom was a small cove created by indelicate hands, the upper curve bearded with black stalactites. Murky water lapped at the shore. There was actual sand there. Sadly, Wren thought this must have been all that remained of the desert that once had been.

Cinders fell like snow outside the cove, dissolving into the gentle sea.

Against the far wall, a strange-looking boat bobbed in the shallows. An engine hung over the back, a long handle protruding from the mechanical mess.

"What is it?" Wren asked, catching the rope Sagan tossed his way.

"Steam skiff from the Veil Islands," the man muttered, shoving the boat the rest of the way into the water.

Wren hopped into the front, boots drenched. At the rear, Sagan unfurled the crimson sail with practiced ease. Placing a knee on the back bench, he started the engine, and the skiff took off with a cough of steam as they sped into the sea. As the skiff sailed from the cove, the water faded to a crisp robin's-egg blue, and the sky brightened to a cloudless afternoon.

But when Wren glanced up to the Nest, his heart turned to stone and sank to his gut.

Thick globules of ivory melted down the face. The lip of the cliff drooped under the scalding heat. The deep-set foundation caved under the castle's monumental weight by the sheer force of violence. Fading spots of bismuth gray dotted the white miasma, hissing on contact with the water. Soon the Great Memories were but a smear of burnt color in the geode gash. The accumulated knowledge of thousands of years and a constant record of the present, gone in a matter of minutes. What remained of the tower finally crumbled into the sea, sending a wave rolling toward them. It swept them farther from the destruction of the Chronicler's work.

The eyes of Sagan's mask dimmed. His shoulders fell, and he shoved down the engine's handle with the tense line of his swollen arm, guiding the skiff east.

To the north, Yuri's ship sailed away. They were already so far out that the people aboard were but spots in Wren's vision. Atop the mizzenmast he spotted a dark figure and knew from the pulse in his brand that it was Asaru. Limp wings spread out on either side of the figure, seeming from that distance to be made of midnight. What were once feathers were now dripping with slick, roiling pitch.

Smiling sadly, Wren clutched his heart. The brand sent a flare of anxiety through him. The southern heat warred with the sea spray along the sides of the skiff. Cool water threaded loss through him as a tapestry of resolve unfurled. He touched the pocket at his breast and was sure of the choice he'd made. The pitiable one. But when they met again, he would have the power to mend his mistakes—to save Asaru.

We'll see each other again.

IV

BRILLIANT FACETS

RISHÉ

"Put it to your ear and hear the water for me, mior little ceurer," Jarha had signed to her daughter as they roamed the shore. *"Aulkit'an'tios coshi cainr'an-kolle. Be my ears, and tell me of her song." Listen to how she sings.*

Down the woman's arm was stitched an intricate display of threads in varying iridescent shades to form a bower of sticks. Burnished-copper fringe obscured her eyes as she pressed the striated conch to young Rishé's hand. She was indistinct, not quite right in this watery recollection.

The child reached up with chubby fingers, giggling as the tide shushed in and out of her ear. Practiced hands forming the words of her second language, she did her best to describe the voice of the susurrating sea to her mother. Beside them, Jarha's shadow-faced husband looked up from his primer, features equally unclear.

"Actually, it's not—" Isile's signing was interrupted by his wife's foot knocking the side of his ankle, hard. He winced, rubbing with his blueberry-stained fingers at where she had jammed

him. He couldn't hold the expression for long, his face softening at the sight of their daughter as she grinned at him.

Jarha knelt and plucked something from the surf. Cupped in her hand was a gem with silver whorls. It pulsed, a glowing flame contained.

She tried to show it to her daughter, but she toddled away, more interested in the shell than anything else. It was just a gem. What did a child care? The child should have cared. For mere moons later, her mother would be gone, and that crimson stone would be all that remained.

"Vuan'kon." *Look.*

A little Rishé looked back at her mother with bright-eyed intensity.

Jarha's face blurred, torn like a waterlogged painting. Colors dripped, umber melting into amber and sapphire—and red. Burning, *burning.* Isile, too, was a smeared mess of strokes, his voice indistinguishable from the rush of blood.

A single drop of water fell. Then another. The drops morphed into a flood cascading down, the image in her mind a smudge of memories. As the memory melted, Rishé exhaled. On the water, contentment went hand in hand with grief.

Her fingers brushed Jarha's last keepsake; she clasped it. The stone leeched warmth from her hands, and light glinted off the shallow whorls. At certain angles, it had the translucent quality of ice.

She pressed it to her lips and wished her mother were still with her. More time—she just wanted more time. They should have had more time together—unearthing the secrets of the gem, knowledge passing from mother to daughter like a primer passed through generations. But she was alone. Because the world didn't care what anyone wanted. It went on carelessly, and it was her self-appointed duty to steal from it any meaning she could.

Sighing, Rishé breathed in the sea, tasted its salt. She watched the murky Lethean waters melt into that of the pale yellow Nectarian. Silver sailfish leaped by the ship, and in the depths, silhouettes of behemoth beasts glided at a ponderous pace before disappearing.

In her mere sixty-five years, she'd never left the continent. Hadn't even considered it until the madam's offer to send her to Fa Djain. The farthest she'd ever traveled was the stony shores of southern Bartrom. Her mother had always wanted to see the world beyond the horizon. In a way, she was—through the eyes that her daughter inherited from her.

The temperature dropped and her nape prickled. Wind whipped her braids into her eyes.

They'd been at sea over a week, but only during the last three days had the sky darkened. It grumbled testily with a storm that didn't seem to want to break. Somehow, though, she felt it would soon. A twinge from an old shoulder injury gained in the forge told her so.

She looked down at the waterlogged tome. On one knee she balanced her journal, pages brimming with notes. Her neat penmanship gave way to hasty graphite scribbles, curving across the page as she tilted it to accommodate her overexcitement. How could she be blamed when this was everything she'd been searching for?

Her lips rounded over the incantations she'd interpreted thus far. Without sound, they felt strange in her mouth—with, they sounded even stranger. Like something sparking along her tongue, popping overly warm and sour as a badly made tart.

The language, she'd found, bore a *very* distant similarity to

Emedu, the Chilawari tongue. Using her thin knowledge of it and her proclivity for linguistics, Rishé translated another line into a vague approximation in Akiki and jotted it down. She had no idea if her translation was anything close to correct.

So far, she had deduced that the page described a location. Or a ritual. Or a location of ritual significance. Most of this was done through diagrams, which depicted a series of mirrors arranged in a hexagon. There were what she assumed to be numbers calculating lengths and widths and other formulas, as well as a caricature of a drake doodled in the corner. Spiraling—her pen followed its coiling body—spiraling.

It wasn't like anything she knew of khetry or Suvaun.

Biting the inside of her mouth, Rishé thought back to the pamphlet sitting on her desk in Ausre. If this was what it truly seemed, the writers of *Amanuensis* hadn't been far off—they just didn't have the Great Memories to supplement their speculations. Then again, no one else would either. Her lips thinned at the recollection of black snow as the Nest melted. Pale stone stained by night stuck in her head. Centuries—millennia—of history, gone in minutes.

She shook away the sight of the collapsed tower and pulled off her necklace, setting it in the center of the mirrors. *Not just a theory anymore,* she mused. *What about practical application? How, and for what, were the incantations used?*

These and many other questions ran through her mind.

At a yell, Rishé jerked and glanced down ship. The crew of the *Danaye* hauled cargo from the main deck into the bowels of the ship. *Stolen* cargo, as this was a pirate's vessel. One in an alleged fleet commanded by the so-called pirate king. Or so Yurikhun Taraqaya had said, introducing herself with a mocking salute when they'd handed her the cat's-eye. Only in the north, though—since apparently Tiyam uut Dazraad had laid claim to the title in the south.

Rishé had no idea who either of them were, and she couldn't care less.

She heard retching, followed by a hacking cough. On her other side, Asaru was vomiting.

"You look foul. How're you doing?" To be perfectly honest, he looked worse than that. Covered in the curse from head to toe, he was a walking obelisk of unforgiving black mineral. Jewels clinked when he walked, accompanied by the faint echo of metal.

"Bad," he replied with a stare as flat as his voice. He choked on another surge of vomit, which he promptly emptied over the railing. He hacked and spat with a pained gasp. Throwing her arms up, Rishé stretched out her spine as Asaru wiped his mouth and slumped against the rail with a grunt. "Thank you for asking."

"No problem."

Wind wailed where there would have been silence.

In her periphery, Rishé watched him shiver under the banded snakeskin mantle he had shared with Wren. Thin scaled fabric clung to his thighs as he spread them out, then pulled them up under his chin. Talons scraped against wood. The furry end of his tail crusted with the diamond dew of the sea. Casting a critical eye over his curled form, she surmised they were similar in size. Setting her books aside, she sauntered over before removing her suman and laying it atop his shoulders.

Asaru watched her like a wary, feral wolvencat. Ears pricked forward, tail stiffening at his side. It didn't loosen until she stepped away, granting him a wide ring of space. Satisfied, Rishé wore something like a smile when he donned the hood.

"Thank you." His voice was almost lost in the gale.

Her sleeves reached her wrists, and she tugged them down to her palms, doing her best to hide her own shiver. The veilari tunic fell in verdant petals to her ankles, and she was thankful for her trousers, for her boots, and for her gloves.

"You shouldn't be up here," she said, looking at the clouds. Below them, she imagined the Broken Spine. That treacherous thrust of rock that marked a fearsome path between Anticarta and Trinacrios. She'd heard it was lit at night by the unbroken ceylonite beam of the Lighthouse of the Evolutionary, which was located on the western coast of Aedyton. Rishé glanced to Asaru again, a little ball of brown wool with her suman, wondering if he'd ever seen its alleged ceylonite glow.

"I'm cursed," he deadpanned, dropping his forehead onto his knees, "not sick."

"You're cursed and sick." She narrowed her eyes with all the heat she could muster.

They stared, then blinked at each other. After a moment Asaru folded like a fate card and gathered himself unsteadily to his feet. Her hands hovered at his back, but he waved her off and grasped the rail. Through his teeth, he exhaled, long and drawn out, like the whistling of riverside reeds.

"Go rest." She waved him in the direction of the great cabin where the captain had sequestered him. Away from the crew, due to fear of Black Diamond. But only eresh keyel appeared to suffer from the curse. Some dead, others dying. Slowly. Painfully, it seemed.

Cruelly. Rishé sighed, watching him shut the cabin's door. From what she had read in Oprekhet's ancient primer, the cruelty was the point.

Still, she had trouble making peace with the fact that Oprekhet was alive. As in not dead. As in probably never dead at all. Or maybe she was, and she'd been resurrected as some sort of revenant. Neither dead nor fully alive. But revenants were fiction. Or so she would have said half a year earlier. The last two moons had taught her such things shouldn't be discarded so quickly—there had to be some truth in stories that remained unchanged throughout the ages.

The Nest, for instance.

Which no longer existed.

A raindrop fell onto her cheek in tearful imitation.

With a mournful huff, Rishé gathered her books against her body to keep them dry. Her necklace warmed, feeling fleetingly like a pair of arms. The embrace of her mother, both imaginary and remembered.

As she fled below, several crooked forms appeared on the horizon. Half hidden by the weeping fog, they marked the beginning of the Broken Spine. Water frothed as waves prepared to drive the ship onto those craggy rocks. The wise crone that was the sea whipped up a frenzy, a test only the most foolhardy of mariners dared.

The gray sky split open, a storm spilled free, and Rishé shut the door above her, hoping this test was one they would pass.

The Nectarian Sea roared and surged around the *Danaye*. Wood moaned with each dangerous shift. Thunder clapped and lightning flashed, ringing as Rishé picked her way between rows of hammocks. The swaying canvas slings were hung from the thick beams of the ceiling by sturdy rope; some were occupied, most were not.

She glanced around the cabin, lit by swinging lamps burning seaross fat.

In a hammock by one of the windows she found Palenisa curled up, a black ball beneath her cape with her eyes clenched shut, muttering soundless prayers.

Another boom rang out; it sounded close. In her head, Rishé envisioned burning fish, cooked to perfection by the storm's strike. But the laugh halted in her chest when Palenisa began shaking like a sick bird. The ship lurched, and she paled, pressing her face to the cradle of her arms. Once in a while, the tremors that racked her body were interrupted by a jarring flinch.

"If you've come to lecture me again, just fucking don't," she groaned, scratchy voice wobbling.

Rishé hid a wince.

"May I sit?" she asked, hooking a finger beneath her chin in question as she spoke. The ship rocked, forcing her to press one hand to the wall for balance.

Lifting her head, Palenisa squinted as though staring into the dazzling glare of the sun. A heavy moment later she rolled her shoulder in a half shrug. Even covered in a sheen of sweat, there was something deeply appealing about her.

Radiant, Rishé told herself as she clambered into the hammock, tucking her books at her side. The silence was a porous thing. Spilling in, pouring out, swelling with the thundering of water against the sides of the straining ship like one great heaving beast. Waves sprayed through the window and fell over them in a fine misting of salt. She hugged her arms around herself. Her pendant provided a bit of warmth, but not nearly enough to stave off the chill.

"I *am* sorry, by the way," Rishé said quietly. Though she still stood by the fact that misery was poor company to wallow in—this should have been said sooner. Was this how Wren felt all the time, why his every second word was an apology?

Palenisa looked grimly amused. "I don't think you were entirely wrong."

Perking up, Rishé leaned forward, intrigued.

"Not about my faith—fuck you for that, by the way."

Snorting, Rishé shook her head wordlessly. She didn't fully agree, but she wasn't going to say that *now*.

"Just, maybe . . ." Palenisa trailed off, looking aside. Her mouth formed something of a pout, lower lip jutting out. "Maybe you weren't wrong to question my desires for the coterie. Recently, there are some things . . . some things that made me question them myself."

"I'm—"

"If the next word out of your mouth is 'sorry,' I'm going to start calling you Wren." A smidgen of emotion bled back into Palenisa's face.

Incredulous giggles bubbled from both their throats. As they laughed, breathless, the storm seemed to fade away. The momentary distraction shattered when the ship rolled. There was a sudden far-flung crack, a startled groan, and Palenisa's hand darted out.

Rishé stilled, her eyes blown wide at the ebony grip tightening around her wrist.

"Don't go."

So quiet was the plea, Rishé almost didn't hear it. With precious gentleness, she pried away the grip and set Palenisa's hand on the hammock at their sides. On a whim, she brushed rough knuckles with the backs of her fingers, which earned her a shaky sigh. And as much as she wanted to entangle their hands, she forced herself to draw away. *Too much—not yet.*

"I won't."

Biting her lip, she waited until the other woman calmed.

Pale wisps escaped beneath the black shadow of a hood, curling along the sides of a haunted face. On the back of the hand balled against the hammock was a cross bound by a circle. An earth suvaugram.

Rishé glanced out the window and watched sallow water sweep in to splash a thin layer across the damp floors.

Huh.

"You're scared of the open sea," she said, waving her hand up and down to represent the sign for waves.

"I am *not* scared of the open sea." Palenisa glowered, a tense blue gaze above the rise of her knees. "I just *dislike* it."

Rishé opened her mouth, rebuttal on her tongue. It was clear that Palenisa was scared; Rishé would have been a fool not to notice the obvious tells. But the ship creaked, wood splintering with a squeal, and Palenisa hunched in on herself. And Rishé knew the rebuttal wasn't worth it.

No arguments, not right now.

Her mouth snapped shut, and she thought for a second. White curls caught her attention again.

"Turn around."

"What?"

Rolling her eyes, Rishé twirled a finger after double-checking that she was speaking Akiki. "Turn—"

"Spirits, I heard you the first time," Palenisa hissed. "Why?"

Cheekily, Rishé reached out and tugged a springy curl. A hitch of breath fanned the inside of her wrist, sending her toes curling. She gulped, something heavy sinking to her core as she doffed Palenisa's hood. The look she received was unrecognizable. The flush, though, was unmistakable. It made the other woman look fevered. *And beautiful.*

"Trust me."

Palenisa searched her face and, when it seemed she found what she was looking for, sighed. Then, to Rishé's mild surprise, she complied. It sparked something curious in Rishé's brain to know that she was trusted.

Turning, Palenisa loosed her hair from its tie. Ivory flared out like bleached petals straining for the sun. She looked delightfully small all bundled up, and it made Rishé want to cup Palenisa in her hands like a duck. And though Palenisa crossed her arms like a petulant child, she'd still relented anyway.

As she combed through the white curls, Rishé hummed. She passed strands of hair between deft hands, forming unrefined braids. There was an intimacy to this kind of act. Among the Norvatti, parents braided the hair of their children. As did friends—perhaps even ones that hadn't seen each other in nearly a decade. As did lovers.

Rishé saw the tips of pointed ears flush and knew she wasn't alone in this warmth swirling and shuddering in her chest. At the silent realization, her own cheeks darkened.

Oh. Well then.

The hammock swayed lazily with the movement of the ship. And she formed more unrefined braids. And the rain pattered, drumming soft and sonorous above.

PALENISA

Shearing wind bit Palenisa's face as the island slowly rocked into view through the fog.

Treveyna was a bone-white spit of weathered rock that cut up from the sea in the midst of the Broken Spine, all sharp lines and crooked angles. She squinted as their skiffs sailed toward the silvery shore, each forward surge accompanied by the dip of oars in and through the water.

The island was too small to safely moor the ship, so they'd lowered two boats into the water to land. In one, she sat with Yurikhun and first mate Rayet, whom Palenisa pettily disliked—totally unrelated to the fact that Rayet had implied a past situational relationship with Rishé. It was, of course, because they were pirates, and they wore the title prouder than they should have in her opinion. The pair grinned at each other as if the cold was a mere inconvenience.

Grumbling, Palenisa tugged lower the hood of the coat she'd been given. It was a faded heather and was heavy with a lining of dark seaross fur. Embroidered along the collar and hem were flowers she didn't know the names of, the thread fraying with age.

A shiver crawled down her spine. She tipped her head back. *Cold.*

As the weather ate at her, she grew a greater appreciation for the humid heat of the south. Sometimes Ilon blazed, dragged sweat from places she didn't even know she could sweat, dried her eyes to painful points of sand. But it was home.

Pinching her thumb and index fingers together, Palenisa conjured a ball of sunlight. Gold glowed along the bottom of her face. Her numb fingers flexed in her lap as warmth dispersed into her extremities. *Thank you, spirits.*

In the other skiff, Asaru and Rishé huddled close together as the navigator and another crew member rowed in large, heaving pushes.

"Looks like there's someone here," Rayet said, far too lightly for her liking. She shifted aside, what little she could in the small boat, hugging her arms around herself. In her periphery, the redhead grinned, saber teeth chipped as if she'd lost one too many fights.

Palenisa looked for the signs of life the first mate's keen eyes spotted. It was hard to make out with everything swathed in varying shades of gray and more gray, but she discerned smoke wafting over the eastern side of the island from what looked to be a lighthouse. Every so often its beacon would wink, though it was far too weak to cut farther than a few yards into the fog.

"Could be those researchers from the tablet," Rishé called. "Maybe they've unearthed the diamondglass for us."

Beside her, Asaru hunched beneath his coat, the engulfing fabric making him look less substantial. He was there, but barely. Black covered him to his cupped chin, arm resting on a restlessly bouncing knee. "If we could be so lucky," he muttered, almost too low to hear over the constant dip and splash of oars. He frowned at the island with intensity, as though staring would bring it close sooner.

As if sensing her stare, Rishé looked over. A strange swarm of butterflies fluttered up Palenisa's throat. Absently, she caught the lone two braids framing the sides of her face. The rest had fallen out while they slept, but she felt the way they'd been plaited deftly, though haphazardly. She didn't feel as cold when she recalled waking up with Rishé splayed across the hammock at her back. The way her hair clung to the sides of her drool-crusted face, which contorted in a frown every so often, lips smacking and nose wrinkling. The way her arm lay slung around her, and the chest rising and falling under her head.

Purple flooded Palenisa's face, leaving her warmer than the sunlight had. Her heart clenched as small hands danced behind her lids. They transformed into a larger, calloused pair, suvaugram marked—and the smile curdled on her lips. She glanced away as the image of Ada surfaced, aged to a haze by time. Guilt tasted sour as she breathed in. It felt like a betrayal to even indulge the possibility of moving on. She'd been driven by devotion to being the Sister of Faith for so long, it was hard to consider a life where the memory of Ada wasn't the most important thing *in* it. Who was she without the Crocodile Coterie?

The crunch of wood on sand threw Palenisa back to the present.

As their skiffs slid ashore, fog fled like a wary creature, slicing thin pieces of visibility through the drear. Instead of sand, the beach was made of granular stones, tiny as pupils. The island's coast was a feathery ring that skirted the border like hoarfrost.

The air felt thick on her tongue as Palenisa stepped unsteadily from the skiff, into the surf. In place of sandals, she wore fur-lined boots that climbed up to her calves; and in place of her wrapped skirt were a pair of trousers, though her chain rings still rattled as she moved.

Their footfalls hissed. Sibilant stones crunched as they dragged the boats farther aground with them. Their careless mash of footsteps left messy pits on the untouched land. If not for the lighthouse, Palenisa would be hard pressed to think anyone had ever set foot there.

Ears flicking, she darted to the other boat, balancing Asaru as he stumbled.

"Hey, hey," she mumbled. "Are you sure you can handle this?"

Pebbles shifted beneath him, and he shivered, pulling away until their only points of contact were his hands on her forearms. Wisps of sweat-soaked hair stuck to his temples as Asaru looked up at her from beneath the shadow of his hood.

"I have no choice." His breath fogged the air. He straightened, failing to hide a slight wince. His tail brushed his boots, stiff from either cold or pain. For a moment Palenisa wondered where he was hurting, before realizing he hurt everywhere. Head to heart to heel.

Cold nipped her nose as she looked out at the rugged island ahead. There was a light dusting of snow and an air of utter loneliness. This place felt like the shattered shard of something greater. A vertebra in a broken spine.

Once the last of the crew had disembarked, they made their way to where the stony shore graded into colorless dirt, seamless as the blend of sky at sunrise. Gray kissed the unmarked path, which crept along like beckoning fingers. The road, if one could call it that, rose in parts as if someone had cracked a geode in two and draped the contents all over the terrain.

They stayed close to Rishé as she glanced up from her

compass, turned aside, then glanced back down to it. Following, the crew chattered in the cursive of their native tongue, long and drawling like a melting slurry. Every so often Palenisa tossed them a suspicious glare, which was met with amusement. She trusted them as little as she did Sagan, and rightly so, considering what the masked shit had done. Parts of her brain still felt tender.

Stuffing gloved hands inside her pockets, Palenisa peered over Rishé's shoulder at the compass. The needle swung aside, swaying as they followed its marrowstone line.

"You know where we're going?"

"Kimberlite pine trees grow near diamondglass on Anticarta. They're nourished by the gems, I think," Rishé said, guiding them beneath an overhang of rock that curved like a crooked back.

The mist opened up on the other side, and the island seemed to unfurl like a rough tongue. Treveyna was much larger than expected, so they found themselves walking for hours, pausing only to eat dried meats and warm themselves by a fire when night fell, much to the chagrin of their companions. For the three of them, though, this had been their lives for the last two moons.

By the time they got to the "forest," blue and pink were filtering through the relentless cloud cover, casting the island in the suffused hues of dawn. Somehow everything was bright, yet dull and gray, a contradiction of equalities.

Morning frost misted their breaths as they came upon the mouth of what some might call a forest. A thin sheet of snow had fallen overnight, coating the hundreds of stone pillars that jutted from the uncompromising earth. Wide bases spiraled up into many-armed points, like candelabras, the breeze clattering a discordant tune between them. Some pillars rose neatly, others fell across the path like crossed bars sprinkled in white. Trailing through the thick crowd of columns, their reflections stretched and smeared across the silvery surfaces in a myriad of smudged colors.

Tall and commanding, at a certain angle they looked almost like suvaunoors. The sight reminded Palenisa of lying prostrate before the monuments to her faith at the foot of the kharess's manse. But she would never get to do so again. Not while she wore dishonor as a coat, slathered in the effluent of shame.

As they ventured deeper into the island, the features on the pillars clarified and she saw what they truly were: trees. Petrified kimberlite trees. Palenisa reached out, brushing a trunk ridged with whorls resembling suvaugrams. Where she expected to hear the cries of the earth—there was nothing. The once- trees were shorn to sharpness by centuries of icy winds. Gone for longer, millennia maybe, like a living person once their aether had evanesced, irreparably destroyed in death. The touch left her with a gap in the cavern beneath her ribs. Snatching her hand back, she exhaled and rushed back to the others.

"This place feels familiar," Asaru said quietly. Something glinted in his black-drowned eyes when he trailed them up the stone roots to the peak of a massive kimberlite.

In the very center of the forest, the enormous fist of a fossil reached for the overcast sky. Its circumference must have been the length of five, maybe six, of Palenisa's wingspan, and it was the only member of the stony horde that appeared to have branches. Thick gray growths with the consistency of hard light dipped low to form an arch of rock that resembled the legs of hunkering spiders. From the undulating tangle of stone roots half buried in the earth in a windswept spiral, this seemed to be the origin from which the rest of the forest had once sprawled.

"It's like a dendrite forest," Asaru said in a breathless murmur that stuttered into coughs. The fit ran through him, shaking sacred silence from the air. Black bile stained the back of his hand, then his coat when he wiped it at his side. The gruesome smear stood stark against the fabric.

It hurt to look at.

When Palenisa's concerned gaze swept back up, she found him dazed, eyes fogged over. Too much like Khensu, his unfortunate kin found in the worst place to die. Alone.

Stay alive, alive, alive. The refrain reeked with a need matched only by her desire for the Zodiac's approval. *A fool's errand,* she envisioned as their reply. But surely once they had the diamondglass, the end to all this would be that much closer. Not a cure, not a break. An end. To the curse, her promise—*promises,* plural. Everything, neat and final.

Shafts of sun dappled a pale, watery light through the branches as she rounded the central kimberlite . . . and came face-to-face with an Antorcan. Equally wide mismatched verdant and red eyes locked onto hers.

Lulaik, said her mind.

"Wuh," said her mouth.

The Antorcan gasped as a pirate's sword shot out from behind Palenisa. Steel flashed in the corner of her vision, and she wrenched the wrist of the attacker, forcing their sword loose. It clattered to the ground, echoing loudly through the forest. She then gave the Antorcan researcher a swift, hard kick, knocking them out. They slumped over their journals. Reams of paper fanned out, covered in a strange script and annotated diagrams of the kimberlite.

"The fuck is wrong with you?" The words sparked off Palenisa's tongue as she glared at Yurikhun. A grin split Yurikhun's face wide, wrinkling the blue scales that hatched her cheeks, faded, likely due to her age. The tall, thick woman rolled a shoulder. *Infuriating.*

Shaking her head, Palenisa leashed her tongue. She took the fallen researcher beneath the armpits and dragged them aside. They loosed a snore, their lashes fluttered. Her feet left sandy footprints across their notes.

"Shouldn't we keep going?" Palenisa asked when Rishé crouched to examine the base of the tree. When Rishé rapped the stone with a knuckle, it sounded strangely hollow. Slender hands felt along the tangle of roots, between the earth hardened by time and something that felt far more arcane. Rishé stilled and looked over a shoulder with a grin that sent heat swooping to just above Palenisa's navel. Blue eyes met amber, which crinkled in smug delight.

"There are markings! It's here."

Curious, Palenisa wandered closer, her shadow falling over the smaller woman. She jumped slightly at their proximity when Rishé suddenly stood.

"Everyone, um, you should step back. I want to try something," Rishé said, raising her hands, fingers spread wide, like an Aspect might. A pink tongue peeked from the corner of her lip as she drew that waterlogged tome from the Nest out of her coat. It hadn't stopped dripping since, still soaked by some unnatural enchantment.

Immediately, the crew took a step back.

"Try what?" Asaru asked, though he, too, made room. As did Palenisa, but only after Rishé sent her a heated look that sped the thrum of her heart. She discreetly pressed a hand to her chest to still it. *Seriously, what is wrong with me?*

"An experiment." Rishé flipped the book open and turned to a page.

She pulled off her necklace, squeezing the pendant tightly in her palm. The gem seemed to glow, causing the space around her fist to shimmer in a heat mirage. The way the air warped when Rishé began to speak must have been a trick of the distorted light.

The tree shook, the shuddering speeding up until the disruption was a constant buzz under the earth. It vibrated beneath Palenisa, trembled through her, jarred her teeth in her skull. Long-dead roots shivered, writhing as though they'd come back to life to pull free under Rishé's command. But stone remained stone—until it didn't. A crack formed, rising from hidden markings.

In a flash, the trunk splintered, and it sundered apart with a terrible shudder. Light poured from within, a divine vein severed through the earth by a vicious dagger. Tumbling from the dendritic cavity was a cascade of diamondglass, glittering as the beacon did—brighter even. Gems clung to the flayed edges of the kimberlite like dew, an overflowing waterfall of wealth. A crystalline glow beamed the sun in all directions, flaring, throwing twinkling spots wreathed in rainbows across the pillars around them.

Palenisa shielded her eyes against the glare and stepped closer. She would have taken another step, but she was snared by Rishé's voice. Crisp, her words drifted in one ear and melted out the other. The language was unlike any she'd ever heard, blanketing her with a heady power. It didn't smell like khetry with its pungent petrichor and irritating essence.

It didn't smell like anything at all.

The nonsmell soaked revulsion into her bones as it muffled her senses. Different from the tunnels, but no more appealing.

A cough broke through the air. A bolt of sound that shocked her from the trance.

Turning, Palenisa found Asaru doubled over as his legs buckled. He collapsed with a wounded cry. His hood fell back, revealing the unnatural red, far more striking than that of the Antorcans, and his back convulsed, his wings rippled and jerked, threatening to break free of the thick seaross coat he now wore. Though it looked more like vermin pulsing through decaying flesh.

The scent of Black Diamond filled Palenisa's nose as the curse flared through his body, attacking every part of him with the cruel and pointed hand of its creator. It thickened, the world slowing to a crawl as her every sensation narrowed to a single point. As strong as the spell that summoned him—*stronger.* It swelled over her in a startling black wave. Death—he smelled of death. She knew that smell well, better than most.

Stricken, Palenisa whipped back around to the lack of smell. Then to Asaru coated thickly in the curse, clutching his middle as pain daggered him.

"Stop," she yelled. "Rishé, stop!"

As she was snapped suddenly from her chanting recitations, Rishé's head shot up. There was a glaze over her eyes, peeling away like scales as she registered Palenisa's cry. She wore an expression equal parts stunned and apologetic as her pendant fell into the folds of the tome.

"By the spirits, what *was* that?" Palenisa knelt by Asaru, unsure what to do as his face tightened, furrows notched deeply in his brow.

With a sharp intake of breath, Rishé clapped the tome shut, swallowing her burning pendant within its pages. She shook as if she were flinging away rivulets of water, turned. Diamondglass silvered the sly contours of her profile in a pale glow.

"Something I think the world used to know." Her voice had lost its clarity, coming out in a croak, as though she'd gargled a generous mouthful of sand.

Palenisa's response was interrupted by a sharp whistle.

Behind them, Yurikhun twirled a finger, spurring her crew into action with a shout in her native tongue. They moved like smooth, dark water through a clock, a machine with every part in perfect unison as they loaded the mass of diamondglass into large nondescript bags that may have once held flour. Covetous eyes flickered over the gems as they disappeared into darkness.

Palenisa bristled at the slavering desire painted on their faces. She bore no great hatred for pirates on the whole, but this crew? By their mere association with Sagan, she distrusted them innately.

"Don't even think about it," she snarled.

"Testy, testy," Yurikhun tutted, rolling her eyes. "Pull that staff out of your ass." Swinging an arm like she was looping rope, Yurikhun snapped at her crew in Vulgar Antic, the Anticartan tongue. The jeweled glow dwindled away as the small spark of divinity faded, leaving in its place the island's creeping cold, which wrapped its fingers around Palenisa's neck. And Asaru's neck as well, latching him in place as black spittle dribbled from his panting mouth.

Rishé rubbed the top of his spine between where his wings lay, waiting for permission before pressing her other hand to his damp forehead.

"Fevering," she said, wriggling her fingers upward. "Fevering badly."

Cupping the lower half of his face, Asaru hacked into his gloves. Spirits, what a horrible sound. The drag of claws on glass, the cacophonous rumble of a storm, the scream of a dying horse. His gloved hands came away utterly *drenched* in black, as dark as a burnt desert. Chuckling, Asaru smiled grimly at the pool of bile dripping onto the rocks.

"I suppose"—he began weakly—"I might have to break a promise I never made."

His eyes rolled back in his head, and he fainted into Rishé's side.

Palenisa's lips pursed at the thin line of blood trickling from the corner of his mouth. Rishé wiped it away and looked up at her in barely restrained worry. It was getting worse faster, and they didn't know how long he had left.

Palenisa moved to his side, knelt, and placed her staff on the ground, not once taking her eyes off her . . . charge. *Friend,* she admitted. Closing her eyes, she hovered a hand over his midsection. Though she was first and foremost a warrior, as Sister of Faith, some of her duties had been of a religious nature. It was her calling, ingrained in every facet of her life: honoring the Zodiac for her blessing, for the life she almost lost in pursuit of revenge, for the coterie.

But they'd excommunicated her. It was the only place she'd felt the scaffold of true belonging. And they'd put her out in the gutters as a drunken sobbing mess. Her chest seized with the ache of wanting. Ada's gift—she wanted it back more than anything. Many other things she wanted too. Off this desolate, frigid island. To make it to Aedyton in time to meet Wren. For Asaru not to die.

A volley of prayers swirled in her thoughts. Under her breath, Palenisa lingered at the end of each orison. All twelve spirits were present. Somehow, she felt them, as real as the chill seeping into her bones. She heard the layers of their imagined whispers coiling in her ears. Piety kept her going. Belief kept her strong.

Thinking was one thing, but saying made it thus. Into existence, Palenisa spoke it. And desperately, she hoped it would work—that Asaru would live.

WREN

On their third day at sea, Wren woke to a sharp pulse in his brand. The persistent throbbing was broken occasionally by an acute stab of pain—*Asaru's pain*—filling him with regret that he had ever agreed to leave. Like a lulaik needed physical contact, some part of him needed to feel Asaru's hands cupping his face, skirting lightly over his nape as if hesitant to touch. It both disturbed and ate away at him how much he yearned, a bottomless hunger and a quenchless thirst.

A different kind of friend, whispered a soft voice at the back of his bleary mind. Furtumbér take him now, he was a fool.

Groaning, Wren rubbed his palms into his eyes and recalled an ivory tower. Black swept in, and the tower toppled, dissolving into the sea like foam. The destruction of millennia of history and the present as it was written. The scarred geode on the cliff became a faint stream of smoke.

Had he not seen the ship sailing off in the opposite direction, his heart might've dropped like a stone at the thought that his friends still remained in that melted mass of black and white and bismuth gray. But he'd seen them leave, he told himself. Though he was less reassured by their being in the hands of pirates. They were teetering on a bone point, and his anxieties only grew along with the distance between them.

The brand tugged his chest, and he turned on the stiff bench, trying to fall back asleep despite the insistent glare of the sun. A crooked staff was shoved none too lightly into his stomach, jarring him back awake.

"Tios'dov-sovi'dem inust." *Wake up.*

"I am," Wren groused, sitting up. Drowsiness drew his lids to half-mast under the weight of poor rest. He felt laden with grime, damp from the constant spray of the sea. On the other hand, Sagan looked frustratingly fresh once he shucked his mask. There were thin bags beneath his lower lids, but little else to indicate he'd spent the last two days only occasionally snatching rest. It was mildly irritating.

"Doesn't look like it."

As he peeled open his bleary eyes, Wren's lower lip popped out. "I. Am."

Sagan grinned slyly. Violet hair fell into his mismatched gaze, and Wren was caught for a moment. He'd never met a lulaik that wasn't from the continent, so to him, purple was a unique color for a khetry eye. Striking and vaguely unnatural, forcing him to avert his own to the crimson waves of the Red Gulf. Water sprayed into the bottom of the boat, warmed by the Volcanic Steps, a small peninsula cradling eastern Peskelos, whose molten mountains boiled from the depths.

"Tut-vaneran takeš?"

"I'm fine."

"Someone's cranky." Sagan blew up his fringe and glanced at the island they were approaching.

Centuries-old stores of iron oxide seeped into the water, lapping at bloody beaches. The rest of the island was an impressive ruddy sprawl smothered in coconut palms and feathered fox trees.

Wren planted an elbow on the side of the boat, rested his chin on it, and watched daily life on Peskelos pass along either side. Shaded stalls and steps of marble descended into the water. Bodies draped in coral fabrics crowded near the edges; children splashed in the shallows, picking up pink cowries, while adults huddled in groups over low tables covered in food.

"Where are we going?"

A notched brow rose. "Where do you think?"

Wren tilted his head at the central hill—which, with its massive eye-catching size, was more of a mountain. A waterfall cascaded down one side to the river they were sailing toward. As the gulf narrowed into the tributary, they began to see other vessels. Their skiff rocked in the tight gap between a boat from which merchants hawked jars of spices and jewelry and the lunar-powered trawler hauling a woven net of fish.

"Specifics would be nice."

"Lake Alhena, at the top of Adranza Hill."

"That's—"

A flicker of a smile, a halted eye roll. "A mountain, I know. Everyone knows. We get it a lot."

Flushing, Wren felt a touch ashamed. He should probably have shut up, but this was the first time he'd ever left Estyria, and he had questions. Damnable curiosity gnawed the inside of his mouth.

"Does anyone, um, *know* the Chronicler's here?"

Cocking his head, Sagan tilted his hand side to side with a hum. "They're quite good at keeping secrets," he said, adding under his breath a bitter-sounding "even from me, apparently."

Pushing the steering lever down, Sagan guided the skiff into a busy receiving port.

Docks stretched in ramshackle rows across which a constant swarm of common folk shouted. Lining either side of the dock were statues of oily black stone, twelve of them, with long, thin bodies and crown-shaped crests. Basilisks, Wren's mind provided at the memory of an all-nighter at the guild spent poring over a tome of folktales with Rishé.

The skiff bumped against the dock, and Sagan leaped out, dragging a rope after him. He looped it around a metal ring on a mooring post and planted his hands on his hips, looking right at home amid lilac- and lavender-haired wraiths. Many humans had also dyed theirs to match, an island of people united under a common shade.

"We don't have rogue Aspects," Sagan said, holding out a hand. "You'll be fine. Trust me."

Just because Wren was there to learn the ritual didn't mean he trusted the man. He just wanted to do right. Part of this he was doing to return to the guild and regain a place among their ranks, and yet . . . and yet. For all he thought constantly of them, did they do the same?

Tightness laced his middle, drew him taut like a thread of khetry.

After a lull, he took the offered hand, adjusted the strap of his satchel, and doffed the hood of his suman, as apprehension congealed his blood. Wren wondered, not for the first time, what the Chronicler was like. The usual weight of his hideous self-worth told him that he wouldn't be enough, that he couldn't fulfill whatever part he needed to play. That he would once again fail, and he would bring something worse than a backlash down on all of them.

Breathe.

As Sagan glided onto the island proper, Wren squeezed after, thankful his height allowed him to keep the shorter man in sight. His feet found sand, and he stumbled before being steadied by Sagan. The other huffed, smirking up at him through dark lashes.

"Watch your step."

Something about Peskelos seemed to loosen Sagan's lips. It made him no less cryptic, but there was something homely about the way he wove around the crowd, returning waves with smiles and gentle kisses.

Everyone contains multitudes, Wren supposed. When he tried to piece together the contradictory, incongruous, frustrating parts of Sagan, all he conjured was a formless red beast impenetrable as the fathomless deep, with an adderowl for a head and two blazing purpled eyes.

They trailed to a nearby bridge, crunching bright red sand underfoot. In the middle of the beach rose the commanding line of an obsidian suvaunoor carved with scarlet suvaugrams. Common folk rested in its long shade and prostrated themselves at its feet.

The bridge rose over a canal, one of many the river split into. While crossing, Wren took in the brightness of everything. It brought to the surface his few memories of his birth clan. The crush of people, the music, the floral fragrance. He didn't think air could feel different, but yes—even that felt substantially different.

The way up to the peak of the hill-that-was-not-a-hill took them under the arch of an aqueduct. Sandy dirt bled to cobblestone in various shades of flaming sunset, inlaid with what looked to be red diamonds. The same way he saw some common folk veiled in pink cowrie coins—*kurigand,* his memory supplied—the island itself was wreathed in jeweled splendor. Excessive, but it seemed they had the gems to spare.

As they stepped onto a jungle path, a cluster of thin pastel buildings packed in Bartramian fashion came into view, and the cheer on Sagan's face faded. It felt as though the both of them were holding their breaths by the time the village was behind them. When it was a good distance away, Sagan stilled by a fox tree. The feathers dappled him in shadow.

On instinct, Wren made to reach out, but paused as Sagan gathered himself, unease melting away. They resumed their trek, and the incline steepened.

"*Tut*-vaneran takeš?" Wren asked.

"That village," Sagan replied, his voice a steel bar without inflection, "forced what remained of my clan to work as 'fortune tellers' when our guardians died. Indentured servitude. It was an insult to our way of life, to our actual Charmers. Then again, when it comes to the Norvatti, it's always *us*. Always the Vana."

Wren gaped. He . . . hadn't actually expected an answer. Much less one so honest it was soul baring. *Indentured servitude?* That practice was said to have died out centuries ago—everywhere. He instantly felt horrible for asking, even though he hadn't actually asked. So he fell back on what he knew best.

"I, um, I'm sorry." His hand brushed Sagan's shoulder.

"It's fine. Someone stopped them, and Inone took me in. Everything's fine now."

It didn't sound fine. But Sagan shrugged him off and sped up.

Over the crest of the incline, peeking out from a bower, emerged Lake Alhena.

Boulders ringed the border, climbing atop each other to form a cave-riddled perimeter over which the jungle drooped. A column of light shone straight down through the break in the canopy onto the water. Flowers floated across the surface, boiling such that steam warped the air.

Ten crimson-cloaked figures meditated at the lakefront. On the hoods of their cloaks was stitched an eye like the one on the Nest. The figures sat before a half-submerged figure that, at first, Wren thought was a massive statue.

Then it moved.

He started when the figure rose, a torrent raining from sleek, straight hair. Crystal-fly wings sprouted from their back in a drape of lace membrane. Each flutter was the dissonant chime of a bell. A wizened bronze face turned his way. Painted across their nose was a band of gold, looping around their neck was an unusual halo, striated by onyx, and their eyes . . . their *eyes.*

Shades of indigo with spinning silver stars for pupils, strange constellations formed with each blink. Khetry threads swam through the liquid iris like blood clots swirling down a drain.

Wren's own eyes widened. Nerves choked the words from his mouth. His many shortcomings and deficiencies filled the emptiness left behind as he stared upon the grandeur of the Chronicler.

He wondered if he was looking upon divinity made flesh.

They extended a sun-browned hand. Water showered from their fingers, dotted in gold and ringed in silver all the way up the wrist. Wren wasn't sure when he moved, drawn closer by their reverent nature, as if he were one of their cloaked supplicants. Unsure what to do with his own hands, which spasmed at his sides, Wren clasped them together at his front, then folded them behind his back.

"Wren Anemone du Ingoscu-Velanescu, bonsou," they intoned. *Welcome.* "I am Niekthe."

If Wren's eyes got any wider, they would pop out of his head.

The eresh keyel who disappeared after killing their sister,

who ended the Founding War but let their name fade from the minds of the masses, as Wren's ancestor crowned herself in their absence.

"Um," he stuttered. "Just Wren is fine. And, um, I'm . . . not a Velanescu?"

They cocked their head with a secret smile. "Oh?"

At his side, he heard Sagan snicker and wanted to sink into the ground. His lips thinned as he looked at his boots.

"Why are you here, Wren?" Their resonant voice thrummed through him, layered atop itself both impossibly high and impossibly deep. A shudder rolled up from Wren's feet to a spot at the base of his brain, unraveling him like a spell knotted into khetry.

A shaky exhale escaped. "T-To . . . to learn the ritual?"

Glancing up through his fringe, he saw the Chronicler smile. Their eyes crinkled, lines deepening at the corners. Despite their placidity, the upward canting of their lips resembled the deadly curve of a scythe. The expression shot a bolt through his abdomen feeling somewhere between mild terror and awe.

"Try again. The truth this time, if you please."

Absently, Wren brushed his heart. Somehow, he feared they knew about the bone that drank his blood, the pathetic desperation he'd plunged into in order to repair what he'd so badly broken.

"To make up for what I did . . . what I've done. At any cost," he said, determination woven into his words. His fingers tightened, itching to reach inside the brand—to the needle, calling to him to finish it. "Especially to myself."

Resolute, Wren raised his head. The Chronicler's smile sharpened, and they nodded. Power emanated from their form, rawer and older than any spell he'd felt before. Almost as wild as the living web itself.

"Come. Join us." They sank into the lake until only their calculating eyes remained.

Wren's heart beat a fraught rhythm as he knelt. The brand burned. He closed his eyes. On the backs of his eyelids, he saw an amethyst halo, gentle hands that held so much strength, and the fondness on Asaru's face, soft as a grazing kiss.

Days passed like rushing water, and soon so had a week.

From dawn to dusk over seven days, Wren woke to join the Doyisha, the Chronicler's crimson-cloaked supplicants. During the morning, they studied the mechanics of the ritual, drawing its spellwork over and over until the symbols were deemed acceptable. And in the latter half of the day, they meditated until the sky turned as blue as the swirl of emotions inside him.

Nausea took him and he heaved, expelling the contents of his stomach into the lake.

Meditation sickness. The thought was interrupted by another swell of vomit, which he promptly emptied. Boiling heat fanned his cheeks, unbearably warm.

Vaguely, Wren heard Niekthe call for a break as he rinsed out his sour mouth.

The Doyisha dispersed, including Sagan, leaving him alone with Niekthe. They swanned closer to rest their chin on the rocky embankment before him.

"I can keep going," Wren groaned.

"You cannot."

"But I—"

"Wren." Their voice left no room for argument.

Frustrated, he frowned at his rippling reflection. Black curls fell to his upper back and hung over his shoulders and around his face, the ends trailing the water. The person staring back was him, but it was also his father. He'd never seen Zaosha, beyond half-accurate depictions on holographic screens, and the wistful descriptions his mother had given the few times she was willing to talk about his father.

Wren frowned and broke the image before sitting back on his knees.

"How is your study progressing?" Niekthe asked. The corner of their lips quirked, but their face remained impassive.

"A little more every day." The studying wasn't the problem—Wren had spent years at the guild. In fact, he gained an almost Rishé-like delight each time he drew the correct spellwork, each little discovery feeling like an advancement in personal knowledge.

But learning the mechanics was one thing. Actually understanding the ritual, the meaning of the sacred geometry, was another thing entirely. It strained every bit of focus he possessed to keep his mind on this sole task, to not wander off in worry about his friends. Or the perhaps not-so-irrational fear that everyone could see the needle burning a hole through his pocket.

Wetness dripped down his chin. Wincing, Wren pinched the bridge of his nose and let it dribble into the lake, three red dots vanishing in the water.

"I *was* wondering, though . . . about the nature of curse breaking?" He licked his upper lip, tasted blood. His face was most surely a smeared mess. Fitting, since one needed blood to work a curse.

Niekthe hummed, amused. They opened a single large eye, pupil white as bone. "Well, we're not breaking the curse."

"But you—we're . . . not, um, killing the creator either."

Their appraising look seared straight through him. For a delirious second, Wren thought that it fell to his chest pocket. *They know; they know.* "Do you think you could kill someone?"

Biting the inside of his cheek, he glanced at the reflection. Him, his father, and also his mother.

"No," he said softly.

There was a whisper in the silence, like the whisking of leaves on stone. He felt more than heard their breathing, each a gale in its large lonesomeness. They moved with the rustle of wet fabric.

"We know black diamonds are the cursed object, and diamondglass its opposite in every way—heal to its hurt, the light to its dark," they explained. "The ritual allows us to use this connection to void the effects of the curse."

"How?"

"By transferring it into a new object. A crucible."

"Crucible?" He was short on words but rich with anxieties.

"Whatever, *whomever,* khetry deems deserving of it."

Wren gulped, feeling a chill rise. "And what . . . who deserves it?"

Niekthe locked eyes with him. The unflinching stare, empty as a void, forced him to turn aside. His brand stung at the thought of the crucible being anyone *but* him. The thought of someone innocent burdened by the consequences of Oprekhet's retribution. Unlike him, for he was all too deserving. Wren should have offered himself in service. Another opportunity for rightful self-flagellation as the chronic vessel of sole blame for this sorry mess—and Asaru's misfortune.

But he remained silent, and his fingers formed lax shapes as he picked at a fingernail.

"All this," he said, "are you truly doing all this to stop your sister?"

"Oprekhet and I . . ." They trailed off, equally soft. "You see, my sister and I are . . . alien to this world. We are the last two feyinesh left, precursors to the eresh keyel from another realm, and our arrival was an accident."

Reeling, Wren was lost for words as everything they said rewired his brain. What was he supposed to say? *Oh, it's all right, thank you for upending my very understanding of the natural order of the world.*

They continued, anger threading their words in a delicate balance. "I remember fragments of fighting—*cleansing,* we called it. Cleaning corruption from another realm. I remember a time when our older sister, Madib, was not your goddess or a warden. I remember stepping through a rift ripped in reality, being stranded here when khetry was but a whimper."

"That's impossible. Khetry is older than *everything.*"

Impossible, impossible, impossible. The refrain leashed his senses.

Waving a hand, Niekthe tugged at khetry. Threads snaked across their arm, an old creature coming to meet a familiar friend. It looked almost sentient. More than alive—it had a thinking, feeling, reeling mind of its own.

"On our home world, we were deathless. I suppose that afforded us a longer-than-average lifespan here. To be honest, I am not sure we would have learned we were mortal had Madib not . . . passed. Mysteriously."

Mysteriously, Wren echoed. He swallowed. Unable to meet their eye, he watched them in his periphery.

"Oprekhet also passed."

The lake rippled as Niekthe sank lower. There was knowing, and there was *knowing.* Desperate for the truth, Wren let his need come ashore in a question he feared the answer to.

"But *how* is she still alive?"

Beams of twilight fell through the canopy, fallen leaves suspended on the lake. Niekthe locked eyes with him.

"Because I resurrected her."

What?

Wren's eyes were hot—was he crying? He felt like crying. At a sudden gust of anger, his stomach sank. In it gurgled revulsion and rage. If the lake weren't already burning, it would have burst into flames.

"Why?"

The Chronicler sighed. "I did not even know I could, that I was a Weaver, until it happened."

His heart stopped. *Weaver.* They knew, he feared, they knew, they knew.

"Now she is a revenant detached from khetry, aetherless. She cannot die. She cannot be killed. But she is still my *sister.*"

A tear slipped free, and Wren wiped it away. He was a ball of hatred and despair, all the bitter emotions he was often too muffled by his melancholy to feel. To truly feel. They rumbled across his skin, cored grooves through him.

She was the reason Alvarys was dead, the reason Asaru was dying—and she had been resurrected. By the same sibling who ended her life. To break the three cornerstones with such flagrant disregard warranted more than just a backlash. It was to court the wrath of reality itself.

Wren knew he would do anything, *anything,* to rectify all he had done.

He wasn't sure he would do this.

The sibilant spread of frost crusted still waters. Moonlight danced across the slick surface where hot met cold. Infinite anger consuming itself only to surge again, brighter.

Standing, Wren turned away from the Chronicler. Without another word, he stalked off. The needle pricked his skin, thirsting for blood.

There was more work to be done.

In a cave hidden behind the waterfall, Wren was soaked in red to the elbow. It dripped down his nose, into his mouth, coloring the edges of his vision. The world was a scarlet glaze that doubled as he swayed, dizzy.

Less than a finger's width of bone remained to fill the needle. There was no going back.

He grasped his wrist, shoved down harder, splitting his finger on the tiny point. Steam rose from the pool to obscure his vision. Its murky water darkened the bottom of his trousers up to the knee, thighs stained with spots of red.

Khetry pulled blood down from his wrists, from his fingers—and the needle drank it with great vigor. It hurt. Badly. The pain sizzled in his bones, like he was being cut open with cauterizing shears. But that didn't matter, because it was *real*. The ritual, Weavers, the powers they were said to gain for their piteous sacrifice. All real.

Wren's determination was then tempered by a subtle misery. Look at him—driving himself into the arms of death so long as he could do this one thing for the man who held half his heart. His mind floated to Asaru. He ached, starved for the kindly touch at the other end of the brand that had become so precious to him.

They were friends. They were something different from friends. They were irrevocably bound.

As he imbued the needle with living liquid, Wren closed

his eyes and listened to the sounds in the cave. The steady drip of water from stalactites bearding the upper curve, the echo of his pained panting, the padding of slippered footsteps that approached him. He cursed as his eyes shot wide. He pulled his hand from the page and hid it in the folds of his suman while shoving the needle up his sleeve. It scraped his inner wrist, but he was too agitated to acknowledge the blood it may have drawn.

Someone sat beside him. They remained as quiet as sleep.

"It's time to descend," Sagan said in a muted tone.

"To descend?"

"The last step in the Chronicler's teachings."

Sagan's legs were splayed aside, crimson suman trailing in the water. He stretched his toes over the pool. From an inner pocket, he produced a white sprig surrounded by evergreen leaves. It resembled the mutant sun seen through a viridian filter.

"Qhat. It lets you breathe underwater and opens your mind. Allows you to grasp the fullness of the ritual and allows it to grasp you in turn."

"Why now?" Wren asked, tracing a bloody loop over the cornucopia embroidered on his suman. What a morbid sight, it looked almost like he'd killed someone. Like himself, slowly exsanguinated for the sake of another. But this would all be worth it—he was more sure of that than his desires for the guild.

"Your friends have done their part. It's time to do yours." Sagan flipped the flower over the backs of his fingers like a coin and held it over his mouth. Stitched on his glove was the severe circle of a flame spell. He charged it with a single finger, light turning white, then red.

The qhat burst into a green cloud, hiding Sagan's face and intentions. Through the mist, Wren met his eyes, swirling dark.

They were the only two people in the world of this cave, and the water lapped at their feet.

Before he could pull away, Sagan grabbed Wren's chin tight enough to bruise and pressed their lips together. Searing smoke passed between their mouths in a sweet puff.

Vapors clouded Wren's head, eyes fluttering. Neither moved as Sagan held on for just a moment longer before pushing away with a set to his jaw. His irises were warped around the pupil by thin green lines that seemed to breathe. Inhaling, exhaling. He brushed down Wren's spit-slicked lip, thumbed at its corner.

He smiled, but all Wren saw was a smear of color. Inhaling, exhaling. Smoke wormed through his body. His fingers flexed in his lap, desirous to run across his lips, to see if that had been real. It felt like blood loss. It felt like a lucid dream. Then he blinked.

And he was drowning. No. He was just underwater.

How did I get here?

There was water in his lungs and mouth, but he breathed just fine.

Where is *here?*

You're descending, came the answer in a voice not his own.

He was immersed in the lake, cradled as if by a mother; it was warm in the descent, but nowhere close to boiling. The weight of watery fingers tried prying Wren's lips open, and his heart beat a thousand times, shivering in the cage of his ribs, threatening escape.

This all felt like an illusion.

Knees curled up, arms wrapped around them, he tilted his head back. Moonlight circled around him, wavering through the depths. He was surrounded by rocky walls with caves carved into them. Inside those caves hid monsters—his fears, his awful desires, the worst of them formed from his mistakes. The darkness was heavy, as if something great lurked within. It felt like he was being watched. The assessing gaze of a wanting predator crawled its way beneath his flesh, wriggling with the sensation of maggots. Or maybe that was him. He felt like a mass of walking vermin.

Something sinister prodded at the reaches of his vulnerable brain. Weak. He was a weak and tender creature. After one more testing caress, the presence receded.

In the space it left behind, the ritual streamed into his mind, understanding accompanied by concentric circles. Sacred geometry, the base that formed the language of a spell. Spiraling and spiraling and spiraling, the glowing circles worked, built the ritual spellwork atop itself. See and know, touch and understand. With disembodied hands, Wren reached. The tips of his fingers grazed a strand. He tugged, intangible hands drawing the knowledge close, tucking it against his chest over the wreath of acorns.

Sparkling stones fractured into dust. The dust formed a tight coronet of thorns around his head.

All was silent. In this underwater world, he was the only living creature.

A trident shot from the dark caves and stabbed through his chest.

Wren's eyes shot open.

He gasped, pain sparking through him until he was a raw, living nerve. Suddenly, he was so startlingly alone that for a split second he almost didn't realize it.

Water bubbled into his throat. And he began to panic. Because he was drowning. He was drowning and he was alone.

Where—his air-starved brain sought answers. *Where am I?*

The Sky Court revealed itself, a wash of stars. The lidded eye of the moon glared at him.

Wren gasped, horrible spurts of breath drawn back into his lungs. Sound crashed into his ears, popping as pressure released. Pools formed under his knees as he coughed up water. What if he had drowned down there and this was the waking dream of death?

It had to be.

For what else could hurt as much as knowing—feeling—that there was nothing on the other end of the bond? *Alone.*

A voice whispered at the edge of his perception. Something seized in his chest, sending waves of pain radiating outward from the brand like the tendrils of a dying star. The brand burned and burned and bit through his skin. He froze, fingers curled and jaw clenched. He was being flayed apart, serrated by a super-heated blade cracking his heart in two.

He wasn't in pain—he *was* pain.

Drawing his arm in, Wren bunched the fabric over his brand. It was dulled. Constant and chronic, he sobbed for—

"Asaru . . ."

Khetry clung to his skin, and his nose felt warm from the streams pouring down his chin. On his tongue was the iron tang of fresh blood. With the amount of it, his face must have been drenched. He felt like he was dying.

"I . . . I can't feel him anymore."

Everything passed in a discordant blur of unreality after that. Time twisted, swirled.

Someone lifted Wren to his feet, another someone placed a cool hand on his forehead, while yet another tied his hair into a tail. He was dried and dressed. A red cloak was fastened at his neck, and then he was pushed into the scores of Doyisha, who moved as one. They were a grand mass whose purpose was greater than the individual parts from which it was formed.

Through it all, Wren was alone. *Alone.*

His body either hurt or was numb, or the hurt was the numb. Mostly, he was tired.

So. Very. Tired.

Dazed eyes blinked as sand softened under his boots, before they adjusted at the sight of a structure of slate and jet half buried in a crimson desert. A true desert. Millions of tiny burning granules.

He was gathered with them, gathered with the Doyisha before a trio of wraiths clad in black, an abundance of slit strips fluttering by their legs. The shadows themselves seemed to writhe at their feet. Checkered masks hid their gazes. They raised their arms, and a midnight substance oozed from their fingertips. It arced up and spilled over, pooling in a mirror of dancing starlight on the sand. Moonlight beamed silvery blue onto the polished surface. One by one, the Doyisha entered the blackness and were subsumed in liquid shadow. Sagan was the last to step through the starlight. His unmasked face glanced over his shoulder, but he turned away quickly and disappeared.

Outside of himself, Wren took a step. He stood at the edge of nothing. He was nothing. Then a hand snatched his wrist. A steadying hand caught his lower back. It was a wonder he could still stand the way his watery legs shook. Through his glassy vision, he saw Niekthe at a similar height to him. Gray fabric fell to their feet, a gauzy shimmer cloaking their body as they locked gazes with him.

They reached inside his chest and pulled out his secret, holding the needle up between them. The small shard of bone was barely larger than a finger and as red as a hearth.

"Are you sure?"

In a faint glimmer of clarity brimming from the dissonant

haze, Wren clasped his hand around theirs and tightened. That grasp kept him present, in the here and now, a living pillar of perpetual pain. His finger pricked the pale glinting point. Blood welled. And it was done.

"More than anything."

Khetry looped around Wren's neck, trapping him in its taut web. All red and red and red. An ominous glow cast their faces in long shadow. Made them look like monsters creeping out of the cavernous darkness.

In that light, he wondered how he had ever thought Niekthe was eresh keyel. Splendor thickened around them, tasting as ancient as the ages. Tasting of centuries of crossed steel, of the conflict from which he was descended.

Niekthe pushed the needle against his chest and nodded. No more words passed between them.

A vortex of black gurgled at Wren's feet, whirling hypnotically. He was pushed forward, and the darkness enveloped him.

ASARU

On the fringes of lucidity, Asaru felt them guide him onto a bed—who were they? Rishé and Palenisa, his fading mind supplied. But the doubled chanting of his mother drowned it out. Tenat—she wanted him to *come home, come back.*

The ground swayed. Right, he was on a ship. Cherrywood, black flag, crewed by northern redheads. They'd sailed through a broken spine and found gleaming bright treasure in the heart of a stone tree. His recollection was a blur as the events bled into each other, less sequential and more all at once, like a long unbroken line of golden blood.

Come home.

He tried to. Tried to move through the miasma of hurt, but he found himself wrapped mummiform in pale sheets that reminded him of grave cloth, charnel houses, and ash, and of a slab shrouded in mourning white.

Everything was laced with a persistent ache—constant, constant, constant pain. Buzzing beneath his skin, inside him. Asaru felt like a raw nerve subsumed in dreamless waters. His protests died prematurely, released instead as a wounded moan as the two women buried him in layers of cloth.

"You're sick," one said, her voice low as a valley at midnight.

"Rest," said the other, curling up at the ends like spoken cursive.

Their voices slithered into unintelligibility as the waking world quivered. Both weightless and leaden, Asaru fell away from clasped hands. There, then—gone.

The nonplace was tinted with shades of darkness. A myriad of colors swirled around him. Patterns shifted behind his closed eyes as reality splintered into something not so real.

Am I sleeping?

There was no response.

The ruby web hung around him. Black tainted the net like corrosive sores. Floating in the substance, Asaru held the indistinct ball of his own aether in his hands, close to his chest like a fallen star. It would have cast him aglow in silver if this place had something approximating light. Khetry threads tightened around his limbs until he lay there—wherever "there" was—supine.

As always, he was at the mercy of endless chanting. *Warrior.* The endless chanting of his mother's voice. *Prince.* His mother's distorting voice as it cradled him. *Son.* Cradled and swathed him in the gauzy tones of eternity. *Come home, come back, come home.* Asaru was adrift for an eternity. Whatever time meant in this nonplace.

Something wet dripped from his nose—blood. But when he reached up—at least he thought he did—there was nothing there.

He peeled his eyes open—did he even have eyes? In this unreality, he hadn't thought to do that. Looking down, he saw a thin layer of water above the ground that didn't exist. Below it were many intangible hands writhing like phantom maggots.

Stagnant water flowed into him, drenched and drowned him like a ritualistic fount. It receded, and through the blur it left behind, a figure approached.

"Alvarys?" Asaru tried, throat tight. The words came from the mouth he didn't have. It took considerable effort to speak. A static pain throbbed at his extremities, and he was far too tired to try lifting his head.

"Asaru."

His vision cleared, and he tried to peer through the clouded pitch in the direction of the voice. A form materialized from the void, larger than life. Every inch of skin bound in gray bandages and limp rings of gold hung like rotting streamers from a corpse. Behind the shadow of a veil lay sparkling black eyes inset in a jackal face—or a mask. Or both.

Khertote—comrade, companion, and guide to fallen eresh keyel.

Ah, I am not sleeping, Asaru realized faintly, *I am dying.*

Moribund, he was halfway between life and death, a talon toeing the threshold as bleeding wings fluttered black. He could almost see the veil where the divine Triumvirate resided, where his brother resided.

"I have been waiting centuries," Khertote said. "But I am glad you have finally returned, though They have made it difficult."

Asaru wanted to ask the illusion what it meant, but his tongue swelled thick and fat in his mouth. Everything was pressed beneath a turgid layer of sleep. He blinked—at least, he thought he did—and found himself enveloped in giant hands, looking up rather than down.

The figment watched him with the focus of a vulture picking at carrion. For a figment, it was so clear, though the dying mind could create intricate hallucinations. It opened its mouth; it opened its mask. "This is for your own good."

What do you mean?

The thing resembling Khertote lowered its head, colossal hands outstretched before them. Twisting its wrist, it conjured chains from the fraying dregs of khetry.

Lead fell across Asaru's neck, his wrists and legs weighed by the crimson bonds. His body yearned to move, to rage against the fetters as they smothered his protests. *I still belong to myself.* A limp refrain. Unyielding chains pulled him to the wet ground of this void space. His vision doubled, blurred into a kaleidoscope of smoke and crimson energies.

"This is not only for your own good, but that of khetry itself." The voice of the simulacrum was a harmony of ululating birdsong above the relentless intonations of *My son, warrior, my son, come back.* "You, a traitor made, were never meant to exist until *Her.*"

What little remained of Asaru grew numb. The eyelids he didn't have drooped.

"Return to dwell in the Red Web of Life once more and be content."

Fading, he sank into the viscous embrace of ceaseless black hands. A hundred thousand tiny fingers trailed every inch of him with their malicious intent. Unkind and insistent, they dragged him down. Farther than he thought possible in this dreaming place.

The allure of the veil called to him. Soon he would be reunited with his brother. He could almost imagine a blue-eyed smile and an outstretched hand welcoming him to the beyond.

As his heart slowed, a familiar sensation pierced his moribund mind. Golden blood gushed over the colossal fingers of his possessor. Their bloody caress lingered at his nape. Cursed tendrils emanated from a stark black triangle, needling into the very fabric of his being. His mother's voice swept in with fury as the chants began anew.

Asaru, warrior, son, prince. Come back, my son, come home—mine. Mine.

For a moment, Asaru's vision went dark. Touched by cold, he trembled. Then he saw red. He saw himself in the celestial pools of Khertote's canine eyes. Water shivered at his knees.

"No," he sighed, every fiber of him resisting the void with keen desperation. *"No."* He tore the collar from his neck. Exhaustion became raw fire in his veins. "I'm not done," he said, staggering to his feet. Chains disappeared into the distance on either side, his arms splayed like wings. They threatened to wrench him back down, but he fought and forced his wrists free. The threads flickered as they peeled away like embers. "I am not . . . fucking . . . *done*."

Above and below him, the entity resembling Khertote nodded. Then it vanished, wiped away like a broken circle.

A crossed pair of flaming blades sheared Asaru in two. Fingers pried apart his flayed remains, forming him into an imperfect totem. Then he was remade by a chorus of chants. *Asaru, come home.* They droned in one tone from everywhere. Their volume climbed until he *was* the voices, an unceasing harmony. *Prince, son, brother, warrior, mine.*

A hand wreathed in black shot down. The bright red claws of the presence sank deep into his chest. Through flesh and bone and violet stone. Burrowed to his innermost places. Gripping tight, it ripped out a trident with a cruel indifference.

Come back to me.

Hardened mineral crawled across him like frost. Black diamond crept up his neck to cover his face. As the cocoon came to a stop, Asaru tilted his head back to meet a pair of crimson eyes.

And his body no longer belonged to him.

One moment he was. The next he wasn't.

Come, my son.

Asaru shot up.

His eyes were black and hollow, lacking the red spark of life. Cold pulled at his pallid skin. He barely felt it; he barely felt anything. Blinking, he looked around, taking in his surroundings. There was a bed beneath him and shredded sheets atop him. Beside him a human clad in changeant blue started with a yelp.

Static threatened to numb his entire being as the possession bound him. The fleeting part of his mind that was his alone struggled under the overwhelming presence. The prickling perception of many eyes on him deepened as Asaru examined his arms. They were covered in midnight, speckling at the elbow like broken glass.

Where had he seen this before? Where had he touched this before?

It was difficult to think clearly, so he rubbed his nape. Felt the keloid-scar remnants of his halo.

What had he become?

As sure as his heart did not beat in his throat, he was dead, a revenant facsimile of a man. A warrior adorned in diamond.

Intense need screamed through his head—*Home. I need to go home.*

No, that wasn't right—yes, it was. Urged forth, Asaru's body followed the directive. His bare talons touched the floor. The ground swayed. *Remember: You're on a ship.*

A whimper came from the human cowering in the corner. *Silence them.*

Sliding a hand down his nape, Asaru drew a line of black. Smooth as water, liquid black diamond snaked from the dark jewel after his fingers. He twirled the bleeding trail around his wrist. When he flicked his hand, it snapped aside with the sound of a whip.

He turned to the door as the human gurgled. They clutched their throat, blood spilling from the column of punctured flesh. Three blades of diamond protruded from their neck. One embedded so deeply it jutted through their nape.

Hand curling into a fist, Asaru created a shimmering pane. Bringing a finger to his lips, he divided the pane into sheets. The sheets became spears. He crossed his arms at the wrist, then flung them out. One spear shattered the door in an explosion of wood and metal. The other shot to the side, and the gurgling ceased. An edge sharper than any knife sliced clean through the human. The top of the bisected head slowly slid aside, revealing a sopping mass. Brown and red mingled with stringy brain matter.

For a moment, Asaru stared at the sight.

Shock thrummed dimly through him. *He was a—person—he wouldn't kill*—the thought was overridden by the command of the one whose desires superseded his own.

He scrutinized the blood beneath his claws. Then stalked forward from the cabin.

Come.

Things had to be done. Anyone who got in his way would have to die.

Square shafts of sun dappled the corridor from the barred ceiling. Down a set of stairs rushed several pairs of feet. At least three.

Knees bent, Asaru dashed forward as the trio came into view.

Fingers pinched, he punched up. A long diamond shard

lanced a human from chin to cheek, and another tore the arm clean from the body of a shorter one. The last human swiped a rapier, which Asaru swiftly dodged. He kicked their knee with such might it bent backward. White bone jutted through fur and leather coverings. Such delicate creatures.

Snatching at the air, he wrenched the spears from the first two. Blood gushed from their wounds, voluminous as water. They screamed, horrendously irritating noises. *Quiet them.* He slammed a swift foot behind him, connecting with the smallest one's jaw. Another kick and they thudded against the wall with a crack. Arcing his clasped fists above his head, he brought them down. And down. And down. Until the human no longer had a face left with which they could scream.

The first human paled, and Asaru snapped a spear through their wailing mouth, pinning them to the ground. A fountain of red frothed down a missing jaw. He rounded on the third, who knelt and wept, and planted a foot against their neck to knock their head back. They slumped at an unsettling angle, eyes emptied of light.

Viscera splashed the walls, offal brown and biting cherry red. Bits of white bone littered the floor alongside other pungent bodily fluids.

Asaru shook his head, continuing.

A torrent of black diamond spilled from his arms as he maneuvered through the bowels of the ship and left a trail of bodies in his wake. Mere remains in some cases. Most cases. Kneeling over the back of a human, he snapped the spear free of their skull with a brown spray. It spattered into his mouth, tasting of venison.

Flipping the spear, he blew up a lock of hair and bounded onto the main deck.

In every direction was the tranquil sea and the empty sky. But for all the warmth of his surroundings, his skin was a land of ice.

Movement in his periphery. Glancing sidelong, he spied a small woman huddling behind a barrel. Wide amber eyes stared up at him, a tome clutched to her chest like a shield.

They blinked at each other.

He took a step forward, then jerked back to avoid the swipe of a staff.

Catching the metal in midair, Asaru frowned in the direction of the attack and was met with a tall brown-skinned woman. Small white braids hung on either side of her face, agape with some expression he couldn't identify. Muscles shifted under her cape as she shoved the staff down harder. He resisted, but her strength strained equally to his.

That was a complication.

He clamped his fingers around the staff. Clenched them tight to break. Tight to crack. Tight until the staff split into pieces. A thin tube of hard light clattered to the deck, followed by both halves of the weapon, raining flecks of metal dust. Placing a palm on her chest, Asaru shoved her back like swatting a fly. She slid across the deck, hand planted between her legs as she panted. Wintry eyes scanned him.

"What have you *done*?"

A voice his mind knew. But he could not tear himself free of the grasp of the possessor enough to make sense of it. Had he been able to think on his own, he might have considered her words. Alas, he was an undead machine programmed to perform one task. *Come home.* Blood or bone, he would spill it all before failing.

His senses told him there were others on the deck. Redheads

brandishing swords and short blades, one swinging a hook on a chain in a loop. They closed in, but the white-haired woman held the entirety of his focus. She slipped a pair of daggers from the sides of her thighs. Lowering her stance, she crossed the short distance in two determined steps. Though their strengths may have been of a kind, he was faster.

Ducking easily around her swipes, Asaru somersaulted. His foot connected with the underside of her chin, and the white-haired woman reeled back. As she stumbled, he whirled his arms up and over his head, creating two slender black ribbons. Black diamond had a life of its own, the serpentine mineral glittering in shifting shades.

Spinning, he slashed outward.

The ribbons sliced every person that crowded him. An ocean of red and violet splattered across the deck. The possessor wanted to admire the play of colors on wood; the rational speck of him wanted to look away. In a tiny victory, Asaru averted his gaze. But he wasn't sure if the victory was truly his own.

Dropping to a crouch, he slammed his hands down and black diamond radiated up in a perfect circle, undulating in sharp spikes like magnetic fluid. He stood smoothly, locking eyes with the white-haired woman. His stare was uncomprehending, hers tinged with a strange emotion. The part of him that may once have known her name was boxed into submission as his body became an extension of the possessor's will.

"Asaru," the woman whispered. His name sounded curious in her mouth. "Please . . . stop."

Gaze unbroken, he raised an arm high. Streams of darkness followed in rippling waves of sunlight. All the black diamond within him coalesced into a cloud, rolling and wriggling, heavy as death.

Someone shouted, seconds before he snapped.

The cloud shattered. A wave of black projectiles rained across the ship. Thousands of notched arrowheads thundered onto the deck like droplets. The noise blended with the screams of the wounded, static in his ears.

Through the noisy film of possession, he watched it all. The destruction he so thoughtlessly wrought. Not that he could think.

COME.

The shout tugged at his mind. The instinctual call to return to where he belonged. Another, louder:

BACK.

Asaru watched his head snap to the side, black diamond echoing the movement. He watched himself drop to a kneel, head bowed reverently as if before a great and ancient power. And he watched himself melt into a shower of sparks. In that moment, he was unmade, slipping into the nebulous grasp of powers greater than he.

I'm coming.

PALENISA

“Fuck!” Palenisa yelped as Rishé tightened the bandage around her upper thigh. Her perfectly apt reaction to the pain earned her a dull stare. She clamped her jaw shut as the sting of her wound echoed down her leg, causing her toes to spasm. “That. Hurts.”

“Stay *still* or it’ll hurt more,” Rishé murmured. She twisted the bandage once more around before tying off the cloth, which had been ripped from the end of her tunic, and then tucked in the stray ends. Purple blood soaked through, but it was the best they could do in the bilge. The creaking and whining turned Palenisa’s stomach as the ship rocked.

Down there, wastewater was their companion. They sat in a swaying layer of scum that stank strongly of brine. At least she knew this experience somewhat well; it was not too dissimilar to her gutter awakening, though that felt distant in her memory. The bilge was all she could smell, and the pain in her leg was all she could feel. It throbbed at her neck, her head. But also in her heart.

In her heart was a miasma of anger, hurt, and confusion that oozed as she tried to comprehend what had happened. Moments after the disaster—*massacre,* her mind provided images of a burning clan—the remaining crew of the *Danaye* had rounded on the two of them. At the ends of swords and hooks, they were marched down there despite their injuries and locked away to sit in filth.

A shiver skittered up Palenisa's spine as she recalled the bodies they'd passed. All of them mutilated with vicious efficiency. Blood painted the walls and floors in grotesquely artful splatters. The hands of betrayal—Asaru's betrayal. It was the only explanation her scrambled mind could supply. No other reason could pierce the emotion that pervaded her thoughts.

All that power at his fingertips. Unlike anything she'd ever seen from him before. Any other time, she might have chuckled at the irony—the thing that killed him he had controlled with brutal efficiency. As if he'd done it all his life.

The look in his eyes painted the backs of her lids. His chest hadn't risen with the breath of life. *Revenant,* came the thought, *a spiritless thing.* An affront to who the deceased was—*once.* Because that was no longer Asaru. Just an empty vessel wearing his body.

Weak satisfaction overcame her as she cursed his name. It was petty, startlingly so, but Palenisa wrapped herself in the vindictive act as a shield against the hurt. Thinking it was one thing—saying it made it thus. So she spoke again, spitting his name in all three languages she knew for further emphasis.

"How did I get it so wrong?" she mumbled, half to herself, half to the Zodiac. It felt like she'd made yet another wrong choice. Each successive decision cascaded into a chrysalis of regrets as she thought of her losses. The Crocodile Coterie, Asaru—and if experience served, likely Wren too. Her promise, broken; she, a miserable failure. Spiraling downward, ever more downward.

A weight landed on her shoulder, and Palenisa stiffened as Rishé's breath fanned her clavicle. As the ship listed dangerously to the side, she wasn't sure whether the swoop in her belly was fear or fluster.

"We don't . . . fully know what happened," Rishé whispered. Her voice lacked inflection, as if all the strength had been drained from her. Since the attack she'd barely spoken, in any of the languages she knew, save clipped responses and the hesitant flutter of her hands. Mostly, she had just stared off blankly and bound Palenisa's injury.

"I think it was pretty clear."

Sighing, Rishé shook her head. Her cropped curls brushed the underside of Palenisa's chin.

"I don't want to argue. Not right now."

One of Rishé's hands rested loosely near Palenisa's own. In the gruesome fluid, their smallest fingers were close to touching. It would take little to bridge the gap and interlock them. Neither did, but Palenisa remained ever aware of the steady press of Rishé's body to hers.

They lapsed into silence, and the rush of water against the sides of the ship crashed in to fill it. Through the headache pounding around the sensitive interior of Palenisa's skull, she fought against the thrall of sleep. She needed to stay awake to wallow in her anger a bit longer. But the fatigue was much too strong, and honestly, she felt far more betrayed than anything else.

Why? Why? Why?

Knocking her head against the slick wall, she lost the battle with exhaustion. The weight on her shoulder slumped, her eyes shut, and fitful rest took her. What felt like only seconds later,

Palenisa was jarred awake with a kick to the side. Accompanied by the pain of her injuries was a headache bandying the tender insides of her brain.

"Both of you, up. Now!"

She hid a wince at the voice's volume and squinted away dancing spots.

Above them, Yurikhun stood bearing a raw scar that cut viciously across her scowl. She held a blade in one hand and a snarling hound, white as fresh fallen snow, waited at her side. Its tarry eyes narrowed as the two of them were forced onto unsteady feet.

An arm looped through hers, and Palenisa glanced down as Rishé blearily gathered herself. Their gazes met, and she was sent a trembling half smile that quickly faded.

As they were shoved through the bowels of the ship, Palenisa did her best to ignore the stormy rumbling of the crew. She couldn't blame them—in lieu of the true source of their rage, she and Rishé were the next best thing.

Ascending topside, she shaded her eyes from the glare of the sun. Midday rays dappled the main deck, highlighting the aftermath of the carnage in gold. Someone had attempted to clean the blood but succeeded only in spreading it around. On the deck lay fourteen figures, each shrouded in spirit-white sheets.

As she stepped past the remains of her staff, Palenisa's chest tightened. Shattered in two, slivers of metal dusted the cracked solar tube. It had been a gift from Ada, and it was beyond repair. Most things, she had come to learn, were beyond repair. The Nest, Asaru—and especially, her honor.

His fault, your fault, said the mirage voices of the Zodiac.

Shaking free of them, she scanned the Sea of Tranquility.

The sea was a polished crystal reflecting sunlight to warm

the ache inside her. Water, water, water, then—there. In the near distance. Land broke the horizon, and she laid eyes on Aedyton for the first time.

Awed, she took in the island. Two-thirds of it floated, suspended by some preternatural power, dark clouds forming the topmost ring. Thick roots clung to the bottom of the middle ring, a fragmented loop made of smaller hunks of uneven rock. To the east, a disconcerting mist spilled from the valley between angular mountains swathed in forest. The green faded to the golden sand of a broken atoll around a shimmering lagoon. The lowest ring was sprinkled with pyramids that rose high through the center of the middle ring.

The grip around her arm grew taut as Rishé staggered. The other woman stared with curious wide eyes, drinking in the island hungrily.

They were shoved from their reverie to the side of the ship where a skiff teeming with overfull bags of diamondglass waited. Palenisa tenderly inched her way to the front, careful to avoid jostling the precious cargo, while Rishé planted herself in the rear. They were lowered none too gently into the water, sinking a bit before the vessel readjusted itself.

"Trade amulet," Yurikhun called. "Catch."

The pirate tossed something into Rishé's hands. Lifting it, she saw a disk resembling an eye bead. The blue, white, and black amulet seemed to stare accusatorily, as if it could see all her faults. Spinning at the end of a string, the eye bead winked at her.

"As payment for the crew I lost, I took half the diamondglass. You're lucky I'm so gods-damned generous." Yurikhun planted her hands on the rail and leaned over to sneer. "That's the last fucking favor Sagan will ever get from me." As the *Danaye* drifted back north, she flipped them off. "I hope I never see you again."

"Feeling's mutual, bitch," Palenisa said once they were some distance away. Across the boat from her, Rishé frowned at the bags, then at the island.

"It won't be enough."

"It'll have to be," she said before dipping the oars into the water to row. *Back, down, through; back, down, through.* It wasn't as if they could do much else, all but stranded as they were—there was only one direction to go.

As they approached, the Sea Gate distorted what was behind it as if they were looking through rippled glass. At a certain angle, it warped the air the same way the ward that once protected the Nest had. How had something so innocuous kept the eresh keyel barred on their island for a millennium? It seemed as though it had stood for a hundred thousand years and would be there a hundred thousand more after she was gone.

When it was right above them, Rishé raised a brow and lifted the amulet. Tendrils of electricity emanated outward where it connected with the barrier, as if something monumental had snapped into place. Passing through the Sea Gate was like falling from a great height and stopping suddenly. Wincing, Palenisa's ears popped from the pressure. The barrier stretched like a gummy film, and once they emerged on the other side, it rebounded back into place with a snap.

Lurching forward, she cupped her nose as an onslaught of pure, concentrated khetry flared to life. Spiced water and iron mingled with the pungent odor of water-struck stone. The closer to the shore they floated, the stronger it became.

The boat squealed like a dying creature as it came aground with a garbled crunch. Waves whisked the beach, so clean it was hard to tell where the water ended and the pale sand began.

From down the shore, a cluster of figures approached. As

they came into view, Palenisa realized they were eresh keyel, each a head or more taller than her. They moved like a flock of white-robed swans, adorned in gold. From their backs fluttered a wild assortment of wings: stained-glass flies', moths', falcons', and even a pair that resembled a bat's. At the head of the group was a woman with soft wheat ringlets cascading from her crown. Instead of a tail, her most striking feature was a pair of horns draped in a net of jewels like cobwebs. Her neck was ringed with a citrine halo, and on her face, she wore a smile that didn't reach her eyes.

After disembarking, Palenisa steadied the sides of the skiff to help Rishé. The boat sank deeper beneath the weight of their quarry. Half what it should have been, she feared it wouldn't be enough. All that effort, and she didn't know what she'd do if it wasn't.

"Well," the woman said, scrutinizing the two of them, the boat, and the bags. If she was surprised to see a wraith, it didn't show. "You may call me Xerqet, the warden, and considering what the Chronicler told me, I expected . . . more."

"Unforeseen circumstances. Sorry," Palenisa muttered, extending a hand to the warden. Dainty fingers gripped hers, fingers that had never seen conflict. Smooth as the caress of velvet when they parted. "There was an incident."

"An incident . . ." The warden's lips pursed, and she appeared to readjust her expectations. Disappointment tinted her gaze—what a familiar sight. "Come along: The Doyisha have been awaiting your arrival at the temple for some time."

Snapping, the warden gestured to her attendants with a slight tilt of her head and spun on a talon. Each move she made brought to mind the kharess, as if both women were layered atop each other.

It tugged at something bitter in Palenisa's chest.

The sour-faced attendants unloaded the boat with a series of seamlessly cast spells. As petrichor clouded her senses, Palenisa cupped her mouth. She and Rishé glanced at each other before following the warden to a temple that bordered the beach. Conspicuously separate, it was pale as bleached bone, lacking the limestone and green-clay coating that dyed the distant structures in the ring. The entryway was a wide, colorless portal framed with raised carvings. Atop the lintel sat a relief of an eye, blending into the stone like the island's foamy glass shoreline.

Through the arch stepped the warden, her attendants, and Rishé, but Palenisa hesitated beyond the threshold. As her throat bobbed, she swallowed down the scent that drifted from inside.

Rot.

With each breath, the smell of death thickened like smoke.

A chill crawled its way up her spine like the spindle legs of a spider. The somber air that hovered over the entire island came crashing into her. If she hadn't seen the effects of the curse firsthand, she might've believed it could be stopped in time. Where she expected to hear the clamor of a city, it was all so still, tense. Though they tried to hide it, she'd glimpsed a tiny flicker in the eresh keyel's eyes—*fear.*

Clamping her eyes shut, Palenisa inhaled sharply, exhaled deeply. And entered.

Inside the temple was just as pristine and unblemished. Horribly white and horribly clean, it looked more like a necropolis than a temple. The floor was a marble ocean brimming with cursed bodies. The densely packed cots thinned out at the edges of the room, creating a passage along which healers and Doyisha navigated, carrying medical swatches and diamondglass.

A constant stream of pain reeled into Palenisa's ears. They

pricked to the sides of her head, but she couldn't hide from the moans and groans and choked-off sobs. Somehow the sterile, bloodless nature of it all made it that much worse.

She froze in the entryway, her eyes flitted around. On either side of her were stacks of swaddled bodies rising up the walls like a morbid mountain of flesh. Her breaths quickened. She was overwhelmed, and the scene blurred. From white and white and white emerged another image. Flashes of Chiroyn between blinks. Flashes of the other men she'd killed. She remembered her bloated near corpse as she lay there among them.

Everything inside her screamed to run, to leave this place and the memories behind. But her trembling knees held her in place, thigh wound pulsating. Legs like water, she clutched the frame of the arch to stay upright.

What she wanted more than anything right then was for things to make sense again. To know once more the way the world—*her* world—was supposed to work. What was she supposed to do with all that was spread before her? She could pray to the Zodiac. Then what? What use were her blessings *there*?

Heat formed in her eyes. She was a pillar of granite primed to crumble to pieces.

"Palenisa?"

The call of her name snapped her back to the present. She blinked and found Wren cocking his head at her. *Wren.* At least one thing hadn't been lost in this whole mess.

In an atypical urge, she pounced. Wren started as she wrapped him in a hug. She hadn't properly hugged anyone in decades; the movement felt stilted, even to her. But eventually his arms found her waist, and the embrace became less rigid the longer it lasted. The scent of blood lingered on him like a second skin.

After a heavy moment, she pulled away and coughed. The smile he sent her was a fragile thing, and the bags darkening his eyes were atrocious.

"What are you *wearing*?" Rishé asked, gesturing to all of him with a mild uptick of the lips.

"I . . . um, don't fully know." Wren smoothed a hand over his clothes as if just noticing he wasn't wearing his coat. "I wasn't all there when they dressed me."

"They?" Rishé drew her finger out to the side and spoke aloud.

"The Chronicler. I think." He doffed the hood of his scarlet cape. Glancing between the two of them, he bit his chapped lips and asked the question she'd been dreading. "Where's Asaru."

Well, it wasn't really a question. Not with the detached affect of his voice. Looking closer, Palenisa noted his subdued eyes were bloodshot, like he'd been crying. Like he already knew and all she had to do was confirm the terrible truth.

"Dead," she said in a husky croak. "Revenant. He attacked us on the ship, then fled."

"Oh."

"I'm sorry."

"Not your fault. He must have been possessed . . ." Wren stared blankly over her shoulder. His fingers twined together like black worms at his front.

Possessed. The one thing she'd forgotten to consider. As much sense as it made, a stubborn part of her didn't want to accept the possibility that something—*someone*—had made Asaru do all that. Savagery—overkill to an indulgent degree. She knew the difference well.

Brow furrowed, Rishé frowned at her. She could have worded it better—but they didn't need better. More than ever, they just needed honesty.

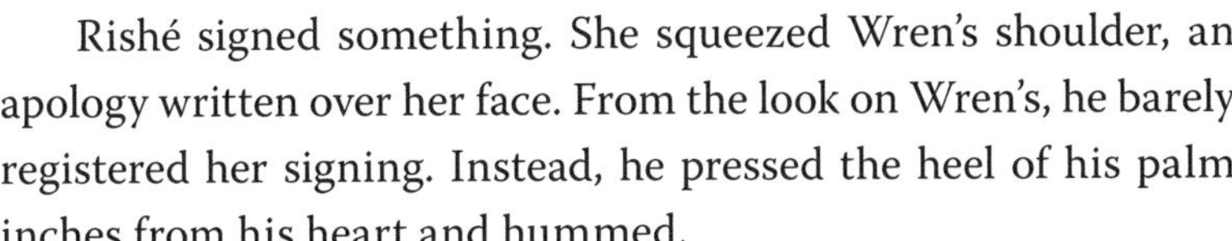

Rishé signed something. She squeezed Wren's shoulder, an apology written over her face. From the look on Wren's, he barely registered her signing. Instead, he pressed the heel of his palm inches from his heart and hummed.

"I'm fine. Really, I am." He shrugged off their concern. "I should, um, I have to get back to work."

Cape trailing behind him, he rejoined the effort, moving to a cot an eresh keyel similar in age to him lay on. There were too many people who needed his help for him to dwell on the betrayal. But that was exactly what discomforted Palenisa. It felt like it discomforted the Zodiac too. Their weightless presences curled around her neck like the drape of a snake.

The air shifted, and Palenisa felt a presence approach. She whipped around to grab it before it made contact.

Mask hanging from his neck, Sagan eyed her grip on him placidly. Damnable mismatched eyes examined her and Rishé. Lavender hair fell over his nose, and he blew it away. Two of her fingers wrapped nearly the entire span of his wrist, the rest held aloft to avoid as much contact as possible—she didn't trust those palms, glowing or not. Frustratingly, she couldn't read his expression.

"We could use a couple more hands," he said casually.

Rishé jumped at the opportunity, though Palenisa took a ponderous beat before scoffing and shoving him free.

While Wren assisted the Doyisha, Rishé aided the healers tending to those in recovery. In place of mineral black, the ritual left their skin with a glowing prismatic sheen like mother-of-pearl. Palenisa herself had been guided by a ruddy Doyisha with mousy yellow-green eyes in preparing the cursed for the ritual. In rote motion, she performed ablutions on the afflicted, running silk soaked in oils over cursed faces, arms, and legs, dabbing away both bile and sweat.

The task was simple, but it slung a yoke of sadness across her back. The act reminded her of the coterie. Frankly, everything reminded her of the coterie, but the almost sacred nature of this was too similar to the funerary rites ashmakers performed, which she had occasionally seen as the Sister of Faith. Rites neither Ada nor her mother had received. The former because her body had been too badly desecrated, and the latter because there'd been no body at all.

"What is your name, miss?" asked the child whose fevered brow she wiped. Their glossy eyes watched her with the wonder only children had. Wings of black blood stained the clean sheets, fluttering with a child's thrill of meeting a strange new person. And that round face reminded her of the Vana who had run from the wrath of her former sisters.

Broken bodies. Burning clan.

Screaming internally, she plastered on a thin smile. "Palenisa."

She brushed a loc behind their ear and moved on before she could burst into tears.

In the next cot over was an elderly man who looked far too much like Khensu. Her hammering heart swelled as she knelt at his side. Fogged eyes stared at nothing, and delirious ramblings accompanied with bile spilled from his parted lips.

"So kind, so kind, so kind," she caught him saying as she cleaned the blood from his halo. It made her feel like a liar as well as a failure. The spirits knew what she was; she knew what she was—a dishonorable fraud mimicking the kindness of others.

Don't say that, she wanted to shout at him. *It couldn't be further from the truth.*

Sometimes he muttered about children, grandchildren, the threads he could no longer see. He looked through her, but she sent him a strained smile, nonetheless. This was worse than Khensu. At least at her end, the warrior had mind enough to remember who and where she was. This man seemed to drift in the haze of visions that weren't there.

He was too close to the end for the ritual to work.

The thought spiked the hurt in her.

Numb, Palenisa sat there holding the man's hand. Just holding him. In a way, it felt like she wasn't looking at him, but at her mother, at Ada. With their deaths as abrupt and violent as they'd been, she never got this. Never got to be there at the end for them. It was a poor substitute for the real thing.

"Excuse me," someone called softly.

Over her shoulder, Palenisa saw an eresh keyel with brown hair across which rainbow light banded. A tan tunic was tied at her hip and collar below a blue halo. Worried cornflower eyes alighted on her as the woman gave a lukewarm smile. Shuffling, she meshed her fingers together in nervous patterns.

"My apologies, but I just arrived. I am searching for my sons," she said, toying with numerous bangles. "Their names are Asaru and Alvarys. Have you seen them?"

Spirits damn it all.

Palenisa's hand coiled into a fist on her thigh, pressing, pressing at the injury she deserved. Her lead heart sank under the knowledge she would have to disappoint Asaru's mother. A childless mother and a motherless child. *Oh, cruel merciless fate.*

"They're dead," she blurted indelicately, and regret immediately swept in like a rogue wave. She tried to tack on an apology, but Asaru's mother looked stricken. Clearly falling apart at the seams, trying to hold it together—failing to hold it together. Her thanks was a garbled mess as she fled. Not fast enough to hide the tears carving down her weathered face.

Pressing the dying man's hand to her cheek, Palenisa groaned. It took every bit of her to keep from crying.

Through the pervasive smell of khetry, something sharp and acrid flared—her eyes grew wide.

Dead and sweet and all too familiar. Like death come walking. *The curse.* As the smell grew, she bit the inside of her mouth to keep from gagging. But she wasn't alone in her olfactory daze. The temple had quieted enough to hear a pin drop. Everyone held their collective breath.

Then it started. The low buzz like hundreds of thousands of bees. Louder and louder—the hair on her nape rose as the sound stung her skin. Her head shot back, and she looked up through the glass capstone. Crimson flecks of energy swam in her vision. Above, where there should have been light, darkness blotted out the sun. Not night, more the absence of light.

The black cloud draped the temple in cold shadow that scooped a cavern inside her. It was formed from what looked to be hundreds of individual particulates. No—hundreds of revenants. Uncountable dead things melding together and pulling apart like viscous, magnetic liquid. As the swarm closed in, the sizzle of burning skin filled the temple.

From outside came a yell: "Deathless!"

The wails of the afflicted rose in a crescendo. And the ceiling shattered. Glass showered the temple in splintered rainfall.

The hand in hers seized and went limp. Terror plunged ice into her veins as Palenisa whipped around to see the man—her mother, Ada—convulsing. A black arrow transfixed his throat. It was buried so deep his head was nearly torn from his neck. What if he hadn't been too far gone for the ritual to work? She would never know. He sputtered, once, twice, then slouched onto the cot—*dead.*

A scream echoed, high enough to break a heart. It almost didn't sound real.

Was it her? Was her face wet? Why was her face wet?

Blood.

Rotted golden gray spattered her face, and Palenisa found herself back with the Vana. They were burning, and they were fleeing, and as her former sisters advanced, she stood in the rear watching them all, horrified. *No, no, don't,* she tried to call out, but the words stuck because she was not there. She was in the temple as death descended.

The temple burst into frenetic commotion, wailing and shouting. As more deathless touched down, arrows flew and swords sheared and lances skewered. Darkness sprayed in every direction.

"Palenisa!"

She spun to the twin cries of Rishé and Wren. Sparks rained from their skin. Panic pulsed in dilated eyes as their edges faded into a sparkling white.

No. Not this. Not again.

Palenisa's heart wrenched in two. She shot forward, hand outstretched, desperately reaching and reaching and *reaching.* In turn they mirrored her, reaching and rushing for her as their bodies dissolved. Amid the violence, there was less than a breath between their fingers. So close. Not close enough. She was a precious moment too late.

The sparks enveloped them entirely, and they vanished, no trace left but ash and amber.

WREN

Wren did and did not feel the heat of the sun and the shift of sand beneath his knees.

He did and did not know where he was; the thin stretch of land that was Hadii, sea lapping the sand in fervent licks. He was within and without, static fuzzing the edges of his vision. In his periphery were indiscernible smudges that may have been people.

He did not belong to himself.

In his hand was a burning needle. In his hand was a piece of bone that resembled a needle. Ceremonial in nature, glinting with the sheen of fresh ichor. It was the sun, it was the molten heart of a forge—it was blood.

At his knees, Wren saw and didn't see the woman. Fogged eyes took her in uncomprehendingly. Black curls haloed her in splendid night. Her hands crossed daintily over her stomach, skin inked with blooming flowers through which silver stitches swam. One finger was adorned with a ring resembling a pair of hands clasped.

Resist.

He knew this woman. Knew the lines of her face, the freckles numerous as the stars, the warmth of her touch. He'd known her all his life.

Resist.

In her sleep, the woman looked more peaceful than she had in years. The sight sparked something in the back of his mind. He searched for a name and came up empty.

Resist.

But why was she there?

Who was she?

Something clicked in his brain—and he caught it. *Mother.* She was his mother. What she meant to him . . . there was no more precious thing. She was to be the central piece of what he needed to be, of what that niggling presence *needed* him to be.

Its intangible hand brushed his nape with flaming claws banded in blackness as the presence rooted around his skull. Wren struggled for sense, but it clenched tightly on his will. Indistinct images floated in a pool of hazy thoughts. An image clear as midday floated to the forefront. A tome soaked in blood, and spidery strokes as antimony kohl hands turned a page.

An intrinsic understanding swaddled him.

He didn't want this. But the presence ate away the many vulnerabilities that made him. What a ripe vessel, it must've thought, perfect for consumption, corruption—possession. Clarity crumbled to ash in his head as he grasped and grasped but could not seem to pull himself from beneath the presence pressing down on all sides.

Fool, the dregs that were his tried to scream. He was screaming into the void, watching himself move. Watching as the thing moved him.

Wren sliced the meat of his palm. Skin parted, crimson

flowed over the woman's arms, scarring the sand at her sides. The blood warped and roiled before his eyes. The blood was breathing, and the sand was breathing, and he was breathing. And life hung suspended for a moment, captured within the web of khetry like a lone insect.

Threads wrapped around his wrist—tightened. His hand stilled, coated in various shades of red. It stung, but he barely registered the pain. It, or perhaps the possessor, commanded him forward.

Tense as a bowstring, Wren tried to fight it. He strained within the recesses of his own mind against the substance that strung all life itself. But it snared his being ever tighter like the coils of the sky serpent. A thread lashed his cheek. The substance rippled like a beast unbound. Wild and red as iron flames.

You wanted this.

You are a creature to be pitied.

You cannot escape the fate you made for yourself.

The senseless hands of possession held all of him but the deepest part, which screamed to take, take, *take* back control. He was very much aware, and that was the worst part.

He watched himself form a six-pointed star around the woman. Blood drenched the sand, and the sand drank it like bone. As the circle around the star was completed, a glow rose to cast his face in gaunt shadow. Part of him screamed. But the dread was suppressed with such speed, it had no time to blossom. An overwhelming pressure squeezed his mind into a cage. Aching, Wren watched in vivid, horrifying detail as he lifted the needle.

What did it need?

Sacrifice.

Why?

Because this is what you deserve.

What else is a point, a blade, an edge to do but whet its hunger?

The needle was a knife, and before he knew it, a red mouth yawned across the woman's neck. He slashed his mother's throat with careless ease, metal swimming through flesh like cloth.

Thread ripper. Life taker.

Ah.

He always did have a penchant for making a mess of things.

The needle was pulled out, blood weeping beneath the blade. Her chest slowed to a stop, breath leaking in waves as the threads surrounding her peeled away, like a scab from a wound. The threads surrounding him thrummed in agitation. A relentless buzz filled his ears, and red heated his eyes.

Was he crying?

There was no feeling in his face, so he wouldn't have been able to tell.

With numb ease, Wren tilted his mother's chin and cupped the side of her neck to gather a handful of her blood. His wound mingled with hers. There was power in blood. Heart lurching, he watched the atrocities of his body in dull horror. His hands did not tremble, though his mind screamed like the splintering of a mirror.

Stop. He needed to stop.

No. He needed to continue.

A scalding thread snapped at him. This was what he had to do. There was nothing more important than what he had to do. An unseen hand ripped away any opposition as it appeared, forcing him deeper under the steadfast control of the possessor. An innate compulsion guided him forward.

Twining their blood together, Wren connected the six points

of the star and painted a spiral of sacred geometry in a series of concentric shapes, each smaller than the last. By the time the heinous deed was done, blood covered his hands to the elbow. The macabre fluid seeped into his skin as though it could soak through the flesh to mingle with his own. Insects crawled over his arms, invisible, untouchable, but present if only in his mind.

The spellwork resembled a web. All around and everywhere.

The satisfied curl of a warped thread raised his head. *Nearly there.*

Outside himself, he watched his palms press into the circle. Red undulated upward from the edges. Raw tendrils of khetry licked down his arms like hungry flames. A strange new power filled him—consumed him. More than he'd ever experienced before—Wren bloated with power to overheating. Hot blood fell from his nose and stained his teeth wickedly. He was dizzy with loss he couldn't fully comprehend.

Quickly, quickly—quickly! screamed a disembodied voice made of white noise.

Gales whipped and whirled, and black spikes rose from the circle to cradle him. The false imitation of an embrace, too warm to be comforting and too tight to be loving. Thin cracks glowed up his arms. Brilliant light shone into blurred eyes, revealing to him knowledge of life itself, of death itself. Wren swallowed them both down—and they tasted like ashen regret.

Now, now, now—now! screamed the energy coagulating in his veins.

For a second, he felt like himself again, recoiling at the carnage at his feet.

See what your curiosity has wrought.

Demanding threads cinched breath from his throat, and unyielding fingers wrenched back control. Wren belonged to the thing that hovered at the edges. A silhouette with eyes the color of viscera splashed upon the walls of his brain, ripping him apart from the inside.

Blood dripped from his fingertips as his hands rose. In a sharp motion, the circle turned white, growing to entirely encase him and his mother.

It *burned*. Oh, how it burned with a passion. Worse than any needle, any knife.

The Red Web of Life hummed. The life with which khetry was animant. Wren wasn't sure the two of them were separate entities any longer. Was he connected to the world, or was the world a living part of him? Maybe they were one and the same.

A single thought throbbed in his skull, and suddenly he knew the awful truth of what he'd done—what he was.

Weaver.

Everything happened like he was moving through water.

Wren was tugged to his feet. Crimson glowed down his outstretched arms to widespread fingers. A pair of golden eyes with stars in place of pupils blinked. In his bright vision, he saw the unusual detail woven into khetry like actual coils of rope, thousands of thin strands braided together to make something more than itself.

His body walked along the beach to the Sea Gate. Vaguely, he sensed three people on his left and another on his right. Through the web, he saw the thread that looped the five of them together, just one of many that made the world.

Those to the left were no ordinary people, though. Weavers alike. Their robes fluttered in the dying wind as a fervent spectrum of colors swam through their hair, green and violet and dusk blue. To the other side, Wren saw an umber-haired woman. In one hand was a tome that dripped to darken the sand, and in the other she clutched a necklace. The ruby pendant dislodged something familiar that fell to the wayside in his memory. But as much as he tried, he couldn't hold on to it. It was painfully beyond his reach.

Wren's head was tilted upward as his glazed eyes stared at the Sea Gate.

The barrier flickered to life and shimmered between streams of unforgiving sunlight. Below was a smaller gate formed of three distinct slabs that arched across the sand like a bridge. Carved into the silver-streaked ironwood was a constellation of symbols. Both magnificent and horrendous, it was the legacy of an ancestor whose name was lost to him. One thousand years ago, a queen stood on these shores and, with the southern drakes by her side, called for this gate to be built.

Four Weavers had raised it. Four were needed to fell it. To untangle the work and smooth the strands straight again. The possessor seeded this knowledge into the depths of Wren's mind, made it such that what they knew, so too did he.

Commanded by their whim, he lifted his hands in tandem with the others. Red bands slithered up their bodies. Flexed fingers manipulated the substance delicately. From khetry, the Weavers pulled the spell that kept the barrier standing. Each of them was the limb of a horrendous whole. They wrenched their hands apart. And the spell ripped free in an explosion of scarlet ribbons.

Khetry shimmered as it pulsed. Power coiled in the caverns of his tremulous heart.

Wren tried to plead, but resistance was fleeting. He was forced to stand there, forced to watch as the Sea Gate crumbled.

It began with a shiver that stirred up sand in small clouds. Thousands of tiny hexagons raced across the curve of the barrier.

A crack thundered as the gate split into two, and the jagged edges glowed until the sky was more white than blue. Water stirred around the smaller gate, quaking like cold bone. As it disintegrated, Wren heard it.

Whispering. The woman on his other side was speaking. Chanting. At first low, then rising like a bell chiming through soundless winter. Her fist glowed with waves of shifting iridescent light. The ancient words that left her mouth daggered through his ears.

A black rift slit the air. Ripping the gate apart and warping reality itself. Staring unblinking, Wren saw the void, saw darkness frothing inside that nothingness. Where the sky once was, there gaped a rippling tear. Red crept at the edges, curling like bleeding maggots.

From within, electric tendrils licked along the shuddering gate. Crimson tongues of lightning snatched at the remnants of ironwood, and the maw swallowed it all. Into the void went every single piece of the Sea Gate. Once the structure that had withstood a thousand years was gone, the rift sealed itself back up as though it had never been there.

Then out of the sea emerged a massive hand.

It slammed down and shook the surf. Another hand. Followed by a head. An enormous being crawled from the sea. Their dripping form blotted out the sun. The earth quaked, the rumbling of an ancient being awakening from millennia of slumber. Water cascaded from the hunched body, and virulent streaks of black diamond spidered up their arms. Shattered fetters hung from the hands clenching at the sand. Two wounds slashed the blades of their back, gruesome things riddled with grayed gold.

They looked over their shoulder at the floating island, then turned their indifferent gaze onto Wren. Through a colossal curtain of crimson hair, a pair of hazel eyes peered down at him, drowning in black, with a silver slit notching the center.

The presence in Wren's mind tightened its uncompromising grip. Its claws pierced his tender head, squeezing until he gasped—until the possessor let him gasp. The pain of the realization was dazzling as a single name bubbled into being.

Oprekhet.

She reached out, enveloping him beneath a giant shadow. Terror shook through his immobile form. He couldn't move, could barely think through the cloud that smothered his senses. At that moment, he was not a person, but a vessel of her will, whose only purpose was subjugation.

Her hand grew closer. The flat of her palm hovered above his head, and she paused. A chill crawled through Wren's veins as a grin widened her lips. An open curve revealing a clustered row of twinkling shards. Malice wafted from her, dripping into him like an intermittent stream of tainted water. Slowly, she shook her head and pulled away with the hiss of sand. Dark tendrils snaked from the corner of her eyes, aglow with a cruel satisfaction. She spread her hands and vanished in a shower of sparks.

The moment she was gone, the possession snapped like an elastic band.

Dazed, Wren returned to himself, suddenly alone in his head again.

First there was silence. Then the screaming began.

It wasn't his screaming, but he felt it boiling up his throat all the same. He clutched his face, his vision nothing but red. Blood leaked from the corners of his eyes and fountained from his nose, his tongue tasting of bitter iron. It crusted thick under his nails. He was stained, never to be clean again. The blood was as much his flesh as it flowed through him. Collapsing to his knees, Wren leaned forward, retching. Sludge swelled from his mouth and oozed down his chin.

Through a smear of color, he saw the other Weavers stiffen. A drawn-out death knell escaped their chests as their bodies swayed. They dropped to the ground in three haphazard lines. Their faces were frozen in horror, mouths agape in an endless scream. They died terrified. For the rest of eternity, that was all they would be. Wren's heart trembled as he felt it, felt the call to join them in their endless stillness. There was nothing left for him. He was better off following them, because death would be kinder than the horror he glimpsed through blurry eyes.

Not too far away lay his mother, her gentle face cold with death. Scarlet jewels drew a path across her neck, bright and accusing.

Sacrifice.

Reality splintered into pieces. A guttural sob tore through him. It was all too much.

Why? Why? Why him? Why leave him to suffer the horror of being alive?

This was his punishment for all he'd done. He deserved the cold that burned in his hollow chest, deserved the ache of his panting sobs.

Was it fate? Destiny? Foul luck? He didn't know. He didn't know anything anymore.

Wren's mind belonged to himself, and it was the worst thing imaginable. Because being alive was the most terrible burden of them all.

PALENISA

Palenisa cut a weak line across a revenant's abdomen with sunlight. Its bleached spine protruded from the eviscerated torso, soaked entrails spilling out as gray-gold blood poured from the wound. The upper half of the deathless slid to the ground. Blackened teeth snapping, it crawled across the sand with the single arm attached to its bisected remains.

She slammed a foot onto the revenant's eye. Once its head was crushed, she kicked it aside and collapsed to her knees. The thing continued to drag itself forward. Skull caved in, eye hanging from the socket by a slick, sinewy thread—it just kept *crawling.* A grotesque line painted the sand from where it was halved.

That was the problem, wasn't it? They were already dead. Arms and legs could be lost, heads chopped clean off, but they kept coming. Relentless. The best she could do was try to divide the unnatural creatures into so many pieces there would be nothing left to move. Try to slow them down to give the afflicted a sliver of a chance.

Panting and tasting iron, Palenisa wondered why she even

kept fighting when the living were no match for the deathless. Thousands of deathless had descended to scour Aedyton. Inside, the temple was stained in bile, viscera painting the white walls, floor strewn with the bodies of the afflicted who hadn't managed to flee. Very few had escaped.

The beach was a bloodbath. Littered with the living and the dead, the latter clawing their way to another fight. Embers flitted through the smoky air, blood trailed in multicolored streams. In the distance, pyramids crumbled to ruin. Past them, the sky no longer shimmered. It was gone—the rippling where light had hit the barrier across the burning horizon.

The Sea Gate was *gone*. She didn't know when it had fallen. Likely somewhere between the massacre in the temple and the one outside.

Sand shifted unsteadily beneath her, and she blinked back tears of pain as her thigh throbbed. She clutched the injury Asaru had given her. It was bleeding heavily as a result of her recklessness. Adrenaline gave way to fatigue, and her muscles seized, her back bracketed in pain. The cuts along her side stung, shooting up to throb between her brows.

A boom rang out from above as eresh keyel manning manticora ballistae rained down ytterbium darts that detonated upon impact. From the ground, the deathless retaliated. They slung back fire and burned the warriors with their corrosive presence.

Another ear-shattering burst thundered.

Spirits, help me. Palenisa clenched her teeth, struggling not to hyperventilate as dismembered limbs landed around her. Hands and feet and the lower portion of a head twitched with inanimate life.

Her head rose to the source of her sluggishness. It was bathetic how pleasant the sky seemed. Save for the black mass of writhing bodies that blotted out the sun. A chill tremored through her as she pressed two fingers to her palm. The sunlight she produced flickered dimly as it appeared. With its blade she sliced the neck of a revenant whose spear aimed for her nape, and the body tumbled. Teeth gnashing, the head rolled down the beach.

Letting out a sharp cry, she curled over her knees. A chill scooped her core hollow, and she felt like she was dying.

The deathless flashed. Here one moment; the next, transformed into the men who murdered her mother. Her powers had been weak then too. This time Ada wouldn't come to save her. It was the wishful dream of a foolish child so driven by vengeance she risked her own life to drown in blood.

What if she let it happen? What if she let the tide swell and the deathless take her?

Then you'd break your promise, whispered the Zodiac over the arch of her shoulders, sounding more real than they ever had before.

They were right. If she died there, she'd break her promise to Wren, as well as the secret ones, the prayers, made to herself. Her word would be dirt. And one's word was a contract writ into reality. The ability to speak a thought and make it so. Breaking her promise meant living in dishonor. There would be no hope to regain her title, her emblem, the life she once knew.

The sudden cry of the earth pierced her skull.

The earth—it was in so much pain. Pain she felt as keenly as her own, filling her every vein with lightning. A scream ripped from her throat. Blood swam in her agonized mouth, dribbling from the corners. She trembled from the constant thrum of hurt, hurt, *hurt* in her head. Her senses overwhelmed her as the cry reverberated through her in successive quakes until her face was wet and her breath came in stuttered fits.

Blearily, Palenisa gazed beyond the beach. On the other side of the Phiari River stood Asaru. What was once Asaru. Crouched low, his right arm swept to the left and his left to the right. With each movement, black tendrils whipped through a massive rift. As the rift yawned into a crevasse, she realized that he was trying to carve the island apart. He was shearing it in half with a wide saw of black liquid. He alone was bisecting the atoll, and from the wail of the earth—*it was working.*

The Zodiac roared in her ears. More than just imagined, their voices were clear as the smoke that clung to her lungs. Earth, sunlight, ward, water, fire, air, mind, blood, spirit, chaos, dream—and starlight. They were saying one thing.

Save him from himself.

"Save him from himself," Palenisa whispered. Again she said it. Repeating the words until they were her own.

There wasn't a decision to be made. Only what she had to do.

She fought the pain and struggled to her feet. The muscles in her legs ached as she dashed across the beach, a strain pulling at her shoulders. So much was lost already. She doubted she would be able to stop him, but she had to try. This she would do, what little it mattered.

A revenant whirled into her path. Though her body screamed in pain, she had enough fight left. Palenisa roped a line of sand around its neck. Noticing her, another jerkily approached. She buried her last dagger in its arm, wrenched it back out, stabbed the revenant's stomach, and dragged the blade down. Guts spilled from its pelvis. Still it lurched for her. In turn, she slashed its throat to the bone.

A snap of her wrist flung the head of the first into the sky. Spinning on a heel, she rounded on it and kicked a hole through its chest. The body broke apart down the middle. A nauseating concoction of viscera and offal clung to her boot.

Wiping stringy blood from her lips, Palenisa advanced on Asaru.

He hadn't seemed to notice her yet. The soil at his feet was drenched in darkness that leached into the river, turning the crystal waters opaque. On the other bank, Palenisa mirrored his position. Planting her feet wide, arms splayed, she pushed every ounce of her aspect into knitting the island closed. Each of his movements she countered, calling earth to fill in the gap, reflecting his unnatural power with her blessed one.

Fighting for control of the widening gap, Asaru frowned at her, notching deep lines in his brow as his claws curled.

Finally—she had his attention.

His tail flicked side to side, giving him the appearance of irritation, and her eyes narrowed. Was there some give to the possession? Some part of him that lingered after death? Before she had time to ponder each question, a shadow fell over them. Warily, Palenisa watched it drop behind him. From all the legends, there was only one person that could be. Someone whose name was an omen she dared not say aloud.

The murderess. Oprekhet.

Sentient strands of her hair danced like scarlet ribbons. Black mineral spidered up her arms and legs from under the scrap of linen she wore as a sorry excuse for clothing. Her red-tipped claws slid over Asaru's shoulder and spun him. For a breathless second, horror bled into Palenisa's veins. But it turned to shock when Oprekhet dragged him into an embrace. She was so much taller that his head only reached her shoulder. Stranger still, Asaru returned the embrace.

Palenisa blinked once. Then twice, thinking the sight must have been a figment.

The murderess wore a smile that was disconcerting in just how banal it was. More chilling than any of the deathless or the gore that littered the sand. Rubbing her cheek against Asaru's, the murderess tightened her hold, then froze. An ugly sneer marred her expression as she placed her chin atop his head. At first Palenisa thought the glare was aimed at her until she followed the murderess's gaze.

From a pool of stars, another figure materialized down the river. Hidden by a nondescript cloak, they resembled a crooked vulture. Footholds formed across the surface of the water where they walked. A silver sheaf of hair trailed their delicate footsteps.

"Niekthe," Oprekhet growled.

As they moved from the riverside, Palenisa strained to hear them over the incessant drumbeat in her ears. A painful heave rumbled up the trunk of her body. The sheer strain of keeping the landmass together pulled at her shoulders. Dry sweat dripped from the wispy hair that feathered her forehead.

The flatness of Niekthe's voice slithered above the clamor of battle.

"I did not bring you back to destroy what Madib created," they admonished, thick emotion dripping from every deliberate syllable.

"You have no right to accuse me of anything," Oprekhet rebutted, her hair lashing like a wild snake. "You murder her, stab me in the heart, then have the gall to claim I destroyed our sister's legacy?"

Niekthe took another step, and Oprekhet dragged Asaru back, hissing. If she was a baleful storm, they were its eye, slow but no less dangerous.

"*I* am not the one killing our progeny."

"Everything you did, you did to spite me," she said, choking on the words with a pain that surprised Palenisa. "My work would have brought glory to Aedyton, but you couldn't stand that I actually cared enough to stay and cultivate what Madib made for us. That I was better at this *one* thing."

Stretching out a hand, Niekthe tilted their wrist. Variegated violet spread down their fingers into a glowing beam. The light grew, throwing long shadows across their impassive face. As it faded, they curled their fingers around the crooked head of a staff made of diamondglass. They pointed the glinting jagged end at Oprekhet like a threat.

"Let's be honest, Sister. All the glories in this world and ours wouldn't hide how rotten you are."

For a moment, Oprekhet almost looked hurt. Heartbreak flickered across her face before it settled into a feral mask. Ducking to whisper into Asaru's ear, she reached out to his chest. *Through* his chest. As her hand plunged inside the layers of leather and cloth, Palenisa's eyes widened. From within, she pulled out a trident of black diamond.

"Have it your way," she spat.

In a blink, Oprekhet was across the bank, plunging the prongs down on Niekthe. The pair met in a clash of sparks, black and white like an eclipse, as their fight dragged them farther from the river.

Palenisa's knees shook, forcing her focus back to the crevasse. The most she'd managed to do was to keep it from widening farther. It felt like futility, holding the earth together as liquid diamond frothed over the flayed edges. Glancing up, she cast her bloodshot eyes on Asaru.

The man stared up at the mass of deathless as it swelled and shrank, a breathing ball of darkness. Slowly, he raised a hand. One snap, and the deathless ceased fighting. Across the island, as far as Palenisa could see, hundreds of dark faces turned upward. Two snaps, and every one of them hearkened to the silent command of their master. By any means possible, the undead horde swarmed to the sky. Even those torn to pieces followed suit as best they could. Already bereft of sunlight, Palenisa grew frigid as the hive increased exponentially.

Then Asaru shot off, bolting beside the river in retreat.

Flinching, she dropped her hands. Without her effort, the crevasse peeled farther open, but that mattered little if he escaped.

She wouldn't let him. Couldn't let him. Maybe if she stopped him, not all hope was lost. *Save him from himself.* The refrain rang like a prayer. Palenisa burst into a sprint, running parallel to the crevasse to keep Asaru in sight. It was longer, larger, deeper than she had initially thought. Her resistance really had been useless, hadn't it? Merely delaying the inevitable.

No matter. If she succeeded, then maybe it wouldn't all be for naught. *Maybe.*

Gritting her teeth, she drew an elbow back. Despite the lack of warmth, Palenisa tried to conjure sunlight. But when she flung her hand out, starlight burst forth from her fingertips.

Startled, Asaru tried to avoid the rays, but her aim was true. An explosion shattered her eardrums, and the impact sent them both flying. While she was hurled backward, he recoiled silently, black ooze spiking over his form like the raised hackles of a wolvencat.

Three silvery-blue lines scarred the sand as Asaru staggered.

Something fell into the water between them—Asaru's arm. Severed at the shoulder, the limb twitched. The mineral encasing it evaporated as if averse to the amputated limb.

Palenisa hadn't realized what she'd done until she blinked

away crimson swirls. For a fraction of a second, it felt like the Zodiac had flared to life. She was one with the aspects of the world. Understanding slid into place. It felt right. It felt . . . heretical.

Terror shivered up her spine at the memory of a shadow in a glistening desert.

Sulfur wafted to her nose. Ashes and fetid swamps, but also the smell of the crisp air after fresh snowfall.

The last reserves of her energy fled, and Palenisa's legs buckled. Though she tried to collect her wits, they dissipated like mist. Dazed, she pressed a palm against an eye. A headache pulsed, pounded, swallowed her whole.

Unaffected, Asaru gazed at the putrid arm as if it hadn't been part of him. His face set into blank determination, and he waved his remaining hand, swiping a retaliatory wave of black diamond at her.

Sodden in weakness, she couldn't avoid his shot. His aim was true too.

The dark flood threw her into the river. As she crashed beneath the surface, cold water elicited a gasp, rushing to fill her lungs. Bubbles screamed out of her mouth, her body convulsing as she scrabbled for air.

No, no, no, she pleaded to the spirits, *please, no.*

Was she dying?

You're not, the twelve replied in discordant tandem. *Swim—and live.*

Raging against the blackness threatening to snatch her consciousness, she thrashed toward that pinprick of light above. That salvation. As she broke the surface, her hands met silt and the pain of the earth enveloped her. The longer she dug in for purchase, the more it twisted her head into knots.

Crawling to her knees, Palenisa shuddered. Wait, not

her—the ground. Plates shifted deep below—it was the ground that shuddered. Black plasma gurgled from the crevasse like lava, scalding hot. Her cheeks blistered from the heat, and it felt like she was being slashed to pieces by her own scythe. It was burning. *It was burning.*

She rolled away as the gaping crevasse yawned like a mouth slit open at the sides. Shakily, she rose onto her elbows and searched for the source of the earth's pain. The cold stone of her heart went still.

Too late. She was too late.

Water fell into the empty nothing. There was no more river, just a sudden drop in the earth as Asaru swung the saw one last time. Palenisa buried her fingers into the sand and formed handholds as Aedyton split in half with a succinct crack.

A loud cry drew her attention, and she caught the end of Oprekhet's bout with her sibling. The murderess thrust a fist forward, knuckles riddled with shards of diamond. The force sprawled Niekthe across the other side of the once-crevasse. A liquid limb wrapped around their neck and slammed them into the ground—once, twice, until they went still. But not dead. Though it looked close, so terribly close.

Before Palenisa could react, Oprekhet reached for the sky in an imitation of supplication. A glossy wall of black diamond shot up before her. Curving her arms back, she stretched the darkness into a dome. The dome expanded, racing to cover one half of the bisected island in a thin, translucent sheen.

Flexing her fingers, Oprekhet pulled harder, tugging with visible strain until the landmass slowly split from its earthly moorings. It shouldn't have been possible. And yet. And *yet.* Palenisa watched in horror as half of Aedyton was cruelly ripped apart and began to drift away.

A harsh wind came in from the sea as the island drifted. Beyond the dome, the land was cast in gray. Crystal trees toppled to shards when they hit the ground. Pyramids shook apart into mounds of rubble and burnt bricks. Sunlight bounced off the faceted bubble as the few trapped survivors pounded helpless fists against the translucent stone.

Soon the dome was too far away for her to make out the abject terror on their faces. But it would haunt her. The image had seared itself on the backs of her eyelids.

Kneeling on the edge of the newly formed shore, Palenisa stared at the horizon. Heat gathered in her eyes, blurring them. Hopelessness caged her incoherent mind. There she sat, a pathetic pale speck on a broken island surrounded by death, destruction, devastation. Even when she tried, she failed.

"Save him from himself," she whispered. The echoing voices of the Zodiac wrapped her in their imagined comfort. But no matter how many times it was repeated—speaking the words didn't make it so.

Once more she said it, and a tear slipped free, rolling down her ashen cheek.

WREN

The limp hand in his felt more unreal than real. Disconnected, Wren watched the fractured pieces of himself. Like a mirror, they reflected his totality: the uncertain future, the horrible present, and the bittersweet past.

The past he so longed to return to. Back when everything made sense.

Wren was thirty, a bright-eyed child traipsing down the grassy hill of his new home as he carried Dakazna like one would a loaf of bread. The wolvencat yawned, revealing gummy infant teeth. Half-formed wings twitched at her back. She was only a year old and couldn't fly yet.

Once he'd found the perfect spot, Wren dropped to the ground. Green smeared his freckled arms as child Wren dug through the earth. Dirt was crusted beneath his nails from earlier when he'd been digging up flowers. He was going to plant them for his mother. Because she liked flowers—black ones and blue ones—and lately, she'd been looking really sad.

Wren was finishing his sizable hole when he accidentally

knocked the nubs atop Dakazna's head. The wolvencat yipped, swiping up with blunt claws, catching his rolled sleeves.

"Scavite, Daka!"

As he comforted the animal, a click reached his ears. Tilting his head, he looked up to see his mother peering around the crooked door of their moss-covered home. Curious eyes alighting on her, he broke into a smile, revealing the small gap where he'd just lost his first fang.

Returning the smile, Sabine stepped outside and planted her hands on her hips. The deep creases made her look really pretty. Despite the heat, she wore a suman embroidered with thorny flowers that glittered in the summer sun. Beneath it was a tunic, bright as pomegranates, that fell like petals over loose trousers. Her skin was brown as precious jewels, dotted with the stars themselves. Like him, her hair was a curly ocean, braided with a blue ribbon to rest over one shoulder. She was as beautiful as our Lady Blessed Sunnai, she of the thousand thousand suns.

"Tios-demovan loi, Anemone?" *What are you doing?*

Shyly, Wren presented the haphazard bundle of flowers to her. He couldn't find dahlias or the unique blue buds that were his namesake, so he'd pulled whatever looked close enough to the images in his botany tome. That they came from the garden of a neighbor located higher up on the hill was neither here nor there.

"Chei." Sabine kissed her teeth. "Mior dorai, the thief."

Shaking her head, she picked her way over to him. Uncaring of the dirt, she dropped to her knees and embraced her child. She pressed her cheek to his, transferring warmth between them, then kissed all over his face as he giggled. Lips like butterfly wings brushed his skin.

Pulling away, Sabine ran a tender finger above his brows with a drooping smile. Often she did this, stared at him like she was searching for something. Wren wasn't sure if she'd ever found it. The look was one he didn't understand the meaning of. Adults could be quite confusing.

"Tut-vaneran takeš, D'ya?" *Are you all right?*

Mussing his messy baby curls, Sabine turned to gaze over the undulating landscape of Sika. The only home he'd ever truly known, having left their clan when he was little more than an infant.

"Mis vaneran," she said. *I am.* "Don't you worry your head."

Her attempt to comfort him fell like leaves at harvest—she *wasn't* all right, and he thought he might know why. Clutching Dakazna to his chest, Wren frowned. He buried his face in her sleek back. Purring, Dakazna pressed her wet nose to the crook of his neck, tail wrapped around his arm.

Voice muffled by smooth, smooth fur, he probed further, "Are you upset because of Daj?"

It was a question that occasionally ran through his mind. He knew nothing of the man heredity claimed to be his father. Save his name—and what he was.

A king. *The* king.

Wren didn't quite know what that meant. Other than the fact that it made his mother sad. And anyone who made his mother sad couldn't be family. Didn't deserve to be family. So he decided then, with the simple logic that came easily to children, there was only one person in the world who mattered. His mother. And Dakazna of course—he couldn't forget the spoiled beast who lay stretched liquid across his lap.

A large hand tangled with his, snapping his gaze back up to Sabine. The tips of her fingers were covered in scars from sewing needles and spells, her palms thick from calluses born of the labor it had taken to get them there. And she wore her ring on her hand rather than around her neck like she used to. It was made from cracked bone—"an antler," she'd once told him when he asked what it was. Though she hadn't told him who had made it for her.

"Not quite. Zaosha isn't *always* on my mind," she chuckled. Cupping his cheek, she pressed their foreheads together. Shining brown and gold eyes bore into his. "I was actually thinking about how much I love you." Sabine's voice was unshakable, unbreakable, but with a thin, desperate undertone. "Venan'tios sunnai ci sterr, movenuem dahlila du apua." *You are my sun and stars, little water flower.*

There was once again that strange look on her face as she thumbed his cheeks. Her touch was loving, a comfort the child sank into.

A comfort that Wren still remembered clear as day. That was the last time she'd ever said his father's name aloud. He could ponder the reason for days and days, but that wouldn't change the past—all that remained was the present.

By the time he came back to himself, the battle that raged on the island was over. Time had passed so quickly that it felt as if he'd been there forever.

Clutching his mother's hand tighter, he pressed it to his face as he sobbed, shoulders shaking with each pained heave as bountiful tears rolled down his cheeks. He had meant to suffer for his mistakes, but not like this. Not like this.

Khetry glowed far too bright, pulsing warm and alive, even though the world over which it was woven was full of cold things, dead things. The sludge of possession still clung to him like a putrid scent. The actions had not been his own, but he bore the consequences all the same. It was *his* blood imbued in the needle, *his* fingers that painted the spell in the commingling of their ichor. And his damnable curiosity that had led there in the first place.

What had he to show for it?

His mother dead, Asaru dead. Nothing but failure and failure and failure. Wren drowned in the mire of every mistake he'd ever made and every hurt he'd ever caused. He was a pathetic, misshapen mess that didn't deserve to exist. The world would be better off without him.

One couldn't hate themself more than he did in that moment.

Shuddering, he shut his eyes. To look was to confront reality. The reality that monsters weren't born—they made themselves, born of blood and light.

Norvatti grew up hearing tales of certain lulaik. So weak-willed they yearned for power, so desperate they sacrificed themselves for the devastating allure of a myth. *Sacrifice*—it wasn't themselves they had to give away, but that which was most precious to them. Pitiful. In all the folktales, in all the stories, they were pitiful beasts.

Stories had nothing on what it meant to be a Weaver, though.

It was torture. To know that in one act, one senseless wrench, a thread could be shredded to pieces, stealing life from some blameless being. Mastery over life and death. All the wishing in the world couldn't take this profane power from him. No prayer would be his salvation.

Sorrow pierced his heart as he buried his face in his mother's beautiful black hair. The fraying khetry threads around her withered like dry worms in the substance. Her body was growing cold. It felt like she'd never once been alive. Never been that beautiful woman who blanketed him in unconditional love, kissed the nightmares away, held him close when the melancholy was at its worst while he healed from a poison of his own making.

Sucking in a breath, Wren tried desperately to pull his fractured being into alignment. His heart shook from the force of his sobs. Pain lanced the aching pillar that was his body, hammered his tender skull. Grief welled up his ashen throat. Hiccups dotted his cries, and a headache beat at his temples.

For minutes, for hours, for days, he cried. Cried until his tears were more blood than water. Cried until his mother's body grew stiff.

A sudden tremor flared through khetry, a cobweb disturbed. With these wretched new senses, he could almost feel the contours of the individual members of the incoming throng, as though each of them was a stone rippling the red substance like water.

Through endless tears, he blinked at the flood of bodies, of what remained of Aedyton.

The island was broken in half from the verdant atoll to the cloudy uppermost ring. Something that had stood for thousands of thousands of years had cracked like the fragile shell of an egg. A testament to the impermanence of everything—death and destruction an inevitability.

Many of the incoming crowd were injured, missing wings and limbs. Among their numbers were dotted crimson cloaks. The ivory of a shattered skull. And a familiar figure that sparked a faint connection in his brain. Even beneath a coating of gray gold and black blood, Wren recognized Palenisa.

She split from the crowd and rushed to his side, dropping to her knees with a soft wince. Her hands hovered over his shoulders, her wintry eyes wide. A popped blood vessel darkened the left one to indigo as glistening tears rolled down her cheeks in heavy drops. Violet soaked through the olive cloth wrapped around her upper thigh.

Was her expression one of horror? Anger? Some other forlorn expression? Everything looked the same to him when the world was a grim blur.

Overcome with a wave of emotion, Wren drew in a ragged gasp and pulled her close. He clung to her, felt her materiality, smelled the iron of her blood. Resting her chin on his shoulder, Palenisa held him as his mother once did. But it couldn't compare.

After a moment, Wren pulled away to press his forehead against hers. They stared at each other, and he could almost imagine hearing her thoughts. Hearing the same refrain of sorrow that swirled through his.

Her eyes flitted aside, and she whispered, "The Black Order."

Releasing a shaky breath, he wiped the tears from his face. He only succeeded in smearing blood across his cheeks, shouting to the world what he had done.

As the survivors from Aedyton gathered where the land bridge met the continent proper, the Black Order stopped them. The large contingent of sentinels formed a black line in the sand. Hundreds of them stood along the border to Estyria, an unwavering, overwhelming show of force from the realm.

The sentinels parted like a wave, and a woman emerged. With bronze skin and umber hair braided neatly into three, she looked to be Ausran. She wore a stern but peaceful look. Platinum studded her uniform, and a long sword hung sheathed at her side.

Her voice rang clear and high as a hush fell over Hadii.

"I, Paramount Commander Elizer-Kaite Godefrei, protect these lands—and *you* should not be here," she intoned, tipping her chin up with an authority that froze Wren to the spot. Likewise, he felt Palenisa stiffen and curl her arms around him. They were alike in their wariness of what was to come, glancing at each other and drying their tears as they waited for the officer to continue.

From the gathered eresh keyel stepped a statuesque woman. Her robes may once have been ethereal, but they were riddled with holes and covered in so much bile they were more gray than white.

"I thought you had this under control, Warden." Godefrei clasped her hands at her back and moved forward, looking up since she only reached the warden's chin. She circled the other woman and cast a derisive glance over the beach with shimmering orange eyes.

"Please tell me what gave you the illusion that any of you will be stepping foot into Estyria?" She continued, giving the warden no time to respond. "The Sea Gate may be gone, but there is a curse actively raging. One of yours *assassinated* our king."

An ache tugged at Wren's chest, and the breath left him in a hiss of air. His heart quaked. Water pearled at the corners of his eyes, smudging the scene before him into a morose watercolor.

"The curse is . . . quelled for now."

For now. It would have been nullified completely had they just had more time. More time before death descended in a black swarm to desecrate the temple. Before foul fortune wreathed him in sparks. Before the cruel presence snatched from him all sense of self and meaning in life.

"And what of the other item?" Godefrei asked, interrupting his thoughts.

The throng shifted, wings fluttering and cloth rustling to fill the silence. The steady thump of footfalls, the familiar stuttering shuffle of a limp, beat into his ears. Through the crowd, the Chronicler approached. Looking worse for wear, they leaned on a diamondglass staff tucked beneath their armpit. Gently pushing their kin aside, they moved into the circle of sand at the front, where the two women stood. For a second, their gaze darted to Wren, and he averted his eyes.

A small pool of anger still whirled inside him. Part of him sought to lay some measure of blame at their feet—this, the destruction of Aedyton, was their fault. But he was no more innocent. In fact, he was worse. For as horrid a thing as they'd done—he bore an equal part. After all, it was *his* hands that were stained in blood.

"If I may," the Chronicler said, their voice cutting the tense silence. "I have a solution to both problems."

A hollow feeling curdled in Wren's gut. In an instant, all warmth fled him.

Crossing her arms, Godefrei frowned. "A solution?"

The hollow in Wren yawned wider. Gruesome tendrils crept into every part of him.

"A solution." The Chronicler nodded. The world slowed to syrup as they turned, lifted a hand, and pointed.

At him.

Thousands of eyes followed. Thousands of eyes fell upon him like a flock of birds. Thousands of eyes devoured every inch of him. Cowering, he looked down with a sudden intake of breath. The red web sang. It flared, demanding his attention with the insistence of a selfish little creature. Quivering threads caressed his senses. He trembled beneath the force of all that life. The sensation of their many eyes needled under his skin, flaying him apart to expose him in all his miserable truth.

"No, please, don't do this," he whispered desperately. "Anything but this, please."

"That is Zaosha's son." *No, please.* "And the last living Weaver in the known world."

Wren stilled, his eyes widening slightly. *That's . . . a lie.*

"A baseless claim. You can't possibly be insinuating the late king was . . ."

Though her words were incredulous, Wren could tell from her tone she already half believed it. That was the worst part. The fact that it *was* so easy to believe.

They didn't all look the same. But Wren was his mother *and* he was his father.

Clamping his eyes shut, he took Palenisa's hand. Pleas bandied through his head, rising and ringing and clouding all other thoughts beneath a constant chorus of *don't, don't, don't.*

"Take a look at him—and you'll know."

Staring into the dull eyes of his mother, Wren blinked. But she did not blink back. His tears dripped onto her face, rolled down her pallid cheeks. That empty gaze stared accusatorily at him. *I know what you are,* it seemed to deride. Is that how she was? Is that what she would have said? Already his memory of her was warping from his ruinous self-hatred.

"Look at me, child," Godefrei commanded, sounding closer than before.

Through his fringe, Wren saw the metal toes of her boots in the sand before him. He could feel the heat from her body, the threads that wove her into the living world. He loosed a breath as Palenisa tightened her grip. Her thumb pressed into the center of his palm. Her presence at his side was grounding, clearing a path through his hazy mind.

"Did you hear me? *Look.*"

If he did this, his fate was sealed.

But his fate had been sealed long before this moment. Had been so since the moment he was born. There was never anything else for him but a legacy drenched in death.

Wren exhaled. Swallowed. And raised his head.

RISHÉ

Rishé woke up in stages.

First, she felt the cold.

Next, she felt the solid ground against her back.

Then, she felt the pain as awareness careened full force into her.

Feeling like kicked shit, she clutched her head against the raging storm threatening to split it open. Her body screamed; something felt broken.

An ache snapped between her shoulder blades. As she curled into herself to try to stand, her ankle throbbed. Ah, there it was. Rishé smacked her lips to wet them and swallowed. Teeth gritted, she pressed a hand to her ankle and immediately recoiled. A large, tender bulb indicated it was at the very least sprained if not completely broken.

Cupping her ear, she let the pain tremble through her like the aftershocks of a quake.

Her head spun as fragmented, nonsensical images swirled on the backs of her eyelids. It was almost too dark to tell if they were truly closed at all. Blinking back tears, she saw the indistinct outline of her body rising from the dimness. She looked to be whole, though it felt more like she was several disembodied limbs. Shifting her legs, she realized the ground was slick with water. It drenched her to the bone. Wet sand clung to her every uncomfortable crevice.

Confused questions ran through her mind, but before she could answer any of them, she had to deal with her ankle. Once more, she touched the swollen limb. Taking stock of the rest of her body, she found nearly every part similarly aching. She pushed up to an elbow, swimming through that syrup, and it left her panting from the effort and feeling more like she'd run through the desert. Sweat dampened her brow, small curls clung to her temple from the new growth at the sides. Gathering her weary strength, Rishé sat up and reached down to remove her boot. Her jaw worked as she laced the wrappings from the boot around her ankle instead. She let out the breath she'd been holding when the small knot was tied. It was a poor job. But she wasn't a healer, so it would have to do.

From somewhere, water dripped and dripped and dripped. The metronome bore into her skull as a headache threatened to beat her into submission. Pressing her head to the cool floor, she tried to ignore the symphony of *hurt-pain-hurt*. For a moment, her memory was a dim haze until everything came rushing back in a wave.

The temple. The deathless. The Sea Gate.

What have I done?

Blood poured from her nose as she doubled over. Horrified, Rishé cupped her mouth against a swell of nausea. Red and hot, blood trickled down the back of her hand. The lingering taint of possession splattered the caverns of her mind like carrion. "Violated" was too kind a word. She'd been stripped bare by

Oprekhet's will. She hadn't belonged to herself, merely a limb in a greater, mad design to thoroughly and completely annihilate the Sea Gate. There had been nothing left of the stalwart barrier that had stood for centuries. Not even marks in the sand where the slabs once rested.

The memory of the incantation tasted foul. Her tongue warmed just thinking of it, burning with regret and bile like she'd just expelled the contents of her stomach. Everything she'd spent countless years researching had led to destruction. In the end, the tome hadn't brought revelation—only devastation.

Her head whipped up in alarm. *The tome!*

Hurriedly, Rishé searched for the tome. For her journal. Her fingers found low, stagnant water and nothing else. Frustration boiled up inside her. Hurt and alone in this dank, dark place, she was colder than she'd ever been in her life.

This place . . .

Where exactly was she?

Shaking her head, Rishé looked around and flinched at a flash of white light. She moved toward it and was met with a wall. Whimpering, she clutched her nose to stymie the fresh gush of blood. She shut an eye and felt along the wall. Finally, her vision cleared like a cloth wiped across dusty glass. An apt description since she found herself peering through what looked to be a window.

Through the rectangle of light was a silvery-blue room, almost like the Nest. Unlike the Nest, crimson cracks spread across the floor and up the six walls. On each wall a mirror was inset, reaching to the domed ceiling. A broken fountain receptacle sat in the middle of the room, formed from the hands of various creatures—human and otherwise—which held up a large bowl with countless fingers.

It must have been beautiful *once*, all the ruination hinting at past grandeur.

Stranger still was the fact that it was entirely underwater. The faint blue cast was really the gloom of fathomless waters, shivering with nearly imperceptible ripples.

Rishé started at the realization, then winced at the lightning that struck her ankle. Exhaling shakily through her nose, she pressed a hand to the glass. Her fingers left red dots behind.

After the pain subsided to a moderate hum, she squinted back through the window. But to her further surprise, she didn't see her reflection in the mirror opposite her.

Instead, where *she* should have been was reflected in the polished length of another mirror.

Six walls, six mirrors, each of them perfectly identical.

And she was trapped behind one of them.

This didn't make sense. She didn't understand. Like light splitting through a prism, her mind scrambled, spinning off in various directions as fear skittered up her spine. Her panic stared back at her as she pounded on the mirror. Every flaw on her person shone in the glass. Injuries, blood, panic scarring her face like wounds.

Harried fingers pried along the edge of the mirror, but there was no delineation between glass and wall, just a smooth transition into darkness. The space was a little smaller than she was tall, and the water across the floor had no source through pipe or vent.

For the first time, Rishé didn't know what to do next. In these depths, she was out of hers.

She raised a fist again but paused when a hooded figure swam suddenly into view.

Their dark form appeared warped by the water in an unreal wobble. They wore a midnight cloak, leaves feathering along the hem as it floated around them. Beneath the shadow of their hood was a golden glow, like the roving beam of a lighthouse. When it alighted on her, she froze.

Rishé's hands rested against a mirror streaked with bloody palm prints. Gulping, she tilted her head. She would have thought the stranger a statue, until they followed, cocking their head to imitate her.

"Who—" She coughed to clear her scratchy throat. "Who . . . are . . . you?" Speaking felt like gargling razors.

The figure swam closer, disturbing the water. They towered above her before doffing their hood to reveal the face of a furious drake. Braids like seaweed interwoven with the bones of tiny fish framed a faintly glowing face. Iridescent scales covered their cheeks and down the sides of their jaw and neck. Four striking yellow eyes, a pair atop another, narrowed to angry slits.

Water splashed as Rishé scrambled back. Pain flared from her leg to her skull, dropping her to her knees and elbows. The heat of their glare prickled the hair at her nape. Fear darkened the corners of her vision when she saw the drake lift their hand.

Hanging from their grip was her necklace, pendant winking like a dying sunset.

With a sharp intake of breath, Rishé threw her hands up. Her chest felt empty. Looking down, she saw it *was* empty, bereft of the precious heirloom. The last piece of material connection to her mother. Instinctively, she grasped for it. But her fingers met the crystal barrier between her and her necklace. That was all she had left of her mother, and it was so close. On the other side of the mirror, yet far beyond reach. Impossibly beyond reach.

Please no, came the desperate thought as she slammed a hand to the mirror. *Please, don't.*

"That's . . . *mine*. Give it . . . back." Harder, she hit the glass.

Harder and harder, until the skin of her palms split and blood smudged the surface. "That's . . . my mother's; that's mine," she ground out through the shards that lined the insides of her mouth. She tasted iron. "You have . . . no right! You have *no right*!"

Rishé watched with increasing dread as the drake lifted her necklace in their fist. Stern eyes scrutinized the pendant, a spot of color burning like the heart of a forge. The chain drifted as through wind. Their gaze flitted back to her, and their frown deepened.

"No," they said, voice muffled behind glass and the pressure of the depths. "*You* had no right."

With a single careless act, they crushed the red stone to dust.

Rishé was obliterated.

Tears brimmed, overflowing from her eyes. Her heart shattered into pieces, innumerable as the crushed particles that filtered through the drake's fingers when they opened their fist. Dust floated off in the water like nothing. Like her whole world hadn't been utterly destroyed.

Gone was the last connection to her mother. The last physical reminder that her mother once lived. It felt like Jarha was being taken from her again. Like the consumptive taint had once more wrapped wretched fingers around her mother's neck to slowly and cruelly wring life from a woman so vibrant and deserving of more.

Throwing her one last sneer, the drake pulled their hood up and swam away, leaving Rishé only with her tears. Devastation dragged her into the water. Sobs racked her body. Heaving cries cascaded pain through every inch of her. She hurt, she *was* the hurt, she couldn't breathe. Trapped in darkness, lonely and alone, she sank into sorrow. Nothing mattered anymore. Not when her mother's memory was ash in the water.

Only emptiness remained.

ASARU

Patiently, Asaru watched as a pair of attendants prepared him for the showing. Through the steady buzz of static and the low hum of pain, he faintly realized he was naked. He let them move him as they liked. He let them wash gray-gold blood from his incorruptible body. He let them clean the jagged hole where his arm had once been. All this he let them do because he did not belong to himself—and neither did they.

Though the deathless retained some sense of who they were in life, the will of another had become their own. They were malleable clay bending to the whims of their possessor. If this was what She commanded of them, it was what they would do. This and more. This and anything else.

When the ablutions were complete, the two revenants dressed him. Bound an ayashif around his breasts, wrapped him in a black tunic that fell to mid-thigh, slipped onto his limbs wraps made of flexible metal that winked in the light.

As one cinched a belt of chain links around his waist, Asaru stared at the mirror across the room. But he did not know the man who stared back. In the fractured glass were the facets of someone who both was and was not him.

The door clicked open. In the mirror, he watched a lieutenant enter. Asaru searched for a name, but they were just another piece of dead flesh in the faceless mass. This piece of flesh was similarly clad in ruddy leather. A trident spearing a sun lay stitched on their upper arm—it was familiar in a way that made little sense. With the help of the newly infected members of their legion, the deathless had been uniformed. Not all of them were warriors, after all. That was good, he'd been told. An army required diversity to function, he'd been told.

He took the lieutenant's hand and was led down a corridor pitted with cavernous gaps. They stepped over ivory debris and tumbled columns. Finally they emerged in the light, grayed due to the dull sheen of the dome.

Ruination spread before him. The broken bowl of the Odeum that once floated among frozen clouds lay splintered in half, a stage rising from the midst of the rubble. Scores upon scores of the dead lined the crude amphitheater. Endless columns of darkness were stacked high in the neat rows, disappearing into the distance.

The crowd was thunderous.

As he climbed the stage, Asaru looked out over the deathless horde. Their eyes were dark and empty, their cries robbed of true vigor. The sight inspired nothing within him.

On stage Oprekhet waited with a glint in her eye. The smile she wore revealed rows of needle-sharp teeth. She gestured him closer with barely restrained glee.

Pressing a fist to his chest, Asaru lowered his gaze and bowed. Why did she deserve such reverence?

"Hello, Mother."

His mother's smile grew so wide, it strained her face. A flush of satisfaction spread across pallid brown cheeks. Snatching his wrist, she dragged him to the middle of the stage. The touch scarcely registered as painful beneath the static cloud that consumed him.

"My son," she shouted.

The crowd roared, their emotions fueled by hers, by her unwavering voice.

Son.

For a moment the notion felt wrong—a sudden surge of *not right*—but it was swept away. Oprekhet was his mother. She was his mother, and he had no one else. This knowledge was pushed into his mind, and he accepted it. Was made to accept it.

"Though my traitorous sibling snatched him from my arms when he was but an egg, through blood and diamond and death, he has at last been returned to me!"

Oprekhet tilted her head to the sky. Her hair danced, forming a wild spiral that expanded and contracted like a panting beast. Liquid blackness undulated around her body in waves of power. The same power with which Asaru had split apart the island they were standing upon. The recollection of a duel over earth and rock surfaced through the fog of possession.

A fleeting part of him screamed in horror, trying to grasp the depths of what he'd done. But an unrelenting presence pressed him into compliance. What resistance remained was smothered. His body was not his own.

It was *Hers*. Had always been. Would always be.

"Asaru, warrior, brother, son," the deathless chanted. The sound reverberated through his body, extremities tingling with sparks. Oprekhet basked in the attention, throwing her arms up. Then her head whipped back down, and—

"Silence."

The crowd quieted instantly.

"A thousand years ago, Niekthe turned humanity against me. Turned our own people against me. Jealous, they killed me to try and destroy my life's work. And driven by sentimentality, they resurrected me. They thought I could be controlled, would be indebted to them. That was their folly—"

As she spoke, Asaru felt the hold on his mind weaken slightly. His will was still *hers*, but with the bit of him that was still *his*, he fiddled with an object at his back.

A poorly folded paper flower.

He'd found it tucked into the pleats of his ayashif, so small it went unseen by the attendants. As he'd examined it, something clicked in the untouched parts of his mind. This nameless flower had a meaning. Some confusing part of him hadn't wanted it destroyed, so he'd hidden it away. Why and *how* he did so, he was unsure. It felt as though the sight of the blossom rocked him free for less than a split second. Then the static swelled back in, and Asaru was lost to himself again.

"Now he shall become what he was always made to be. My masterpiece, my greatest weapon, forged for one sole purpose: *Retribution.*"

The noose of possession tightened around his neck, and all thought fled like mist.

Instinctively, Asaru turned to Oprekhet—his mother. *Your mother, remember that.*

She clasped her hands, light pouring from the cracks between her fingers. A glow cast her face with baleful shadows, her grin the arc of a scythe. Slowly, she pulled her hands apart, uncovering a circlet of black diamond. The jewels glistened, rising like mountains to the center, where a triangular shard rested.

With a smile gesturing vaguely at tenderness, Oprekhet placed it in the crimson sea of Asaru's hair. Cupping his cheeks, she pressed a kiss to his forehead. Hidden in the back of a small part of his mind was the urge to draw away in revolt. It was replaced with appreciation and thankfulness. Emotions pushed into his body and made to feel like they were his.

"Let Estyria have their bastard king," she murmured. "We have a prince of our own."

"Warrior, brother, son. Home, you're home, Asaru." The persistent drone streamed into his ears like through water. He heard them in discordant unity, voices all one and the same. The horde and his mother, his mother and the horde.

The corner of Oprekhet's lips quirked up. Pressing the jagged scars of his wings, she pushed him forward. Her other arm flung out as she presented him to the legions. Her mindless, obedient followers. "I give you Asaru! Prince of the deathless, heir to my sister Madib—my magnum opus!"

An earsplitting cheer shattered across the island. Revenants cried out in clattering cacophony. Writhing hands waved, fluttering in his honor. Pitch-covered wings dripped, and thousands of feet stamped an arrhythmic tune. Distantly, Asaru watched the horde congeal into a rising tide of black. Black that screamed. Black with hollow faces and gaping maws. Black as diamond.

The din rose and rose and rose. Until all he knew was the scream of a thousand living corpses. As the deathless showered him in his mother's glory, a name resurfaced in his waterlogged thoughts.

It's a crystal lotus.

A beautiful name, unfurling like a blossom. But try as he might, Asaru was unable to wrap mental fingers around comprehension. Whatever it represented, whatever it meant, drifted away on ethereal wings. As possession crept back in, he pushed the name into the tiny part of himself that he still owned, senselessly protecting it.

Any coherent thought he may have had was obscured beneath a will that he was forced to take as his own. The only thing that mattered was the cold caress commanding him under the guise of gentleness tinged with retribution.

The man that used to be Asaru was a body without a mind, a vessel of pure violence. A tool to be used. A weapon to be directed at enemies. His enemies, her enemies. Anyone who stood against them.

Nothing—and no one—would stop him.

ACKNOWLEDGMENTS

Like most of what I write, this book came about as a result of way too many ideas that probably don't belong together, stuffed in a blender and synthesized through years of single-minded writing. Sometimes I find myself stunned by the fact that other people . . . actually like it. (But despite my anxieties, they do, and I'm amazed.) I'm also super grateful for all the people who inspired this story—none of whom will read this, though I'd be over the moon if somehow they did. Thank you for putting your art into the world, for being self-indulgent without cringing and for inspiring me to do the same. You always have to be your number one fan—I don't know if I'm quite there yet, but I do like this little book I wrote. I think it's neat.

Thank you, Shira, for completely ruining my five-year plan (/pos)! I appreciate how patient and understanding you were at the beginning of all this, and I still have to pinch myself to make sure it's real.

Thank you to my agent, Emily: A million praises for standing in my corner since our very first call, despite the circumstances—you're seriously an absolute rockstar, and I'm amazed by everything you've helped me accomplish so far!

Shout-out to the editing and production teams! Thank you for making this feel like a "real novel" even before I held a physical copy. Special thanks to Sara, my publishing manager, for answering my ELI5 questions and making this process less opaque; Alicia, my developmental editor, for literally reading my mind with suggestions that strengthened the story I was trying to tell until it was polished like a diamond (get it . . . ?); and Charlotte for designing an amazing cover—I have a new appreciation for typography and just want to stare at it all the time. Thank you also to Emilie, Alyssa, Wanda Z., and Janice for handling this book in its uneven transitory states.

Thank you, Jaysen, for being the catalyst that set this whole thing in motion! Hearing the enthusiasm in the way you spoke about the book almost brought me to tears. I'm honored that you took a chance on *Black as Diamond* despite it being unlike your first two acquisitions—there aren't enough words to describe how much that means to me. I want to keysmash, but it would be improper for a published book, so imagine me endlessly screaming THANKS in your ear.

Thank you to Julia (Seoyeon), who didn't follow the journey of this specific book but has always supported my writing in her own way despite our differing career paths. I'm soooo happy we didn't allow a certain obstacle to keep us from becoming friends. Thank you for checking in during the lulls, sharing your interests, and ranting about your fixations with me. ♥

And thank you to N. B. and N. P., the teachers who kept me writing: the one who quietly sparked the dream of being a novelist and the one who ensured that I would always love being in a library.

GLOSSARY & PRONUNCIATION GUIDE

- **adderowl**: A large serpentine owl commonly found in the Veil Islands.
- **aether/spirit**: Immaterial concept that animates living beings.
- **aetherstones**: Prayer spots for members of the Church of Queen Mab found all across Estyria, said to have been built by Ariadine.
- **Akiki**: Official language of Estyria, formalized by the linguist Koa nadu-La Schei.
- **Antorcans**: Humans originating from and mostly found in Anticarta, have distinct physical evolutions adapting them to the cold.
- **Aspects**: Wraiths with spirit-blessed abilities gifted by the Zodiac, identified by the red suvaugrams on their hands. They can control up to two different aspects.
- **aur** (ohr): Currency of the continent of Trinacrios.
- **ayashif** (aya-sheef): Stays made from leather, silk, and metal that act as both armor and chest binding for eresh keyel.
- **Black Order, the / Black Fleet, the**: Estyrian military and naval force. Its members are called sentinels.
- **Chilawari**: A hybrid ethnic group native to the Veil Islands, descended from humans and drakes.

- **choramelo** (kora-melo): Domesticated chameleon equus.
- **Crocodile Coterie, the**: Private order whose sole task is to protect the kharess and carry out her commands. Each member is given a title, such as Sister of Peace, Coin, Faith, Might, or Body. They are identified by emblems, which they cannot remove, though they can be stripped from them.
- **Dis**: Afterworld where the aethers of the forgotten dead are said to be sent, ruled over by the god Disan.
- **dolomites**: Ancient precursors to the wraiths.
- **Doyisha, the** (doy-ee-shah): Lulaik curse breakers under the tutelage of the Chronicler. Identified by their red cloaks with wide-open eyes sewn onto the hoods.
- **Ela Prinâza** (ella prin-aah-za, prin-ee-za): One of the primary deities of the Norvatti faith. Also known as our Lady Blessed Sunnai.
- **Emedu** (em-eh-doo): Primary language of the Chilawari.
- **Eșarpe** (esharp, etsarp): One of the three primary deities of the Norvatti faith.
- **Eslang**: Estyrian sign language.
- **feyinesh** (fae-yee-nesh): Alien race of originally nameless entities from another world, the progenitors of the eresh keyel.
- **flintrock**: Mineral that cloaks the scent of khetry, used to construct Birinuyi.
- **fox tree**: Tall palm-like trees with feathers instead of leaves. They grow from the feathers shed by feather foxes and sprout feather foxes from their own fallen feathers.
- **freelancers**: Aspects who take on kill contracts to make a living.
- **Furtumbér** (foor-toom-bear): One of the primary deities of the Norvatti faith.

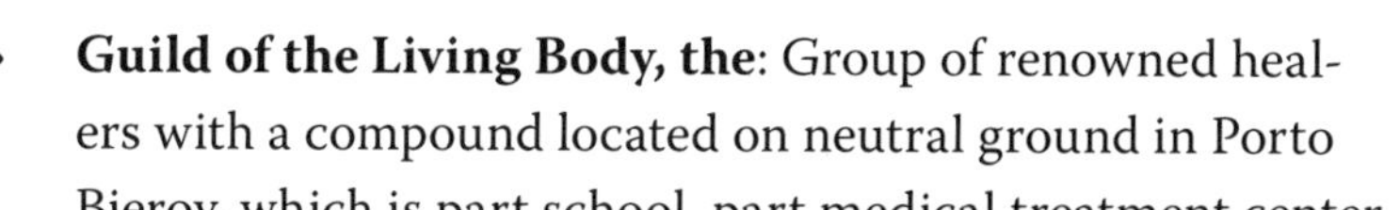

- **Guild of the Living Body, the**: Group of renowned healers with a compound located on neutral ground in Porto Bierov, which is part school, part medical treatment center. Founded by Eírtat Warda.
- **hexe**: Public shrine dedicated to any number of the Six, covered in decorations associated with a god or gods, usually contains a statuette with an offering bowl at its feet.
- **Inachie** (ina-chi): Primary language of wraiths.
- **Ishmer**: Afterworld where the aethers of the beloved dead are said to be sent, ruled over by the god Disan. All eventually sink into Dis.
- **Kestrel**: A celebration that takes place over three days at the end of summer. It also correlates with the coronation day of the rulers of Estyria and is rooted in historical worship of Disan.
- **khetry** (keh-tree): Warm substance resembling a web of red threads woven over the world that connects all living things. It is raw and wild and pulsating with life. Visible only to those who can manipulate it through drawing and casting spells.
- **kurigand** (koo-ri-gand): Currency of Peskelos, made of pink cowries.
- **major**: Economic hub or central square of a town or city.
- **Maronwuchi** (mah-rawn-woo-chee): Celebration to revere the Zodiac that occurs once a year on the first half-moon. In Ilon, the beginning of the festival is marked by a gala.
- **marrowstone**: Wraithian term for "obsidian."
- **Melarhone** (mel-a-rown): Humans originating from and mostly found in the south.
- **minor**: Residential districts of a town or city.
- **Neyari** (nay-ari): Ilonese nobles. Most highborn Aspects are Neyari, but not all Neyari are Aspects.

- **Nomyrs** (noh-mirs): Language of the Norvatti. There are slight variations among the tribes of Estyria, as well as an alternate dialect spoken by the Vana of Peskelos.
- **Norvatti** (nor-vah-tea): Comprises three tribes of humans, and some lulaik, that originated in the Anticartan Silver River region before migrating to Sterrock Valley in Romia. The Eihron are mostly sedentary, the Rosatay are seminomadic, and the Vana are mostly nomadic.
- **panmi** (pan-me): Norvatti dessert of circular sweet bread filled with fruits and decorated with floral shapes made of pastry.
- **primer**: Khetry spellbook. Many of the surviving primers have been passed down within lulaik clans.
- **qhat**: A psychedelic from Peskelos known for its ability to aid underwater breathing when smoked (or at least induce the feeling of breathing underwater).
- **remnants**: Type of sentient protoscience contamination, essentially a waste product.
- **seaross**: Dumpy mammals from Anticarta whose fur, skin, and fat are used to make secondary products such as clothing and lighting.
- **Shadows of Anajera, the** (ana-yer-a): Controversial Suvaun cult. Not much is known about their practices save for the fact that they drink blood. They work under the blessed will of the Shaded One.
- **Sirrah**: One of the primary deities of the Norvatti faith.
- **Six Facets of Being, the**: Primary religion of Estyria, named for its six deities, who are referred to as the Six: Gadgifah, Armasin, Mab, Disan, Bahdab, and Jalorun.
- **strategos**: Captains, each leads a legion of foot warriors.

- **suman** (soo-mawn): Traditional Norvatti outerwear, floor-length, slit-sleeve cloaks with hoods, embroidered in motifs unique to each tribe.
- **suvaugram** (soo-vah-gram): Symbols of the Zodiac painted on the suvaunoors. When marked on skin, they indicate what powers an Aspect has.
- **Suvaun** (soo-vahn): Primary religion of Peskelos and Ilon, named for the suvaunoors.
- **suvaunoors** (soo-vah-noors): Also called the Pillars of the Gods. Twelve monoliths dedicated to the Zodiac, covered in suvaugrams and made from obsidian. Constructed by the dolomites as a physical representation of the spirits. The twelve in Ilon are replicas of the originals on Peskelos.
- **Tetrarchia, the**: A small, specially selected group of elite warriors. Led by a strategos who is chosen by a section leader.
- **three cornerstones, the**: Rules of manipulating khetry. Breaking any of them is met with a backlash, a negative reaction in khetry as it tries to protect itself.
- **thunderstones**: Alternate name for red diamonds. Found in the waters of Peskelos and Fa Djain.
- **Triumvirate, the**: Three legendary eresh keyel akin to gods that the people of Aedyton pray to. They are likely myths and represent abstract concepts related to khetry.
- **veilari** (vay-lar-ee): Breezy material harvested from the bark of silkwood trees, used to make cloth that cools in the heat.
- **Velanu**: Diamondglass sword wielded by Rhenitha, which some songs and legends say felled the last of the dolomites.
- **Vesisto, the**: Dreary sect within the Church of Queen Mab that attends to the bodies left near aetherstones, preparing

the dead for their journey into the Afterworlds. Their job is to collect, cleanse, cut, and bury the bodies, as well as tend to the burial sites.

- **wealthies**: Universal slang term for people who are far more wealthy than common folk. The most powerful are nobles, though not all are of the nobility. The specific meaning varies in every nation.
- **Weave of Fate**: Deck of cards that Norvatti Charmers use for primarily religious purposes. Has been appropriated by non-Norvatti for use in fate games.
- **wejat** (weh-jat): Wide pupilless eye with markings beneath it that is tattooed on the hands of warriors from Aedyton. The symbol of Chert Ouadjet.
- **White Sand, the**: Highly specialized group whose sole job is to monitor the Sea Gate and escort eresh keyel who cross into the Sterrock embassy.
- **wolvencat**: Furry domesticated house pets with small bat-like wings and curling horns.
- **Zodiac, the**: Twelve spirits of the religion of Suvaun. Each represents one of the twelve aspects of life (air, blood, chaos, dream, earth, fire, mind, spirit, starlight, sunlight, ward, water).

THANK YOU

Abby Smith
Amanda M Harwood
Bookspokenly
Brett Foster
BRYN
Fowzidragneel
Jmlavoie7
Kari Frazier
Katie Krishnamoorthi
Lanamalia
LibCraft
Manda Dwyer
Megan K
Micky
TheTammuz

ABOUT THE AUTHOR

© 2025 Caleb (littlestpersimmon/@sethpuertoluna)

U. M. AGOAWIKE is a Nigerian Canadian author from Calgary with a BFA in creative writing from the University of British Columbia. The spark for their love of reading—and eventually writing—was born in their first-grade class, where they preferred devouring the contents of their teacher's corner bookshelves over the mortifying ordeal of being known. When not conjuring speculative new worlds, they dubiously enjoy stressing over lines of code and geeking out about fictional characters with their best friend.

Ezeekat Press is an imprint of Bindery, a book publisher powered by community.

We're inspired by the way book tastemakers have reinvigorated the publishing industry. With strong taste and direct connections with readers, book tastemakers have illuminated self-published, backlisted, and overlooked authors, rocketing many to bestseller lists and the big screen.

This book was chosen by Jaysen Headley in close collaboration with the Ezeekat community on Bindery. By inviting tastemakers and their reading communities to participate in publishing, Bindery creates opportunities for deserving authors to reach readers who will love them.

Visit Ezeekat Press for a thriving bookish community and bonus content:

ezeekat.binderybooks.com

JAYSEN HEADLEY is a content creator on TikTok, Instagram, and YouTube known as Ezeekat, who celebrates and curates diverse voices in books, games, and other media. Jaysen is listed in the top five BookTok influencers in the world, with over 760K followers on TikTok, over 320K on Instagram, and over 70K on YouTube, as well as over 13K members in the Ezeekat Book Club. He reads and enjoys a wide range of stories but focuses on fantasy and contemporary middle-grade to adult fiction, with a preference for queer storylines.

TIKTOK.COM/@EZEEKAT

INSTAGRAM.COM/EZEEKAT

YOUTUBE.COM/@EZEEKAT